"I do not look for love in marriage.

"Merely respect—friendship, if we are fortunate. Tolerance, if we are not. I believe that Katherine Harley will be more than suitable as a wife."

His mother sighed. "Be kind to her, Marcus. Her childhood cannot have been quite comfortable."

"I will." She instantly knew that she had touched a nerve. His tone took on a sardonic note. "It is not my intention to be cruel to her."

"Just try not to overawe the poor child. It would be so very easy for you to do."

"I will do my poor best. Nor is it my intention to punish her for past sins. So don't fret."

"Very well." And that was as far as Lady Elizabeth dared push the issue.

"So, madam. What shall I bring you from the fleshpots of London?"

A bride with whom you have fallen hopelessly in love and who will love you in return.

* * *

Puritan Bride
Harlequin Historical #762—July 2005

PURITAN BRIDE

*is Anne O'Brien's dramatic debut novel
in Harlequin Historical*

Look for

THE DISGRACED MARCHIONESS

Coming September 2005

ANNE O'BRIEN

Puritan Bride

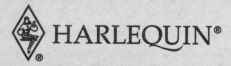

TORONTO • NEW YORK • LONDON
AMSTERDAM • PARIS • SYDNEY • HAMBURG
STOCKHOLM • ATHENS • TOKYO • MILAN • MADRID
PRAGUE • WARSAW • BUDAPEST • AUCKLAND

ISBN 0-373-29362-3

PURITAN BRIDE

Copyright © 2004 by Anne O'Brien

This edition published by arrangement with Harlequin Books S.A.

® and TM are trademarks of the publisher. Trademarks indicated with ® are registered in the United States Patent and Trademark Office, the Canadian Trade Marks Office and in other countries.

www.eHarlequin.com

Printed in U.S.A.

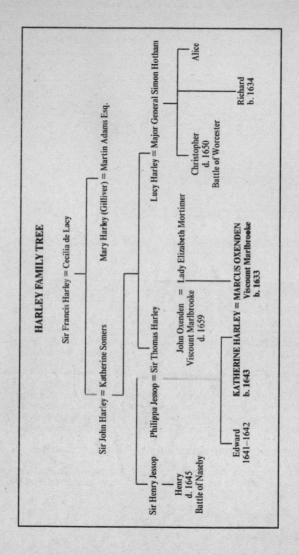

HARLEY FAMILY TREE

Sir Francis Harley = Cecilia de Lacy

Mary Harley (Gilliver) = Martin Adams Esq.

Sir John Harley = Katherine Somers

Philippa Jessop = Sir Thomas Harley

Lucy Harley = Major General Simon Hotham

John Oxenden = Lady Elizabeth Mortimer
Viscount Marlbrooke
d. 1659

Sir Henry Jessop

Henry
d. 1645
Battle of Naseby

Edward
1641–1642

KATHERINE HARLEY = MARCUS OXENDEN
Viscount Marlbrooke
b. 1633

b. 1643

Christopher
d. 1650
Battle of Worcester

Alice

Richard
b. 1634

Chapter One

'And how long do you expect to be gone?' Lady Elizabeth Oxenden, seated in the window embrasure of the library at Winteringham Priory, addressed her son.

'Two weeks. Possibly three.' Viscount Marlbrooke stood behind the desk, leafing through a sheaf of estate papers. He was dressed for travel, his cloak, gloves and flamboyantly plumed hat cast negligently on the chair by the door. 'I trust that you will be quite comfortable during my absence. Verzons will see to all your comforts. And there is, of course, Felicity.'

Indeed there was. She did not care to dwell too much on the thought. The grey light that dulled the brocade curtains and barely crept into the distant corners of the room matched her mood perfectly.

'I beg you will not leave me too long at Felicity's mercy. I need someone I can talk with, without having to watch my every word in case it offends her sensibilities.' She deliberately kept the tone light. She would not burden him with a need to dance attendance on his mother.

'Would I do such a thing?' He raised his eyes to hers, humour glinting, his expression one of surprised innocence. Studying the slight, pretty woman with sable hair, now heavily streaked with silver, he allowed her to set the tone and direction of the exchange.

'Quite possibly.'

'Find her something to do. There must be enough attics to clear out in this place to keep her from under your feet.'

But then I would be lonely. 'What an excellent suggestion. Felicity excels at organisation. I will tell her you suggested it.'

'I wouldn't, if I were you. She would immediately balk at the suggestion.' They smiled at each other, in perfect understanding.

'I suppose, Marcus, that you will find the opportunity to visit Whitehall?' Lady Elizabeth deliberately turned her eyes to the view beyond the window. Although she might wish herself back in London with its distractions and glamour, she found it difficult to hide her censure of some of the more extreme elements of the Restoration Court.

'Of course. Do I detect a hint of disapproval?'

'Well...'

Marlbrooke cast the papers on to the desk and moved with agile grace to sit opposite her. 'You should know, madam, that it pays me to keep my name and person in the King's mind. Charles is gracious and affable, but notoriously fickle. And since I need his favour yet for the security of my inheritance here at the Priory, I will pay my respects to him with due humility and considerable flattery.' His black brows rose in faint mockery. 'I find that I have become adept at it. Do you not approve?'

'I would—' she frowned '—if our esteemed Sovereign Lord were not such a bad example for any man to follow. There, now! I don't suppose I should have said that, should I?''

'Certainly not! Can this be his Majesty King Charles, our beloved monarch, brought back from exile, who has earned your displeasure in three short years? Are such opinions not treasonable?' The gleam in his eye was most pronounced. Conversations with Elizabeth Oxenden were always stimulating.

'Most definitely. Rumour says—and I am sure that it is true—that he lost one hundred pounds at cards in one sitting last Twelfth Night.'

'But, as you should know, *I* do not gamble. Not unless the cards are definitely stacked in my favour.'

'And as for that baggage Barbara Villiers...'

Marlbrooke laughed aloud. 'And what do you know about the Lady Castlemaine? Have you been indulging in scandalous gossip again?'

'Of course I have. This place may be some miles from London, but I frequently receive interesting news by letter. Some of it I could blush for!''

'So now you are critical of our new King's taste in women. Barbara Villiers is a very attractive lady. Ravishing, in fact. A riot of auburn hair, deep blue eyes. And such a figure...'

'And such a trollop!'

'The Villiers blood is as good as yours, Mother.' He grinned his appreciation of her assessment of the lady who had installed herself so effectively as Charles's current mistress.

'That may very well be, but she is still—'

'A trollop. As you said. But she has a passionate nature—and Charles is attracted. The lady has presented his Majesty with two healthy offspring already.'

'And neither of them legitimate.' Elizabeth wrinkled her nose in distaste. 'Of what use is that? The man needs a legitimate heir. My heart goes out to poor Queen Catherine—how she tolerates it I know not. I only hope that *you* do not bring home such an ambitious, self-seeking harpy as your wife.'

'Mistress Lovell is not an ambitious harpy.'

'Mistress Lovell?' Elizabeth's eyes widened, searching in her mind for the last name to be linked in liaison with that of her son. 'I thought it was Dorothea Templeton.'

'No. That was last month.'

'Oh, Marcus. I wish you would not!' But she could not prevent a ghost of a smile from warming her expression.

'I know. But allow me a little freedom and pleasure. I promise that while I am at Whitehall I will neither gamble away my fortune nor bring our name into disrepute. Nor marry a trollop. Does that satisfy?'

'I suppose it must.'

'I shall marry soon enough and produce an heir to the estate and grandchildren for you to spoil.'

'It is time.' She hesitated and then broached the delicate subject that had been on her mind for some days. 'You will see Sir Henry Jessop?'

'Yes. It is my intention to go to Downham Hall.' The humour immediately vanished from Marlbrooke's face. 'It is more than time that the matter was settled.'

'And so you are fixed on this marriage?'

'Of course. It is the perfect solution. For both our families.'

'She may reject you, you realise.'

'I doubt it.' His shoulders lifted in the slightest of shrugs. 'It is as politically advantageous for the Harleys as it is for the Oxendens. Perhaps more so. The girl's situation is not enviable. Not everyone is as tolerant of erstwhile supporters of Parliament as King Charles. I am sure they will have suffered their share of slanderous gossip and malicious revenge, so I would be amazed if Katherine Harley did not leap at the chance of so advantageous an alliance.'

Elizabeth was compelled by good sense to agree. She looked at her handsome, charming, *infuriating* son who resembled so closely his father. And remembered the days when, as a young girl, she had been swept off her feet to fall headlong into a love that lasted until death had parted them. What girl in her right mind would reject Marcus Oxenden? Katherine Harley would be either a fool or blind to do so.

'Would you not consider marrying for love?' Her suggestion, for once, was tentative. It was not, she knew, a subject open for discussion.

Marlbrooke smiled at her, making no attempt to hide the deep affection between them, understanding her anxieties. He leaned forward to bracelet her wrists in a light clasp. 'It may not be. I know that you adored my father. And he you. But such a blessing is not for everyone. I do not look for love in marriage. Merely respect, friendship if we are fortunate—tolerance if we are not. I believe that Katherine Harley will be more than suitable as a wife. Now, let that be an end to it. There is no need for your concern.'

Elizabeth sighed, but accepted from experience that there was no good to be had in pursuing the matter further.

'Be kind to her, Marcus,' was the only comment she allowed herself to make. 'Her childhood can not have been quite comfortable. And tell her...tell her that I will welcome her here as my daughter.'

'I will.' She instantly knew that she had touched a nerve. His tone took on a sardonic note. 'Many would tell you that I have no such finer motives, but whatever they might say about my character, it is not my intention to be cruel to her.'

'I know all about your character! I would not accuse you of such things!'

He showed his teeth at her response. 'But you are biased, my love.' Then made her smile again as he raised her hands to his lips and kissed them lavishly.

'Just try not to overawe the poor child.'

'It was not my intention.'

'No. But it would be so very easy for you to do.'

'I will do my poor best. Nor is it my intention to punish her for past sins. So don't fret.'

'Very well.' And that was as far as Lady Elizabeth dare push the issue. She stood and made her way slowly towards the door, now followed by Marlbrooke.

'So, madam. What shall I bring you from the flesh pots of London?'

'Anything?'

'Anything your heart desires.'

A bride with whom you have fallen hopelessly in love and who will love you in return. 'Books, if you will. Poetry. Whatever is fashionable.'

'Whatever I think Felicity will dislike?'

'You are too astute for your own good.' Elizabeth chuckled, allowing her hand to rest for a brief moment on her son's shoulder, smoothing the dense nap of his velvet coat.

'I will do it, with much pleasure.' He bent to kiss her cheek.

'Take care, Marcus.'

'Of course.'

And he was gone, leaving her to worry over a proposed marriage that had such cold expectations. A suitable wife, indeed! It seemed to her to be damned before it had even begun.

And now, a week after Marlbrooke's departure, Elizabeth Oxenden made her way slowly and painfully through the Great Hall in the oldest part of Winteringham Priory. She leaned heavily on a cane, her knuckles white with the effort and her lips compressed into a firm line. Today she felt every one of her forty-eight years. It had been a long winter. Every joint and muscle ached with the persistent damp and cold. The flaring agony in her left hip caused her to limp heavily and doubt that she could reach the distant doorway without aid.

How embarrassing! It seemed such a short time ago that she

had been able to ride with her husband, to dance until the candles guttered, to play in the Long Gallery with her boisterous son. She paused to rest against the heavy oak table. Her skin was still soft and clear, her eyes arresting with green flecks in their luminous grey depths, all remnants of her earlier beauty. But pain had left its imprint, strain had touched and deepened the lines around mouth and eyes. She felt so tired. Elizabeth sniffed in an instant of weakness and self-pity and tears threatened to spill from her eyes.

But self-pity was not in her nature. She would *not* call for Felicity. She straightened her spine and continued her clumsy route, surveying the heavy linenfold panelling and oak floorboards that stretched before her. They looked polished and well cared for to her critical eye. She did not to any degree dislike the house. She simply wished that she was not there. She would much rather be in London where her home was familiar, far smaller without the inconvenience of long corridors and vaulted ceilings and so, of course, much easier to heat and eradicate draughts. Where friends came to visit and cheer her through the dark winter days, where there were shops, and companions and entertainments now that the King had come into his own and made it clear that he intended to rejoice in his new powers.

Her own house in the country—not this one, but Glasbury Old Hall—had been destroyed in the war, razed to the ground after a year of bitter and violent siege in 1643. All her furniture gone, her treasures and her comforts, everything but the most personal of possessions, which they had managed to carry away in a night of frenzied packing and flight.

As for this house, Winteringham Priory, her husband had valued it greatly as an object of conquest. He had wrested it from the Harleys and taken it for his own in the same year that they had lost their own home. Sir Thomas Harley had been absent with the Parliamentarian army and his wife Philippa did not possess the backbone to withstand the siege as some beleaguered wives had done. And then Sir Thomas had been killed at Naseby—so young, such a waste... And so Elizabeth had come to live here, comfortably enough, if a little shadowed with guilt. It had seemed like justice, she supposed—if she could close her mind to the fate of Lady Philippa and the baby. But everything had changed so quickly. The house had been confiscated by Parliament under the authority of the Rump after the execution of the old King. And John, her beloved John, was now dead. Memories were too painful and Elizabeth would not willingly have returned to the Priory, no matter how magnificent its rooms, how valuable the estate.

But since King Charles had seen fit to gift the Priory to her son rather than the Harleys, here she was, uprooted from London and restored to this place of edgy memories and icy draughts. She winced and gasped in pain as she had to pull with some force to open the door from the Great Hall to the kitchen regions. It should please her that her son had the ear of the King, she mused as she rested again on a convenient window seat. But she wished he was here with her now, rather than indulging himself in the dubious pleasures of the Royal Court. Not that it was any hardship to him, to immerse himself in Court life, if rumour did not lie. Drink, cards, women, all the delights of the flesh—John would turn in his grave if he knew what Marcus was about. And if she remonstrated with her son, the love of her life, he merely smiled that particularly charming smile, his eyes warming his handsome but frequently unnervingly austere features, assuring her that there was nothing for her to be concerned over.

Raindrops ran down the window with icy monotony, blurring Elizabeth's view of the formal garden and the distant skyline. She knew the landscape well, of course, had always known it. After all, the outer reaches of the Priory ran with the Old Hall on its western side. Once, before the war, their families had been close neighbours, friends even, enjoying each other's company in hunting and evenings at home. She remembered Lady Philippa Harley, a gentle girl, perhaps a little weak, always afraid of criticism from those around her and with no real interest in the world-shaking events taking place in London and nearer to home. But pleasant enough for two young women to exchange girlish gossip. So how had it come to this—death and division between neighbours who once bought christening gifts for each other's children? The War had a lot to answer for, and here they were, back with a King and Parliament, irrespective of the death of John, and of Sir Thomas.

The voice of Felicity interrupted her thoughts as it echoed along one of the corridors above, querulous and harsh in complaint against some hapless servant. Elizabeth struggled to her feet to make good her escape before she could be discovered. Felicity was not the most amenable companion in the world, but without doubt she needed someone. Some days she could hardly lift her arm to brush her own hair. Or even push herself out of bed. The fear of increasing pain, of growing dependence, gripped her with sharp talons. *Oh, Marcus! Let me go back to London where it is easier to forget my infirmities, where I am rarely lonely.* She knew that she would never say those words to him. He would listen and try to make life more comfortable for her, but he was determined to make his home here at the Priory and she knew better than to voice her dissatisfaction. She understood the loss in his life, the devastation, the driving force within him, and loved him far too much to stand in his way.

She struggled through the doorway to avoid Felicity's approach, and turned into the passageway to the kitchens. As for this marriage... Elizabeth pursed her lips thoughtfully. She could understand only too well the logic of her son's decision. Katherine Harley was the true heiress to the property, even if her inheritance had been overlooked in the present political climate. It would certainly consolidate her son's possession, not that he needed it with the courts and the King's pleasure behind him. But marriage... How old would she be? About twenty years? Elizabeth vaguely remembered the birth of the baby just before Sir Thomas had died. A babe in arms when Philippa had been driven from the Priory to take refuge with Sir Henry Jessop, her brother over at Downham Manor. What sort of upbringing would the child have had there? Little warmth and pleasure, Elizabeth imagined. Sir Henry had a name for staunch Puritanism, even though he might be a fair man. And Philippa would probably not stand against him in the matter of the upbringing of her child.

But nothing was settled as yet. It was all still in the hands of the lawyers. And what would the girl make of her profligate son? A slow smile eased the tension of Elizabeth's face at the prospect. Perhaps Katherine Harley would be a true daughter to her, to replace the still-born child she still mourned after all these years. But what if she was a hymn-singing, Bible-reading girl, all duty and service with no love of music and pretty clothes? She shuddered at the prospect. Not all the legal intricacies would make her a suitable wife and daughter, whatever her promise to Marcus.

She hesitated outside the kitchen door and would have retreated if she had not experienced a particularly sharp twinge of pain from her hip to her knee. Did she really want to enter Mistress Neale's domain? She was pleasant enough, a sturdy, capable body, elderly now but still able to run the household efficiently, but she was an old family retainer of the Harleys who had stayed put through all the upheavals and changes of ownership, like Master Verzons, the steward. Always polite. Always cooperative. But Elizabeth felt that, as a newcomer, a usurper in fact, she was an intruder. They could run the house and did not need or desire orders from her. They smiled. They showed all due respect. But she sometimes caught a gleam in Mistress Neale's eyes—not unwelcoming, exactly, but assessing, even after all these years.

There was no help for it—she could not stand here for ever in this draughty corridor. She pushed open the kitchen door.

'Good morning, my lady. Can I be of any help?' Mistress Neale broke off her conversation with the cook, wiped her hands on her apron and approached with a quick curtsy and a calm welcome. The kitchen was warm, a blessing to Elizabeth's chilled flesh, and hummed with well-ordered activity. Something fragrant steamed over the fire. Lady Oxenden would have liked nothing better than to sit and exchange news and gossip with her housekeeper.

'Why, no. I thought...' Why did she feel so inadequate? 'I might take a look at the still-room.' *And Felicity will not find me in there!* 'I do not have the key. Perhaps you have it, Mistress Neale?'

'Indeed, my lady.' She took a ring of keys from her belt and selected the appropriate one. 'Was there anything in particular you were needing? I can always send Elspeth.'

'No, indeed. I am sure you have an inventory, but I would like to see what is still of use. I doubt that anything has been bottled or stored for a good number of years.'

'No, my lady. It has been sadly neglected since the house has stood empty. My own preserves are kept here in the kitchen larders. Mistress Adams never used the still-room—she thought it too small and inconvenient for the storing and drying of herbs—and she had no interest in preserves.'

'No. I do not suppose she had.' Elizabeth sighed and avoided

the opportunity to discuss the likes and dislikes of Mistress Gilliver Adams. Some of them were most disturbing and did not
bear close contemplation.

She took the key and, since there was no forthcoming invitation to stay in her own kitchen, she closed the door quietly and
retreated.

A blind passage led off from the corridor to the still-room.
With stiff fingers Elizabeth applied the key and found to her relief
that the lock had received some recent care and opened smoothly.
The door allowed her entrance to a small room, lined with
shelves from floor to ceiling, with a work bench along one wall
and an old cabinet fixed to the wall in one corner. The only
window was small, mullioned, letting in a poor, grey light. How
long since anyone had ventured in here? she wondered. Dust and
cobwebs covered and draped from every surface, as did the spi-
ders, and she tried not to notice the mouse droppings along the
surface of the bench.

For the most part the shelves were empty, but there were a
few jars at one side, some with faded labels, most without. Elizabeth remembered enjoying this little space in happier days to
store the products of the kitchen garden and the orchard for the
onset of winter. Presumably it had not been made use of any
time in the past decade. Above her head hung bunches of herbs,
perhaps collected and put there by herself. They were dry and
brittle now, too dusty for use, but the scent of sage filled the air
as she crumbled a sprig in her hand and allowed the leaves to
drift to the floor. She had seen that the herb garden was totally
overgrown, but it would be pleasurable to resurrect it on warm
afternoons in spring—if she could find it physically possible.

The bottles had dark, sinister contents. Possibly plums...or
damsons—she remembered a particularly fine specimen by the
wall in the kitchen garden. She would not care to risk sampling
them after all these years. Perhaps she could get Felicity to help
her take stock and clear out. It would give her something to do
other than complain and read pious passages from her limited
collection of books. Her eyes closed, the aromas of herbs around
her, Lady Elizabeth wished with all her heart that she had her
health back.

Finally Elizabeth opened the cabinet. On one shelf was a pestle and mortar. Beside it a sheaf of yellowed pages, perhaps a collection of old recipes, but nothing she remembered. Otherwise there was a general clutter of spoons, dishes and a cracked glass container.

She was about to turn away, somewhat disappointed at the cabinet's meagre treasure, when it caught her eye, tucked into the bottom corner of the cabinet. It was a handsome pottery jug, quite old, undecorated and cloaked with dust, but with an elegant neck and handle. She had no recollection of this. There was no label that she could see, so she bent carefully to lift it out and place it on the bench. It was well sealed with wax and there were traces of an official seal stamped into it, but it was brittle enough to begin to disintegrate at her touch. She carried it to the window to squint at the imprint. Impossible to tell. She moved to replace it in the cupboard. Perhaps Mistress Neale would know more about it.

Felicity's voice calling her name from close at hand caught her attention. It was enough to herald disaster. She fumbled, the pottery too smooth in her grasp and her swollen knuckles unable to keep a firm pressure.

She dropped the pot. It shattered on the tiled floor at her feet, sending shards of painted clay in every direction.

Elizabeth groaned in frustration and self-disgust. Now she would have to clear it up, whatever mess it contained—apart from having wilfully destroyed a handsome jug. Relief and some surprise swept through her, however, when she realised that, in spite of the stopper and the seal, the jug was, in fact, empty. All she could see around her feet were broken pieces of pottery.

It took no time for Elizabeth to accept that her hips and knees would not allow her to stoop to the floor to sweep up the pieces, however much she might like to hide the evidence. Never mind, Mistress Neale would see to it. Or even Felicity. After all, it was her fault, calling out in such a fractious voice that Elizabeth had dropped it in the first place. At least the vessel would not have been worth very much. It was not as if it was a family heirloom. Old, yes, but surely not of any great value.

As she closed the cabinet, Elizabeth was touched by a prickle of ice all the way down her spine. She shivered, experiencing a sudden desire to leave the still-room and take refuge in the warmth and familiarity of the kitchen. Nothing tangible. Just a natural discomfort, brought on by the cold and damp. And guilt, probably!

She closed the door, locked it, and retraced her steps to the kitchen—but she was unable to throw off the faint chill of unease. She resisted an urge to look behind her.

Chapter Two

The formal gardens of Downham Hall were awash with spring sunshine, the clipped box hedges spangled with diamond rain-drops. An attractive prospect after the gloom of winter months, but the chill wind and threat of further showers was sufficient to deter any but the hardiest of gardeners or the most determined seekers of natural beauty. Or solitude.

The lady, protected by a hooded cloak, was oblivious to the perfect symmetry of neat flower beds or the impressive vista of rolling park land. Her attention was clearly fixed on the man kneeling at her feet.

'Kate! Will you marry me? You must know that I love you. It cannot be a surprise to you after all these months—years, even.' The urgency in his tone surprised her: her cousin could usually be relied upon to remain calm and unruffled in any even-tuality.

'I... Oh, Richard! Do get up! If my uncle sees us, it will only make matters far worse than they already are. Besides, you are kneeling in a puddle.'

Richard rose to his feet, but kept a tight clasp of Kate's hands.

'Be serious, Kate. Marriage could solve all our problems, whatever Sir Henry believes. Besides, I know that you love me. I am certain that I have not been mistaken in this.'

Releasing her hands abruptly, Richard pushed back her hood so that Kate had no choice but to look at him when she answered.

There might have been traces of tears on her cheeks, but she raised her eyes to his with no shadow of uncertainty.

'You know how I feel, Richard. I have always cared for you. When we were children, you were my magnificent cousin. In recent years...I have come to rely on you far more than I think you realise.'

Richard returned her smile, but grasped her shoulders insistently. Kate became intensely aware of the pressure of his fingers through the worn velvet.

'Then if that is so, why are you so anxious?' He gave her a little shake. 'Why will you not give your consent to wed me? To allow me to approach your uncle?'

Kate sighed and turned away, forcing him to release her. She appeared to survey the distant landscape, but her violet-blue eyes were focused on unseen horizons.

'You know it is not possible.' she explained patiently. 'Come. Let us walk a little. I feel that walls have ears and there are too many people in this house who are willing to carry tales to my uncle. And none of them would wish us well.'

Richard offered his arm with a graceful bow. They crossed the paved terrace and descended the shallow steps to stroll amongst the wintry flower beds. By mutual agreement they came to a halt at the centre. Kate wrapped herself more closely into the heavy folds of her cloak and seated herself on the stone edging of an ornamental fountain.

'Are we far enough from the house now to be out of earshot? We only have these underclad nymphs for company.' Richard raised his hand in the direction of the marble mermaids and sea horses, silent witnesses who continued to release sprays of water from their conch shells. There was a teasing note in Richard's voice, but Kate did not respond to it. Instead there was an unexpected depth of bitterness in her immediate reply.

'No! We are not! I can never be far enough away. I know that I should be grateful, but gratitude has a finite quality—and I have been everlastingly grateful for twenty years!'

'Then marry me. That will enable you to live sufficient distance from this house to give you all the freedom and independence you desire.'

Kate shook her head. 'But don't you see, Richard? Independence is the crux of the matter. I owe everything to my uncle.

So does my mother. Since the day Winteringham Priory was besieged and overrun by the Royalists we have been dependent on Sir Henry for everything. From the food that we eat to the clothes that we stand up in.' She smoothed her fingers over a worn patch of velvet and pushed a frayed ribbon edging out of sight. 'How old was I when it happened? Three months? I have no recollection of my own home. My father's death at Naseby simply complicated an already impossible situation. For twenty years Sir Henry has fed, clothed and housed my mother and myself. His plans for my future can not be lightly disregarded. And then, of course, there is the question of money!' Kate's eyes sparkled with anger. 'And the land settlement!'

'But surely our marriage would help to smooth over the inheritance problem?' Richard joined her on the parapet and once more took possession of her cold fingers. 'You are the direct heir to the estate. We know that a female claim brings its own difficulties but, after my father, I have the most direct male claim. Our marriage would ensure that Winteringham Priory returns to our family where it rightfully belongs. I can not accept that Sir Henry will be so antagonistic to our union. It would also be an excellent opportunity to get you off his hands for good!'

Richard's persuasive argument did little to calm his companion. 'Oh, I agree. I know all the arguments. How should I not? I have heard them so often over the past three years since the King returned. But I'm not at all sure that what is legal and rightful will play any part in the final outcome. My uncle certainly does not think so. Oh, Richard! Why does it all have to be so difficult?'

'Politics, of course. And, as you so rightly said, money.' In spite of Kate's obvious distress, Richard rose abruptly and walked away from her. She watched him as he strode to the balustrade which separated them from the sunken garden. He leaned his hands upon it, his back to her. The rigid set of his shoulders spoke of his frustration at his inability to solve the problems of a financially ruined and disgraced Parliamentarian family in this time of revival of Royalist fortunes.

Her heart went out to him. Her own father had declared for Parliament, but his death in battle in 1645 had effectively removed the Harley family from the political scene. Her brother Edward, a baby, had died of the sweating sickness before she was born. Except for local events her uncle, Sir Henry Jessop, had deliberately remained uninvolved throughout the Interregnum. 'A sensible man stays at home and keeps his head down!' became his frequently expressed opinion.

Time had proved him to be right. For Richard, of course, it was an entirely different matter. The Hothams had always held to strong views and strong actions, in both politics and religion. Simon, Richard's father, had a reputation for uncompromising Puritanism and, as a military man, had become a figure of significant importance in Cromwell's New Model Army. Sir Henry even suspected him of supporting the execution of King Charles back in 1649. The new King would assuredly recognise the name of Hotham as that of a sworn enemy.

And now the Royalists were back in power, which promised little in the way of restoration of wealth or political advancement for any of those who had chosen to stand for Oliver Cromwell. The pardon for all sins committed in the name of Parliament was the most they could hope for.

As if aware of her scrutiny, Richard turned and walked back towards Kate. The fitful sun glinted on his fair hair, which he wore curling on to his shoulders, and highlighted the worn patches on his severe black coat. He no longer wore the distinguishing white collar of his youth, but no one would regard him as any other than an impoverished country gentlemen of a Puritan persuasion. And as such, he could not possibly figure in Sir Henry's plans for his niece.

Once more standing before her, Richard demanded, 'What of your mother? Has she no views on your marriage? Has she no influence with her brother?'

Kate's immediate laugh expressed anything but amusement. 'How can you ask it? I love my mother dearly, but I can expect no help from that quarter. She is entirely dominated by my uncle. She will go along with exactly what he plans and will be far too timid to voice even the slightest objection. She fears argument and dissension more than anything.'

'You clearly do not take after her!' Richard observed with more than a hint of irony.

'No.' Kate sighed with a wry smile and tucked her wind-blown curls back into her hood. 'It might be more comfortable for everyone if I did. I am, my uncle frequently states, a true Harley.

All self-will and determination, and a refusal to listen to good advice. He does not, of course, intend it as a compliment.'

'My lady!' Richard swept a mock bow with his broad-brimmed hat. 'I would not love you half so much if you were a meek little mouse. And were you aware that you have the most charming smile?'

'Thank you, sir!' Kate stood and swept him a regal curtsy, extending her hand for him to kiss, which he promptly did. Her troubles were momentarily swept away, a smile lighting her face with an inner glow.

'You shine as the sun in my life, dear Kate.'

'And you, sir, are a flirt,' responded Kate with a delightful chuckle. 'What would your severe parent say if he could hear you?'

'He would say that it is God's will that you become my wife and that we restore the Harley fortunes together.'

'I fear that it will depend more on the influence of Sir Henry than on God in the end!'

'Katherine! But that's blasphemy!' The glint in Richard's eyes did not quite rob his words of criticism of her flippant attitude. 'Indeed, my father is very strongly in favour of our marriage. He would welcome you as a daughter-in-law, as would my mother. Let me approach Sir Henry,' he urged once more. 'We cannot plan for the future unless we give him the opportunity to accept or reject me.'

'You are very determined, sir. And persuasive.' She took his arm and they continued their perambulations, abandoning the nymphs to their watery frolics.

'Why not? I can see nothing but advantage for us. Do you agree?'

'I find the idea of marriage to you most acceptable, dear Richard,' Kate assured him. 'It's just that...' She hesitated, then turned towards him as she made up her mind to speak. 'If my uncle disapproves, he could rake over all the old bitterness of past years. And he might forbid you the house. How could I exist if I could never see you again? I have no confidence in Sir Henry's compassion or tolerance.'

Before Richard could respond, they became aware of footsteps crunching on the gravel walk. Swynford, Sir Henry's steward, approached. He studiously ignored the closeness of the pair and their joined hands. With an impassive countenance, he bowed to Richard and then Kate. His words were for Kate.

'Forgive me, Mistress Harley. Sir Henry has sent me with a message. He and Lady Philippa desire your presence. In the library.' He hesitated and then added, 'Sir Henry would wish to see you immediately.'

'Thank you, Swynford.' Kate smiled her gratitude, picking up the note of warning in the steward's demeanour through long custom. 'Tell me…is Sir Henry aware that Mr Hotham has called on me…on us?'

'No, mistress. I believe that he is not aware of this circumstance, although Mr Simon Hotham is with him now. I do not believe,' he continued imperturbably, 'that there is any need for his lordship to know.'

'Thank you, Swynford.' The steward returned to the terrace and Kate faced Richard for a final farewell.

'I think that you should not speak with Sir Henry now,' she stated. 'I don't know why he desires my presence so urgently, but I have a premonition that it will not be an agreeable experience. It rarely is! To discuss marriage now would be to stir up a viper's nest.'

'So you wish me to leave you to face Sir Henry alone?'

'Indeed, it would be better.'

Richard was reluctant to release her. 'Remember that, whatever happens, I love you more than life itself,' he assured her. 'I promise that I will always stand by you and protect you.'

The garden was suddenly silent, magnifying the tension between them. Even the blackbirds in the adjacent cherry hedge stopped their scufflings. Whatever encouragement Richard read in her eyes, he drew Kate firmly towards him and kissed her, first on her forehead and then, as he received no rebuff, on her lips. It was a gentle, undemanding kiss, a mere promise of future passion. Her hair, whipped into a tangle of ringlets by the persistent breeze, caressed his face as his arms encircled her waist beneath the folds of her cloak. She felt a flicker of response surge through her body as his hands stroked her sides, her arms and then reached to smooth her hair. It was an intimately possessive gesture, leaving Kate in no doubt about her cousin's feelings towards her. Then, before she could respond further—and, indeed, she was unsure just how she wished to respond—he let his arms fall from her and stepped back, releasing her, leaving everything between them once more unresolved.

'Then I will say good day, Mistress Harley.' Richard had himself firmly under control and spoke formally. 'Or perhaps I should say adieu.'

He bowed once more with one hand on his heart.

'Adieu, Mr Hotham,' Kate whispered in like fashion and held out her hand.

Richard raised her palm to his lips in a final salute, aware of her trembling fingers. 'I give you my word,' he affirmed in a low voice, 'one day you will be my wife. You will belong to me. I will not allow anything or anyone to stand in my way.'

With that, Richard released her, turned on his heel and strode through the flower beds towards the distant stables. Kate was left to follow him with longing in her eyes, her heart beating a shade more quickly than usual. She had never believed Richard to be capable of such intensity, such determination. She traced the outline of her lips with one finger and smiled as she remembered the firm pressure of his mouth on hers. He was so certain. She wished with all her heart that she could be equally so.

Richard's disappearance through the ornamental gateway recalled Kate to the more immediate situation. A small frown creased her brow. Whatever it was, it had to be faced. With characteristic squaring of the shoulders and not a little forboding, she turned her steps towards the house. It was only then that she noticed how the sun had been obliterated by dark clouds and the first heavy drops of rain were beginning to fall.

'No!'

The single word hung in the sudden silence. Kate slowly drew in her breath, eyes fixed defiantly on Sir Henry Jessop, and waited for the storm to break. She did not have to wait long. Not even the presence of Simon Hotham, hunched and brooding in a high-backed chair beside the fireplace, could restrain her uncle from expressing his displeasure toward his errant niece.

'No?' Sir Henry rose from his chair behind the desk with a distinct air of menace. 'Perhaps I have misunderstood you, madam?'

Kate bowed her head, but not in submission. She remained straight-backed, alone and defiant in the centre of the room.

'No,' she repeated it with commendable calm. 'There is no misunderstanding. I will not marry Viscount Marlbrooke.'

Sir Henry thrust back his chair, which lurched violently, rounding on his sister who shrank back in alarm.

'What's this? Did I not tell you to instruct your daughter in what is expected of her?'

'Well...of course, Henry, but...I haven't...that is to say...'

'I understand only too clearly, madam! I hoped that I could rely on you in matters concerning the welfare of this family. It seems once again that I was wrong. Is it too much to ask?'

'But indeed, brother—'

Kate intervened to save her mother from any further distress.

'My mother did not have the opportunity to inform me of your wishes, sir. I have been engaged with the housekeeper this morning.' She risked a quick glance at her mother to plead her compliance with this obvious lie, but received no recognition. 'But whether I was aware of your plans or not,' she continued, 'I will not comply.'

'Indeed. It is high time you were married with a husband to teach you obedience and good manners since your lady mother has so clearly failed. You will accept Marlbrooke's offer or I will have you locked in your room and whipped until you do.'

Kate's eyes flashed with anger, her usually pale cheeks washed with a delicate colour.

'How dare you! I have been obedient to your wishes all my life. But this is a different matter. My father fought for Parliament against the King and served the cause loyally.'

'I am well aware of your father's unwise commitment.'

But Kate refused to be deflected by the sly slur on her father's memory. 'He gave up his life for his beliefs at Naseby. How can I tarnish his memory by marrying a popinjay of a Royalist? A courtier who concerns himself with nothing but pleasure.'

'You know nothing about him, girl! How should you? As for the rest, it is all history and must be buried with all speed. It will do us no good to hang on to past loyalties.' Sir Henry might be too well aware of Marlbrooke's reputation, but he had no intention of acknowledging it before his wilful niece. The less ammunition she had against this marriage, the better.

Kate turned to her mother in despair. 'My father would not have wanted this. Would he?' She sank on her knees beside her mother's chair in a swish of blue velvet skirts. 'Have you nothing to say to support me in this?'

But Lady Philippa refused to meet her eyes or respond to her daughter's anguish. She simply sat, continuing to pleat the lace edging of her handkerchief, and ignored Kate's grasp on her arm. Kate watched her in exasperation, wondering not for the first time how she could have so little in common with this nervous, faded lady who had given her birth. Her face was still unlined and her figure had the trimness of youth, but her soft brown hair, severely confined, and her blue eyes had faded with time as if she might slowly disappear from view. Even her grey damask gown added to the illusion that it was her wish to become invisible, to merge with the furniture and hangings. Widowhood had not treated her kindly. She needed love and support to bolster her self-esteem: her brother's blustering spirit caused her to wince and cower. Even now she turned her face away from the intense emotions expressed around her.

'Your father is dead,' continued Sir Henry as if Kate had not interrupted him. 'As your uncle, your marriage is now my affair. The war and your father's death ruined us. We must restore our fortunes—and this is the obvious opportunity.'

Kate rose to her feet and swept round to face her uncle, seizing the obvious weapon for attack, to Sir Henry's dismay. 'I have been told of the state of our family fortunes since childhood. Surely the chief cause of our ruin was Viscount Marlbrooke himself? And now you wish to marry me into the Oxenden family. His son, I presume? I find the logic of this beyond belief and it smacks to me of hypocrisy.' The sarcasm was heavy on her tongue and her direct gaze issued a challenge to Sir Henry. He picked up the challenge immediately.

'Your memory is perfectly sound. Marlbrooke took possession of Winteringham Priory in 1643 and—'

'I know it! Mother, how can you countenance this match? Surely the events of the past were too painful for you to lay aside now without comment? Driven from your home by the direct orders of Viscount Marlbrooke, unable to make contact with your husband, your baby son dead and myself only a few months old—how can you tolerate this?'

Lady Philippa raised her handkerchief to catch the tears that had begun to flow down her cheeks. 'Indeed, my love. It is all true. But...' she sniffed and blew her nose '...your uncle believes that this marriage will be for the best and will secure the Priory for our family. I don't quite understand...but pray listen to him, my love. He is thinking of your comfort as well as the restitution of the family.' She began to sob in earnest to Sir Henry's evident disgust. He cast his eyes to heaven.

'So how can my marriage to Viscount Marlbrooke be in any way advantageous?' Kate demanded of her uncle as she abandoned any hope of a sensible response from her mother.

'Your niece has the truth of it. I am unable to support you in this proposal, Sir Henry.' The words dropped into the heated atmosphere with the sizzle of hailstones into a dish of mulled ale.

Simon Hotham had remained silent, his crippled fingers, talon-like, resting awkwardly on the oak carving of his chair. His pale grey eyes settled on his brother by marriage, fierce and uncompromising with a depth of contempt for the argument developing round him. Once he had had an enviable reputation as a soldier in Cromwell's Army. But that was before the destruction of Republicanism and Puritanism, the two great causes of his life, and, after taking a bullet wound in his thigh in the Battle of Worcester, the destruction of his health. Now his once tall, well-muscled body, used to a life of action and authority, was bent and wasted, his face lined with pain. Now he found difficulty in walking even the shortest distance without the aid of sticks and rarely travelled far from home. Bitter disillusion, a dark cloud, now cloaked his every move and thought, his driving ambition being to restore the power and authority of the Hotham family, through his son Richard. Richard, his first born and light of his life. Simon's fair hair was lank and thinning, his lips pressed into a thin line of austerity, his cheeks hollowed. Yet Kate saw Richard in his face and build and smiled her gratitude for his championship of her cause. She was surprised to receive help from this quarter.

'I find that I must agree with Mistress Katherine,' Mr Hotham continued, ignoring Kate and addressing his remarks to Sir Henry. 'I cannot believe that you would even consider marriage to an Oxenden. It brands you a traitor to the name of Harley and negates everything that your sister suffered in her exile from her home.'

'Forgive me, Simon—' a nerve twitched in Sir Henry's jaw as he strove to control his anger at this unwarranted interruption '—but this is not your concern. And even you must see that the marriage would guarantee to restore the Priory to us and our descendants.'

'Perhaps.' Hotham's lips curled sardonically. 'But would it not be better to fight for the inheritance through the Courts? Do you really wish to be beholden to the family of Oxenden, who despoiled the Priory in the first place?'

'I do not see that we have any choice.'

'You do. You know it. Let Katherine marry Richard. It is a union made before God. He is the direct heir to the property after Katherine—and marriage will provide a male claimant. That would sit strongly with the Courts. And it would unite and strengthen the family. I can think of no better means.'

'I will not countenance that marriage.' Sir Henry shook his head impatiently, but refused to meet Simon's jaundiced eye. 'I have no criticism of your son. Indeed, Richard is as fine a gentleman as I could wish to meet. If my own son had lived... But that is irrelevant. Such an alliance would not be of advantage to the family and nothing you say will persuade me differently.'

'I would still say that Katherine has the matter correctly,' Simon continued to develop his argument, 'however much I might disapprove of her manner of saying it—such forwardness in a young woman is to be regretted. And I would hope that in marriage to my son she would learn to conduct herself with more seemly dignity and respect for those who know what is best for her.' He ignored the flash of anger in Kate's eyes as she strove to remain silent, but kept his own cold gaze fixed on her uncle. 'But I agree with her that to unite with this Royalist family in the circumstances is despicable. I would have thought better of your sense of loyalty to the cause, Sir Henry. Do reconsider before it is too late.'

'I will not.' Sir Henry was not to be moved from a decision that had lost him some little sleep.

'Then I have nothing further to say on this topic.' Simon all but spat the words. 'It is beyond my comprehension that... But it is not my wish to quarrel with you, Sir Henry, so I will take my leave. If you would arrange for my carriage... I find it difficult to express my displeasure in mild words.'

He struggled to his feet, wincing at the pain that attacked his twisted limbs, Lady Philippa hurrying to retrieve his sticks from beside the chair. He took them from her without comment and sketched a clumsy bow before hobbling from the room, his rigid shoulders expressing his intense disapproval.

Sir Henry sat silently for a long moment, contemplating his clasped hands, and then with the slightest of shrugs continued where he had left off before Simon Hotham's departure. 'It is a matter of inheritance and politics.' He fixed Kate with a stern stare. 'The future of Winteringham Priory is still in doubt. If your father had been more aware of his domestic duties and had been present to fight off the attack in 1643, this would never have occurred.'

'But we did not give up our land willingly. No one could ever say that. Why should it not be restored to us now? Who can possibly have a better claim than I have?'

'I am sympathetic to your family pride, Katherine, but we have to face the realities of the situation.'

'Surely the reality is that the house was snatched from us: we were driven out with Royalist cavalry at our backs.'

'Very true, my dear. And it became to all intents and purposes a Royalist estate, used by Viscount Marlbrooke to aid the King and his cause. Where do you think the rents went in the years before Charles was defeated? Why do you think there is no trace of the family silver? Sold! Or melted down! The result is the same.' Sir Henry shrugged, extracted a document from a pile before him and held it out to Kate. 'Here is the latest intelligence from London concerning the settlement of claims. If you can understand the legalities!'

Kate carried the letter to the window to struggle through the legalistic words and phrasing. The implications were only too clear.

'I understand,' she finally admitted with a sigh. 'It seems that my inheritance will be given to whoever has the largest purse or the loudest voice at Court.'

'Exactly. It will not be the Harley family, I fear.' Sir Henry retrieved the document from his niece with a slight shrug. 'A female claim is always unsatisfactory. And, of course, your father left no will, presuming that the entail would stand. If the land had been willed to you, it might have been different. But as it stands, there is little hope.'

'What about Richard?' Lady Philippa had recovered from her bout of tears and had followed enough of the discussion to see the possibilities for her favourite nephew. 'Is he not the male heir to the Priory?'

'Never! A foolish suggestion, which would be a disaster for the family. Besides, his claim is also through a female line, through his mother. But it is beside the point.' Sir Henry threw back his head in an impatient gesture. 'Marlbrooke is rich. He has the ear of the King. He has submitted his claim to the Priory and the Courts are likely to uphold it against us.' He slammed his hands down on to the desk, sending up a cloud of dust motes to dance in the slanting sunshine. 'It appears to be a hopeless case.'

'Would the new King really be so unfair?' Kate's voice registered shocked surprise.

'Ha!' Sir Henry's bitterness was clear. 'Is it unfair to reward your own followers at the expense of those who took the sword against you? I think not. That, Katherine, is what I meant when I spoke of realities.'

He crossed the room towards her. He was still tall and upright in spite of advancing years, his hair showing only the faintest sprinkle of grey. His objective was now clearly to make amends and apologise for his earlier harsh approach to the problem. He stretched out a hand in supplication.

'I'm sorry, Kate. I have fought hard for your rights. Not simply for the family, but because you have been the daughter I never had. It would have pleased me to see you re-established at the Priory in your own right. But we must now of necessity revise our plans to match present circumstances.'

'I can see why you wish me to marry Viscount Marlbrooke.' Kate's tone indicated a dull acceptance of the inevitable.

'Of course you do! You're an intelligent girl. So come, let us work for a propitious outcome. What better way to restore out fortunes and mend our relations with the Royal Court than through this one marriage?'

'I understand. Might I ask what Viscount Marlbrooke's feelings are?'

'That is immaterial. He has made an offer. It provides an excellent settlement and I will not allow you to throw it away. It is a political marriage and you should not look for emotional involvement. You will grow to like him well enough, I expect, and if you don't—well, it will still have served its purpose and your children will give you plenty to occupy your time!'

Kate took another deep breath and threw caution to the winds. There was little point in doing otherwise. 'I feel that I should tell you...' she was angry to note the uncertainty in her voice but ploughed on '...I wish to marry Richard. I love him. And I know that he wishes to marry me.'

Any sympathy that Sir Henry might have felt came to an abrupt end as he swept aside her admission with an impatient gesture and returned to his chair behind the desk to take up his habitual position of authority.

'Forget your cousin. And any of those ridiculous notions expressed by Simon Hotham. Richard has no claim on you.' He began to shuffle the documents before him into a neat pile as if Kate's announcement was of supreme unimportance.

'But I love him,' she whispered, struggling to prevent tears from gathering as she realised the strength of her uncle's will.

'Marriage to a Parliamentarian traitor would be less than advantageous to us at a time like this.'

'Surely Richard's family were no more traitors than we were,' Kate pleaded in despair. 'We have all been pardoned. How can you condemn him like this? Please let him speak to you.'

'It is not the same at all. Simon was too close to those who signed King Charles's death warrant for my liking. I would hesitate to discuss this in his presence—but it is none the less true. If there is a renewed demand from the Anglican Church to pursue a policy of revenge against those still alive, Simon Hotham's name might just head the list. And where would that leave us, if you were married to Richard? It is not a situation I am willing to risk.'

Kate, acknowledging the truth of Sir Henry's reading of the situation, found that there was nothing she could say. Sir Henry, sensing her hopelessness, tried for a more conciliatory tone, hoping to win her acceptance of a marriage that he had always known would be distasteful.

'Come, my dear. You will do well to put Richard out of your

mind. Look at the advantages in marriage to Marlbrooke. Wealth. Status. Recognition from the new King and a position at Court. You will be able to return to the Priory as your rightful home. You are twenty years old. It is high time you were married, you know.'

Kate shook her head, anything but co-operative. 'I will not marry Viscount Marlbrooke!'

'Then I have no alternative—' Sir Henry was interrupted by the quiet opening of the library door. Swynford entered with some reluctance.

'Well? I thought I gave orders we should not be disturbed.'

Swynford inclined his head respectfully, well used to his lordship's peremptory tones. 'Indeed you did, my lord. But a visitor has arrived. And I believed it best to inform you immediately.'

'Well?'

'Viscount Marlbrooke, my lord.' Swynford opened the library door wider to admit the unexpected guest. Three pairs of eyes were riveted on the figure in the doorway. The unexpected visitor paused, supremely aware of his audience.

Kate received an instant impression of wealth and elegance— and of confidence. Marcus Oxenden, Viscount Marlbrooke, only son of the villain of her childhood and her proposed future husband, made a worthy entrance in the deliberate magnificence of full Court dress. Unfashionable as it might be, he wore his own hair, black and dense as midnight, fashioned to fall elaborately in ordered waves and curls to his shoulders. Otherwise he wore the latest Court fashion: a black velvet, knee-length coat and waistcoat, heavily decorated with silver embroidery and ribbon loops at the shoulder. Kate's lips took on a derisory twist at the obvious French influence. His white shirt, visible below the wide cuffs of his elbow-length sleeves, was of the finest silk, as were his stockings. He had obviously made no concessions to the dusty journey from London. His shoes, flamboyant with black rosettes and crimson heels, merely added to his height and consequence. Light glinted on the jewels in his cravat; priceless lace cascaded over his hands. It was an impressive entrance and, Kate suspected, had been deliberately stage-managed to achieve maximum effect.

Cold grey eyes, at present watchful and perhaps a little judgmental, swept the room, hardly touching on Kate. He was younger than she had expected, perhaps around thirty years, but the fine lines around his unsmiling mouth betrayed a worldly cynicism. Kate swallowed as the pulse in her throat increased its pace, and as she realised that Viscount Marlbrooke was everything a bride could have dreamed of in the secrecy of her heart. He was tall, taller than Richard, broad shouldered with the muscle development fitting for a soldier and swordsman, and, of course, with the superb control and elegance essential for a courtier. His face commanded immediate attention in its austere beauty, not only the clear grey eyes but the planes and angles of cheekbone and jaw. As his hair, his brows were dark, his nose straight and masterful.

Viscount Marlbrooke, apparently unaware of the critical assessment from the lady of his choice, swept off his plumed hat and bowed with exaggerated, polished grace to the assembled company. He was, without doubt, the most handsome man Kate had ever seen. She sighed in disgust that this man who had dared to petition for her hand should be so outrageously attractive.

'A painted popinjay!' she repeated it, not quite below her breath, watching him bow towards her uncle. As he rose to his full height with a flourish of an elegant, long-fingered hand, he gave no sign that he had heard her opinion but instinctively, perhaps by the slight stiffening of his shoulders, she knew that he had and wondered momentarily at her temerity in antagonising this palpably dangerous man. All in all, it seemed of little importance that she hated him on sight.

Kate was immediately conscious of her dishevelled appearance. Her assignation in the windswept garden had done her no favours and had whipped her ringlets into a riot of curls. She feared that there were obvious smears of mud and dust along the hem of her skirts. As for any remaining tear stains on her cheeks... Kate fumed inwardly that he should have caught her at such a disadvantage on their first meeting, especially as, she surmised, his only reason for travelling such a distance from London was to look her over and assess whether she was worthy of marriage to a royal favourite! And no one, as she continued to view him with hostility, could believe that he had travelled any distance at all. Certainly not in that impeccable outfit. How dare he put her at such a disadvantage!

'My lord!' Kate was silently amused to realise that her uncle was flustered by the sudden appearance of their previous topic of conversation. 'Please forgive our lack of welcome. We were not expecting you. Well, certainly not today.' Not only flustered, but over-conciliatory. Kate set her teeth as she listened to her uncle's determined attempts to secure this marriage at all costs. He returned Marlbrooke's bow and then approached down the length of the library to extend his hand in a polite gesture of greeting.

'I understood that you were expecting me.' Marlbrooke's response was bored, languid. It seemed that it could not have mattered less. 'We have a matter of business to arrange. But, indeed, I should not need to encroach too far on your time or privacy.'

So, thought Kate. At least I know where I stand. A matter of business indeed! She caught her mother's vague gaze across the room and was surprised by the sympathy for her plight that she read there. But sympathy would not bring her the means of escape. Kate smiled reassuringly, even though it was a mere tightening of her lips, and then returned her attention to the central tableau.

'Permit me,' her uncle was saying, 'to present you to my sister, Lady Philippa Harley...Viscount Marlbrooke.' Lady Philippa smiled nervously at her brother and the Viscount and extended her hand. The Viscount bowed low and touched his lips to her fingers. 'I am delighted to make your acquaintance, Lady Philippa. I believe that you were acquainted with my mother, Lady Elizabeth.'

'Why, yes.' Lady Philippa looked startled. 'I had forgotten... It was many years ago, of course.'

'My mother remembers your friendship with pleasure.'

'Why...of course.' She became even more flustered, casting a glance towards her brother, seeking approval for this friendly overture. She did not receive it and promptly lapsed into embarrassed silence.

'And this,' Sir Henry intervened impatiently and turned to Kate, 'is my niece, Mistress Katherine Harley. She, of course, is the sole heir of Sir Thomas Harley, late owner of Winteringham Priory.'

Kate found herself, for the first time, being observed in such an impersonal manner that she felt a need to repress a shiver that ran down her spine.

'Of course.' Marlbrooke bowed again and Kate responded with the slightest of curtsies within the bounds of good manners. 'Mistress Harley. I have heard much of your beauty. Allow me to tell you that it was accurate in every detail.' No trace of emotion crossed the smooth features, no hint of a smile touched the firm mouth and his glance in her direction was cursory in the extreme.

And who could possibly have told you anything about my appearance? questioned Kate silently. He was certainly adept in the art of flattery, even if he hardly looked at her. She determined to give him no pleasure in her reply.

'Thank you, my lord.' Her dark brows arched to express utter surprise. She ignored a warning glance from Sir Henry.

Marlbrooke appeared to be unconcerned with her cool response, but accepted Sir Henry's invitation to sit, taking the chair beside the fireplace recently vacated by Simon Hotham and crossing one well-shaped leg over the other. Swynford was despatched to bring refreshment for the guest.

'We were, of course, expecting a visit from your lordship,' Sir Henry explained, 'but hardly so soon. It has not been clement weather for travel.'

'I stayed last night at the house of a family acquaintance, only a little distance from here.' He shook out the lace at his wrists with a politely distant smile. 'It was an engagement of long standing. It seemed to be too good an opportunity to miss.' Kate's raised brows once again registered his lack of enthusiasm.

'Indeed, indeed.'

Swynford returned with pewter tankards of ale.

'Let us hope that we shall be able to drink to the successful outcome of this matter,' stated Sir Henry. Marlbrooke inclined his head in agreement as he accepted the tankard.

'It seems to me a simple matter.' The Viscount's gaze swept the three players in the game. 'Let us be honest about the possible outcome of the settlement of Winteringham Priory. We have both put forward a claim. It is most unlikely that the Commission will look with any sympathy on yours, given the history of recent loyalties and involvement in the War.'

Sir Henry knew that he was fighting a last-ditch stand, but rallied valiantly. 'The estate belongs by right to the Harley family. It was not sold, but wrested from them forcibly—by your father, my lord. My niece has the legal right to the land. You cannot refute it.'

'Possibly not.' Marlbrooke remained calm and relaxed, sure of his ground. He could afford to be generous in victory. 'The estate was sequestered from my father by the county committee in 1651. If you had made a push for the title then, it might have been a different story. As it is, my father compounded for the estate: indeed, he paid a far greater fine than the land was worth.'

Marlbrooke raised the tankard to his lips, drank, then continued. 'For the past decade we have been excluded from politics and government until the happy restoration of our King. We devoted out energies to developing our assets. With considerable success, I might add.' He smiled without humour. 'I am in a far better position to bribe the Commission judges than you are, you understand.'

Sir Henry raised his hands, palm upwards, in defeat. 'So. I have no choice but to accept the situation. I presume that you have not come here merely to gloat? What is your offer?'

'All I ask is that Mistress Harley do me the honour of becoming my wife. I would not be so discourteous as to gloat,' he reproved gently. 'That will produce an immediate and satisfactory solution to any inheritance problem. She...' he bowed his head slightly in Kate's direction '...has the claim *de jure,* I have the estate *de facto.* What better solution? It is a valuable estate. We should not allow it to be harmed by interminable legal wrangling.'

Sir Henry looked with distaste at the composed and arrogant courtier before him. It was all too true, but it stuck in his gullet to accept it. 'Very well,' he stated, breaking the short silence. 'Your offer has my consent. Katherine?' He turned towards his niece who had remained silent and motionless throughout the negotiation, which had apparently settled her future without any reference to her own feelings in the matter. 'You understand the situation. What is your reply?' His fierce expression dared her to refuse the offer.

Kate continued to remain silent. What could she say? Her brain seemed to have frozen and she had lost the power of speech.

'Katherine?'

Before the hiatus could become totally embarrassing, it was broken by Marlbrooke.

'Perhaps I might be allowed to have a private word with Mistress Harley? I would not wish her to feel pressurised into this marriage against her will.'

A range of emotions flitted crossed Sir Henry's face, not least the hope, quickly suppressed, that this arrogant young man would be refused out of turn by his volatile niece. Since the upstart Royalist was so confident, let him try!

'Certainly, my lord. With pleasure. Perhaps, Katherine, you would care to show his lordship into the parlour.'

There was little point in arguing. Kate stalked out of the library, defiance writ clear in the erect spine, the proud carriage of her head, and into the pleasant panelled sitting room, which overlooked the front drive. She walked to the window where she turned to face her suitor, her back to the light so that it would be almost impossible for him to read her expression. Marlbrooke followed her more slowly, closing the door gently behind him.

The room echoed with a silence that neither party seemed to be in any hurry to break.

Kate stood motionless, acutely aware of her nerves stretching to breaking point, when Marlbrooke spoke. 'So, Mistress Harley. You have had nothing to say so far about this transaction. I would be pleased to know your sentiments.' His voice was soft but firm and Kate heard in it a command. She found her voice at last and was grateful that her anxiety was not evident.

'Do you expect me to welcome this marriage?'

'Hardly!' He laughed gently. 'But I do not desire a totally reluctant bride. That would lead to a most...uncomfortable relationship, would it not?'

'So it would matter to you if I was pushed into this by family dictates?' The surprise in her voice was clear.

'Of course it would. I am no monster, in spite of any rumours to the contrary.' Marlbrooke smiled slightly, a wry curl of his lips. 'If you refused, if you could not possibly tolerate my person, I would accept your refusal.'

'That's all very well, my lord, but my uncle would not be so understanding!' Kate was horrified to feel tears begin to sting her eyes and admonished herself at this emotional response to a practical matter. She swallowed and looked down, hiding her imminent distress with a sweep of dark lashes. 'You are very kind,' she managed in a low voice.

'Is your heart perhaps given elsewhere?'

Richard! Oh, Richard! She shook her head. 'No,' she whispered, acknowledging the guilt of betrayal. She could not tell him. She could not allow him any knowledge that might give him a hold over her. She dare not trust his sympathy.

'Your mother appears to see no objection.'

'She wouldn't, of course.' Her tone was bleak.

'I see. So, do you accept my offer, madam?'

It is like negotiating a good price for a beast at market, thought Kate wildly, swept by a sudden desire to laugh hysterically. Finally she raised her eyes to his across the growing shadows in the room.

'My lord, I cannot refuse your offer.'

'Then let us be practical.' Perhaps he had heard the vestiges of panic in her voice, seen the ivory whiteness of her clasped fingers. 'The marriage will bring you benefits. I am sufficiently wealthy to provide you with all the comforts of life that you could wish for. If it is your ambition to experience Court life, then so be it. Most importantly, you can return to your family home and be mistress of it. You must have affectionate memories of it.'

'I have no memories of it!' she was driven to reply bitterly. 'I was only a few weeks old when we were cast out. How can I see it as my home?'

'Then perhaps it will become so with custom. Come, Mistress Harley. These are the obvious advantages. What is your answer? You cannot put the blame on my shoulders for events that happened before I attained my majority. I would make recompense if possible.'

'What do you gain from this?' Kate's bald enquiry appeared to take him as much by surprise it did her. It prompted him to hold out his hand. 'Come here,' he ordered. Kate found herself compelled by an overwhelming force to cross the polished expanse of floor between them and place her hand in his. He raised it and formally pressed her fingers to his lips. She was instantly reminded of a fair head rather than the dark one before her before she closed her mind to such painful comparisons.

Marlbrooke raised his head, continuing to hold her fingers lightly and at last replied to her question. 'Since we are beginning this relationship on a point of honesty, madam, I will tell you

what I will gain. I will gain security of tenure of the Winteringham estate. No descendants of yours will make a counterclaim
against my inheritance at any future date. Your descendants will,
of course, be my heirs. Furthermore, the King believes that it
would be an excellent ploy to recompense my family whilst at
the same time making clear his concern for those of his subjects
who had, unfortunately, committed themselves to treasonable acts
against the Crown.'

So there it was. Kate felt the blood run cold in her veins. A
business deal expressed in a voice totally devoid of emotion. But
what else had she expected? She snatched her hand away from
the Viscount's light control.

'How fortunate that such intricate matters can be settled so
easily.' She failed to control the scorn in her voice. 'If it is also
the King's wish, then how can I possibly refuse? I should certainly never receive another such flattering offer. I perceive that
I should be honoured that anyone of your standing should wish
to enter into an alliance with my family in the present political
climate.'

'Indeed, madam. After all,' he reminded her in the smoothest
of tones, 'your uncle was one of Cromwell's closest henchmen.
Hardly the best qualification for advancement in the circumstances.'

Kate accepted the implied rebuke—indeed, she had no choice.
'Very well. You have persuaded me where my family could not.
I accused my uncle of misreading the situation. He obviously had
not.'

'I am afraid not. So? Your decision?'

Again she turned her face away. And then, 'I accept your offer,
my lord. I will agree to the marriage. I must thank you for
your…condescension.'

Marlbrooke ignored the barb and bowed slightly. 'I am most
gratified. Perhaps I should have added that I shall also acquire a
most beautiful wife?'

Kate looked up. In the evening light his face was still clear.
She searched his eyes and fine-featured face. And such splendid
eyes, she thought inconsequentially, dark grey and thickly fringed
with black lashes. But there was no warmth or encouragement
here for her in her distress, merely a cold, calculating strength
of will.

'Thank you, my lord.' She could think of nothing else to say. She kept her voice as colourless as his. 'I hope that I shall prove to be a conformable wife.'

'I am relieved to hear it.' Did she detect a flicker of amusement for the first time, the slightest twitch of his lips? But then it was gone, to be replaced by dry cynicism. 'I am certain that we shall deal well together, madam. I will inform Sir Henry of your compliance. I believe that he will be greatly relieved. I will also inform you of the necessary arrangements in due course when the legalities are complete.'

He turned on his heel and walked to the door, halting to look back once more to where Kate stood motionless before the leaded window. The evening sun gave her dark curls a halo of gold, but left her face in shadow. Marlbrooke hesitated, his hand on the latch, appeared to change his mind and calmly, deliberately, retraced his steps until he was standing close before her. Kate's immediate reaction was to retreat, but before she could do so she found herself held fast by the Viscount's arm around her waist. She caught her breath in utmost surprise and was considering the most effective way to regain her freedom when his free hand wound itself into her tangled hair to pull her even closer.

'Look at me,' he demanded and when she automatically obeyed, his lips sought hers. It was a brief, cool caress, a fleeting touch of mouth against mouth, as insubstantial as a butterfly's wing, but when Marlbrooke lifted his head his expression was not one of total disinterest. Kate could not read the fleeting emotion in his eyes, but was aware that his grasp showed no evidence of loosening.

'Well, Mistress Harley? Nothing to say?'

'No. I...'

'Despite my admittedly short acquaintance with your delightful self, I would wager that you are rarely lost for words. Am I correct?'

A flare of anger lit Kate's eyes. 'I can think of any number of things to say, my lord. But good manners prevent me from expressing them.' *How dare he mock me!*

Her confusion obviously amused Marlbrooke for he laughed, a gleam of white teeth in the dusk, tightened his hold further and bent his head to kiss her once more. But this was different. His mouth was demanding and urgent, melting the ice in Kate's

blood whether she wished it or no. It was as if he was determined
to extract some reaction from her beyond her previous resentment
and reluctant acceptance—and she was horrified at his success.
Her instinct was to resist him with all her strength, but she was
far too aware of the lean hardness of his body against hers beneath its velvet and lacing. His hands caressed her hair, her
shoulders, sweeping down her back to her waist, but all the time
holding her captive.

Her mouth opened beneath the insistent pressure of his and
she found herself responding to a surge of emotion that spread
through every limb as he used the tip of his tongue with devastating effect to trace the outline of her lips. A strange fire threatened to engulf her, at odds with her inner fury at so intimate an
invasion. In the ensuing war between mind and senses, Kate was
horrified that her senses should be so easily victorious. Her hands
seemed to move of their own accord to grasp his shoulders more
tightly, to savour their strength...when suddenly she was free. As
quickly as Marlbrooke had taken possession of her, he released
her and stepped back. Kate found herself standing alone, her
breath tight within her laced bodice, the only certain thought in
her mind that this experience bore no resemblance to the one in
the garden in Richard's arms.

Ultimately the decision of what to say, of what to do next,
was made for her. Marlbrooke executed a perfect Court bow with
impeccable elegance and grace and a flourish of his plumed hat
which he had recovered from the oak side table. 'Adieu, Mistress
Kate,' he said. 'Until our marriage.' Then he walked towards the
door, giving Kate the opportunity to recover sufficient dignity to
respond with a deep curtsy and an echo of the 'adieu.'

'I had almost forgot,' said Marlbrooke suddenly from the doorway. He halted and turned in one fluent movement, the folds of
his velvet coat gleaming softly in the dying light. He watched
her where she stood in the shadows and was surprised by the
shadow of guilt that touched his heart. Hers was indeed an unen-
viable position after all, as his mother had intimated. She was
very young and would be a mere pawn in the vicious game of
politics and power being played out in this time of transition from
one regime to another. And he was as much to blame for her
present predicament as was her uncle. But he had to admire her
spirit. He suppressed a smile as he remembered her defiance to-

wards her family and himself. And remembered with pleasure the softness of her mouth beneath his when she had recovered from the initial shock of his touch, the clear translucence of her skin under his fingers. The memory of the scent of her damp hair, the sweetness of lavender with the sharper overtones of rosemary, tugged at his senses, surprising him with a tightening of his muscles in thighs and belly. He frowned a little at the unexpected response. Perhaps their marriage need not be as bleak and fraught with tensions as he had feared. Beneath the solemn exterior he might discover a bride of surprising qualities. If only he could make her laugh a little.

From the pocket of his velvet coat he produced a small package, wrapped in linen. 'I had brought you this, to seal our bargain. Perhaps you would like to unwrap it when I have gone. I hope that you will like it. It belonged to my mother, you see, and she considered it to be suitable for a young bride. She treasured it when she was a girl, but sadly she can no longer wear it.' He hesitated for a second. 'I believe that she will like you.'

He bowed again with a final flourish of lace at his cuffs.

'The stones will, I believe, compliment your eyes.' His mouth curved with genuine humour. 'A gift from the painted popinjay! Your servant, Mistress Harley.'

Upon which, he opened the door and left the room. She heard his footsteps die away in the direction of the library. As in a dream, she listened to the distant ebb and flow of a conversation, but remained where he had left her. Finally she heard more footsteps, then the slam of the front door followed by the beat of a horse's hooves on the gravel drive. She stood at the window to watch the powerful figure of her future husband spur the gleaming bay thoroughbred into a controlled canter towards the gate. She watched until he had disappeared into the dusk and the sound of the hooves lapsed into silence.

Only then did Kate walk slowly to the table. She picked up the package and unwrapped the linen to disclose a small velvet box. Opening it, she studied the enclosed jewel—a ring, a fragile flower of tiny sapphires and pearls mounted on a gold band. She caressed the delightful ornament with one finger. It was beautiful. But then Kate shut the box with a snap. She had had quite enough of love and emotion and romantic gestures for one day. Perhaps Viscount Marlbrooke's mother was a romantic lady, but she had certainly misread this planned union between her son and the enemy. And yet he had said that Lady Elizabeth Oxenden would like her. He had given her much to think about.

On impulse, Kate reopened the box and pushed the pretty ring defiantly on to her finger, watching the sapphires as they caught the final gleams of the day. *You have committed yourself to this marriage,* she told herself sternly. *You will wear the ring. You will forget Richard and become a loyal wife. But you would be wise not to lower your guard before Viscount Marlbrooke.* She closed her mind to the sudden vivid memory that rose, unbidden, of the possessive touch of his hands on her arms and shoulders, the imprint of his lips on hers.

She took a deep breath against the ripple of reaction that feathered over her skin. Choking down the sob that rose in her throat, she left the silent privacy of the parlour and prepared to accept the felicitations of her family on her good fortune.

Chapter Three

The coach shuddered, jerked, stopped. The moon, bright in a clear, frosty sky, illuminated the coat of arms on the door panel. Three silver falcons, more grey than silver in the refining light, wings spread in flight on a sable field. A device instantly recognisable in the vicinity as that of the Royalist family, the Oxendens. Then the coach lurched forward again at a faster pace than was sensible for the icy conditions, only to be hauled once more to a precarious standstill. The voice of Jenks, the coachman, could be heard bellowing instructions, spewing out curses and oaths as Viscount Marlbrooke leaned from the window. The horses were plunging, snorting, eyes wild, manes tossing, a danger to themselves and anyone who might venture near. Jenks hauled on the reins, uncomfortably aware of their volatile temper.

Footpads?

Marlbrooke could see no one in the fitful moonlight, but it was always possible. Thieves and robbers, quick to prey on unwary travellers, had spread in the lawless months between the death of the Lord Protector and the return of the King, months when local government had lost its grip in many local areas and it was taking time to rid the countryside of this scourge. But he could see no one in the deep shadows cast by the stand of trees or on the open road before them.

'What's amiss, Jenks?'

'Can't rightly say, my lord. But something spooked 'em for sure.' Jenks was too preoccupied for long explanations. 'God preserve us! Don't just sit there, Tom. Get down! But watch that devil at the front. He's got one of his forelegs over the traces. If you don't hold him, he'll have 'em all down—and then where'll we all be?'

He pulled hard on the reins, bracing his feet, but the horses continued to sidle and plunge on a knife edge of control.

Viscount Marlbrooke sighed, removed his gloves and shrugged off his heavy cloak and coat in anticipation of some intense physical action. Shirtsleeves would freeze him to the marrow, but they would be far more serviceable than braided velvet. It had been a long day of travel over poor roads and ice-edged ruts, but now he was almost home and he had been anticipating a warm fire and hot food, allowing his thoughts to wander. The moon had enabled him to recognise some of the local landmarks: a small copse, the old oak by the bridge, now missing many of its branches, the Wyvern brook. Soon they would reach the crossroads. If they turned left, Marlbrooke knew that Glasbury Old Hall was within an hour's journey. But now there was no reason to travel in that direction. Nothing of value or comfort remained there. He had brooded in silence, eyes veiled by heavy lids, wedged into a corner of the coach. If they turned right, as they would, he would be at the Priory within fifteen minutes. Only Winteringham Common to cover with the village in the distance and he would be home. It was still difficult to think of the Priory as home. But he would work on it. The coach had slowed even more as it began its descent of a small hill to the parting of the ways. Marlbrooke had stretched his limbs in impatience to reach the end of the journey. Perhaps his mother would still be awake, certainly if the pain was bad. She would be keen to know of his visit to Downham Hall. To hear of his assessment of his prospective bride. What would he tell her? As little as possible other than that she was young and not totally unwilling. Indeed, there was little more that he could tell her, other than that the lady had dark hair. And a somewhat confrontational manner. And any number of decided opinions, one of them a devastatingly cynical view of the motive behind his offer of marriage! He had smiled a little at the vivid picture that came to mind, sighed and stretched again in growing discomfort.

Then he had been shocked into alert wakefulness.

Now as he watched Tom leap to obey Jenks's orders, the Viscount jumped from the carriage to help the young groom.

'What in hell's name got them in this state?' he shouted up to Jenks, who still wrestled with the reins. He grabbed hold of the head of one of the lead pair, preventing it from snatching at the bit.

'Couldn't make it out, my lord. Somethin' over there, at the edge of the trees. One minute we was travellin' sweetly enough—next, two dark shapes bolted across the road under our very noses, and then all 'ell broke loose as if the devil 'imself was after us. Begging your pardon, my lord.'

The horses began to quieten, enough for Marlbrooke to give his attention to the young lad—Jed, he thought—sitting next to Jenks on the box. His face was bone white in the moonlight, his eyes glazed, wide with shock, and his mouth dropped open. He was paying no heed to the crisis at hand, but had his gaze fixed on the group of elms next to the signpost. In his rigid fingers he grasped an old pistol, which Jenks had ordered him to take up at the first sign of trouble. His whole body was paralysed with terror.

'What is it, lad?' Marlbrooke shouted. 'What did you see?'

The lad shook his head, witless, unable to speak beyond a croak. When the moon suddenly disappeared behind a rogue cloud, plunging them all into black darkness, it was too much. Jed shrieked and raised the pistol in a wild swing, causing Jenks to haul heavily on the reins, jabbing at the horses' mouths.

The lead horse began to plunge again, pulling its harness out of Marlbrooke's grasp. He cursed and momentarily stepped aside out of the range of the flailing hooves, dragged Tom to his feet away from any obvious danger.

'Put the gun down, lad,' Marlbrooke ordered, but was given no time to see the result of his command. The horse trembled beneath his calming hands and sidled in a frenzy of panic. The Viscount braced his legs, clenched his hands, now slippery with sweat, on the loose reins and hung on. There was nothing here of the effete courtier who had earned Mistress Harley's censure at Downham Hall. The muscles in his shoulders and thighs strained as Tom risked life and limb to untangle the traces from beneath the deadly hooves. Sinews corded in his forearms and sweat broke out on his forehead as he fought to prevent them making a dash for freedom. Jenks continued to handle the reins with all the skill born of thirty years' experience. Then their combined efforts prevailed. The horses steadied. Marlbrooke focused again on the source of Jed's terror.

'What did you see?'

'Take no heed of the boy, m'lord. His granddad's been telling him the tale of the highwayman, Black Tom, hung in chains at this very crossroads twenty years ago—until his eyes was pecked out by the crows and his flesh rotted on his bones. Jed thinks that he's still hanging there, creaking and rattling. Or his ghost is lurking in the bushes.' Jenks clipped Jed on the back of the head with a large hand and ignored the squawk of pained surprise. 'And his granddad's a fool for filling his head with such stuff.'

Marlbrooke released the lead horse with a final gentling caress down a sweat-slicked shoulder.

'Ghosts and skeletons, is it? Now. Hand me down a lantern and let's see what the problem is.'

'Take care, m'lord.'

He took the lantern handed down by Jenks, lit it, and went towards the shadowed verge. He would wager he would find no footpads lying in wait. Or decomposing skeletons. And it was as he thought. He returned to the coach, handing back the lantern.

'Nothing to alarm you, Jed. Just a night kill. A young deer who did not run fast enough. And the shadows you saw under the horses' feet would be foxes, I expect, as we interrupted their feast. The horses would have smelt the fresh blood and panicked. Far more prosaic than a chained skeleton, I'm afraid. Take us home, Jenks.'

Just as he made to swing up into the coach again his attention was caught by a distant sound, carrying clearly in the frosty air.

'Horseman approaching fast, my lord,' Jenks confirmed. 'From the south.'

'And travelling too fast for such conditions,' the Viscount agreed grimly. 'We had better stay and warn him.'

They waited as the rattle of hooves drew nearer, saw a dark shape emerge from the darker surroundings and Jenks called out, either a greeting or a warning. The rider reacted and began to rein to a halt beside the coach. No one could have foreseen the outcome as the moon emerged once more to bathe the road in its stark and unforgiving light. Disturbed by the commotion, a hunting barn owl lifted from its perch in the elms to glide across the road, large and shadowless, its white shape and soundlessly flapping wings ghostly in the moon's illumination. In a return of mindless terror, without waiting for any orders, Jed raised and fired the pistol.

Chaos erupted around them once again. The ridden horse shied, reared, plunging as its feet came into contact with an icy patch on the road's surface. Caught without warning, the rider cried out and was instantly flung to the ground with bone-shattering force. The horse made off, maddened, coat flecked with foam, the moon glinting on the whites of its eyes as it determined on putting distance between itself and the source of its terror, but the rider remained slumped on the floor, a dark shadow, motionless. Jenks once again, with renewed oaths, became engaged in a struggle for control of his restless team as they reacted to the sharp crack of the pistol above their heads, ordering Tom to look lively whilst berating Jed in colourful terms for his gormless stupidity.

This left Marlbrooke, the horses once again manageable, if it was possible to ignore their bloodshot eyes and fiery nostrils, to approach the still figure on the road. He crouched beside it. A young man, perhaps little more than a youth, as far as he could see. It was too dark to assess any real damage, but he ran gentle hands over the prone limbs to determine any obvious injuries. There seemed to be none, although one arm felt to be swelling under his searching fingers. Probably a blow to the head had caused the unconsciousness, he presumed. He pushed aside the rider's hat and gently turned the pale waxen features to the searching moonlight. His hand came away dark with blood and there were clear signs of bruising on the temple and above the eye. Marlbrooke grimaced. If the wound had been caused by the horse's hoof, then matters might indeed be serious. But however dangerous or life threatening the injuries, they could do nothing for the rider here.

Tom was hovering at his shoulder and moved to kneel beside the still figure. 'Mr Jenks says we should get out of 'ere, my lord, as soon as may be. While the horses are quiet. They're still spooky.'

'Very well, Tom. You've done well tonight. You'll have to

help me here.' Marlbrooke rose to his feet and gave the young groom an encouraging grasp of his shoulder. 'I think he's sound enough apart from a bang on the head, although his arm might be broken. Help me get him into the coach as gently as we can. I doubt he'll weigh much. We'll deal with this at the Priory.'

'Yes, sir.' Tom stood tall under the praise, swallowing his nerves.

They wrapped the still figure in Marlbrooke's cloak to cushion the limbs against any further blows. Then between them they manoeuvred him into the coach where they wedged him onto the seat.

'Right, Jenks.' The Viscount nodded to his coachman as he pulled on his coat and gloves once more and Tom swung back into his seat on the coach. 'Let's get to the Priory before our young man dies on us. It's been a long day.' He moved to grasp the open coach door and then turned back. 'On second thoughts—' he held out an imperative hand '—give me that pistol, Jed. On balance you're more of a danger than any ghostly highwayman or passing footpad.'

'Yes, sir. Sorry, sir' The moonlight failed to hide Jed's blushes or his sheepish smile as Tom nudged him and Jenks guffawed. The tale would not lose in its retelling in the stables over the coming months.

Marlbrooke dropped the pistol into his pocket with an answering grin. 'The Priory, then!'

Master Oliver Verzons, steward of Winteringham Priory for as far back as any of the local families could remember, swung open the great oak door at the sound of the approaching coach. He was a stern, austere figure, clad in unrelieved black, his dignity a testimony to his position of trust and responsibility. His white collar and cuffs, seemly and precise with no hint of decoration, were as immaculate as when first donned that morning, despite the late hour.

'Good evening, my lord. Can I be of any assistance?'

He stood back into the entrance hall as Viscount Marlbrooke carried the inert cloaked form up the shallow flight of steps.

'Verzons!' Marlbrooke conserved his breath until he had lowered the young man to the high-backed oak settle beside the door.

He flexed the taut muscles in his back and arms with a grimace before turning to his steward, struck anew by the incongruity of the situation. Why Verzons would have been prepared to remain in service at the Priory under Royalist authority was beyond his understanding, unless loyalty to the estate took precedence over loyalty to family. Or perhaps he hoped and prayed that God would deal out justice with a fair hand and one day a Harley would return and oust the hated Oxendens. Meanwhile, he would keep faith and oversee the estate to the best of his ability, which was considerable. Whatever the reason, he had proved to be an excellent steward and Marlbrooke could see no need to trouble himself further over any dubious motives that Verzons might secretly nurture. As ever, he rose to the occasion, no matter how unusual the circumstances.

'Is the young man badly injured? I can fetch Elspeth from the kitchen if you deem it necessary.' Verzons bent over the settle with some concern.

'No. I think not.' Marlbrooke stripped off his gloves and shrugged out of his coat for the second time that night and handed them to his steward. 'He fell from his horse at the Common crossroads and hit his head. There is no need, I think, to disturb the rest of the household at this hour. I'll carry him up to one of the bedrooms if you would send some cloths and warm water, and some wine—for me, if not for him.'

'Certainly, my lord. And there is food prepared when you are ready.'

Marlbrooke nodded. 'Is my mother still awaiting me?'

'No, my lord. Lady Elizabeth retired some little time ago. I believe she has not been well today. Mistress Felicity is, I understand, still in the parlour.'

The Viscount grimaced in recognition of his steward's bland expression. 'We will not disturb her!'

'Certainly not, my lord. It will not be necessary.' Verzons bowed his understanding and vanished into the shadowy fastness of the house.

Groaning at the strain on his tired muscles, the Viscount bent and lifted the youth, climbed steadily up the main staircase and shouldered his way into the first unoccupied bedroom on the first floor. The lad might not be heavy, but the events of the night were beginning to take their toll. The room was cold and barely furnished, not from neglect rather than simply long unoccupancy, but the bed had fresh linen and newly laundered curtains and a fire had been thoughtfully laid in the hearth. The panelled walls had been recently polished, as had the floor. There was a pleasant pervading scent of beeswax and herbs. As he thankfully deposited his burden on the bed, a servant arrived with candles.

'Robert!' Marlbrooke smiled his thanks. 'Perhaps you would light the fire. Even the mice could die of cold in here.'

'Yes, my lord.' Robert grinned as he knelt to comply. 'Master Verzons asked if he should send up food?'

'No. Not yet. Let's see how much damage the lad has done to himself.'

He took a candle and placed it by the bed as he freed the youth from his enveloping cloak. He had been correct in his first assessment. He was indeed young with a light frame and slender build. His face was ashen, waxy in texture, which roused Marlbrooke's immediate fears, but his fingers were able to detect a faint but steady pulse beneath his jawline. The short dark hair was matted with blood from a deep gash to the skull. Marlbrooke investigated with gentle fingers. It had bled copiously, as did all head wounds, but was now beginning to clot. A deep bruise was developing on the forehead and temple where the stony surface of the road had made hard contact and removed a layer of skin in a deep graze. The collar and sleeve of his jacket, as well as the sleeveless jerkin worn over it, were soaked with blood, but hopefully from the head wound only. He appeared to be otherwise unharmed, but the shallow breathing worried Marlbrooke—a blow to the head from a horse's hoof could be fatal, but there was nothing to be done in the short term but clean the wound and wait for time and nature to take its course.

But who was he? His clothes were of good quality, if plain and serviceable. Most likely from a local gentry family—of Puritan inclination, since there was none of the lace and ribbons adopted by Royalists. The jacket was buttoned to the neck over the now bloodstained linen shirt. His leather boots were worn, but soft and well made. No clues here. The pockets of his coat, quickly searched, yielded nothing to identify the traveller.

With deft movements, as gently as possible, Marlbrooke manoeuvred the boy's arms out of his coat. No signs of further wounds were apparent apart from an angry swollen wrist that was probably nothing more than a bad sprain. Elspeth could dress it on the morrow. He pulled off and discarded the boots. No sprains or broken bones. He ripped open the ties at the neck of the stained linen shirt, hoping that the blood here was merely from the head wound and nothing more sinister.

And his fingers froze.

Exposed before him in the flickering light from the candle were the unmistakable delicate bones and obvious form of a young girl. He took a deep breath and expelled the air slowly as realisation hit him. Small firm breasts with exquisite pink nipples. Sharp collar bones. Fragile shoulders. A tapering waist, the rib-cage visible under the skin. Skin as pale and silken as any that could fill a man's dreams or fantasies. He drew a fingertip along one delicate collarbone in a whisper-soft caress. She reminded him for all the world of a fledgling tipped from its nest by some malignant force. He sighed, touched by compassion, before drawing together the edges of the shirt with great care and respect for her modesty.

The Viscount lifted the candle to give his attention to her face. With knowledge it was distinctly feminine. It was an arresting face, cast into clear relief by the short revealing hair, which, with hindsight, showed signs of being inexpertly hacked off at back and sides with a less than sharp blade. Long dark lashes, well marked brows, a straight nose. Her face was relaxed, but shadows marked the fragile skin beneath her eyes and the bruising on her temple was outrageous. As he pushed her hair gently back from her temples he noted its tendency to curl round his fingers. Her hands, which he lifted and turned over in his own, were fine boned, long fingered and clearly those of a well-born lady. This was not a girl who had worked for her living on the land or in the kitchen. As he released them he felt a strange tug at his senses. She was beautiful. How could he possibly have thought that she was a boy? He touched her cheek, so pale, so soft, with the back of his hand.

The girl opened her eyes. They were a deep blue, the colour of delphiniums, and now almost indigo with pain and confusion. They were blurred, uncomprehending, as they moved searchingly over her line of vision. Then her gaze stopped and focused on his face. Suddenly they were filled with fear, a nameless terror.

Tears gathered and began to trickle down her cheeks into the pillow and her ravaged hair. She said nothing.

He was caught in that blue gaze for the length of a slow heart-beat, trapped in their sapphire depths, unable to do anything but wipe away the spangled drops from her cheeks.

'Don't cry,' he murmured. 'You are quite safe here. There is no one to hurt you here.' What terrible circumstance could have driven her to cut her hair and ride the perilous roads at the dead of night dressed as a boy?

The girl gave no recognition that she had heard him. She closed her eyes as if to shut out a world that threatened to engulf her in nameless horrors.

Marlbrooke swallowed and rose to his feet from his seat on the edge of the bed. He turned to the hovering servant, who was as yet unaware of the deception unfolding in the quiet room.

'Has he come round, my lord? Doesn't look too good, does he?'

'No, Robert. He does not. If you would rouse Mistress Neale with my apologies, ask her to come with all speed. It would seem that I need help here.'

The Viscount lifted and spread the embroidered bedcover over the still figure and stood, hands on hips, looking down on her. Then he moved to the chair by the struggling fire to wait. But he could not take his eyes from her.

Chapter Four

'Good morning, madam. You look well. And remarkably fetching in rose silk. Is it new? Ah, Felicity... I have brought you the books you requested. I believe that Verzons will have taken them from Jenks last night and have them in his keeping. And these—' holding out a number of slim volumes to Lady Elizabeth with guileless grace '—should keep you entertained and make your heart beat a little faster, my lady.'

The ladies were seated in the magnificent library at Winteringham Priory. Chairs had been placed for them in the window embrasure where the light was good and a fire crackled beside them in the hearth. Warmth and light glowed on the leather-and-gold volumes and reflected softly from the polished oak table on which lay a quantity of embroidery silks and pieces of tapestry.

'I see you have not lost your capacity to charm in your absence,' Elizabeth responded in dry tones, but smiled with quiet pleasure as she returned his light kiss on her cheek. 'Did the delicious Mistress Lovell not attempt to detain you at Court?'

'Why, no. Your gossip is distinctly out of date, my dear.' The Viscount's eyes, so like his mother's, held a decided twinkle. 'The delicious Mistress Lovell has decided to cast her eyes and fortunes higher than a mere Viscount. She was fluttering her remarkable eyelashes in the King's direction when I made my departure. And he was showing a distinct and lamentable tendency to engage her in conversation whenever their paths crossed.

Which was frequently. Lady Castlemaine is even now sharpening her claws.'

'I hope that she will not live to regret it! Or perhaps I do. Such a rapacious female in spite of her undeniable beauty.'

'I doubt that Charles will notice her avarice as long as he has access to her equally desirable physical charms. I do not believe that she will have to wait long for him to accept her offers.'

'How demeaning for you, dear Marcus...' Elizabeth chuckled '...to be thrown over for the King!'

Felicity sniffed, lips downturned in disapproval. 'Really, Marcus. Such disloyalty to your King!' She frowned at Elizabeth, but directed her censorious gaze at the Viscount. 'We have been expecting your return any time this past fortnight, have we not, dearest Elizabeth? Your long absence has been a severe trial to your mother—and a source of grave concern. We hear such tales of footpads and robbers, as Elizabeth will tell you. Could you not have sent us word of your safety and intentions? Then your mother's mind would have been put at rest—you must agree, dearest Elizabeth!'

Elizabeth Oxenden suppressed a sigh, refusing to comply with her cousin. She shook her head slightly to deflect any sharp remark that Marlbrooke might be tempted to make in reply, a rueful smile touching her lips as she met her son's sardonic gaze. Secretly Elizabeth was delighted that Marlbrooke had returned home and even more so that he should have noticed her extra care with her appearance that morning. Crippled she might be, but she retained a young woman's interest in fashion and the latest styles at Court. Living in London had some distinct advantages. The deep rose of her full skirts and boned bodice compensated for the lack of colour in her cheeks. The lace edge at collar and cuffs was truly exquisite, if a trifle expensive. It was no good Felicity lecturing her on the sin of vanity. She enjoyed fashion and would do so until the day she died! If Felicity would only take more interest in her own appearance, she might be far more content with life. How could anyone be other than sour dressed in a gown of such unfashionable dark-green watered silk, and at least twenty years old? And with only the minimum of decoration. Felicity, an angular lady of more advanced years and thin features, grey hair scraped unbecomingly beneath a lace cap, managed a tight smile and dropped a small curtsy as the Viscount bowed politely to her and took the time and courtesy to salute her hand.

'So what have you been doing in my absence? Nothing scandalous, I presume, or Verzons would have informed me on my arrival.' He picked up a length of tapestry that had slipped to the floor. 'More bed hangings? You could soon furnish Hampton Court! Have you been well?'

Lady Elizabeth could not prevent her lips curving in a smile.

'I find the cold weather attacks my fingers— ' she hid her swollen joints from his hawk-like gaze in her lap '—but I shall come about with the warmer days.' She deliberately kept her voice light. How could she tell him of the pain that kept her awake and prevented her from doing all the things she had loved to do in the past? Her embroidery was a nightmare of perseverance and she dare no longer approach the spinet. The snowdrops and daffodils in the gardens bloomed without her care.

But, indeed, she did not need to tell him. He had already discerned the fine lines around her eyes—were they perhaps deeper than when he had left?—and the haunted glaze of pain in her eyes.

'I know you would wish to return to London, ma'am.' He was as forthright as ever in his dealings with her. 'I think you are lonely here and would far rather enjoy the visits of friends and the Court gossip. But if you could agree to remain here at the Priory until arrangements for my marriage are finalised and the bride has arrived, then I would willingly transport you back to town again. Can you bear it for a little longer?'

'Of course.' She smiled as he bent to brush her fingers with his lips. She could not hide the obvious signs of suffering any longer and did not attempt to. She adored her handsome son, and, even if not blind to his faults, she was aware of his love and concern for her well-being. But if she was unwilling to tell him of the pain, how could she possibly explain to him her growing discomfort in this house, a house which he prized above all things? She had not felt it when she had first arrived—of that she was certain. But it had developed gradually in recent days. The sensation that her footsteps were being watched, if not actually followed, by a silent presence— a presence that chilled the air with the keen edge of winter frost. And brought with it such a sense of despair, of utter misery, enough to touch her own emotions in reluctant sympathy, almost to reduce her to tears. The word *haunted* did not seem too extreme. She could not, would not, admit that her sleep was disturbed not only by physical discomfort, but by a fear of what might lurk in the shadows in the corner of her room. Of every room. He would think she was fanciful in the extreme and merely making excuses to escape back to the city.

'Well, tell me.' She mentally admonished herself and turned the conversation into happier channels. 'Tell me what she is like. Katherine Harley. Will I like her?'

'I expect so. You are predisposed to like everyone!'

'That makes me sound witless!' she complained with a wry twist of her lips and not a little impatience. 'Is she pretty?'

'I don't really know,' he answered with a slight frown, surprising her. 'I only saw her once and she looked dishevelled, as if she had come in out of a rainstorm. And she scowled at me for most of the interview.'

'Oh, dear! Were you not made welcome? Surely Sir Henry was expecting you!'

'I suppose the answer has to be no and no.' Marlbrooke's expression and voice had a derisive edge as he remembered the reaction of the household at Downham Hall. 'Sir Henry was discomfited and flustered at having to enter into such close dealings with a Royalist. Lady Philippa withdrew into nervous silence and flinched every time I looked in her direction. My prospective bride could in all truth be described as hostile and likened me in a most uncomplimentary way to a frippery bird, without pretence to style or elegance! And they would all have willingly consigned me to the devil.'

'So?' Elizabeth failed to suppress a smile at the picture, wilfully ignoring Felicity's snort of disapproval at the whole distasteful situation. 'Do you then still intend to pursue the match? Apart from the hostility, was Katherine pretty enough to tempt you into the married state?'

'I have to admit that the lack of candles—in the interest of economy, I presume—and the growing dusk made it difficult to pick out anything but a general impression. But she has a good figure and holds herself well. And she has a cloud of dark hair. I told her she was pretty, at any event. I am not sure that she believed me. Her opinion of me did not appear to be overly complimentary!' He grinned at the memory of Mistress Harley's barbed comments.

'Oh, Marcus! You are very like your father.'

'But is that for better or worse, my lady?'

'I will leave that decision to you! And did you overawe the poor girl, in spite of my excellent advice, with full Court rig—nothing less than lace, velvets and those appalling shoes with red heels?' She cast an appreciative eye over his more restrained jacket and breeches, more suitable to a country gentleman than the excesses of French fashion. The shoes in question had been abandoned for serviceable black boots.

'My dear Mother, you could not expect me to pay my respects to my future wife in anything less.'

'And will you go ahead with the marriage, now that you have seen Sir Henry?'

'Why not? He is willing enough, no matter Mistress Harley's sentiments. It brings my claim all the advantages of legitimacy. And she did not seem totally unwilling.' He did not seem too convinced, but shrugged his shoulders. 'I expect we shall brush along fairly well.'

Elizabeth chose not to comment, once again effectively hiding her concern on this sensitive subject. She changed tack again as Felicity, unbidden and always solicitous, poured and served small ale in pewter goblets. It sounded a bleak prospect, although Marlbrooke, lounging in an armchair before the fire, boots propped comfortably on a fire dog, appeared to be unaware.

'Mistress Neale has told me of the occurrence last night. About the young girl you found on the road.'

Marlbrooke looked up from his contemplation of the flames. 'Of course. I had momentarily forgotten. I am sure Mistress Neale has furnished you with all the details. You had retired when I arrived home. When I realised that she was a girl and not the young man she wished to be taken for, I asked for Mistress Neale's help.'

'That was very considerate of you! I believe that many would not expect it, Marcus, if gossip speaks true.' There was a degree of disapproval in her voice.

'My delicacy and thoughtfulness can be relied upon on such occasions.' The gleam in his eye held a degree of cynicism not lost on his mother.

'You could have fetched me, dear Marcus,' Felicity interrupted with a fluttering of hands and an avid gleam in her eyes, always receptive of gossip and intrigue. 'I believe that I was still sorting dearest Elizabeth's embroidery silks in the small parlour. I could have come to your aid.' Her voice was as thin and dry as her appearance. 'There was no need for you to be concerned with some runaway girl—so indelicate, do you not think?'

'Thank you, Felicity. I know. I suppose I did not think of it.' *And I certainly did not want you prosing in my ear about the morality of modern youth.*

'A most unsavoury circumstance, I am sure. Doubtless the girl will be recovered and well enough to leave today.'

'Mistress Neale suggested that her head wound was quite unpleasant. And a damaged wrist, I think.' Elizabeth closed her mind to her cousin's perpetually querulous voice, sipped her ale thoughtfully, and directed her comment towards her son.

'I suggest it was merely a ruse to get herself into this house,' Felicity continued, impervious to the lack of response. 'That type of female might sink to any level to gain the interest of her betters.'

Elizabeth sighed. 'Are you suggesting that we should lock up the silver? I think not. If you please, Felicity, I find it rather cool in this room. Please would you be so good as to fetch me my quilted wrap from my bedchamber? I am sorry to put you out.'

'Of course, dear Elizabeth. It is always my pleasure to be of service to you.'

'She is so judgmental!' Elizabeth regarded the retreating figure with disfavour. 'And always so obsequious towards me. Sometimes I find myself wishing that she would curse me so that I could curse her back! But she never would, of course. She is far too grateful.'

'I do not know how you tolerate her day after day. All her petty criticisms and ill wishes. Does she ever say anything pleasant about anyone?'

'Rarely! But she helps me with all the intimate tasks that I can no longer do for myself! So I have to be grateful and tolerant.' There was an astringent quality to her reply that her son could not ignore.

'I know. Forgive me for my lamentable insensitivity.'

'Besides, she has nowhere else to live. I try not to pity her or patronise her.'

'You have more goodness than I have.'

'So, what of the girl?' Elizabeth asked somewhat impatiently. 'Could she have come from the village?'

'I think not. My impression is that she is of good family—her clothes, if a little unconventional, her hands, her features, all speak of money and breeding.'

'Is she seriously injured?'

'It was difficult to tell when I left her in Mistress Neale's capable hands. She was comfortable enough and Mistress Neale had bathed and cleaned the head wound but it was deep and her face is badly bruised. We must wait. She had hacked off all her hair,' he added inconsequentially.

Elizabeth raised her fine brows. 'Then she won't be pretty enough for you to flirt with!'

'Never fear! I am now betrothed to be married and so beyond the levities of youth. And, as you know, I never flirt!'

'Well...!' Lady Elizabeth's views on handsome young men who were ruthless and arrogant enough to use flattery to gain their own ends would never be known for they were interrupted by a quiet knock quickly followed by the opening of the library door. Mistress Neale entered in her usual calm fashion, hands clasped before her over her enveloping apron, the jangle of keys at her waist marking her every step. She stopped inside the door.

'Excuse me, my lord, my lady. I have brought the young lady. She says she is recovered sufficiently to rise from her bed— although I did tell her you would understand if she rested today, in the circumstances. In my opinion, she is far from well.'

Lady Elizabeth registered the faint expression—of what, anxiety or disapproval?—on her housekeeper's homely features, but with a mental shrug presumed that it was merely concern for the health of their unexpected guest.

'But yes, Mistress Neale. Please come in. Is she with you now?'

Mistress Neale turned, beckoned and ushered in the young woman who had been standing in the shadows in the hall. She paused, framed by the doorway, her own ruined and unsuitable clothing discarded, now clad in ill-fitting skirt and bodice, borrowed from Elspeth, tied and tucked to take into account her slender figure. Her harshly cropped hair was uncovered. The extensive bruising down one side of her face was shocking to see, but the wound in her hair, covered by some neat bandaging, appeared to be giving her few ill effects. She held one firmly bandaged wrist awkwardly at her side. Exhaustion was printed on her face, the pallor highlighted by the plain white collar, and there was a faint frown between her brows, but she waited with apparent composure for her hostess to make the first move.

'Come in, my poor child. What an ordeal you have been through. Come and sit with me.' Lady Elizabeth stretched out her hand in instant compassion.

Mistress Neale curtsied and left. The lady remained standing in the doorway as if she had not heard the invitation. Viscount Marlbrooke saw the instant bewilderment in her expression and so rose and walked across the room, to take her hand. It was icy cold. She did not resist as he led her further into the room but neither did she respond to her new surroundings. His eyes searched her face, but he could detect no emotion. Perhaps she was unaware that she grasped his hand hard as he led her into the room. He felt compelled by he knew not what impulse to raise her hand and brush his lips over her rigid fingers in a formal salute.

'There is no need to be anxious,' he reassured her in a gentle voice as he applied a comforting pressure to her fingers. 'I was at the crossroads and brought you here last night after the accident with your horse. I am Marcus Oxenden. This is my mother, Lady Elizabeth. You are at Winteringham Priory. Perhaps you know of it?'

Her eyes flashed to his face as she shook her head, wincing at the sudden lance of pain. If anything she became even paler, the blood draining from beneath her skin.

'Thank you. You are very kind.' Her voice was clear and steady but toneless as if her mind was engaged elsewhere.

'Forgive me that I do not rise.' Elizabeth held out her hand and smiled in welcome. 'I find the cold weather difficult. You must tell me where you were going. I am sure that we can help you reach your destination. You must have a family—and friends—who will be concerned for you, to whom we should send a message. What is your name, my dear girl?'

The result of the concerned enquiry was devastating. It was

not composure that held the girl in its rigid grasp but naked fear born out of blind panic. She pulled her hand from Marlbrooke's light clasp to cover her face, to suppress a sob of anguish.

'But what is wrong?' Elizabeth struggled to gain her feet, ignoring the discomfort, moved immeasurably by the plight before her. 'I am sure that whatever distresses you so can soon be put right.'

'No!'

'But what is it that causes you such despair?' Marlbrooke raised his brows, glancing hopefully towards Lady Elizabeth, but she merely shook her head. 'Surely it can be remedied?'

The eyes that the lady raised to Marlbrooke's face were wide, stark with terror. 'I don't know where I was going,' she explained, her voice breaking on a sob. 'I do not know who I am. I cannot even remember my own name!'

'I cannot remember my name,' the lady repeated the statement in barely a whisper. 'I don't remember anything before I opened my eyes here this morning.'

She looked at the two strangers before her, panic turning her blood to ice, freezing her ability to assess her position with any clarity. The lady with her faded beauty, kind smile but awkward limbs. The gentleman, eyes intent, dark haired, with a distinct air of authority. Both offering compassion and support, but both total strangers. How could she be so dependent on them? She shook her head, wincing again at the sharp consequence, unable to take in her surroundings or the enormity of her predicament. In response to the mute appeal in the girl's face, her pale lips and cheeks, Elizabeth put a gentle arm around her shoulders and steered her towards the fire. She was trembling, but obeyed as in a trance and sank to the cushioned settle. Elizabeth sat beside her, keeping possession of her hand, stroking the soft skin in comfort.

'You must not worry so. You have had the most traumatic of experiences. You must know that you were struck on the head when you fell from your horse. I am sure your loss of memory will be temporary and you will soon remember everything quite clearly.'

The lady looked into Elizabeth's calm grey eyes, clinging to sanity as she clung to her hand. 'But what am I doing here? Please tell me what happened last night.'

The Viscount had come to stand before the fireplace, leaning his arm along the heavily carved mantel, pushing the smouldering logs with his booted foot until sparks showered onto the hearth.

'I am afraid that I can tell you very little. You were riding from the south, but from where exactly, I know not. You arrived at the crossroads on Winteringham Common at the time when my coach had stopped because of an incident. We waited to warn you of possible danger on the icy road. You were travelling fast.' He frowned, watching her closely to see if there was any hint of recognition of the subsequent events. There was none. 'When you came abreast of us, your horse shied badly on a stretch of ice and you fell, hitting your head on the road. I brought you here. And that is all I know.'

She nodded in thoughtful acceptance, head bent as she contemplated his answer and the blank spaces in her memory, which his explanation did nothing to restore.

'Do I know you?' The lady raised her eyes to the Viscount's face, but without hope.

'No, my dear.' Elizabeth sighed in answer and shook her head sadly. 'We can be of no help to you in that quarter. I do not think you live in the vicinity, although we have only just returned to the area ourselves after some years' absence. We can make enquiries, do you not think, Marcus?'

'Of course.'

'Did I have any possessions with me? Nothing to tell who I am?'

'No.' The Viscount had moved silently to a side table to pour a glass of wine. He handed it to the lady, who took it and sipped absently. 'Your horse may have had saddle-bags, but it bolted out of sight. I have sent out word to recover it if it is found on the estate or in the village. I expect it will—horses rarely stray far, even when frightened.'

'I...I understand from Mistress Neale that I was dressed as a boy.' She lowered her eyes in some confusion as a faint flush stained her pale cheeks. 'And I have cut my hair.' She lifted her hand to touch in shock and disbelief the shorn strands that lay against her neck. 'I think I had long hair. I do not understand any of it!'

'Indeed.' Elizabeth squeezed the cold hands. There was little she could say to comfort her. 'You must have had a good reason for doing so.'

'Yes. I suppose so.'

The door to the library opened to admit Felicity, who had completed her task and returned carrying the shawl. Her pursed lips and the closed expression on her narrow face indicated that she had, in her absence, made it her business to become well informed of events by Mistress Neale and did not approve.

'Here is Mistress Felicity, my cousin.' Elizabeth made the introduction, her heart sinking as she read the condemnation in her companion's stiff shoulders and tight-lipped mouth. Uncomfortable at the best of times, Felicity could be a damning influence when her sense of morality was outraged. 'This is...?' She looked at the lady beside her in sudden consternation.

The fear had deepened in the lady's eyes as her lack of identity had immediately presented its own problems.

'We must decide what to call you, my dear child, until your memory returns.' Elizabeth smiled and tried to keep her tone light.

'Why, I...I don't know.'

'I do.' The Viscount had been watching intently and now surveyed the delicate features and deep blue eyes with a light curve of his lips. 'You are Viola, for sure. Master Shakespeare had the right of it in naming his masquerading heroine. We will borrow it for you, if it pleases you, if only for the short term.' The smile that accompanied his words held great warmth and charm, guaranteed to put the lady at her ease. He reached down for her hand and bowed elegantly over it. 'Welcome to Winteringham Priory, Mistress Viola.'

She tried for a smile, but it was a poor attempt, and pulled her hand away as if his touch embarrassed her even more. A shiver ran through her slight frame in spite of the burning logs. Seeing it, Marcus took the shawl from the fussing Felicity and placed it round her shoulders.

'Thank you. I cannot express how grateful I am for your kindness.'

'Well, of course...' he grinned '...we had planned to throw you out into the cold and wet to find your own salvation. We always treat our guests with such lack of consideration! Particularly when they are in distress.'

'Enough, Marcus.' Lady Elizabeth frowned at his levity. 'Take no heed of him, my dear. Be assured you are welcome to stay here until we know what is best for you.'

The girl smiled at last with genuine warmth but Marcus had seen the flash of real fear and tried to remedy the effect of his light jest.

'Indeed, Mistress Viola, there is no cause for concern. I have known cases such as yours before—in the war. A severe blow to the head can bring temporary loss of memory. It returns, sometimes gradually in increasing flashes of realisation, sometimes in one blinding revelation.' *And occasionally leaves the sufferer in devastating limbo for ever!* 'You need to rest. You will stay here as long as you need. Meanwhile, as my mother suggested, we will put out the word.'

'I cannot express my thanks.' She placed the almost untouched glass carefully on the table at her elbow. 'I have a headache a little. Perhaps, if you will excuse me, I will go and rest.'

'Of course.' Elizabeth saw the distress and weariness in the young face and understood the need for privacy. 'Mistress Neale will provide everything you need. Perhaps, Felicity, you will show Mistress Viola to her bedchamber, until she becomes more accustomed to the house.'

Felicity moved to comply with bad grace and a sharp inclination of her head, leading the way from the room, leaving Elizabeth alone with her son.

'Well, Marcus? She is so young and defenceless to be put in such a position.'

He shrugged as he returned from the door to pour out two more glasses of wine, handing one to his mother before stretching his limbs again with casual grace in the chair opposite her.

'It is as I said. Her memory will probably return in its own good time. But what can have frightened her to such an extent that she would cut her hair, dress as a man and ride through the night with no companion or protection?' He frowned down into the blood-red liquid as he swirled it in the glass, the light catching in the faceted stem. 'Perhaps her fears are more deep rooted than from mere loss of memory. We must be circumspect in our enquiries. It may be that she does not wish to be found.'

'I agree.' Felicity stalked back into the room in time to hear the final comment. 'A girl who is prepared to dress in such an unseemly manner and take such precipitate action might have all manner of things to hide. I believe that you are too trusting, my dear Elizabeth. We do not know what she might be guilty of.'

Elizabeth raised her eyebrows and caught the fierce challenge in her son's eyes as he prepared to deliver a stinging rebuke. Felicity would only sulk and that would make everyone uncomfortable. She took up the challenge before he could speak.

'Your lack of charity in the circumstances is unfortunate and does you no favours, Felicity,' she chided in a mild tone, but leaving her cousin in no doubt of her sentiments. 'I expect you to treat Mistress Viola with all consideration and compassion until we know for sure who or what she is! I would not like to hear that she has been open to insult in my home.'

Felicity pressed her lips into an even firmer line, if that were possible, and sniffed.

Chapter Five

Viola awoke next morning to the same complete absence of knowledge of her previous existence as when she had taken to her bed. She struggled to quell the all-embracing fear as she became aware of a maid who bustled about the room and drew back her curtains. *You must be calm. You have to accept. You will remember as your head heals.* At least the headache had gone. She smiled uncertainly at the maid, a young smiling person with quick, deft hands, and felt an immediate lift in her spirits as the pale spring sunshine flooded the room. Of course things would soon be back to normal and she would be able to complete her journey—wherever that was. Was someone, somewhere, concerned for her safety? She shook her head as the maid approached the bed.

'Her ladyship has sent you this, mistress. To replace Elspeth's bodice and skirt which you wore yesterday. She thinks it will be a little large, but the length should be good—if we lace it tightly it should do well enough. Her ladyship no longer wears it. And it is too pretty to be packed away for the moths.'

'How kind everyone is. It is beautiful.'

She scrambled from the bed to don shift and petticoats and the gown that the maid held and laced for her.

'There, now.' Bessie tied and twitched with experienced fingers and she was dressed. The deep-blue damask bodice, boned and laced, fit, if not as if made for her, at least adequately, emphasising her small waist and the swell of her breasts. The full overskirt was of the same deep colour, looped up to show a delicate cream underskirt, embroidered with flowers and leaves around the hem. The low neckline, which might have made Viola blush, was made more suitable for day wear by a fine linen-and-lace collar that matched the lace falling from elbow-length sleeves. Viola sighed at the sheer delight of it against her skin.

She stood before the looking glass, letting her fingers smooth down the figured brocade of the skirts. The reflected image shocked her. The dress looked well—indeed, she had the faintest suspicion, hovering on the edge of memory, that she had never worn anything as fine in her life—but she had no recognition of the lady wearing it. It was as if she were looking at a stranger. Then she gasped as she took in the short hair, roughly cropped—hacked, rather!—and unflattering in the extreme to her critical eyes. It seemed to her that in the past she had had hair that curled in ringlets to her shoulders, not this stark crop which threw her face into cruel relief. For there was the matter of the large purpling bruise that disfigured her temple—and would for many days yet.

Her eyes met those of the maid and she flinched inwardly at the depth of pity she saw there. 'I look terrible,' Viola whispered.

'That you don't, mistress. You look so much better than yesterday—what with the colour in your cheeks an' all. Your hair will soon grow. It is very pretty and, now that you have taken off your bandage, you look well.'

'I suppose I do. At least it takes little time to run a comb through it.' She grimaced as she did so, mindful of the tender wound on her skull. What terrible need had made her cut it so drastically? There was no point in idle speculation. She must be practical. Viola squared her shoulders and looked again at the maid.

'Would you do something for me…?'

'I am Bessie. Her ladyship says for me to take care of you. What would you wish for me to do for you, mistress?'

'Thank you, Bessie. Would you trim my hair—to cut away the worst of the stray bits?'

'My pleasure, miss. I will fetch the shears from Mistress Neale!'

* * *

Half an hour later Viola risked a second look in the mirror. Her hair now lay neatly against her neck and curled on to her cheeks and forehead in feathery wisps. She sighed. It was the best she could hope for. 'Thank you, Bessie. I suppose it is some improvement!' She smiled wryly as she swept herself a regal curtsy. 'Do you suppose it will ever look passably attractive?'

'That it will, Mistress Viola. And when the bruise fades you will feel more the thing.'

'You are very good for my spirits, Bessie.' They smiled at their achievements with the shears. 'Now, where will I find Lady Elizabeth at this time in the morning? I must speak to her—thank her for all her kindness and this beautiful dress.'

'She usually sits in the panelled parlour at the front of the house in the morning. The sun makes it warm and comfortable for her—with the pains in her limbs an' all. I will take you there when you are ready.'

Lady Elizabeth sat in the wash of sunlight in the small parlour with a neglected piece of tapestry on her lap as Bessie ushered in Viola. Felicity sat beside her, head bent industriously over a similar pattern intended to cover a chair seat. Elizabeth's face was solemn and pensive as she gazed out over the gardens, but brightened immediately with a welcoming smile as she stretched out her hand in greeting.

'Well, Mistress Viola. You look charming this morning. I knew the dress would suit. Turn round for me.'

Viola did as she was bid, enjoying the swish of damask skirts against the polished oak boards.

'I do not know what to say. You have given me more than I deserve.'

Felicity's curled lips suggested that she might agree, but said nothing and continued to ply her needle with little vicious stabs at the tapestry.

'Nonsense, dear girl. Come and sit and entertain me a little.'

Viola did as she was bid and bent to admire Elizabeth's embroidery. 'Your tapestry is beautiful. The stitches are so even.'

'I could do better.' Elizabeth wrinkled her nose in self-disgust. 'My fingers are so swollen and painful. Can you do tapestry work?'

'Yes, of course. I remember...' She stopped in some consternation.

'There now. I knew your memory would return when you stopped trying so hard. I expect your mother taught you.'

'Perhaps. I certainly know that I have worked tapestry—and needlework—and I remember patterns. One very similar to Mistress Felicity's cover with flowers and leaves, but in darker greens. But I am not sure that I enjoyed it.' Her lips were touched by a faint smile. 'I feel that I applied myself reluctantly and only because I must.'

'It is indeed amazing how your memory is beginning to return.' The sour note in Felicity's voice was unmistakable.

There was a silence in the room for a long moment. And then, 'It is not a situation that I would wish on anyone, Mistress Felicity,' Viola replied in a quiet voice.

So she has spirit. It pleased Elizabeth to hear her young guest stand up for herself against Felicity's unkind sniping.

'Perhaps you would fetch us some wine, Felicity?'

'Of course, dear Elizabeth.' Felicity simpered in Elizabeth's direction, but with a scowl for Viola as she flounced through the door.

'You said, my lady, that you had recently returned to live here.' It seemed to Viola an innocuous subject that would not require any reminiscences on her part.

'It is a complicated story,' explained Elizabeth, willing enough to find a neutral topic. 'We used to live at Glasbury Old Hall—you probably do not know it, but it is only a few miles from here. I went there as a young bride. But it was damaged beyond repair in the war—and then we came here.'

'Do you never go back?'

'Too sad. Too many memories of what might have been.'

'But why did you come here in the first place—and then not remain here?'

'I warned you it had its complications. The Priory became ours after a siege and the original family fled. So we moved here when our own house was destroyed. But then we were on the wrong side after 1649 and the King dead, so it was confiscated by Parliament and the rents used for their own policies. In effect, we lost both houses—I think it helped to bring about my husband's intense melancholy and ultimate death. We went to a property in

London, which I had brought to the marriage in my jointure—and this place stood more or less empty except for a strange lady from the original family who stayed on as a sort of guardian, with our steward, Master Verzons, and Mistress Neale. When King Charles was restored, my son petitioned for the return of the Priory—and the King granted it back to him. So we returned. Not an edifying story!'

'And the lady—the guardian? What happened to her?'

'She would not stay. I cannot blame her. She was very angry.'

Felicity returned, followed by Verzons bearing a tray. He poured the wine, handed the glasses to the ladies and arranged a small table conveniently beside Elizabeth. As he presented Viola with her wine, she looked up at him in thanks to surprise an intent look on his face as he studied her. He immediately dropped his gaze and became once again the self-effacing steward, but it left Viola uncomfortable. It was not a casual look at all.

As Elizabeth reached to put down the glass, she caught the stem with a clumsy hand and the glass fell to the floor, smashing the fragile vessel and spilling the wine in a spreading puddle. She cried out in distress as Felicity leaped to her feet to mop up the mess. 'I am so clumsy,' she fretted. 'Some days it is insupportable.'

Viola was horrified to see tears gather in Lady Elizabeth's eyes and only sheer effort of will prevent them from spilling over down her cheeks.

'Is it...?' She hesitated, unsure of such a personal enquiry. 'Is it the rheumatic disease that causes your suffering, my lady?'

'Yes. So painful! For some little time now—and the cold and damp aggravates it.'

'I believe I can make things easier for you if you would allow me.'

'I doubt anyone can,' Felicity intervened, still on her knees where she dealt with the spilled wine and glass. 'Lady Elizabeth has suffered from such pains for many years and nothing helps. We must pray for deliverance.'

'But I know how to ease the pain.'

'Do you really?' The spark of hope in Elizabeth's eyes and voice touched Viola's heart.

Yes, because...' She hesitated, frowning, as if the reason had slipped away from her grasp. 'I do not know why I know,' she continued, 'but I know that I have the skill and knowledge to ease the pain and reduce the swelling. Someone must have taught me. I remember a number of potions and balms, and a pain-relieving draught, that would be of use.' Viola took a deep breath, eyes closed in frustration. 'Why can I remember such trivial details and yet not know my own name?'

'I know not. But you could make such a potion for me? You could make the pain go away?'

'I believe I can ease it. Do you wish for me to try?'

'If only you would.' Hope illuminated Elizabeth's face. 'What would you use?'

'Herbs and hedgerow plants. Dried leaves mostly at this time of the year when little is growing. It is not difficult to prepare something that should give you relief.'

'But what if her memory is wrong, dear Elizabeth?' Felicity came to stand protectively beside her cousin, one hand on her shoulder as if in warning. 'Her so-called remedies could have disastrous consequences. You could be poisoned and we would not know what to do for you. I advise very strongly against it.' Her eyes, fixed on Viola, were cold and full of implacable hatred.

'Felicity—' Elizabeth's voice was weary in the extreme, but she recognised the jealousy that afflicted her companion and understood it even as she would have condemned it '—I appreciate your concern—and your motives—but some days I would accept a remedy from the devil himself if I thought there was only the smallest chance of success.'

'I never thought to hear such blasphemy from you, dearest cousin!'

'It is not blasphemy.' Elizabeth remained calm, although her eyes snapped with temper. 'It is desperation. Nothing else has any effect. Perhaps Viola is an answer to our prayers.'

'As to that, I know not. But I will use the skill I have. Do you have a still-room?' Viola enquired, rising to her feet. 'And I presume there is a herb garden.'

'Yes. Sadly unkempt, but I make you free of it.' Lady Elizabeth looked at her hands with swollen joints and ugly reddened knuckles, and clenched them in her skirts to hide them from view, even from herself. 'If you could take away only a little of the pain I would be everlastingly grateful. And vanity would hope

that you could improve this unsightliness.' Her smile was a little
twisted. 'I used to have fine hands once.'

Some time later, Viscount Marlbrooke followed directions
from his mother to find Viola ensconced in the dust-shrouded
still-room, her slight figure with its fashionable gown wrapped
in one of Mrs Neale's large white aprons to protect the delicate
material. The streaked glass in the small window was pushed
wide to allow in as much light as possible and a fire burned on
the hearth. Various pots, spoons and dishes, borrowed from the
kitchen, littered the bench and a pot bubbled over the fire. Viola
wielded a pestle and mortar clumsily with her bound wrist, the
small dish clasped by her arm against her body, but none the less
effectively.

He stood in the open doorway to watch her concentration and
neat movements. She was unaware of his presence, but hummed
softly, almost under her breath. It made a pleasant domestic scene
if it were not for the disfiguring bruise. His memory of his first
knowledge of her swept back, surprising him with its intensity.
He remembered her fragility, her total vulnerability, aware of the
tightening of the muscles in his gut and thighs in response. And
yet here she was, wielding pestle and mortar, unconcerned with
the painful sprain, in his still-room. His mouth curled a little in
admiration of her, content to stand and watch.

He knew the moment she became aware of him. She stiffened
slightly, halted in her ministrations and turned her head to glance
nervously in his direction. The flash of tension in her face vanished almost immediately when she recognised him.

'I'm sorry, my lord. I was only—'

'Why should you apologise? I had not intended to distress
you.' He strolled forward into the room.

'No. I had thought there was someone behind me. On a few
occasions I have felt... But perhaps it is simply the close confines
of the room. That is why I had left the door ajar.'

'Perhaps.' He picked up a bunch of herbs from the bench and
sniffed the pungent aroma. 'Do you realise that you are giving
my mother hope for the first time in months—years, even? Will
it work?'

'Yes.'

'It would be a relief, for her and for myself.' He frowned unseeingly at the empty dust-covered shelves before him. 'She believes that she is a burden to me, you see. And I cannot make her accept otherwise. If she were free from pain, could rest well at night and take up her previous interests, she would regain her old spirits. Nor does she enjoy being dependent on Felicity.'

'I can assure you the relief from pain will be effective.' Viola smiled a little nervously, flustered by his close proximity in the small room. But Marlbrooke did not appear to be aware, for which she was grateful.

'You are very confident. What is it?'

'Willow bark. It was easy to collect from the grounds—Mistress Neale sent one of the lads from the stables. If you make an infusion with boiling water, strain it and drink...but I doubt you want to know all the details,' she finished as she caught the guarded expression on his face. She laughed. He was instantly transfixed by the sparkle in her violet eyes and the faint flush the heat in the still-room had brought to her fair skin. And a lightening of mood from the fact that, for a short time, she had forgotten the weight of uncertainty surrounding her existence in this house. He would have liked to touch her short hair where it curled on to her cheek in front of her ear.

He pushed his hands firmly into his pockets.

'There. This is done.' She lifted the pot from the flames with a cloth in her good hand. 'Would you like to take it to her, my lord? If she would drink a little now, it will begin to give relief.'

'Yes. With pleasure. What are you doing now?'

'Making a liniment to rub into sore joints. I cannot make the most effective—it is not the season for many of the best plants, such as angelica or meadowsweet—but thyme is an excellent remedy, readily obtainable. Your herb garden is in a dreadful state and much overgrown, but it contains all the most useful and sweet-scented herbs.'

He accepted her innocent criticism of the state of the gardens with an amused smile and a shake of his head. He picked up a jar and sniffed, investigated the contents of a bowl and frowned down into them.

'If you can make her life worth living again, I will be completely in your debt.'

Suddenly she put down the dish and the sprigs of thyme and

grasped the edge of the bench with tensed fingers, fixing the Viscount with a direct gaze.

'Well?'

'Do you suppose that I worked in a kitchen somewhere? I seem to be very good at this. And I know my way round a still-room.'

'Not a chance!'

'Why not? How can you be so sure?'

He took possession of both her hands in his, and before she could pull away, he turned them over, palm up.

'This is how I know.' He smoothed his thumbs over the slender fingers, the soft palms. 'You have not worked in a kitchen. No burns, no abrasions, no calluses. Does it worry you?'

'Yes... I don't know... If I were a servant in a kitchen, it might explain why no one has enquired about my whereabouts. But the *blankness* fills me with dread,' she admitted with sudden candour. 'Do you know what it is like to look in a mirror and not recognise the face that looks back at you?'

The anxiety that he read in her violet eyes moved him unutterably and he could say nothing to ease it. He kept possession of her hands and raised them to his lips. He felt an urge to do more than kiss her fingers and so acted on the impulse. He turned one hand in his and pressed his mouth to the palm and then to the wrist that was bound against the sprain.

'Perhaps you are indeed a godsend, Mistress Viola.'

She shook her head, the pulse leaping where his mouth had rested, the glow in her cheeks deepening. 'I do not know. But it would please me to be able to repay Lady Elizabeth for her generosity and her kindness.' She tried to pull her hands free, and failed.

'She has an unfathomable depth of compassion,' he agreed gently. And then, brows meeting fiercely in a sudden frown, 'Do you realise that such skills as you wield here could be misconstrued as witchcraft? In the present climate that could be dangerous.' He did not release her hands. 'In the circumstances you deserve more than my thanks.' He watched her carefully as he awaited her reply.

'I did not think of such an interpretation.' Her eyes widened, but were clear and guileless and her voice was calm. 'I do not know *how* I know or where I obtained my knowledge, but I would wager it was not from a witch! Besides, I will do no harm to anyone.' She trembled under his hands and her eyes fell from his. 'I do not need your thanks—it is I who am entirely in your debt.'

And then the words were wrung from her. 'What will I do if no one ever claims me—and I never remember who I am? What will I do?'

'Why, then...' He hesitated only a moment before speaking what was in his heart, for once thoughtless for the consequences, for himself, for the lost girl who stood before him and for the absent Mistress Harley. 'Why, then I would have to claim you for myself.'

Without another word he closed her fingers over the salute on her palm, picked up the cooling bowl of fragrant liquid and left.

The weather lapsed into winter again with rain and gales, severe enough to keep the inhabitants of Winteringham Priory imprisoned within their four walls. For Viola it was a time of intense frustration interspersed with bouts of sharp-taloned fear. Her memories of her past life refused to resurface, deluging her, at the most inopportune moments, with shattering moods of total desolation that she fought against and tried to hide from her concerned and watchful hosts. Any tears that she shed were in the privacy of her bedchamber.

Apparently no search had been instigated for her by anxious relatives. No messages arrived at the Priory, in spite of enquiries made by Viscount Marlbrooke. No one appeared to lay claim to her to put her mind at rest.

It was not all fears and anxieties, of course. Her wardrobe extended as Lady Elizabeth found pleasure in giving her gowns that she decided would be far more becoming to a young girl than to herself. Viola found herself the possessor of satins and velvets, decorated with ribbons and point lace, which seduced her eye and her touch.

But her hair was slow in showing any growth and caused her severe mortification when she looked hopefully in the mirror every morning. It still framed her face in dark wisps and curls. She sighed with Bessie as she tried to coax it into a more be-

coming style and hide the worst of the short ends with a length
of ribbon threaded through them.

Mistress Felicity continued to watch her closely with suspicious eyes and a frequent sneer on her thin lips. Never outwardly
hostile—she was too intent on preserving Elizabeth's favour—
she was adept at asking innocent questions that just might catch
out an impostor who was hiding her murky past for her own
devious reasons.

Master Verzons also kept a discreetly watchful eye on Mistress
Viola. Silent and unobtrusive, manner always impeccable, she
would look up to find his pale eyes fixed on her face.

As for Lady Elizabeth, the wet weather could not dampen her
spirits. She blossomed. The willow-bark infusion, drunk daily,
spread its calming, insidious fingers through her body, gradually,
slowly but undoubtedly relieving the worst of her pain. She was
tentative at first. Afraid that she was imagining the ease in her
limbs. Certain that it could not last. But it did. She walked with
more fluidity. She could brush her own hair. And the oily, aromatic liniment that Viola rubbed gently into her inflamed knuckles was so soothing. And perhaps, although she hardly dared
contemplate it, the swelling was less. Certainly less *sore*. She
even dared to hope that her fingers looked more slender and
elegant as they had in happier times.

And she could sleep. Well, certainly better than for many
months past. In fact, she decided in a moment of introspection,
she felt a certain happiness and contentment with life. That is, if
only she could rid herself of the feeling of...of *sadness* that
seemed to linger in the house. The suspicion of something, a cold
aura, watching and waiting, sometimes in utter despair. She decided that it was simply her imagination, closed her mind to it
and told no one. Thus she was ignorant of the private and detailed
conversations whispered between Mistress Neale and Master
Verzons concerning the return of a definite *presence* to Winteringham Priory.

The Viscount found himself increasingly aware of the dangers
of a man drowning in a pair of trusting violet blue eyes.

On the fourth day of storms, when hail battered the windows
and the spring flowers unmercifully, Marlbrooke set himself to
entertain.

They settled themselves at one end of the Long Gallery with

screens to ward off the worst draughts. A fire of fragrant and spicy apple logs provided warmth. A chessboard, counters for draughts and a pack of cards were produced, together with a flask of wine, and Felicity was persuaded to pick out part songs and madrigals on the spinet, which she did with surprising efficiency.

Viola sat silently within the music and singing.

'Have you no ear for music, Mistress Viola?' Felicity enquired in sweet tones when she did not join in a fashionable ballad.

'I believe I have—but I fear I lack the knowledge. I recognise neither the melody nor the words.'

'Did you not then sing when you were a child?' Elizabeth enquired.

'Why, yes. I can sing hymns!'

'Ah! Definitely a Puritan family.' Marlbrooke surveyed her with some speculation. 'That confirms it. I fear that we are leading you astray, Mistress Viola, and that, at some time in the near future, we shall be called to account by your austere and God-fearing parents.' She had already proved to be knowledgeable at draughts, but had never played cards. Marlbrooke had taught her to play primero and piquet with much enjoyment at her sweet if minor successes and her equally disastrous failures.

'I think that must be so. I know that we had no musical instruments. And I have never played a spinet—but I am very skilled in salting fish and pickling mushrooms.' She met his eyes with mischief in her own.

'Well, I can do neither, nor can I play the spinet, so it seems that we are even.'

'I think not! I am in no doubt which skills have most value. Where would we be without salt fish?'

'I could wish that we were, but Mistress Neale had a liking for it!' Elizabeth joined in the conversation.

Viola laughed aloud, shyness forgotten, for perhaps the first time since her arrival. Her eyes sparkled, her face flushed prettily. Marlbrooke was charmed at this unlooked-for vein of levity in the otherwise solemn lady.

'Would you perhaps wish to become equally skilled in playing the lute? Now there I can claim some expertise.' He experienced a surprising desire to teach her, to watch her slender fingers pick out the notes and pluck the strings. To see the vulnerable curve of her slender neck as she bent to the task.

'I would like to try,' she responded gravely. 'I expect I would find it far more satisfying than plucking and drawing a chicken.'

'Then I will teach you, if it pleases you. But only if I do not have to tackle the chicken later.'

'It would please me considerably.' The shy smile of delight ensured that the Viscount's enslavement was complete.

'So much for your future musical education.' He rose to his feet. 'Can you dance? You should know that my mother is an excellent dancer.' He advanced purposefully towards the lady. 'And perhaps since she is feeling more sprightly, she will stand up with me.'

'Marcus. I cannot. I have not danced for years—and certainly I have no wish to dance now.' But Lady Elizabeth's eyes told a different story. 'You know it is impossible.'

'I am sure that it would be unwise for dear Elizabeth to exert herself.' Felicity frowned her displeasure at the Viscount, her fingers stilled on the keys. 'You know that it will only lead to a recurrence of the pain. She will probably be crippled for days. I am perfectly willing to sit with her—'

'I know no such thing.' He glanced at Felicity with a warning in his eyes, but spoke directly to his mother. 'I have seen you moving with increased ease these past days. You can certainly join me in a pavane. Play something slow and stately if you please, Felicity.'

Elizabeth, with the colour in her cheeks and gleam in her eyes of her younger days, allowed herself to be pulled to her feet by her determined son. The steps came easily to her and she was able to move with only the slightest of twinges, stepping out the stately measures with almost as much grace as she had ever shown. Not for as long as she had once been able, but enough to reawaken the pleasures of youth. Along the extent of the Long Gallery she experienced once again the thrill of music and elegant movement, woven into one beautiful thread. With a final curtsy and a satisfied smile, she sank back into her chair and accepted a glass of wine from Viola.

'You are good for my spirits, Marcus. I never thought that I would ever—' Her voice broke a little on the words. She shook her head and applied her handkerchief, waving her son away. 'Now let me rest a little.'

He bowed over her hand with courtly grace and, to give her

space in which to recover her composure, turned to Viola, a wicked grin warning her of his intent. 'Your turn, Mistress Viola.'

'But I cannot flaunt my ignorance in public!'

'This is in private. If I am willing to risk the health of my feet, so can you.'

'For shame, Marcus.' Elizabeth had duly recovered from her momentary lapse. 'If Viola is from a Puritan family, of course she will not dance.'

'We will remedy it.' He held out his hand. And Viola could not resist, to Elizabeth's delight.

'I think you should, dear child. I give you leave to trample on his feet for his impudence!'

'I fear that I shall—but I should like to try.' Viola moved to stand before the Viscount and awaited instructions.

'Good. Now. Stand there. Hold out your hand so. Curtsy...well done! Now you are too tense...you are not going to the gallows. You are simply going to follow my directions.'

The music of the pavane once more filled the distant reaches of the Long Gallery while the ancestors of previous inhabitants looked down impassively on the dancing lesson from their gilded frames. Viola forgot everything beyond the need to concentrate on the intricate steps and the response of her body to the Viscount's expert guidance. She was graceful and agile, quick to learn, and could soon copy Marlbrooke's assurance even if his elegance was still to be attained. She was guided through the movements by his sure hands, learning to match her steps to his and the measure of Felicity's music.

'When you can forget your feet,' he commented caustically at one point, 'it is possible to exchange a glance with your partner, you know, even to converse with him.'

'I dare say—' Viola swept her silver grey satin skirts in a half-turn to face him, her hand joining his '—but if I did I would certainly cripple you.'

'I will risk it. Look up. Well done...if a little fleeting.'

Viola laughed, warmed by his praise, but equally unsettled by his closeness. He might be as critical and unemotional as the most exacting of dancing masters but the touch of his hands and the weight of his arm around her waist were unnerving, as were the pressure of his thigh and his warm breath on her face as the demands of the dance brought them close together. She swallowed and tried to concentrate on his words rather than on her heightened breathing and rapidly beating heart, which owed nothing to the slow steps of the dance. But he was so handsome, black hair rippling to his shoulders, face vivid and alive. His eyes woke in her such a yearning when he smiled at her or touched her hand. How could she be expected to concentrate when he was so close and exerted such an unlooked-for power over her mind and body?

They completed the measure again and again until Marlbrooke was satisfied at her proficiency. At the far end of the Gallery he finished with an elegant bow and raised her fingers to his lips.

'Do you suppose that dancing is sinful?' A faint line of concern appeared between Viola's brows. 'I feel that I should think it is.'

'Did you enjoy it?' Marlbrooke smiled at her solemn enquiry.

'Yes.'

'Well, then. And before you ask,' he continued as he saw the line developing further between her dark brows, 'I am not prepared to discuss with you the belief that enjoyment for its own sake is a ploy of the Devil to lure us into evil ways! Certainly not on this occasion.'

Viola laughed and shook her head at his accurate reading of her intention.

'But if we are to be serious,' he said, since they were out of earshot of their companions, 'I must express my gratitude to you. Your gift to my mother is inestimable.'

She shook her head 'It is something I found that I could do, to recompense you for all your care and generosity. I can do better when summer brings more plants into growth.'

He smiled down at her, remembering her low, infectious laugh, the way her brows drew together when she was unaware and concentrating.

'Your bruise is beginning to fade.' He reached up and traced her temple with a gentle finger. Then his whole body stilled, the smile disappearing to leave his face stern and aware.

She held her breath. He was close, so close. For one shocking moment she thought he might kiss her; indeed, she found herself hoping that he would. Her eyes were trapped in his gaze, deepest blue in clear grey, and she could not look away, held by an enchanted web that bound her whole destiny to this man whose touch lingered on her face.

Whatever he read in her eyes, Marlbrooke stepped back and dropped his hands.

'Forgive me. I presume too much.' His voice was soft, but clipped with perhaps an edge of unusual harshness. He turned on his heel to lead her back to the end of the Gallery, but did not take her hand. She followed in some confusion at his sudden withdrawal behind a chill wall of formality, unable to explain the feelings that touched her heart and sent the blood rushing to her cheeks. All she knew was that she had been stunned by the fleeting expression in his eyes, had wanted him to kiss her and instead was left cold and empty at his apparent rejection. *How foolish you are,* she chided herself. She'd clearly been mistaken, had misread what, after all, was simply kindness and tolerance towards a guest.

Marlbrooke fought hard to regain his composure. He had felt her tremble beneath his hands. The urge to press his mouth to hers, to savour the softness of her lips, to taste the sweetness as they opened beneath his, had been well-nigh overwhelming. He could not. He *must* not. It was all far too complicated. He had a duty to his distant betrothed, whereas this girl was living under his roof, vulnerable, defenceless, dependent on him for her security. But she was so damnably beguiling.

Elizabeth welcomed them back to where she sat beside the spinet with a smile and a light comment, but a hint of trouble in her eyes. This was not wise. A lady in distress could easily provoke the chivalrous nature of a gentleman however unaware she might be of her charm. And charming she undoubtedly was. Her hair might be beyond what was thought fashionable, but it drew attention to her fine bone structure and those magnificent eyes. Elizabeth sighed. When she was restored to glossy curls and ringlets, she would undoubtedly have a devastating effect on any man—a breaker of hearts, for sure. Her own heart went out to the unknown Katherine, the betrothed lady whom she had yet to meet, surely a dull creature in comparison to this laughing sprite of a girl who, without any deliberate intention, was well on the way to stealing her son's notoriously fickle affections.

* * *

The days passed.

Elizabeth had read the unspoken situation between her son and her guest correctly. And for her son, it was a damnable situation, one which was entirely outside the vast experience of Viscount Marlbrooke. Affairs of the heart were something to be indulged in—and then discarded with no damage or hurt done to either party. The sophisticated ladies of the Court knew how to conduct such matters. Alicia Lovell, pert, pretty and confident, was adept in the use of eyes and fan, if not her glorious body, to attract and invite. And, in the past, the Viscount had been only too willing to respond, with skill and finesse. It was a game, to be played out and enjoyed, without winners or losers. Mutual if superficial pleasure was the ultimate goal.

But this Marlbrooke knew, from the instant that Viola had turned her eyes to his, her fingers still clasped in his after the dance, was not a trivial flirtation, for the moment only. And, he realised, with equal certainty, that it would be wise if he put as much space as possible between himself and temptation.

The estate presented plenty to occupy him, to take him from the house where the ladies continued to while away the cold, wet days of early spring. Estate matters would enable him to pretend that Viola did not exist. It would be better if he were not tempted to touch her hand, to watch her expressive face as she began to relax and forget a little. To be captivated when she smiled at him or laughed at some foolish comment. He closed his eyes against the images that persisted in creeping with sharp-edged insistence into his waking moments. And his dreams. Yes. He turned his face into his pillow. It would be better if he forced his body and mind into different pursuits.

He set his teeth when he heard her delicious voice in the Long Gallery and her laughter echo in the corridors.

She brought light and life into the house and into his soul. But no good could come of it. She would soon recover her memory and be returned to her loving family. Perhaps to a young man who had already claimed her heart and would wed her... He set his teeth in a snarl at the thought of another man having the right to touch her and... And he would not contemplate the complications if she was never able to remember her past.

So he had the Falcon saddled and galloped across the home

park in driving rain. Physical discomfort might succeed in taking his mind off his dilemma.

Because he also, quite deliberately, contacted the lawyers to hurry the documents for his own marriage. To tie Katherine Harley into the suitable, loveless union he thought he had so desired.

Guilt rode him hard. In God's name—what was he doing? Arranging marriage to an innocent, unsuspecting girl when his heart was irrevocably lost elsewhere. Surely Katherine Harley deserved more from him than mere lip service and a legal settlement. He plummeted into a hell of self-disgust and loathing.

And yet the marriage would happen because it was necessary and he was committed to it. He would wed his Puritan bride and care for her and give her children to fill her heart and life—and she would never know. In those dark days he vowed that he would never allow her to realise that he wished he had never made the contract.

And any feelings for Viola would fade with time. It was, after all, mere infatuation at the novelty of the situation.

But his argument did not convince him. He rode across the park in black mood, to return cold, wet and mud-spattered, furious with himself and his sudden inexplicable inability to control his life.

Katherine was not unattractive, of course. They would do well enough together. He cast his mind back to Downham Hall with some difficulty. A slim figure, pale complexion, dark hair. But no matter how hard he tried, he could not remember the colour of her eyes. Viola's eyes were violet blue, the blue of delphiniums, of heart's-ease, of dew-drenched bluebells... Marlbrooke groaned and buried himself in estate papers, dry enough to quench any thoughts of passion.

'Marcus. I wish that you would—' Lady Elizabeth ran him to earth in the library and pushed a pile of bills and receipts across the desk.

'Not now, Mother. I am busy.'

'But I need—'

'Not now!'

Lady Elizabeth retreated with raised brows but no further comment. Marlbrooke *never* snarled at her in ill temper. Her lips curved in a little smile that held more than a hint of sadness and her heart ached for him. She had noted his lengthy absences from her company and believed that she knew the reason for them. Now she was sure. What could she say to him in such an impossible situation? But how ironic that he should have fallen into love with a girl whom he could not, in all honour and duty, touch or claim as his own.

Viola noted the Viscount's absence too. Quite simply, she missed him. She looked for his presence and was disappointed. When they met, which was of course inevitable, he was as charming as ever, always pleasant. But cool, rather reserved, his smile rarely evident. And she had the strongest impression that he never actually *looked* at her. He certainly never touched her! Unlike the early days, when he had put himself out to reassure and entertain. She wondered what she could have possibly done to annoy him. Marlbrooke saw the puzzlement in her eyes and could do nothing to alleviate it. *He* realised the consequences, if she did not. So he continued to keep his distance.

Chapter Six

'Good morning, Verzons. How lovely to see the sun again. Perhaps I shall walk in the garden this afternoon.'

'Yes, my lady.' The steward bowed and placed a small dish of sweetmeats on a low stool beside Elizabeth. 'It is good to see you able to take advantage of the warmer weather, my lady.'

The ladies had taken themselves to the front parlour to absorb the warmth and appreciate a view of the swathe of snowdrops beneath the beech trees along the drive.

'Mistress Neale asks if you wish her to begin an inventory of the household linen. She deems much of it to be so old as to be beyond repair.'

'Yes, of course. Spring weather always makes you think of investigating dark corners. Pray tell Mistress Neale that I will come and discuss it with her—in about an hour, if you please, Master Verzons.'

As Verzons made to draw a curtain a little to shade her ladyship's face from the direct rays of the sun, she enquired, 'Has his lordship gone down to the stables? I know he intended to ride out to the home wood to see if there are fallen trees to be dealt with after the storms.'

'I believe so, my lady. He has sent one of the grooms back to the house with a message for Mistress Viola.' He inclined his head in her direction.

'For me?' Viola looked up sharply from the book of flower illustrations open on her lap.

'Yes, mistress. Your horse has been found. It apparently found its way to the Stamford estate, beyond the village. Mr Stamford received my lord's enquiry and has returned the horse with, I believe, its saddle-bags intact. I have had them taken to your room.'

'Saddlebags! Perhaps they contain...' She looked across at Elizabeth, her eyes very bright, an uneasy mixture of excitement and anxiety on her face.

'Then go, my dear. See what treasure they hold.' She put out a restraining hand as Viola leapt to her feet and would have followed Verzons from the room. 'But don't be too disappointed if they hold nothing of value...or help in restoring your memory.'

'No, of course not.' She smiled reassuringly. 'But I must know.'

Viola almost ran from the room, up the great staircase and into her bedchamber. She closed the door and leaned against it, her breathing heightened, hands pressed against her beating heart, her eyes fixed on the worn saddle-bags that had been placed beside her bed. *Don't be too hopeful. What could possibly be in there to be of any use in solving the mystery?* She swallowed against the dryness in her throat, but her heart refused to settle.

She approached them and lifted them on to the bed. Not very heavy. With almost reluctant fingers she unfastened the leather ties and lifted the flap of one compartment. She pulled out some rolled and creased items of clothing, damp and mildewy now, which meant nothing to her. She shivered, with no desire to wear them next to her skin. A plain, unadorned skirt and bodice in dark blue woollen cloth. An equally plain linen chemise, stockings. She shook her head. Nothing of note here. They could have belonged to anyone. Beneath the clothes she found a pair of shoes. Black leather with silver buckles. At least, if they were hers, she would be able to wear shoes that would actually fit and not rub her toes into blisters. She opened the other compartment, but any remaining hopes fell. A heel of bread, now hard and stale with a suspicion of mould, and an apple, which was brown and bruised. She sat down on the bed as a tide of disappointment washed over her. The saddle-bags had really been her only hope. And they had yielded so little. She battled to prevent the tears that gathered in her eyes from spilling over down her cheeks.

Well, she must make the best of it. With her fingers she wiped them away. Then she slid off the shoes that Felicity had lent her—with ill grace, of course—and picked up the pair from the saddle-bag. Presumably they would fit. She rubbed her fingers over the polished leather and the silver buckle, both a little cloudy from the damp, and slid her right foot into the shoe. It fit like a comfortable, well-worn glove, so at least it must be hers! Then the left. *Ouch!* She took off the offending shoe, turned it and shook it. On to the bed beside her fell a small package wrapped in cloth.

She swallowed against the quickened beat of her heart as she unwrapped the cloth with unsteady but urgent fingers to discover a small box. Opened it. Inside on a bed of worn velvet was a ring. The tiny sapphires and pearls formed the shape of a delicate flower, mounted on a gold band.

She rose to her feet and carried it to the window to study the intricate detail in the sunlight glinting through the glass. The blue stones glittered as their facets caught the light, the milky pearls gleamed. She slid it on to her hand and admired the effect of the dark stones against her pale skin. It was exceedingly pretty. Was it hers? Had she worn this pretty ring? Perhaps it was a family piece, which had been given to her as the only or eldest daughter. Whatever its origin, presumably it was a jewel that she loved, which was precious to her if she had found the need to hide it in her shoe and bring it on this journey with all its risks and dangers. Why had she not left it at home? In safety? But if she owned something of such value, did it not prove that she indeed had a family who might be searching for her at this very moment?

As she studied the workmanship, her attention was caught by the sound of hooves on the gravel of the main drive below her window. She lifted her head. A horseman, dark-haired, broad-shouldered, agile, elegant. Riding a bay thoroughbred in a controlled canter down the drive away from her vision towards the main gate. She looked down at the sapphires and then back at the diminishing figure on the cantering horse.

It was as if a door suddenly opened on to a sunlit room. Or a curtain was drawn back to allow a view of a well-known scene. Detailed, vivid, familiar. And she remembered. Oh, yes, in that instant she remembered every aspect of the past in bright focus. Her name. Her childhood. What had driven her to undertake her masquerade in boy's clothes and why she had cut her hair so drastically. The surge of memory initially swamped her with relief—only to be overlaid with a thick coating of anger and disbelief as she assimilated her past with her present position. She was at Winteringham Priory, of all places, of all times, although she had no recognition of it. And the man who had ridden from her, out of her sight, was Marcus Oxenden, Viscount Marlbrooke. She sank to the floor below the window, regardless of her borrowed finery, her back against the panelling, the ring removed from her finger and now clutched in one hand, a frown drawing her brows together into a black line above troubled eyes. She needed to think, to allow her mind to grasp the realities now laid out before her.

And remembering more, she reached for the folded linen chemise from the saddle-bag. She shook it out to discover within its protective wrapping the single folded sheet of paper that she knew she had hidden there.

She was waiting for him when he returned from the stables. She knew he would eventually go to the library and he found her there, sitting on a window seat to look out over the parkland. Her hands were empty, clasped loosely in her lap, her face turned away from him. He did not know how long she had been there, but the impression was, perhaps in the set of her shoulders, that she had been waiting for some little time. She made an attractive picture, her rose velvet gown, the lace collar and cuffs glowing softly against the dark wood and rich leather bindings of the many volumes, the sun gilding her with a bright halo around her dark hair. He smiled as he approached, touched with unexpected pleasure, and against all his better judgement, that she should come to him. He had no intimation of the imminent storm.

'Well, Mistress Viola. Were you waiting for me?' She heard the smile in his voice.

She stood and turned. She had enjoyed many hours in which to build her rage against him. The range of emotion in her eyes forced him to halt and drop his outstretched hand. Anger, yes, but, far more, a deep underlying bitterness. And without doubt it was directed at him.

'What is it?' His brows snapped together.

'I remember! Everything! My name, my background, where I was going. And I remember who *you* are. You are my enemy, Lord Marlbrooke.' Her voice was low, furiously controlled, but that did not disguise the venom in her words, fuelled by bitter humiliation from the knowledge that she had come to enjoy his presence in recent days.

She stalked past him to his desk, her skirts sweeping the oaken floor, picked up a small velvet-covered box and held it out to him, palm upward. He knew what it was immediately. Not taking his eyes from her face, he took the box and opened it. He looked down at the ring and then once again at the girl standing before him.

Katherine Harley.

'Oh, yes.' She saw the recognition in his eyes even though his face remained austere and expressionless. The disdain in her voice coated him from head to foot, slick and cold. 'I am Katherine Harley! Your betrothed! Your intended wife! And you did not even recognise me!' She laughed, but without humour, rather a touch of hysteria that she quickly suppressed. 'You could not even put a name to my face.' She turned her back on him again, returning to the window to stare out over the gardens as if she did not trust herself to preserve her composure in the face of such betrayal.

'Apparently not.' How could he deny it? If she had looked back at him, she would have seen the dawning recognition replaced by intense regret and contempt for his blind selfishness in his handling of her. But she was too angry to look at him and it would have been too revealing of her own state of mind.

'Can you understand how humiliating, how shaming this is for me?'

He heard the hurt in her voice, saw it in her rigid spine, and blamed himself. Anger would be better, certainly easier for her to bear, and he deserved that it be directed at him. With that in mind, he took hold of her arm and pulled her in spite of her resistance across the width of the room to stand before a mirror on the wall.

'Look at yourself.' He stood behind her. 'Really look. Apart from the fact that I would not expect to find my betrothed riding round the country without protection and in boys' clothes, would I really have matched you with the lady I saw for one short meeting at Downham Hall? I barely saw you. When I took my leave of you, you stood with your back against the light, masking your features most effectively. And I remember long dark hair, which curled onto your shoulders and around your face. No, of course I did not recognise you!'

She looked at the image that stared back at her. Short curls. The shadow of fading bruises. No, she did not look like Katherine Harley. But she would not forgive him. She would not allow his excuse. She fanned her anger as he had intended.

'If I was beautiful, you would have remembered me.' She made no attempt to hide the resentment. 'But I clearly do not come up to the standards of the ladies whose company you frequent at Court, in spite of the flattering words that I recall when you requested my hand in marriage. You even told me that I was beautiful! It has certainly taught me a hard lesson in honesty and the reliability of men!' And how a man could seduce a woman into believing that he cared a little for her.

She dragged herself out of his grasp and put space between them.

Marlbrooke took refuge from the truth in chill formality and in attack. His voice was cold. 'Perhaps you could explain, Mistress Harley, what you were doing on the night I found you. Riding unescorted, miles from home, in the dead of night. Presumably you were not making your way here to me.'

'Hardly, my lord. I would never come to you! And you exaggerate—it was not the dead of night. I was going to Widemarsh Manor and I would have been there within the hour. What a terrible quirk of fate that I should have been thrown from my horse at *your* feet!'

'Widemarsh? The Dower House? But for what reason?'

'My great-aunt lives there. Mistress Gilliver Adams.'

'What? The old witch who was firmly ensconced here when I came to take possession—and apparently had been for years?'

'Aunt Gilliver stayed here throughout the years of the Interregnum when the house would otherwise have been empty,' Kate explained with icy contempt. 'My mother had no desire to return here and my uncle had no interest in the house. So Aunt Gilliver moved in. She kept the house with the help of Verzons and Mistress Neale. They had both been servants to my family before my father's death and chose to stay on in the hope that one day the Harley family would be restored.' She frowned at him. 'And I intend that they shall!'

Marlbrooke decided that it was politic to refuse the final challenge of the angry lady before him. 'I remember Mistress Adams very well,' he reminisced. 'She called down all the curses of heaven and hell on our heads and refused my invitation to stay here, before taking herself off to the Dower House even though she has no right to it. But that does not explain why you would come all this way to see her and presumably in such haste and secrecy.'

'She sent me this.' Kate held out the folded document, which had been wrapped in her chemise. It was now curled and smeared with the effects of travel. 'It is a letter. You should read it.'

He took it from her and spread the page. And read.

It was a letter, short and to the point, the handwriting small and neat with idiosyncratic loops and curls.

My dearest Katherine,
It has come to my notice that Sir Henry has given his blessing for your marriage to Marcus Oxenden. It is hard to believe such insensitivity exists, but I have found that men often act without thought or logic when compelled by greed or avarice. I have some information that may be to your advantage concerning your inheritance of Winteringham Priory. Your father made his wishes plain and the document may be of use in your campaign to oust the Marlbrooke family from your legitimate home. If you wish to know more, you will find me, as ever, at Widemarsh Manor. If you have any of the Harley spirit in you, unlike your Lady Mother, you will find your way here sooner rather than later.
Gilliver Adams

'I see. Does this really mean so much to you? The prospect of finding your father's will?'

She laughed softly. 'Of course it does. I have lived on charity all my life. This is my home and I have no wish to return to it simply through your dubious ownership. I need this chance of possession in my own name, my own legal right. If a will exists, I will fight you through the courts for possession. The King may

have granted it to you, but *I* will have the legal claim. Besides...'
her chin took on an aggressive tilt '...why should I not visit and
speak with Mistress Gilliver?'

'Because she is a vindictive and bitter old woman. If she has
a copy of your father's will, why has she kept silent so long?'

'I don't yet know the answer to that. But Richard thought I
had nothing to lose by agreeing to talk to her.' She met and held
his gaze.

'And who is Richard?' he demanded, the glacial glint in his
grey eyes leaving her in no doubt of his proprietary concern.

'My cousin. Richard Hotham.'

'Ah. I begin to understand.' Marlbrooke looked down at the
ring box, which he still held clenched in his hand, with a speculative gleam in his eye. 'He also would have a legal claim to
Winteringham Priory, I presume. Perhaps he also believes he has
a claim on you?'

She raised her chin further at this, but refused to answer.

'Tell me, Mistress Kate. Was your cousin aware that you intended to ride to Widemarsh alone, without protection, on a journey that could easily have taken you more than one day? A
journey full of danger and hazards in these lawless times?'

'He knew that I had received a letter from Gilliver.'

'I see. Which does not quite answer my question. I find that I
cannot admire his sentiments towards you. And I suppose your
unorthodox appearance was intended to protect you from any
untoward attention. Did Richard also know about that?'

'No. Of course he did not!' she snapped, disliking Marlbrooke's silky tones and the threat of the hard-held emotion in
his thinned lips and raised brows. She had no intention of accepting criticism of her actions from *him*. 'No one did. Indeed,
my mother... But it seemed to me to be the most sensible policy.'

'Did you see fit to inform your mother or your uncle of your
intentions?'

'I left a letter to tell them that I would be at Widemarsh Manor
with Aunt Gilliver. That I would be quite safe and write to them
when I had spoken with her.'

'And presumably that would stop them from worrying! A more
hare-brained scheme I have never had the misfortune to come
across.'

'I did not see the necessity to tell them anything else.' The slightest twinge of conscience put an edge on her voice. She would not make excuses to *him*. 'They would certainly have prevented me from coming to Aunt Gilliver. Both of them are intent on securing my marriage to you, so it was not likely that I would receive a blessing from either of them. And, it is not your concern!'

'Oh, but it is.' He walked towards her and held out the letter. 'You are legally bound to me. It is certainly my concern.' His comment might be expressed in a quiet tone, but she was left in no doubt of his temper. She quaked inwardly when he remained standing before her.

'And what do you wish to do now, Mistress Harley?'

'I will go to Widemarsh Manor as I had planned. As soon as may be.'

'Then I will take you tomorrow.'

'I suppose I must thank you, but I do not see the need. All I require is a horse.'

'Your cousin might allow you to ride off unescorted and unchaperoned, but it might surprise you to know that I have more of a care for your safety.' He frowned at her, a flare of temper quickly hidden.

'It does surprise me. Since you could not even recognise me as your betrothed. Even after you had kissed me!'

It was the wrong thing to say. She realised it almost immediately as she detected a flash of grim humour in his eyes and slight curl of his lips. It was a mistake to expose the real source of her humiliation to him.

So that was it! He should have realised. 'So I did. Perhaps if I had kissed you again, here, I would have noted the resemblance. And there I was, trying hard *not* to kiss you. I resisted kissing Viola very successfully, if not always comfortably!'

She did not understand his implications, but understood only too well his approach and the intent written on his face.

'Well, Mistress Kate, let us discover if this helps me, and you of course, to remember. I do not think we will be disappointed.'

He grasped her shoulders before she could retreat and pulled her hard against his body. Angling his head, he crushed his mouth ruthlessly to hers before she could struggle or resist. There was no gentleness here, as much anger as desire, and directed at himself more than her. He forced her lips apart to accept him, all heat and possession, taking the kiss deeper when she refused to relax into his embrace, but stood rigidly against him, her lips cold and unresponsive. He raised his head and looked down into her shocked eyes.

'No, I fear I would not have remembered. There was far more sweetness in your lips last time. And, in truth, perhaps I was in a better humour. Let me try again.'

He turned instantly from possession to persuasion. His mouth was softer, caressing, seducing her lips to part, her tongue to match his. She found to her shame that she could not withstand the tender onslaught any longer. The force, yes. That could be resisted as a matter of pride. But not this gentle insistence. She felt herself melt and damned him—and herself—for allowing it. Now her lips softened and grew warm, the warmth beginning to spread through her blood to her fingertips.

'Ah, yes.' He raised his head at last to smile at her bemused expression. 'I remember that.'

Disgust whipped through her. *How dare he!* Without thought, without reason, she lifted her hand, struck out, striking his handsome smiling face with a slap of her open hand, the sharp sound echoing in the room. He released her, more in surprise than anger, so that she almost staggered, losing her balance. Shock at her actions swept her face, emotion raw in her eyes. *What have I done? How could I have struck him? How could he humiliate me so?* She could not bear it, the whole sorry situation. With a sob she turned on her heel and ran from the library before she could expose her emotions further.

As she reached the door, it opened to allow Elizabeth to enter. Kate brushed past her with a stricken glance, tears evident on her cheeks, and a murmured apology.

'What is it?' Lady Elizabeth turned in astonishment to look after her. 'I heard raised voices. What have you said to her to upset her so?'

'Thank you for your confidence, ma'am! But for once I must agree. The fault is entirely mine. It is a long story, Mother. You should sit down and I think some wine would help.' He sighed and moved to pour out two glasses of claret.

'It is not an easy tale to tell and does not sit particularly well with me.' He leaned against the edge of his desk and, abruptly and concisely but leaving nothing unexplained, proceeded to enlighten his mother. Elizabeth listened in silence, making no attempt to interrupt, simply noting her son's refusal to justify his actions or lift any of the blame from his own shoulders.

'And so,' he finished, 'you entered on the final unedifying scene. I had remarkable success in rousing her anger against me, did I not?' He ran his hand over his jaw. 'She expressed herself with some force, to my cost. I find I cannot blame her.'

'Nor can I!' Elizabeth might understand the situation, even sympathise with him, but she had seen the despair on Viola's face and could not imagine the horrors of her recent heartbreaking discovery. It would do Marlbrooke good to deal with a degree of guilt.

'And you did not even recognise her, Marcus?' She kept her tone stern and unyielding. 'How humiliating for the poor girl. Apart from everything else that she has rediscovered today, how must she feel to realise that she has actually been living in the house which she believes should be her own? And that she owes her rescue to the one family whom she has been brought up to regard as her enemy? My heart goes out to her.'

'*Mea culpa.*' Marlbrooke threw himself down in a chair and groaned. 'I blame myself. She blames me. You blame me. I shall take to sackcloth and ashes if it will help. But I cannot see as yet how to put it right. In fact, I doubt if I can.'

'So what now?'

'Tomorrow I will escort her to Widemarsh Manor and deliver her to her great-aunt as she wishes. After that...we shall see.'

'Yes, I agree. That is where she wishes to be and it will give her time to come to terms with events.' Lady Elizabeth looked down at her clasped fingers and decided to speak her mind. 'I shall miss Viola.'

'You might come to like Kate just as well.'

'Marcus, can I say...perhaps this unfortunate situation might help to solve a dilemma for you.'

'You need to explain such an enigmatic remark, Mother. My brain feels as if it has been pummelled from Kate's attack!'

Elizabeth smiled briefly in some sympathy. 'I have seen the way you have dealt towards Viola. The way you have looked at her. And yet you kept your distance from her when you might have been tempted to do otherwise. And I believe it was because of Kate.'

'You are far too percipient.' Marlbrooke's returning smile had a sardonic edge. 'But I fear that Viola might have been more receptive to my advances than Kate will ever be.'

'Give her time. Her situation has been impossible.'

'I know. And I will give her the time and space she needs. She mentioned a cousin—Richard—who has some interest in the outcome of these events—and perhaps in Kate herself.' His tone was pensive and caused Elizabeth to raise her brows.

'Indeed?'

'Yes. I need to know more about Richard Hotham. Hotham is a name that was once feared by many in this land—presumably his father. I knew of the connection between the Harleys and Simon Hotham, of course, but did not know of the son. He must be of a similar age to myself.' Marlbrooke tossed off the wine in his glass as if he had come to a decision. 'I need to know what Richard Hotham intends—because, whether she is Kate or Viola, I fear that I have fallen in love with her.'

Kate awoke instantly. Alert, listening to the silence around her. Breathing shallowly, heart thudding in her breast.

There was no sound. The house slept silently round her. Kate groaned into her pillows and forced her muscles to relax. She was merely suffering from an overactive mind after the dreadful revelations and events of the day.

She snuggled under the covers and closed her eyes again. She really was too tired, too numb to re-stoke the anger against Marlbrooke. But the image of him was immediately there, as she had seen him behind her in the mirror. Tall and dominant and devastating. She would not relive his kisses. The possessive sweep of his hands. The lean, firm body pressed hard against hers. She would not think of that. Or of his teaching her to dance, his innate grace, the laughter that they had shared. And she would definitely not dwell on the depth of love and compassion that he showed, but carefully masked, in all his dealings with Lady Elizabeth. It was easier to think of her humiliation at his hands than his caresses. His impossibly handsome face. Those clear grey eyes that stripped her to her soul. His devastatingly charming smile... She turned her face into her pillow and willed herself to sleep.

Her body tensed again. Something *had* woken her. The air

temperature around her had dropped to ice, sending shivers through her from head to toe despite her warm coverings.

Struggling up against the pillows, she prepared to light the candle, which stood in readiness on the night stand. Probably only the skitter of mice behind the wainscoting. Or a hunting owl outside her window. She lit the candle with trembling fingers, acknowledging the relief that swept through her when she found that her room was empty, though she had experienced the distinct impression that she was not alone. But it was so cold, the icy chill pressing down on her to fill her lungs with freezing mist. And then from the chill came such a sense of uncontrolled grief that Kate caught her breath. It surrounded her, filled her head and her heart, pulsed through her veins with her blood. Such sorrow. It was so intense that she expected to hear someone sobbing in despair. But there was no sound, only this terrible sense of anguish and betrayal.

'Who are you?' Kate whispered, but there was no response. 'Can I help you?' Nothing. Kate realised that tears had come to her own eyes. She would weep for this grief-stricken creature if she could do nothing else.

And then, as quickly as it had come, the chill was gone. The room returned to its normally cool atmosphere, scented with lavender and rosemary. It might all have been a dream. But Kate was left with the residue of heartbreak and knew that it was not some trick of her imagination. Her breath continued to catch, the tears to slide down her cheeks.

For a little time she simply sat, not knowing what to do. She certainly could not sleep, as if nothing were amiss. And where had the presence gone? How could it tolerate such emotion without someone to offer comfort? She threw back the covers, snatched up the candle and a shawl for her shoulders, and went quietly out of the room. Whether to give comfort or to seek it for herself she was unsure. But such grief could not, must not, be ignored. She turned her steps towards the Long Gallery where she sensed the presence had gone.

Viscount Marlbrooke was not asleep. He had not even gone to bed, but had shut himself in the library, stretched out in his chair behind his desk, with a series of unsettling thoughts for company. A number of glasses of red wine did nothing to lesson the turmoil within.

By some mischievous quirk of fate, his dilemma had indeed been solved. He had planned to marry Katherine Harley to secure an inheritance. No love, no complications, no commitment other than a legal binding and a need to produce an heir to secure the future stability of the estate. It would serve his purposes very well. And if she had no feelings for him, then so much the better. It was not necessary to find affection in marriage.

But, damn it, he had fallen more than halfway in love with Viola. He remembered the impact on his senses as he had untied the linen cords of her shirt and uncovered her delicate feminine body. He drew in a deep breath. He remembered the silken glide of her collarbone beneath his fingers. And after that he had simply fallen into the abyss. Not the easy lust of desire he had felt for other women, the practised ladies at the Court, but a blow to his gut that had almost sent him to his knees to ask her forgiveness for feasting his eyes on so much beauty without her consent.

But now, although the outrageous complication had been removed, there seemed to be little hope of his love ever being returned. Because he had hurt her—Kate and Viola.

And she hated him. Understandably, in the circumstances! If he had wanted to destroy Kate's self-esteem, he could not have made a better job of it. To converse with her, to stand in her home and discuss marriage settlements, to compliment her beauty, to kiss her—and then not to recognise her! She had every justification for refusing to accept his excuses. Yes—she would hate him. His eyelids masked a gleam of bitter emotion.

Or did she?

He experienced an uncomfortable tightening in his loins as he remembered her unwilling response to his kiss, the soft lips parting beneath his to allow his tongue to invade and possess her sweet and tender mouth. Perhaps she was not as angry as she believed. He was a patient man. Within reason, at any rate. He would be willing to lay siege to her damaged heart and teach her the delights of love. He wanted her and he would have her. He wanted Kate to smile at him, as Viola had done, so that he could sink fathoms deep into her glorious eyes.

His senses suddenly became alert and aware of his surroundings, jerked out of his thoughts. Not a sound exactly, but *some-*

thing had caught at his attention. Perhaps Master Verzons or one of the servants still not abed.

He yawned, rose to his feet and opened the library door. The hall was dark. No one there. And then—a glimmer of light. From the Long Gallery, he deduced—someone with a candle? He walked quietly across the hall, up the staircase and turned to where the Long Gallery ran the length of the front of the Priory.

'Katherine!'

She walked towards him, a slight figure in linen nightgown and shawl, her bare feet making no sound, her candle guttering as she moved.

'Is there something wrong? Do you need anything?' She looked lost and alone in the dark expanse of the vast room.

When she did not reply, he strode towards her, thinking for a brief moment that she might be sleepwalking, a reaction to the stress brought on by the tensions of the day. But her focus was keen and sharp and she responded to his voice, quickening her step. He took the candle from her and lifted it high. What he saw stopped his heart. The tears no longer fell, but there was no hiding the fact that she had wept. Her cheeks were stained, her lashes damp. Coming to the obvious conclusion and cursing himself silently, he set the candle down and took hold of her hands.

'Kate. Don't cry. It was never my intention to humiliate you or distress you. I know that the blame is all mine and I am beyond redemption. It is not worth your tears.'

To his amazement she simply stared at him, uncomprehending, eyes blank.

He wiped away the remnants of moisture with the edge of her shawl. 'I deserve to be thrashed for causing you such pain. I would beg your forgiveness, on my knees, if you wish it.'

'No.' She shook her head, surprising him again. 'No!' More insistently now as she realised his misunderstanding. 'It is not what you think. Can you not feel it? The presence here?' She turned her head to look over her shoulder. 'She is so cold and desolate.'

For the first time Marlbrooke became aware of the atmosphere in the Gallery. His dark brows snapped together. Yes, it was unduly cold. And a wash of some intense emotion touched his senses with invisible fingers.

'Yes. I feel it.'

'I could not rest. I could not imagine so much sorrow. And I did not know how to console her.'

In reply, the Viscount drew Kate gently into his arms, enfolding her close, simply giving warmth and comfort. Anticipating her rejection, primed to release her at her demand, he relaxed when she made no move to resist. Instead she stood, breathing softly within the circle of his embrace, her forehead resting against his shoulder as the taut silence settled around them.

'She has gone now.'

'Yes. There is no need for you to cry, Kate. I was arrogant enough to believe that I had been the cause of your tears.'

'No.' It was little more than a sigh.

For Kate it was as if a spell had been lifted. Embarrassed by her tears, her unconventional attire, her presence in the Long Gallery in the dead of night, she moved to extricate herself from Marlbrooke's embrace. What must he think of her? But he would have none of it. Instead, he bent and lifted her into his arms.

'Just hold on to me. You are quite safe and I will take you back to your room. She has gone, whoever she is, and her sadness is not yours to bear.'

His words had the desired calming effect. She clung to him, face turned into his throat, all the journey back to her room where he lifted her on to her pillows and pulled the bedcover over her. She still trembled a little and her hands, when he took hold of them to tuck them under the quilt, were icy, but the emotional storm had passed, enough for her to attempt to hide her tear-ravaged face from him when he lit the bedside candle. He smiled at her very feminine response, reaching to push some wayward strands of hair from her cheek.

'What a momentous day you have had, Viola. But you are safe now and you must try to sleep.'

'Yes.'

He hesitated, thought better of what he would have said and turned to leave.

'My lord?'

He turned his head.

Her eyes rose to his, shyly, hesitantly, before the words tumbled out. 'Please don't leave me. Stay a little while. She did not frighten me, but...' Her breath caught, although she could not have explained why.

Looking down at her pale skin, enhanced by the dark feathers of her cropped hair, Marlbrooke took a deep breath and exhaled slowly. Did she know what she was asking from him? Probably not. A sardonic smile, heavily laced with mockery, touched his lips. Normally he would have welcomed such an invitation to share the bed of a woman for whom he had more than a passing desire. But this was not normality. He sighed and returned to stroke a finger down her cheek.

'I won't leave you, little one. If that is your wish. You will not be alone tonight.' He snuffed out the candle, allowing the moonlight to paint the room in black and silver. In the darkness he removed his boots, stretched out on the bed beside her, pulling the bed cover over them both and taking her into his arms so that her head was pillowed on his shoulder and her body tucked firmly into the shelter of his own.

'Comfortable?'

'Yes.' A mere whisper, a sigh of relief.

'Go to sleep.'

Silence.

'Marcus. I'm glad you were there.'

'There is no need to thank me. I think I have done enough damage for you to condemn me for my sins.' His voice was soft and gentle and smoothed the soreness round her heart. 'But I will try to make amends. And I will stay with you tonight.'

Her breathing deepened and she fell rapidly into sleep from the exhaustion of the day and the emotional trauma of the night. Without her knowledge, one hand rested on his chest, absorbing the comforting beat of his heart. The warmth from his body spread into hers as he held her secure and safe. He pressed his lips against her temple where the bruising had almost gone, now merely a pale shadow. For now he would give her all the reassurance and tenderness that she needed, but which he knew she would never admit to—and would doubtless reject on the morrow. He had been relieved to see the return of trust and acceptance in her eyes, driving out the hostility and anger of the afternoon. And the terrible humiliation of which he had unwittingly been the cause. His own obvious desires from sharing a bed with her would also have to wait.

He smiled into the darkness, grimacing at his hard arousal, and set his mind to rule his body. 'I will not leave you,' he murmured, 'nor will I readily let you leave me. You are mine, dearest Viola!'

Next morning Kate awoke to bright sunshine and the cheerful ministrations of Bessie, uncertain what she had experienced and what had been caused by an overwrought imagination. But the memory of the grief was there. And the imprint on the pillow next to her reminded her of Marlbrooke's care for her while she had slept. His understanding and tenderness towards her had been beyond belief. But the depression was cold and he had left her. She felt strangely alone and, until she scolded herself, and reminded herself of Marlbrooke's perfidy, she wished that she had not insisted on leaving for Widemarsh Manor.

Chapter Seven

Kate's leave taking of Lady Elizabeth next morning in the sunny front parlour was private and difficult.

'I understand that I must learn to call you Katherine. And that you plan to leave us.' Elizabeth surveyed the girl who stood before her, her spine rigid, her face stern and unsmiling. All the spirited confidence that she had acquired in the past days had drained from her. She looked pale and lacking sleep, which was understandable in the circumstances.

'Yes. I am sorry for all the difficulties.' She continued to stand, eyes downcast, highlighted by the pale spring sunshine, but frozen in embarrassment. Elizabeth's heart went out to her, she had come to like her too well and could not allow them to part like this. And, of course, unexpectedly, there were Marcus's feelings to consider now.

'Dear Viola. Come here.' Her smile was encouraging and she held out her hand in a silent plea.

Kate blinked back tears. 'I do not know what you must think of me. I feel as if I have invaded your home under false pretences. And presumed on a relationship that...' She sighed. 'And I seem to have suddenly become very emotional!'

'Never that, my dear girl. You have been the victim of a terrible misfortune. Can I be honest? It gives me pleasure that I came to know you as Viola, without any of the strains or tensions from your position as my future daughter. And I have liked Viola very well.'

The kindness and understanding in Elizabeth's voice destroyed all Kate's hard-won attempts at control. The tears coursed down her cheeks unchecked. She took Elizabeth's outstretched hand to sink to her knees at Elizabeth's feet. Her own mother had never shown her such easy affection and understanding and yet a stranger could soothe the ache in her heart.

'Come now.' Elizabeth squeezed the slender hand and stroked her hair. 'You must not blame yourself, Katherine. And of course, you are Philippa's daughter.'

'Yes. My family call me Kate.'

'Then so shall I. It suits you. I knew your mother many years ago when we were both young brides, she living here, I at Glasbury. If things had been different, I would have seen you growing up and would know you well. As it is, I believe I remember you a little when you were still a child in arms with soft black curls. A little like now.' She smiled as she ran her fingers through the short hair and tucked a stray curl behind Kate's ear.

'I will not apologise for my son's sins of omission,' she continued. 'He must do it for himself and work out his own salvation with you, but I believe there were mitigating circumstances.'

'Yes.' Kate sighed. 'With some thought, if I am honest with myself, I suppose so. But...'

'I understand. You do not wish to forgive Marcus too easily. But whatever your difficulties with my son, please do not absent yourself from the Priory. It was your family home—come back and reacquaint yourself with the house.'

'I would like that. It seems strange that I have lived here over a week with no sense of recognition, no touch of memory. But I suppose I was too young to form any lasting impression.' She frowned down at her hands. 'I would like to come back to the house. And to visit you.' She glanced up shyly, still unsure in this unlooked-for relationship.

'That would please me more than anything. I have grown to enjoy your company. I would be hurt if you felt that you could not come without an invitation. I accept that Mistress Gilliver has no love for us, but I would hate that she might try to poison your mind against us. There has been too much hatred and bitterness in past years and I would not wish it to taint our friendship. And the Manor is such a short distance away.' Elizabeth pushed herself to her feet, drawing Kate with her so they stood face to face. 'I will not talk about your marriage. It is your friendship I value, freely given. I would not lose it.' She leaned over to kiss Kate's cheek.

'Nothing will do that. Besides, I shall need to visit you, to see that you are still making use of the herbs and still feel their benefit.'

'You cannot know how much better I feel.'

'I know now where I learned the skill. When my mother was…when she left the Priory and my father died, she shut herself away at Downham Hall. She began to study such things—at first, I think, to fill the hours. She became very knowledgeable. My uncle, Simon Hotham, has rheumatism—sometimes far more severe than yours—brought on by a wound in battle, which did not heal well. It can keep him abed in the worst cold days of winter. My mother used her knowledge to make medicines as suggested by Master Culpeper in his Herbal. And they were very successful. I learned from her—there was no witchcraft here, whatever Mistress Felicity might fear! My mother is the gentlest of people and believes the best of everyone.'

Elizabeth gave a unlady-like snort. 'Felicity has some very strange notions that you need not concern yourself with. Your relationship with Master Culpeper has been a great blessing!'

Lady Elizabeth thoughtfully surveyed the young face before her, full of hope and possibilities for the future, and decided to act on impulse. She felt a need to know the answer to one question, but must tread carefully. After all, it was none of her concern. Nevertheless, 'Before you go—Marcus mentioned to me that you have a cousin, Richard. Tell me about him. Are you close to him?'

Kate turned her face away. 'He is…very dear to me.'

She was no longer very sure. Her emotions seemed to be in such turmoil—was she so capricious? 'I have always known and admired him since I was a little girl. He wished to marry me.'

'I see. And what do you think? Do you wish to marry him?'

Kate shook her head, unwilling and unable to answer. Elizabeth let it go, a little disappointed, but she had seen no certainty in Kate's demeanour.

Kate turned to the door. 'I have left some of the willow-bark tea and the liniment with Mistress Neale. Also a tincture of primrose, which will help you sleep if you feel you need it. It will relieve a headache or reduce tension in your neck and shoulders if they trouble you at night.'

'Yes, they do. But it is not the pain that keeps me from sleep—that is so much easier. I don't...' She found that she could not explain. Or could she? She felt an urgent need to speak to someone, to express her fears aloud.

'What is it?' Kate saw the lines of worry deepen around the lady's eyes.

'I dare not speak of it.'

'But tell me. It cannot be so very terrible. Perhaps I can help.'

'Perhaps. I dare not tell Marcus.' She picked at the lace on a handkerchief with anxious fingers, a deep line between her brows. 'He will think I am making an excuse to escape from this house—to return to London. I have never believed in ghosts—' once she had started she could not stop, the difficult words pouring out '—but I feel that this place is haunted and that a cold spirit follows my steps. It is so full of wretchedness and grief. Sometimes at night...and I am afraid. He might not believe me and I do not know what to do. Sometimes I awake and feel it, almost as if it is standing, watching, and the dread prevents me from sleeping again. What must you think of me!'

'But I believe you.'

Elizabeth looked up, a mixture of disbelief and relief in her eyes. 'Really? So you have sensed it too?'

'I have.' Kate hesitated and made a decision. 'Last night—here in the house. Her sadness overwhelmed me—so much that I found myself weeping for her.'

'She frightens me a little.' Elizabeth sank her teeth into her lower lip. 'But at least it is a relief to know that I am not imagining it.' Her soft laugh was nervous, but Kate saw some of the tension drain from her shoulders and her face.

'Talk to Lord Marlbrooke,' she advised. 'He too has sensed her presence. You are not alone in this. He has kept silent because he probably did not want to worry you.'

'And I thought... How like him.' Elizabeth nodded. 'Can we do nothing?'

Kate shook her head. 'I don't think my herbal remedies will cure a wandering spirit. Or even a broken heart. I suspect Master Culpeper would not believe in either of them. But I will talk to

Aunt Gilliver. She may have some knowledge that my mother would frown on.'

Elizabeth gripped her hand. 'I would be grateful. Farewell, dear Kate. Do not make yourself a stranger to me.'

The short journey to Widemarsh Manor took place later in the day, for the most part in an uneasy silence between the Viscount and his betrothed wife. The turbulent weather reflected Kate's mood, so she resisted Marlbrooke's attempts at trivial conversation with references to the scenery and the estate. She would not forgive him—yet. Sensing this, he gave up and the resulting silence lasted until they breasted the rise overlooking a gentle depression with a stream, a group of beech trees and a pretty half-timbered manor house, built in the previous century for a Harley widow. The Viscount pulled his horse to a standstill on the ridge and, when his companion would have ridden on, leaned down to take the bridle of Kate's mount and force her to do likewise.

'There are things I must say before I deliver you to your aunt.'

She remained unhelpfully silent, her eyes turned away from him towards the waiting house.

'I have sent news to your family that you are safe. I do not know their reaction to your letter or your apparent disappearance, but now they will know that you are safe and well and where to find you.'

'You are very kind. My uncle at least will be relieved that I am in your care. His schemes could not have been better fulfilled!'

She did not see the glint of appreciation in his eyes at her wry comment as she resisted his gesture. If she chose to ignore the fact that she had spent the night in his arms, he would allow her to do so—for now.

'I would ask a favour of you,' he continued. 'I would ask you not to cut yourself off from my mother, whatever your differences with me. She has come to enjoy your company. You will not have seen the change in her, but she smiles more than I have seen for many months and looks so much younger. She would hate to lose you—and would perhaps not wish to compromise your freedom of choice by asking you to visit.'

'Lady Elizabeth and I have an understanding.' *Which we clearly do not!*

'I am delighted to hear it!' He read the thoughts that flitted across her expressive features with ease. 'I know she will miss your company.'

'And what about you, my lord?' She turned her head to fix him with a quizzical sapphire stare. 'Will *you* miss me?'

'By God, yes!' He allowed the frustration to surface for a moment before reining in hard. 'I believe I will miss you far more than you realise.' *And far too much for my peace of mind!* For the first time in his life his emotions appeared to be slipping beyond his control.

Before she could read his intention he reached over to grasp her shoulders and pull her towards him. The horses sidled uneasily beneath them as he tightened his grip and took her mouth with his own. It was of necessity brief, but possessive and thorough with hidden depths of fire. A branding of ownership. He released her only when the horses moved apart.

'Understand me, Kate. As soon as the legalities with your uncle are complete, I will marry you. You are mine, whether you discover your father's will or not. Because there is something you should know.' His hesitation was momentary—and then he plunged, for better or worse. 'I love you, Katherine Harley. I fell in love with Viola, against all my intentions, when I was not free to love her. And resisted all temptations to pursue her. But now I am free to love her—as Katherine. And I will not give you up for anything—in this world or the next.' He registered with intense satisfaction the shock and astonishment that swept her face, tinting it with delicate colour, at his unexpected declaration. 'My heart, whether you will it or not, is in your keeping. That should give you something to think about! And in case you should forget...' He pushed a hand into his pocket to bring out the old velvet ring box, struggled with the catch and extracted the fragile jewel. He took hold of her unresisting hand and pushed the ring firmly on to her finger, then, before she could resist, bent his head to press his lips to it in confirmation of the gift. 'That is where it belongs, to remind you of our commitment and my feelings for you.'

He released her to pick up the reins, pleased that she could find nothing to say. 'And now, let us see what sort of welcome the old witch has for us. I hope I live to tell the tale. The last time we exchanged words she threatened to use a pistol against me if I set as much as a foot on her property! I would dislike it if you had to return to the Priory to participate in a burial rather than a marriage.'

'God's bones! Marlbrooke! If you move one inch closer to my house, I will set the dog on you.' The dog, a hound with an impressive display of teeth, growled and snarled under the hand of the diminutive woman who issued the threat. She stood before them, defiantly determined to repel any invader.

'Hold the dog, Mistress Adams.' Marlbrooke was unperturbed and grinned down at her, to her obvious annoyance. 'I have not come to trespass on your property or your time today. I have brought you a visitor.'

'I see you, Marcus Oxenden! I would rather not—nor anyone else who comes with you. Royalist filth!' She squinted up at the Viscount and Kate, head on one side like an inquisitive robin. 'Go away.'

Kate glanced apologetically at Marlbrooke and turned to her kinswoman, who stood before the open door of Widemarsh Manor, one hand clenched on her hip, one restrainingly on the collar of the dog.

'Aunt Gilliver. I am Katherine Harley. I have come in answer to your letter.'

'Mary's tears, girl! What would you be doing in his company? Get down from that horse and come inside before he contaminates you with his Royalist heresies. Why did Richard not bring you?'

Kate dismounted, but hesitated before approaching her aunt. She stood by the withers of Marlbrooke's horse and raised her eyes to his face, but now that she was parting could not find words to fit the occasion or to excuse Mistress Adams's blatant ill manners. He looked down at her expressive face, the generous mouth, her beautiful eyes and found the words for her.

'God keep you, Mistress Viola.' He stretched out a hand in command and she placed hers into it. Tightening the pressure of his grasp over the ring that she now wore, he bowed low to press his lips to her fingers. 'I am always at your command.' Then he released her, bowed to Mistress Adams, 'Your servant, Mistress!' and turned his horse in the direction of the Priory.

Kate watched him, conscious for a moment that she had not said what she intended—but suddenly unsure of what it was she wished to say to him. His family had caused hers such grief. But then the memory returned, bright and sharply focused, of being warm and safe in the arms of this man whom she was determined to despise. She remembered the laughter as they danced, the *frisson* of pleasure with his palm caressing hers. And she remembered the gleam in his eyes when he smiled at her. Yet his outrageous statement had robbed her of all sensible thoughts. He said that he loved her. But how could that be? He had fallen in love with Viola—but was she very different from Kate? And how should Kate react to being the object of Marlbrooke's love, with all the turbulent family history behind them? Her brow furrowed a little as she contemplated the startling scene where the man whom she had been brought up to hate and despise should cast himself at her feet—figuratively, of course—in a passionate declaration of love. How should she respond to that? She closed her eyes momentarily to block out the sight of him as if it might help her to eradicate him from her thoughts. But perhaps he did not truly mean what he had said. Perhaps it was simply a superficial flirtation, prevalent amongst ladies and gentlemen at Court where, it seemed, amusement and triviality were the order of the day. She knew nothing of such things. But love! That was a different matter. How dare he put her at such a disadvantage and cast her mind into such turmoil!

'Come in, then.' The voice behind her was raised in triumph. 'It's too cold to be standing out here in the wind. Now that we have got rid of that spawn of the devil we can be comfortable.'

Kate obediently turned and walked towards her formidable great-aunt.

'Now. Let me look at you.'

Kate turned obediently towards the light from the leaded window in her aunt's parlour. Aunt Gilliver was not what she had expected, but an amalgam of opposites. A small, round, plump lady, but with a sharp face, rosy cheeks, wrinkled like a long-stored apple, but with youthful, mischievous brown eyes that assessed and missed nothing. Kate received the instant impression that old she might be—older than anyone else of her acquaintance—but it would be unwise to stand against this formidable and unknown relative. Her grey hair was untidily scraped back into a knot, her clothes unkempt and dusty, but she was spry and active, her voice full of life, her movements quick and precise like the small bird she resembled. She wore black, from head to foot, but her figure was enveloped in an apron, once white but now grey and well stained from her operations in the kitchen. She smiled at Kate with overt friendliness, encouraging her to respond in kind. No, this was not the vindictive poisonous witch as she had been led to expect, but neither was she a harmless old widow living quietly in retirement. She had seen Marlbrooke off the premises with considerable energy and had enjoyed every minute of it.

But it was the jewellery that caught Kate's attention. Aunt Gilliver positively glittered with it. Ropes of pearls and precious stones were looped round her neck, diamond brooches flashed on her ample bosom and a jewelled pin in her sparse hair reflected the light whenever she turned her head. Bracelets hugged her thin wrists and her fingers, although not very clean, were adorned with a fortune in costly rings. Kate found it difficult to take her eyes from the incongruous lady who had clearly acquired—and wore all at the same time—the complete collection of Harley jewels.

'Well, Katherine, you have the look of your father about you. Thank God you do not resemble your mother. A weaker female I never met and I do not suppose she has improved with age. I could not bear to visit her.'

She walked round her, looking her up and down, Kate flushing under the intense scrutiny, even though she was a good few inches taller than her aunt.

'God's bones, girl! What made you hack at your hair in that way? And just look at your face. Did Marlbrooke force himself on you for you to receive such bruises? Nothing would surprise me about that family! I think we need to talk. Come and tell me all. Mason!' She raised her voice and a female of even more advanced years and untidy appearance materialised in the doorway as if summoned from realms of magic. 'This is Mason.'

Aunt Gilliver dismissed her with a wave of her hand. 'Build up the fire, Mason, and fetch some wine. My niece and I need to become acquainted.'

In spite of sitting at her ease with a glass of wine beside her before a comforting fire of apple logs, Kate spent an exhausting afternoon, between intense interrogation and being the recipient of a range of uneasy information. The house, from what she had seen of it, was as eccentric as its present owner and housekeeping was clearly not high on Gilliver's priorities. The wooden beams were festooned with cobwebs and the plastered walls yellowing and grimy with smoke, which had been layered over many years. A fine film of dust lay over the furniture, masking the heavy carvings, blurring the edges. Kate thought that she could have written her name perfectly legibly on the surface of the oak table at which they sat. Curtains and tapestries were stiff with dust and it was not wise to look too closely at the floor. Mice were evident along the edge of the panelling and Kate closed her eyes against what might have been a rat. They presumably accounted for the presence of a large tabby cat that sat, expression and ears alert, beside the vast fireplace. Even more unnerving were the bunches of herbs and plants that had been allowed to take over every surface. They were everywhere. Dried and fresh. Hanging from the ceiling, stuffed into bottles and jars, spread out to dry before the fire, filling the rooms with sharp or subtle scents of lavender, rosemary, thyme and many of a more pungent nature that Kate could not immediately place. The results were overpowering and made Kate sneeze to Aunt Gilliver's amusement as she sat amongst the chaos, her jewels rendered even more incongruous in such an unlikely setting.

Aunt Gilliver's mind was as lively as her appearance and as unconventional as her name. She had a ready smile, but sharp eyes. Kate had the impression that little escaped her notice. Brought up in the seemly atmosphere of Downham Hall, she was fascinated, shocked and disturbed, all at the same time. Mason sat silent, watchful in a corner, her eyes following the conversation between her mistress and the newcomer. A little like a witch's familiar, Kate decided with a shiver, as she caught a particularly fierce stare from the elderly retainer, which contained no hint of respect for either guest or employer And whatever her duties in Widemarsh Manor, they were not of a housekeeping nature. She thought longingly of the gleaming wood and vibrant, well-tended hangings of Winteringham Priory.

'Why did Richard not escort you?' Aunt Gilliver immediately picked up the conversation from where they had left off on the doorstep.

'I did not ask him to.'

'I have not seen him since he was a child. I expect he will be a well set-up young man by now. And how is Simon?'

'Crippled with pain and swelling of the joints. He rarely stirs from home now.' Kate hesitated. 'Can I ask—why did you not keep in touch with the rest of the family?'

The lady shrugged her shoulders and chose not to answer. 'I am surprised Simon has not approached Sir Henry with an offer of an alliance between you and Richard,' she continued. 'Marriage to Richard would be far more suitable for you than that *misalliance.*' She nodded in the direction of the Priory and the absent Viscount. 'I hope you have not formed an attachment there.' Mistress Adams's brows twitched together as she remembered the manner of parting that she had just witnessed.

'Of course not.' Kate kept her voice even, deciding that it would be unwise to reveal to her aunt too much of what had passed between herself and Marlbrooke until she knew this waspish lady better. 'My uncle Sir Henry sees the advantage of a marriage with Marlbrooke,' she explained simply. 'I am contracted to him.'

'I may be old enough to be your grandmother, but I know a handsome man when I see one!' Aunt Gilliver's mouth curved with sly intent. 'You would not be the first girl to lose her heart to a charming smile and a rich pocket. I see that you are wearing a very pretty jewel. Did he give it to you?'

Kate flushed. 'Viscount Marlbrooke is Sir Henry's choice, not mine.'

'We could soon put an end to that!' The fierce grin sat oddly on the wrinkled face. 'A little belladonna or a touch of aconitum judicially administered would end all your troubles.' She raised her brows innocently at the horrified expression on Kate's face. 'What's wrong, miss? You look shocked. What's the point in knowing about the uses of God's plants if you are going to be squeamish about using them? We know all about the properties of plants and herbs, do we not, Mason?'

Mason ignored the question as if it were too obvious to merit an answer. She kept her eyes fixed on Kate, who tried not to fidget under the intense and not very pleasant scrutiny.

'Well, I... I had not thought of it quite like that.' Kate regarded her aunt with horrified fascination.

'Does your mother still dabble in medicines? Has she taught you the skills?'

'Yes, some, but only to help mild ailments. Nothing dangerous.' She did not know whether to laugh or frown at her aunt.

'Never mind. I can remedy that while you are here. Do you intend to stay long?' Such an innocuous enquiry after a suggestion of administering a painful death! It took a moment for Kate to reorganise her wits.

'I do not yet know. In your letter you said you had a will written by my father.'

'Did I say that? Not exactly.' A crafty, knowing look spread across her aunt's face, at odds with a cherubic smile. 'I believe I said that I knew Sir Thomas had written down his intentions.'

'So you do not have his will? I was pinning all my hopes on that.' Kate sighed; her heart sank in disappointment.

Gilliver studied her, head on one side, eyes bright. 'It is more than likely he hid it at the Priory when he left to go fighting and interfering in matters that were not his concern—typical of a man. He should have stayed at home and minded his own. I doubt he would have entrusted an important document to your mother—only a fool would do that!'

Kate chose to ignore the underlying criticisms of Lady Philippa. After all, she recognised the truth in the barbed comments. 'But where?' she asked. 'Would it have not been found at any time in the years since the siege?'

'Not necessarily. It is an old house with secret caches and suchlike—I remember loose floorboards and panelling in some of the oldest rooms. And priest holes for sure.'

'Are you suggesting I should search for it?'

'Why not? You have entrée to the house. And I have these.' She motioned to Mason, who immediately rose and scuttled to a battered chest that stood beside the fireplace. It had been a spice chest with many little drawers, but now apparently contained a range of treasures. Mason opened one drawer after another, searching quickly, before she found what she wanted and returned to lay them on the table before Mistress Adams.

A bunch of old keys, a little rusty, tied up with twine.

'These open doors at the Priory.' Aunt Gilliver explained. 'By rights they belong to you. I brought them with me when I left last year—when the Oxendens drove me from the door with only the clothes I stood up in! You are welcome to make use of them. And if you need help, Verzons will give it.'

'Master Verzons?'

'Well, of course. He was steward for the Harleys long before the Oxendens seized the house by force. Why do you think I know so much about events at the Priory? He keeps me well informed.' The sly expression slid across her face again. 'Although I did not realise *you* were staying there. All Verzons could tell me was that there was a lady who had had an accident.'

'Aunt Gilliver—' Kate picked up the keys and weighed them in her hand, making her decision '—since you are so well informed, what do you know about the spirit at the Priory, the presence?'

'Ah! I had heard.' She pursed her lips, her eyes narrowed. 'If I am right—and I have no doubt that I am—it is a revenant from our family tree...the Harleys, that is. But I do not know why she is *about* after all these years.'

'I have felt her presence.' Kate leaned forward, frowning down at the keys, which she spread out on the table. 'She filled me with such a sense of sorrow, of betrayal. It touched my heart.'

'Did she now?' It struck Kate that her aunt never questioned the existence of this unquiet soul. 'I wonder about her intent. She was once considered to be a dangerous spirit—before my time, of course.'

Silence fell as Aunt Gilliver ruminated on the possibilities, tapping restless fingers on the table, making little eddies in the dust.

'But who is she?' Kate had waited with undisguised impatience and finally disturbed the train of thought.

The old lady sat back in her chair and glanced at Mason, who stared back and gave a brief nod. 'Did your mother ever tell you about Isolde?'

'No. My mother talked little about the family and never, I am certain, of anyone of that name.'

'No, she wouldn't, of course.' Gilliver's lips thinned in distaste. 'She shut herself off when your father died and she lost the young baby. Well, Isolde was one of the Harley ancestors. A young girl. Way back, in the time of the Old Queen, I think. Is that correct, Mason? When did Isolde live?

Mason did not speak but nodded again, her eyes darting between Mistress Adams and Kate.

'Whatever. I do not know the reason why—it was all hushed up, as you might believe—but one night she took it into her head to throw herself from the roof of the Priory and died on the front courtyard. She was not buried with the Harleys—not in consecrated ground, you see. And so her spirit did not rest. Or perhaps she did not rest because of the reason why she ended her life, if you take my meaning. She became troublesome, disturbing the villagers, the livestock, and the family of course. And she grew bolder as if she absorbed energy from the fear she engendered. A traveller was killed when his horse threw him on the road across the Common. And there was some story of... Well, at the end the head of the family—I don't remember who—asked the church for help. The bishop was persuaded—he brought out the clergy *en masse* and the spirit was reduced and confined for eternity. Not without a struggle, though—Isolde was intent on remaining free to wring her hands and weep sad tears—but it was finally done. I have heard tales that she appeared before them—twelve canting priests in all their finery with their candles and their Latin—in her own form, crowned with light, and then as a black cat, spitting and defiant.'

'So how did they control her for a hundred years?'

'Well, my dear, the authority of the church would not be gainsaid and they reduced her spirit to the merest flicker of light, so small that it could be trapped inside a pottery vessel. Something like that one.' Gilliver gestured with a nod of her head to the simple earthenware jug which stood on the hearth. 'And they imprisoned her within it with a wax stopper.' She snorted her disgust. 'All holy water and ceremonial at the dead of night—just the stuff beloved by the church to keep us mortals in thrall! Rumour said she was kept somewhere in the Priory, but I never knew of its whereabout when I lived there. But now it would

seem that she is released again. How she came to be free I have
no idea. Or what the end might be.'

'It is a sad story,' Kate agreed.

'You can see her in the portraits at the house. Did you realise
that they are mostly of your family?'

'Why, no.' Kate's brows rose as the realisation struck her. 'But
then I did not know who my family were until yesterday when
my memory returned.'

'She is buried in the little copse beyond the village, on the
edge of the estate.'

'She is certainly not at rest, poor lady. There is a terrible heartbreaking desolation about her. I have felt it—and wept for her—
and I know she disturbs Lady Elizabeth.'

'Good. With luck she will frighten them into packing up their
belongings and taking themselves back to London. Perhaps we
should encourage Isolde.' There was a wicked light in Gilliver's
eye.

'Encourage her? If you had been touched by her as I have,
you would not say that! It would be a sin to make use of such
grief. We should pity her.'

'Such a Puritan attitude, my girl! I detect your uncle's influence here. Sir Henry always was too moral for his own good.'
Gilliver sniffed in disdain. 'But see, Katherine, if it gets the Oxendens out of the Priory, it will certainly be in *your* interests to
make use of Isolde.'

'No. I cannot agree.' Kate discovered that her hands were curling into fists. She hid them in her skirts as she fought to regain
her composure and her good manners. It would not do to antag-
onise Gilliver on such a short acquaintance, after all! But nevertheless she continued to argue her point. 'Lady Elizabeth was
more than kind to me, you must understand, Aunt Gilliver. I
would rather do something to make life easier for her than bring
her any further distress.'

'Easier? Do I hear correctly?' Gilliver rose to her feet in a
swirl of agitation and a glitter of facets. 'And from a Harley?
Did you hear that, Mason? A week at the Priory and she is already thinking like a Royalist!'

'Why not?' Kate persisted with the determination Aunt Gilliver would have recognised if she had had a longer acquaintance

with her niece. 'Lady Elizabeth is not responsible for the events that led to our loss of the Priory.'

'Hmm! You are more like your father than I realised. Perhaps you will be an uncomfortable guest in my house after all.'

'I hope not, Aunt Gilliver. I would like to stay for a little while. Can we help Elizabeth? I am certain you will have the knowledge. The presence of Isolde in the house causes her great anxiety.'

'If you wish.' Gilliver's scowl, tightening her wrinkles further, expressed her extreme reluctance. 'But don't expect me to do more than the basics.' She changed the subject adroitly before Kate could make any more demands on her. 'Do your family know you are here?'

'They do now. Marlbrooke informed them.'

'So I suppose we can expect a visit from Richard any day now. That should make life interesting.'

Kate ignored the twinkle in her aunt's eye. Before she left the parlour to be shown to her bedchamber by a silent Mason, acknowledging a sense of relief in escaping from such an unsettling influence, she felt compelled to satisfy her curiosity.

'Why are you doing this, Aunt Gilliver? Why speak out now about my father's will after so many years of silence?' Marlbrooke's words about mischief-making echoed in her ears.

'No reason, my dear.' Gilliver's smile was bland and innocent. 'No reason other than that we would not like the Priory to fall permanently into the wrong hands, now would we?'

Chapter Eight

'Aunt Gilliver has given me these. Forgive me, my lady. I would feel guilt if I used them without your knowledge—or your permission.'

Kate sat once more in the sunny parlour at Winteringham Priory, having ridden over from Widemarsh Manor on a return of the spring-like weather.

Elizabeth had welcomed her with genuine pleasure and found various errands for Mistress Felicity, of a trivial but very necessary nature, to allow them some privacy for conversation. Now she regarded with interest the corroding bunch of keys that Kate had placed on the table between them. She picked them up with a ripple of satisfaction at Kate's amended apology.

'I suppose that Mistress Adams kept them when she left—a final gesture of defiance.' She looked up at Kate with a wry smile and a shrewd expression in her clear grey eyes. 'She does not like us very much, does she?'

'No.' There was no point in Kate hiding the truth. 'She has no good to say about the Oxenden family, and has made it clear that she objects to my visiting you. But she does not care much for most of the Harleys either. Her comments on my mother are illuminating, if not complimentary.'

'Then I am doubly pleased to see you again.'

There was no need to say more, and certainly not to discuss Gilliver's vitriolic words on the forthcoming marriage between a Harley and an Oxenden. Kate had blushed with embarrassment but refused, for reasons that were not clear to her, to give Gilliver the satisfaction of agreeing with her.

'Marcus has ridden to Glasbury, I believe,' Elizabeth continued with an understanding smile. 'I do not know when he intends to return. You are looking well—the bruising has vanished at last. Dare I say your hair appears to be growing a little?'

Kate laughed, unsure of whether she felt relief or disappointment at the Viscount's absence. 'Not as fast as I could wish it. Aunt Gilliver is far more forthright. She has given me some pungent concoction—she would not admit to its contents—which she says will encourage growth and strength. I dare not refuse to use it, despite its unpleasant aroma. If I fail to do so, Mason will surely report me and I dare not put myself further into her black books. Mason is a formidable lady in spite of her silence and small stature.'

They smiled, sharing their experience of managing female dependants.

'But how are you, my lady? Are my potions still effective?'

'Why, yes. I have taken up my needlework again. It is not easy, but I find great pleasure in it once more and my fingers are more nimble. I have also walked in the gardens a little.'

'I have brought this.' Kate rummaged in a leather satchel she had brought with her. 'My aunt has considerable knowledge and a great stock of dried and preserved herbs and roots. You would not believe! They even hang in my bedchamber and rustle when the draughts blow through the window frame! She says that this will be more effective than the liniment I made. If Mistress Felicity will rub it into the sore spots twice a day, you will feel the benefit.'

'How did you persuade her to send such a blessing to an Oxenden?'

'It was not too difficult—if I could put up with the comments about females who were just as hard headed and managing as she was.'

'I am indeed grateful. So what do you intend now?'

Kate's hesitation was slight. She knew Elizabeth would understand and so decided on honesty. 'My aunt says that my father may have hidden his will in this house before he left for the battle and was killed.'

'And you wish to look for it. Well...' Elizabeth sighed '...you are welcome to try.' She pushed the keys back towards Kate. 'I know of no rooms that are still locked and have no keys—but if you wish to satisfy yourself... And apart from that—' she smiled with quick sympathy '—I think you would wish to explore your own home.'

'You would not mind?' Kate's face lit with anticipation. 'I would like it above all things.'

'Of course I do not mind. As long as you come and see me again before you leave.'

So Kate found herself exploring the house which was hers by right of birth. As she had confessed, she had no childhood memory of it. She found it faintly unsettling to stand in rooms filled with furniture that had once been owned, used, polished and cherished by generations of her own family, and yet she herself had no sense of ownership. How should she, indeed? Her earliest memories were of her uncle's cold and loveless home. Even so, as Kate moved from room to room she hoped for some lingering echo from the past. Her mother's withdrawing room. The bedchamber where she was born. The Long Gallery where she had probably taken her first steps. But nothing. Her only memory of the Long Gallery was of learning to dance under Marlbrooke's eagle eye and the terror of Isolde's controlling power. And yet, despite the lack of any *frisson*, Kate still felt that she had come home.

She knew the history of the house of course. Sir Henry had ensured that she be word perfect in her knowledge of her inheritance. Some parts of the house were very old, remnants of an Augustinian priory that had stood on that spot from medieval times. For the rest, it had been built by an ancestor, Sir Francis Harley, a courtier in the days of old King Henry who had been rewarded for serving his master well. He had received his patronage and the granting of the estate, Winteringham Priory, now in the King's gift after the dissolution of the monasteries. In his old age, Sir Francis had taken himself and his family from Court to the Priory and proceeded to build a house that would reflect the increased wealth and his status as an elder statesman.

This was Kate's home. An Elizabethan mansion of some presence. She explored it eagerly. As she climbed to bedrooms and attics, she realised how neglected the house was. In these distant reaches dust and mice competed and so did the damp and mildew. The structure was sound enough, it merely needed to be loved and lived in. The Oxendens had commandeered the house after the siege in 1643, laying claim to it as one of the fruits of conquest, but had spent only a few short years in residence. With the death of the King and the supremacy of Parliament, they had returned to London, leaving the Priory, its rooms closed up, its furniture shrouded in holland covers. The Harley retainers had stayed put, with Mistress Adams moving in to keep as tight a hold as she was able in the name of the Harleys. Kate now realised that Master Verzons had played a major role in holding the estate together. In 1643 he had been a young, inexperienced indoor servant. When his predecessor died in the siege, he had the initiative and ambition to take over the stewardship. And the estate had prospered since old Viscount Marlbrooke had not chosen to bleed the estate dry in the name of the King. During the Interregnum, Verzons had exercised careful husbandry, steering cautiously between all disputing local factions and keeping a firm hand on the purse strings so that Kate, on her personal tour of inspection, quickly saw that she had inherited a smoothly run operation. Why had Lady Philippa not returned? Kate shook her head in disbelief that her mother should not have insisted on returning to her home, but perhaps the more ordered, secure life at Downham Hall with her brother to take on all responsibilities was more to her taste. But not for her daughter. She stood at the top of the oak staircase with mythical beasts carved into the newel posts and vowed that she would open up the house again and banish its chill neglected air. And if King Charles saw fit to gift the house to Viscount Oxenden, then Kate would do all in her power to thwart him!

With such treacherous thoughts in her mind Kate came across Verzons in the Great Hall. He bowed, his face as usual stern, expressing no emotion.

'Good morning, Mistress Harley. It is good to see you returned to the Priory.'

'Thank you, Verzons.' She smiled shyly before this austere figure. 'It feels strange to be here. You must remember my father and mother well.'

'Indeed.' His eyes met hers directly. 'May I say, mistress, that you can have every confidence in my desire to be of service to the Harley family, now and in the future. At any time.'

'Surely you mean the Oxendens, Master Verzons?' Kate frowned a little, unsure of the purpose of this affirmation of loyalty.

'But of course. How could it be otherwise?' The steward remained solemn and respectful and his voice held nothing but calm and reassurance.

'My aunt, Mistress Adams, has told me of your assistance to her in the Interregnum years.'

'I kept faith. If you have an interest, Mistress Harley, the portraits in the Long Gallery are all of your ancestors. The Oxendens never moved them—having none of their own to hang there in their stead, of course. You might care to study them.'

So Kate walked the Long Gallery to peruse the stiff figures and unfamiliar faces of her Harley ancestors. If she wondered why there were no Oxendens, it was a mere fleeting thought and of no matter. Most of the portraits were Elizabethan figures, stern and solemn in farthingales and ruffs, velvets and pearls. There were fewer from the recent past. Most of them held little interest, even the names were unfamiliar. But Kate was drawn back to look again at two. One was a large portrait, a family group of Sir Francis Harley, his wife and children, painted a century ago. They stared down at her in unblinking scrutiny. The children were for the most part small, the boys still clad in the petticoats of their infancy, playing with a small monkey and a goldfinch. But beside them stood an older child, a girl. Kate knew immediately, without doubt, that this was Isolde. She was dressed in a deep blue gown, square necked, tightly waisted and with a farthingale. Around her neck was a string of pearls. Her face was a clear oval, her eyes a deep blue, which reflected her gown, and her hair was long and dark. For so young a girl, her expression was most solemn, no hint of a smile or pleasure, but perhaps that was the whim of the artist. Her slender-fingered hands were loosely clasped before her and she held a small sprig of apple blossom. A charming portrait. And what, Kate asked silently, made you take your own life and return to walk these corridors in such wretched misery? The painted eyes and unsmiling mouth kept their own secrets. Other than this picture, Kate could detect no hint of Isolde in the Priory on this sunny morning.

The second portrait before which Kate returned to stand in profound thought was that of her father and mother, painted to celebrate their marriage. Sir Thomas had her own dark hair and deep blue eyes. She also recognised the hint of determination in his straight nose and firm chin. Perhaps she had inherited that too! His mouth looked as if he would laugh easily. Lady Philippa was simply a young and pretty girl with none of the querulous nature that was to develop through loneliness and loss and dissatisfaction. They stood hand in hand, ignorant of the pain and separation of the future, in a knot garden with the Priory dominating the background, dwarfing the two figures. Kate stretched up to caress the painted face of the father she had never known.

Shrugging off the faint shadow of melancholy, Kate turned from the portrait to see and acknowledge the one new addition to the Long Gallery. It was dominant, making a statement, as it was intended to do. Above the main fireplace had been set a hatchment of the Oxenden coat of arms. Its fresh colour, set against the sombre portraits, blazed in the room. The silver falcons, fierce and predatory, caught the light as they soared majestically, their wings confidently spread. There was no doubting who was master here. She stood before it, contemplating that the falcons were very like their owner.

It was here that the Viscount found her. She heard him first and turned to see him stride down the gallery towards her. He was dressed for riding in a plain coat and breeches, a leather jerkin over all, gloves and hat in hand, the glossy waves of his hair tied back with a black ribbon. She felt her heart pick up a beat and admitted to herself that she had missed him. But she would not show it.

He swept her a bow, as elegant and composed as ever. 'Verzons told me I would find you in the Gallery. How did you come here?' His glance was sharp.

'I rode, of course. You left the horse at Widemarsh when you escorted me there.'

'Did you ride alone?'

'Yes. It is no great distance. And within the bounds of the estate.' Her brows rose at his implied criticism. 'Do you disapprove?' Those dark, expressive brows dared him to do so.

Marlbrooke looked at her as if he intended to say more, then shook his head slightly, thinking better of it. Any expression in his eyes was instantly veiled. 'It is no matter.' He turned to study the portrait beside them. 'Your parents?'

She nodded.

'You have the look of your father.'

'Yes. So I believe. Aunt Gilliver will be here somewhere in the portraits, but I do not recognise her.'

'If you find the portrait, tell me—and I will burn it to rid us of a malign influence.'

She could not resist a smile at the dry comment. 'Come and look at this, my lord.' She led him to the family portrait of Sir Francis. 'That is Isolde. She, according to my aunt, is the uncomfortable presence in the house.'

'Do we know why?' He studied the image of the young girl with some interest as Kate had done.

'No, other than that she took her own life. She fell from the roof of the house here.'

'And is not at rest. Unless Gilliver has specifically sent her to stir up the spirits at the Priory to force us to leave.'

'No. But I would not put it past her—she hates the Oxendens beyond anything else in life. She thinks I should marry Richard.' She did not know what moved her to say that. Unless she was at heart as devious and mischief-making as her aunt.

'Does she, now? And what do you think?' She could not mistake the cooling in his tone, nor the set of his jaw.

'I have no choice in the matter.' She sniffed disdainfully and raised her brows and chin, neatly evading the question. Indeed, she did not truthfully know what answer she would make.

'No, you do not.'

She stiffened at the flat statement and the accompanying chill and turned away. As she did so, the keys that she had been carelessly holding clashed together in her hand. Marlbrooke's eyes sharpened as he caught the faint chink of metal on metal.

'What are those?'

'Nothing that need concern you, my lord.'

'Keys?' He cocked his head on one side. 'Would I be correct in thinking they are keys to rooms in this house?'

Her chin went up again. 'Yes. Aunt Gilliver gave them to me.'

'If they belong to the Priory, they are mine. I do not like the thought of them being in the hands of someone else. And certainly not Mistress Adams.' He held out his hand with an imperative gesture. 'Give them to me.'

Whereas she had willingly handed them to Lady Elizabeth, this was a different matter. 'No. I will not.'

'Give them up, Kate.' His voice was soft, but she could not mistake the implied threat.

'No.' She shook her head and hid her hands—and the keys—behind her back.

He advanced. She retreated.

'Kate. I shall have no mercy if you force me to take them from you.'

'They are mine!' With which she turned and fled down the length of the gallery, her heels clattering on the wooden floor.

'Damn you!' Torn between frustration and amusement, he flung aside his hat and gloves and launched himself in pursuit. She beat him to the end of the Gallery but there the chase came to a precipitate end when she found herself with no escape. She turned at bay, her eyes sparkling with anger as she silently dared him to take the keys from her. With a grin he picked up the challenge immediately, advanced with deliberate intent and pushed her back against the panelling, his hands easily capturing and pinioning her wrists behind her back, the weight of his body holding her in submission.

'That was not wise, Viola!'

She kicked his shin smartly, enough to cause him to flinch and draw in a sharp breath. She saw anger and frustration—jealousy, even—in his eyes, but only fleetingly, to be replaced by a far more intense emotion that she could not identify. He scanned her face intently, the flush in her cheeks, the angry glint in her eyes that turned them dark and lustrous, her parted lips as she gasped for breath. His heart picked up its beat and the tightening in his groin made him take a deep breath and pray for control.

'Little Kat. What penalty shall I demand for that unwarranted attack on my shin!'

Her eyes flashed their defiance at his intimate misuse of her name.

He removed the keys from her resisting fingers and tossed them to the floor where they fell with an ominous clatter. Then he did not release her, but held her firmly against the wood, her soft breast crushed against his jacket, his hard thighs holding her still.

'Well, little Kat?'

'If my father's will is hidden here, then I have a right to search for it,' she spat at him, refusing to acknowledge the effect of his nearness, the spread of heat in her blood, the trembling throughout her body that owed nothing to her previous anger.

'You have no rights other than those I allow you.' His voice was gentle, against all her expectations—but without warning he bent his head and kissed her. It took her by surprise. She had expected him to take his revenge, all flash and fire, searing possession. Instead he touched her mouth with the utmost tenderness, his lips sliding gently, persuasively over hers, encouraging them to open to allow his tongue access. Her mind might resist him, but her body and heart betrayed her. She could not resist such gentleness and found herself sinking helplessly, treacherously into his embrace. He lifted his head and she blinked at him in shocked uncertainty.

'Katherine,' he murmured and smiled down into her face. 'That was not so unpleasant, was it? From a Royalist and an Oxenden!'

Then the heat and passion in his fiercely narrowed eyes took her breath away. He released her hands, changed the angle of his head, holding her face exactly as he wished, his fingers, callused from reins and sword, rasping on her soft skin so that she shivered in anticipation, and took possession of her mouth once more, his tongue hard and deep in its invasion. When her hands were free, against all her intentions Kate found herself sliding her arms around his neck, pushing her fingers into his hair to glory in its silken strength, pulling him closer. She was aware of him as she had never been before, the hard firmness of his chest and belly, the strength in his well-toned muscles. It was so unfair of him to take advantage of her in this way—and for her own responses to be guilty of such betrayal.

When he finally released her he stepped away, his grey eyes dark and watchful, flickering over her stunned expression, her softly parted lips. He raised her hand to his mouth and pressed his lips to her palm.

'You should know, Mistress Harley—the written contracts for

our marriage are complete and I now have them in my possession.' Kate shivered a little at the calm determination in his face.

'So you have everything you want.' He detected a hint of sadness behind the defiance and felt a need to soothe it, but sensed her withdrawal from him.

'I do not need the legality. I have possession.' There was an edge to his voice now. 'I want you. And I learned in past years that you hold closely to what is yours. Do you remember what I said to you on the way to Widemarsh?'

'Yes. I remember.' *I love you.*

'You did not believe me.'

'No.' Her eyes were wide and locked on his. A challenge again. 'How should you love me?'

'I will prove it.' He knew it had been a gamble from the first, but he would risk it. For the first time in his life, when the cards were stacked against him, he would take the chance—to win this entrancing girl who fired his blood and possessed his mind and heart. He would risk the possibility of hurt and rejection. 'There are three things that I find I want from you, Mistress Harley. I want you in my arms and in my bed. That's the first. Second, I want you to carry my heirs.'

'Then the contract is a victory for you, my lord.' There was no softening in her. 'You will get all of that.'

'Does the will matter so much? The legal recognition? You will live here at the Priory and your children will claim it.'

'Yes, it matters.'

'Very well.' He released her shoulders abruptly, turned from her and stooped to pick up the keys. 'I will allow you to do as you wish, search the house for any hidden documents, if that is what you wish, but I will not give you the keys to my house— yet. I will keep these.' He tossed them lightly in the air, catching them, eyeing her with a narrowed stare, before dropping them into a pocket.

'That is exactly what I would have expected from you!' If her upbringing had not been so strict and ingrained, Kate would have stamped her foot. She hissed in frustration like the kitten he had called her when she recognised defeat for her intentions in the implacable grey of his eyes. She turned her back on him and tried for dignity as she marched down the Gallery She did not see the quick grin on his face or the softening of the light in his eyes as he noted the hint of a flounce when she swept towards the door. With a few strides he caught up with her.

'You have not asked me about the third thing, my dear Viola.'

She clenched her teeth at the laugh in his voice. 'So, what is the third thing, my lord?' She fought hard to keep her tone uninterested.

Marlbrooke took her arm in a gentle clasp and drew her to stand before him. 'Why, nothing of great importance.' His eyes mocked her, but not unpleasantly. 'I merely would have you love me. I want your heart, Viola.'

This time the flounce in her step was unmistakable as she pulled her arm free and made good her escape. But she could not quieten her feverishly beating pulse, just as she could not eradicate his words as they echoed hauntingly in her mind and her heart.

The Viscount watched her go, making no further attempt to detain her, his eyes a little pensive and the ghost of a smile touching his hard mouth. He was not dissatisfied with the outcome, sympathetic to the contradictory emotions that tore at her and left her uncertain and insecure. Resist him she would—but not for ever. He turned to retrieve his hat and gloves, haunted by the memory of a soft mouth and reluctant surrender in his arms.

In the following days Kate made the short journey between Widemarsh and the Priory on a number of occasions. She was allowed free rein to continue her explorations of the house and always found time to spend with Lady Elizabeth. She found that she began to look forward to her visits, particularly, if she were honest, with the prospect of exploring her difficult relationship with Marlbrooke. Sometimes he was there, welcoming her with wry amusement in his smile. Sometimes he was engaged on estate business, when she was disappointed and felt that some of the brightness had dimmed from the day. Her mind returned again and again to the central problem. How could she find so much pleasure in his company, in his acerbic wit, the occasional touch of his hand on hers or the brush of his lips against her fingers? How could she desire above all things to be in his com-

pany, when she had vowed never to come to terms with the
Oxenden family in general and the Viscount in particular?

She was forced to accept that she was not immune to his
charm. As she was forced to accept two other important facts. In
spite of her diligent searches, Kate found no trace of family papers or her father's will. And as for Marlbrooke, he made no
mention of his love for her again. Either his fleeting attraction
had dissipated as speedily as it had developed, or he was giving
her the space to consider and question her own feelings as she
came to know him better.

'Kate.' Marlbrooke held out his hand in greeting as Kate dismounted one morning and handed her horse over to Jenks. 'Come
and walk with me.' He drew her hand through his arm to compel
her agreement. He did not need to do so.

'So Mistress Gilliver continues to allow you to return to this
Royalist pit of sin and depravity.' His glance was cool and bland,
hiding the humour. 'I fancied that she might lock you in at Widemarsh and so effectively thwart our marriage arrangements.'

'No.' Kate smiled a little at the not-too-extreme likelihood of
Gilliver taking such action. 'But I admit she has been brutally
outspoken on the subject.'

'Who do you suppose Mr Adams was?' Marlbrooke mused,
taking Kate's hand to lead her along one of the gravelled walks.
The box hedges in the knot garden were beginning to put on
spring growth with bright new leaves.

'I have no idea. I do not remember his being mentioned in the
family.'

'Whatever he was, he was without doubt a brave man.'

'Brave?' Kate bent to pick a sprig of lavender, its scent warming with the sunshine.

'He would have to be to tie himself to Gilliver.'

'All I know is that he is dead.'

'He would be.'

Kate could not suppress a laugh at the Viscount's dry tone.
The breeze whipped colour into her cheeks and her eyes sparkled.
Marlbrooke watched her with pleasure as she relaxed in his com-
pany, crumbling the aromatic leaves between her fingers.

'Does she, do you suppose,' he asked idly, 'dabble in the black
arts?'

'I think not.' Kate took up the point in all seriousness. 'But the only room in the Manor without a layer of dust is the still-room—it is so neat and well ordered I do not like to set foot there without her permission. Everything is labelled and in its place. The rest is a very poor apology for housekeeping, and she does not seem to notice when mice run across the hearth in front of you. But she undoubtedly has great knowledge and skill in the use of herbs and plants.'

'Against my better judgement, I must acknowledge my gratitude to Mistress Gilliver! My mother continues to find relief from her potions. But it is hard to accept that she will never be restored to full health.'

'I know. My uncle—Simon Hotham—is also afflicted with rheumatic pains, brought on by a badly attended wound. His joints become severely inflamed in damp weather. He finds it hard to tolerate his infirmity, I believe. My mother says that it has had a detrimental effect on his temper—indeed, on his whole personality.'

'I remember him as a soldier. He earned a considerable reputation—at the Battle of Worcester he was instrumental in the victory for Cromwell's New Model Army.' Perhaps this was not a suitable topic for light conversation on a bright morning, particularly with a lady who was still a little reserved, conscious of the burden of the past and so reluctant to relax in his company. Marlbrooke adroitly changed the subject. 'You will be gratified to know that your salves and potions—or Gilliver's—have given my mother so much ease and made her life so tolerable again that she is considering a total refurbishment of the Priory—with mention of the beating of tapestries and the clearing out of attics. Mistress Neale is, of course, in close collaboration. It makes my blood run cold to think of it. I *could* believe that perhaps that was your intent from the beginning, my devious child.' He raise an expressive brow as he looked down at her.

'Really, my lord?' She smiled innocently, but the he caught the instant mischief in her eyes.

'Really, Mistress Harley! Should I thank you or damn you for disturbing my comfort, do you think?'

'If I were you, I would thank God for Lady Elizabeth's improved health—and find as many opportunities as possible for business at the far ends of the estate!'

'I will bear that in mind. What a managing person you are. I had not realised.' As they walked a little in silence, his clasp on her hand where it rested on his arm was warm and companionable, calming her uncertainties. Kate found herself having to fight the desire to trust this man, to open up her guarded thoughts and feelings to him, to lean on his strength. It would be so easy—and so dangerous.

She took the rosemary that Marlbrooke had casually plucked and now held out to her, and raised it to inhale the fragrance, contemplating it with a slight frown.

'What is it, dearest Kate?'

'I was just thinking. My uncle is so bitter, so angry, driven by nameless passions. My mother says that the pain has crippled his mind as well as his limbs, that it has destroyed his clear judgement and pushes him to extremes. I think his wife—my aunt Lucy—finds life very difficult with him.' Now she raised her eyes to Marlbrooke's. 'And yet, your mother, Lady Elizabeth—she is so full of courage and joy. The pain has not robbed her of her warm heart or her loving spirit to any degree.'

'A loving spirit.' Marlbrooke smiled down at his intended bride. Her sensitivity held great charm for him. 'You have the truth of it. And I agree. She has all my admiration, although it would not do for me to tell her so.' They turned to retrace their steps towards the house before he continued, somewhat pensively. 'It concerns me that some days my mother finds it difficult—well-nigh impossible—to walk far and so rarely leaves the house, even to stroll in the gardens. She loved the gardens at Glasbury, I believe, although I was too young to pay much heed to such things. It must be a great loss to her.' It was as if he were speaking to himself, voicing a deeply hidden concern.

'Have you thought of...?'

'Of what?'

'No matter.' Kate turned away towards a naked arbour that would soon be a riot of roses and honeysuckle, suddenly reluctant to interfere in matters that some would think were not her concern. 'I am sure you have considered all possibilities for Lady Elizabeth's comfort. I would not presume to suggest otherwise.'

'Yes, you would. Damn it! Why are women so difficult?'

'I am not difficult!'

'You are perverse—and quite delightful! Tell me, dearest Kate, what is it that you are quite sure that I have not thought of—but are unwilling to voice in case you step on my supremely sensitive toes?'

But the opportunity was gone as Verzons appeared at their side.

'My lord. You have a visitor who requests speech with you. The Reverend Peters. He appears to be in some degree of agitation and claims a matter of great urgency for the whole community.' Verzons's mouth bore a sceptical twist. 'Do I say that you are unavailable?'

Marlbrooke's brows rose. 'The Reverend Peters? No, Master Verzons, I will come. If you would show him into the library and provide him with some refreshment, I will be there shortly.'

'What have you done to upset the local clergy in your short residence here?' Kate glanced up at him with a sympathetic twist to her lips. 'Refused to attend church services, perhaps?'

'To my knowledge, I have done nothing. I expect it is the problem of footpads and robbers on the Common—they seem to be spreading like a very contagious rash. The Reverend Peters will expect me to take action. God and the lord of the manor against the devil and all his works, or something of that nature. This is not an interview I anticipate with any joy. Would you care to accompany me and help to soothe his ruffled feathers?'

'Certainly not! I think you will deal with it admirably without me. What will you say?'

'That I will communicate with Moreton, the local Justice of the Peace, and together we will take suitable action. That should satisfy him—indeed, it is a problem that must be looked to and it is within my jurisdiction. Meanwhile, I will leave you to consider the means of helping my mother that you will not discuss with me.' He took her hands, linking her fingers with his, and turned her to face him.

'Do you mean that you are willing to give me a free hand, my lord?' His eyes were full of light and laughter as he considered her request, trapping her own into a union of more than hands. Kate felt her limbs grow weak at the warmth of the bond developing between them.

'That sounds dangerous. I know that I might regret it—but very well. As long as you promise me that it will involve neither Isolde nor Gilliver.'

She laughed. 'I promise. But it might involve Jenks!'

'You are a revelation, my love. Will you not tell me?'

'Never!'

He kissed her hand and then her lips, lingering a little as he tasted their sweetness. 'Then do your worst, dear Viola. I know that you will find enjoyment in it!'

Kate remained for a long moment as he left her, enjoying the graceful elegance of well-tuned muscle with which he mounted the steps to the terrace. A faint smile warmed her eyes and softened her lips as she was forced, even against her better judgement, to acknowledge the pleasure that she could find in his company and conversation—and the disturbing heat that fanned her blood when his mouth touched hers. Such a light caress, and yet her hands clenched involuntarily at the sharp memory. Her fingers bruised the rosemary leaves that he had given her until their fragrance surrounded her and filled her senses, as his kiss had done.

And then, with a little shake of the head, she turned back towards the stables, to speak with Jenks about the little matter of a chair.

Chapter Nine

London!

Marlbrooke had suddenly announced, with typical arrogance and lack of consideration for the occupants of Winteringham Priory, that they would go to London. The King had decided to hold a celebration—he forgot for what reason—but then Charles did not need a reason other than his own pleasure. Kate frowned at the Viscount's highhandedness. The fact that Elizabeth, and even Felicity in her dour way, responded to the prospect with unconcealed pleasure irritated Kate even more.

'When shall I expect you to return, my lord? Or perhaps it is your intention to remain in London.' Kate stood before the Viscount in his library, shoulders braced, her tone light with casual interest. He would not know of the sudden disappointment that gripped her at the news.

'No, Viola. It is not my intention to remain in London.' His face betrayed no amusement. 'A week. Perhaps a little longer. It will depend on how much shopping my mother wishes to do. Or how soon she can drag herself away from old friends.'

'I know that she looks forward to it.' Kate's lips felt stiff when she tried a smile. *I will refuse to admit that I will miss you!*

'London has much to offer.'

'So I am told.'

'And *you*, dear Kate...' he relented '...so that you will do more than know of its attractions secondhand, *you* will accompany us.'

'No!' Was it shock, surprise? Horror, even? 'I cannot.' She

would certainly not admit to the quick burn of excitement in her stomach.

'Why not? You will make your curtsy to his Majesty and allow your Puritan soul to be revolted by all the excesses of the Court and the depravity of the capital. You will enjoy it above all things.'

He watched her carefully, her attempts to hide the leap of pleasure. And then he saw her lips part. His response was both accurate and immediate.

'Don't say it! Don't argue with me. It will do you no good. I have decided.'

After which there was no more to be said, and nothing to do but pack her meagre belongings and inform Gilliver of her destination.

Her aunt's response was colourful and predictable, but Kate found in herself the ability to ignore what she did not wish to hear. She listened patiently to biting comments on the likelihood of her selling her soul to the devil, the relationship between sow's ears and silk purses, and the perils of visits to the Thrice-Damned Den of Iniquity which was the capital.

'Don't let him turn your head.' Gilliver ended her tirade. 'He is still the enemy, and it will behove you not to forget it! You owe some allegiance to the Harley name, my girl, even though it seems to me that you seem to have forgotten that small fact. Allowing your head to be turned by a handsome face and a pocket of gold! You should be ashamed of yourself.'

But she relented enough to gift her one of the remarkable diamond brooches that adorned her person. 'This is suitable for a Court appearance.' Unpinning it, she rubbed the tarnished metal on her shawl, but with no noticeable effect on the lustre. 'You can return it to me when you come home.'

Kate thanked her and eyed its massive brilliance askance. She could imagine no occasion when she would wear it, but meekly thanked Gilliver for her generosity and promised not to be seduced by the pursuit of pleasure.

For Kate, London was an experience for which nothing in her sheltered life at Downham Hall had prepared her. The crowded streets with their mass of humanity, the constant bustle, the squalor and the filth. From the moment of her arrival in Marlbrooke's comfortable travelling coach she was both enthralled and repelled, in equal measure. The shops with their wealth of goods beckoned seductively to a girl brought up strictly with no regard to fashion or luxury. The beggars who struggled to live in the lowest degradation contrasted uncomfortably with the comparative luxury of her own childhood—even when her dress had been threadbare and not of her choosing, she had lacked for nothing. The smart streets that housed the rich made sharp and appealing contrast with life in the depths of rural seclusion. Elegant Palladian façades with pillars and friezes, created from Inigo Jones's designs, entranced her. But the refuse in the streets, with its rank smell and threat of disease, and the ragged children who swarmed in the gutters, without food and without hope, appalled her.

She would not have missed it for the world.

The Marlbrooke town house in the Strand, flanked by other houses of the rich, was, of course, far smaller than the rambling wings and inconvenient corridors of Winteringham Priory, but she quickly realised that it had far more to offer in the way of luxury and comfort. It was now perfectly understandable to her why Lady Elizabeth sighed over it when damp chills settled over the Priory. And so many people were there to welcome them with warmth and easy friendship. No wonder Elizabeth found life in London more congenial and easier to bear. Her high sprits and lively anticipation were infectious as they set themselves to wring every moment of pleasure from a week of celebration and festivity.

It was rendered even more attractive by Felicity's decision to absent herself from the household for a few days to visit a cousin.

'Shall we not then have the pleasure of your company, Felicity?' Elizabeth was all concern as she pulled on a pair of fine kid gloves, turning them to admire the smooth fit. 'I had presumed that you would accompany us.'

'No. I have no wish to attend Court. And it is my duty to visit Cousin Mary, who I believe is unwell.' Felicity sniffed, mouth curled in derision, as she took the opportunity to express her opinions at length. Such lewd behaviour as went on there, if only half the rumours were true! Why, she had heard—and did not doubt it for one moment—of one of the Queen's ladies-in-waiting actually giving birth to a child in an anteroom at the New Year's festivities! What sort of behaviour was that? She eyed Kate with ill-concealed malice. It would do well for the lady to note the society to which Marlbrooke belonged and to which he would no doubt choose to return when the inheritance was settled.

'For after all...' Felicity's lips thinned even further as she warmed to her task '...my lord has always expressed his appreciation of the culture and sophistication to be found here in London. The wit of clever conversation with friends, the music and dancing. The theatre. And the elegance of the fashionable company, of course. Why would he possibly wish to bury himself in the country? He will see no attraction there, I warrant, once the novelty of life at Winteringham Priory has worn off. I am sure that you will soon see this for yourself, Mistress Harley, brought up in Sir Henry Jessop's austere household. It will be very different from your own limited experience.' Felicity folded her hands complacently, having made her point.

Kate could make no reply. The spiteful observations were to remain with her, making for uncomfortable speculation. It was unfortunately true. This was Marlbrooke's world, not hers. Kate closed her eyes and mind to the comments she imagined from Sir Henry on the frivolity of Charles II's scandal-ridden Court. Or, even worse, from Simon Hotham's bitter lips.

'I doubt that Marlbrooke is quite as shallow as your picture paints, my dear Felicity. But we shall miss your company, of course.' Elizabeth responded to Felicity's words, as always, in the handling of her companion, her tone gentle and conciliatory, if a trifle dry.

Marlbrooke, later in private, was not.

'Thank God! It would seem that occasionally the Heavens are pleased to smile on sinners! Let us make the most of Cousin Mary's chronic ill health. She has my utmost sympathy.' And so saying, swept them off to a performance of *Macbeth* at the newly opened and most extravagant Duke's Theatre. Here any concerns that Kate might have had concerning the wisdom of her visit to Gilliver's den of iniquity were swept away by the enchantment of colourful scenery, ingenious devices and dramatic performance of Master Shakespeare's bloodcurdling tragedy.

* * *

They attended the Royal Court at Whitehall, of course. To a ball, to a reception, to a masque. On Wednesday morning they gathered with other privileged members of London society to watch Charles and Queen Catherine dine in formal splendour. Promenades in St James's Park enabled them to admire the avenues of trees and the expanse of water. It was indeed a round of pleasure. Marlbrooke was usually in attendance to guarantee their comfort—but not invariably so. If he gambled and wasted his fortune, Kate did not see it. If he spent his nights alone or in female company, she was not aware. *You have no right to think about it!* The voice in her head was sharp as it lectured her. *What is it to you how he spends his time?* But she was honest enough with herself to recognise the sharp twist of jealousy when she and Lady Elizabeth spent an evening at home without him.

As promised, she was taken to make her curtsy to the King at Whitehall, at a formal reception to welcome the newly appointed Portuguese ambassador. She was nervous, understandably so when face to face with her King, unable to raise her eyes above the gold buttons on his waistcoat as she sank gracefully to the polished floor, her skirts billowing round her. But Charles was quick to put her at her ease. He had been well informed.

'Lady Elizabeth. It is good to see you in town again and in health. And Mistress Harley. The Puritan bride. So I get to meet you at last.'

'Yes, your Grace.'

She risked a glance, to find him smiling at her with complete understanding. Tall, taller than Marlbrooke, loose-limbed and swarthy, the lines of cynicism were already deeply engraved on his harsh face. But his smile warmed her heart: she understood at that moment why many could speak of him with such affection.

'And are you enjoying your first experience of Court, Mistress Katherine?'

'Yes, your Grace. It is beyond anything I had dreamed of.' She fought against the acute embarrassment of knowing that her family had waged war against this man and rejoiced in the death of his father on the scaffold. Charles, with quick intelligence and intuition, was aware and took steps.

'The past is over, Mistress Harley. I hold no grudges for the past. Especially against beautiful women.' His smile illuminated his harsh features to a fleeting beauty. Kate now knew why so many women found it easy to surrender to Charles's demands. She looked up in consternation at his accurate reading of her thoughts, her face becomingly flushed, her deep blue eyes wide with apprehension as her King held out his hand to lift her to her feet.

'You are a lucky man, Marlbrooke.' Charles cast him a sly glance, a knowing grin.

'I think so, sir.'

'If she were not yours, I might consider giving you some competition.'

'I would hate to refuse you, your Grace.'

'But you would, of course. And rightly.' His Majesty laughed with utmost good humour, touched the Viscount's arm. 'Come, Marlbrooke, and play a hand of cards with me for your sins. It will take us out of the reach of our Portuguese visitor with his bad English and inability to stay silent.' He bowed to the ladies. 'Lady Elizabeth. Until next time.' And then, before he turned away, 'I delight in your company, Mistress Harley. And regrettably leave you to the safekeeping of my lord Marlbrooke.'

'And I felt no better than a prize pig, to be haggled over!' Kate announced to Elizabeth when they were alone.

'Never a pig!' Elizabeth laughed gently at Kate's outrage, understanding the conflict of allegiance that pulled at her.

'A filly, then!' She was not to be placated.

'But a very pretty one—or his Majesty would not have noticed you.' Lady Elizabeth saw the answering gleam in Kate's eyes. 'And you have to admit that he has an easy charm.'

Kate was prepared to admit to no such thing, but returned the pressure of Elizabeth's fingers.

Taking a seat against the painted walls to ease her aching limbs, Elizabeth took the time to point out some of the notables at Court. The notorious Barbara Castlemaine, smaller than Kate had expected, but eye-catching with her vibrant hair and sharp features. The Earl of Clarendon, the King's chief minister, portly and already nervous at his master's lack of political interest and disinclination for business. And, of course, Frances Stewart, Charles's most recent mistress, tall and elegant and quite beautiful, setting herself up as Lady Castlemaine's rival with consummate skill. It made for engrossing entertainment. But throughout, Kate could not but be aware of eyes turned in her direction. All assessing. Some pitying. Some critical. Her new court dress gave her confidence, of course—who could fail to admire the tight bodice with its full sleeves and low neckline, to delight in the soft fall of full skirts of violet silk, over a brocaded petticoat? Dressed in the height of French fashion, Kate gloried in its femininity—and deliberately closed her mind against Gilliver's imagined strictures against vanity and avarice. Even the growth of her hair gave her some satisfaction—the style achieved by her maid and a careful application of satin ribbon was almost acceptable.

Yet she still felt vulnerable in the face of such sophistication and more than thankful for Elizabeth's reassuring presence. The arrogant smiles and whispered asides, not quite hidden behind gently fluttering fans, tore at the rags of Kate's self-possession that she was determined to wrap herself in. She might find it difficult to retain her composure, but still held her head high. Ignorant of Court ways she might be, lacking in clever conversation and sophisticated banter, but she had wit and intelligence and so would hold her own. For whatever reason, she was betrothed to Viscount Marlbrooke and so owed something to her new status. And to her father's memory, whatever his political allegiance. She discovered that she had a depth of pride which she could draw on—and it was demanded of her frequently.

'So you are Marlbrooke's bride.' If she had to respond to that observation one more time, delivered by some Court beauty with raised brows, glossy curls and a supercilious air, Kate felt that she would explode! But she learned quickly how to reply. A calm smile. A condescending inclination of the head.

'Indeed. I am Katherine Harley.'

'I believe your family once owned Winteringham Priory? Before losing it to the Oxendens when your father fought for Parliament.' There was invariably an accompanying curl of the artfully rouged lips.

'Yes. Winteringham Priory is legally mine. It was stolen from my father. But I have now returned and my family are once more in possession.' She would raise her chin a little. 'And Viscount Marlbrooke, of course.'

'It is a sudden decision, is it not? We had not realised that Marlbrooke intended to wed. He will be sadly missed if he decides to absent himself from Court for any length of time.'

'Our marriage is an obvious outcome, both desirable and to the benefit of all parties.' The challenge in Kate's eyes dared anyone to contradict her. 'Where we shall live for most of the year will be a matter to discuss after the ceremony.'

'So, when will you be married?'

'Very soon. My lord Marlbrooke desires a rapid conclusion. As I do, of course.' Which effectively put an end to most interested, if patronising, enquiries. And, in all truth, Kate had to admit that she came to enjoy the encounters.

So did Lady Elizabeth, when she chanced to hear the end of such.

'I see that you have the makings of a politician, dearest Kate. I cannot tell you how pleased I was to see Lady Templeton discomfited. She had high hopes for her daughter—a disagreeable girl.' Her eyes glinted in appreciation. 'I do believe that Marcus would be proud of you!'

'Perhaps. But do not tell him.'

The Viscount did not need to be told that his betrothed was the subject of much speculation and comment. And he used his own methods to allay it and smooth her path. For the most part, he remained at her side, attentive and charming, to protect and encourage. When he could not, she was still firmly in his vision, so that he noted the approach of Mistress Dorothea Templeton, once an object of Marlbrooke's casual interest.

'Do you not dance, Mistress Harley?' Here Kate recognised an enemy of some calibre in the flash of blue eyes and the toss of honey curls.

'No. I have never learned these French dances, which are so fashionable.' She decided on honesty as the best policy. But not too much!

'How unfortunate.' They watched the dancers draw to an end in a stately corant and then step into a more lively saraband. The pavane, Kate had already realised with a whisper of regret, was not in fashion. The lovely Dorothea showed her teeth—and a dimple!—in what might have been mistaken for a smile. 'Life at Court is so tedious if one is unable to dance. Do you not find it so? But then, you have not had the advantage of mixing in Court circles, have you, Mistress Harley?'

'Why, no. My uncle, Sir Henry Jessop, would have condemned such superficial frivolity and so ensured that my education was on a higher plane.' Before she could say more, Kate felt a hand rest lightly on her wrist as a smooth voice at her shoulder answered for her.

'Mistress Harley has not had the opportunity to indulge in dancing, Mistress Templeton.' The Viscount stepped forward and bowed with graceful ease. He lifted his eyes to Kate's. She saw the mischief lurking in their depths. 'Her gifts, which you should know are considerable, lie in quite another direction.'

'Indeed, my lord?' Mistress Templeton assayed an arch look, fair brows raised in delicate wings.

'Indeed, ma'am. You would not believe the extent of her skills.'

Don't mention chickens or salted fish! Kate held her breath, but kept a polite smile pinned to her face during the interchange.

'Then I must look forward to knowing you better, Mistress Harley.' The lady was now not nearly as confident.

'I too,' Kate responded as she deliberately placed a proprietorial hand on Marlbrooke's sleeve. 'Lady Elizabeth has spoken of you and told me much about you. I feel that I know you well already.'

On which unsettling comment, and with no encouragement to linger from the Viscount, Dorothea found an excuse to return to her mother's side.

'Congratulations, Viola.' The Viscount eyed her with interest. 'You have vicious claws, I see. And need no help from me to keep the harpies at bay.'

'No, indeed. But I...'

'What is it?'

'I hoped that you would not shame me by mentioning...'

'Chickens?' He laughed aloud, his striking features alight with pleasure, causing others to turn their heads. 'What a delight you are to me.' He bent to press a kiss to Kate's hand where it still rested on his arm and then—to her shock—to her temple.

'My lord!'

'Now what? Why do I always seem to be the object of your displeasure?'

'No...I...' She stammered helplessly, caught up in his devastating allure. 'It is so public. People will see us.'

'I have done nothing improper,' he assured her. 'I am allowed to show my considerable regard to my betrothed.' He pulled her hand through his arm to lead her through the elegant rooms. 'If you do not dislike it, of course.' He slanted a quick glance down to her upturned face. 'I should hate for you to retaliate with your fist, as you once did.'

'I would not!'

'I am relieved to hear it. Then, since we are for the moment in such pleasant accord, let us see if this more than tedious reception can provide us with some refreshment.'

Yes. They were in agreement, she thought, as he procured for her a glass of sack.

But it did not last long.

She was unfortunate to overhear a conversation between Marlbrooke and an elderly, stout lady in opulent satins, who patted his arm in a familiar gesture of long-standing acquaintance.

'So you have brought your future bride to Court. Pretty enough—but a country girl I presume, by her strange hairstyle.'

'Yes. That is Katherine Harley. And there are reasons for the cropped curls.'

'Ah, so you will be mysterious, my lord. I forgive you. You are very like your father, God rest his soul. What a shame that you have to wed her to safeguard your property. I hope that we will still see you—that you will not absent yourself from Court and settle down to the tedium of country life.'

'I expect to spend some time at Winteringham Priory.'

'And is it your intention to rebuild Glasbury Old Hall?'

'It is in my mind.'

'I can understand. But surely, my dear Marlbrooke, the Court holds too many enticements to keep you long in the country?'

Kate did not hear his response as they moved away. But she found herself wondering if the enticements had golden curls and blue eyes, and if so, whether the Priory would be enough to keep him by her side.

She smiled reassuringly at Elizabeth, leaving her to believe that she had not overheard the exchange. But her heart was sore and she could find little enjoyment in the remainder of the evening.

It might have been mended between them.

Next day Marlbrooke bought her a fan, a little half-circular folding device, cunningly crafted and delicately painted with violets.

'It is very pretty.' Kate opened it to reveal the tiny flowers around the edge. 'I have never owned a fan before.'

'Perhaps I should teach you how to use it.' Marlbrooke smiled at her solemn expression. 'So that you can flutter it and flirt madly—and have all the gentlemen in submission at your feet.'

'I could not!'

'Of course you could.' He wilfully misunderstood her. 'You have me at your feet, after all. And I am reputed to be a hard case.'

She looked up, startled, resisting as he captured her fingers and proceeded to slide his teeth along the ends, nibbling gently. When she tried to clench her fingers into a fist to thwart him, he resisted, prised her hand apart and promptly transferred his mouth to her palm. 'I can feel the beat of your heart through your blood,' he murmured against her soft skin. 'It has quickened a little. I hope that I am the cause.' She felt his mouth curve provocatively against her palm.

'I...' She had no idea what to say.

'I think you do not know how lovely you are. That your eyes are the colour of the violets on your fan. But it is to my advantage.'

'I am not like the ladies at court!'

'No. You are not.' Suddenly serious, he released her hand and captured her eyes with his. 'But you are yourself. And you have all my love.'

'I do not belong to this world.' She could not look away or disguise the hint of panic.

'Perhaps not. But you belong to me, and that is all that matters.'

He snatched a kiss from her surprised lips—might have

changed the angle and deepened it—but then stepped away from her as Felicity, returned from her dutiful visit, entered the room.

He left her speechless.

And even more so on the following morning when Kate rose from the breakfast table.

'I think that we should spend a little time investigating the shops in Westminster Hall.' The week had overlapped into two. Lady Elizabeth was now eager to make the most of her time before Marlbrooke announced their departure. 'Will you accompany me? I have need of some new lace—and silk stockings, perhaps a pretty fur muff and...and any number of things that might take my fancy!'

'Of course.' Lady Elizabeth noted the slight crease which appeared between Kate's dark brows.

'Would you not wish it, dearest Kate?'

'Why, yes. Only...'

'What is it?'

'I...I have no money.' Kate was unsure why such an admission made her uncomfortable—except that it drove home the fact that she was totally dependent on the Oxendens.

'Kate!' Elizabeth laughed gently. 'Of course you have money. What can I be thinking of? The pleasure of spending it has apparently addled my brain. I would expect your marriage settlement to allow you considerable pin money to fritter on French fashions. You are—or will be—a very wealthy young woman. And I had forgotten.' She rose from the breakfast table to search in the depths of an court cupboard. 'Marcus has gone hunting with the King this morning to Richmond Park, but he left this to give to you. He knew of my intentions today.'

Kate took the embroidered purse, noted its weight, the chink of coins and read the attached note: *Viola! You are allowed to spend money and enjoy it! It is not necessarily a sin!*

The forceful hand in black ink was all Marlbrooke.

She clutched the purse, her female heart aware of the possibilities. And if she remembered Gilliver's warning, she hastily pushed it from her thoughts. 'I would be delighted to go shopping with you, my lady!'

Once more, Marlbrooke had surprised her by his thoughtful

consideration, when she would have liked nothing more than to find some reason to feed her resentment against him. Would she ever understand him? She doubted it.

But the most abiding picture, one that was to return to haunt her, was far more unsettling.

Her experience of him at the Priory had been of the country gentleman. Now she saw him as the accomplished courtier. Well versed in the ways of Whitehall, charming and urbane, with all the grace and elegance to captivate any woman. His athletic figure, broad shouldered and long limbed, was shown to advantage in the luxurious velvets and satins of court dress, but which could not disguise the tough smoothness of muscle and latent power. His dark hair curled and tumbled to his shoulders, as thick and lustrous as the velvet on to which it curled. What woman would not wish to touch it, to feel it sift through her fingers? And the beauty of his face would trouble any woman's dreams.

Marlbrooke might flirt with her but, as Kate soon learned, he was also capable of flirting with others. With Mistress Alicia Lovell. Mistress Harley set her teeth.

'He does not mean anything by it.' Elizabeth had seen the direction of her critical gaze as they sat together at a Court ball. Her heart went out to the young girl beside her when she assessed the splendid tableau of the dancers. And for once Lady Elizabeth could cheerfully have slapped her adored but careless son.

'Of course not.' Kate turned her eyes from Marlbrooke's figure, her smile bright—and false. 'It is of no matter to me. Marlbrooke is free to dance with anyone of his choice. And as I am unable to master these difficult steps in public, I could not expect him to dance attendance on me.' She deliberately turned her back on her betrothed, but then felt compelled to watch him lead Mistress Lovell into a dance. Compelled to watch him as he bowed with exquisite grace and flamboyant gesture over her pretty hands. As he responded to some flirtatious remark with a bent head and an engaging smile. And then proceeded to execute the complicated steps with elegant finesse. His black brows rose, his lips curved as his hands met hers in the dance...

How dare he!

And then Marlbrooke moved on to partner the exquisite

Frances Stewart, deliciously feminine in an extravagantly low-cut gown...

Whatever else, Kate was forced to acknowledge bitterly, he was hugely in demand.

And equally with the King and the men who frequented the Court—to play cards, to hunt, to while away the time with tennis and fencing.

In her bedchamber, Kate had to accept the truth of what she had seen in this short time at Whitehall. How could Marlbrooke possibly love her when the sophisticated and beautiful were at his beck and call? How could he possibly wish to bury himself in the country away from all this glamour?

But if that were so, why had he told her that he loved her? He was contracted to marry her anyway. He did not have to love her as well.

So why declare himself so openly?

Kate's mind roved over the possibilities, liking none of them. A spirit of mischief? To woo and seduce an innocent and ignorant girl from a sheltered Puritan family. Of flirtation? To while away the days of boredom until he could return to London. Worst of all, was he playing some sort of malicious game at her expense? A continuation of the Civil War hostilities between their two families?

No, she could not think it. In all fairness, she could find it in her heart to accuse him of none of those. Marlbrooke had never treated her with such cruelty. Would never. She was sure of it. He had never been anything but considerate and thoughtful of her difficult situation. It was simply that...she did not know him. And, as Felicity had pointed out, her world was far removed from his.

Her mind continued to be in turmoil. How could she trust him? Did she want to trust him?

She did not know. All she knew was that she resented every moment of the time he gave to other women. And when he smiled, when his eyes glinted with humour or more difficult emotions, she wanted them to be focused on her.

On the return journey to Winteringham Priory, wrapped in furs against the cold, Kate took stock of the sharply etched montage of memories and impressions. Deep in thought, she realised with a sudden jolt that she had not given Richard more than a passing thought. With a sharp twinge of guilt, she instantly condemned herself as shallow and fickle. Perhaps Gilliver was right after all. She could easily be bought by a handsome face and two weeks of frivolity in the capital.

Chapter Ten

Ensconced once more at Widemarsh Manor, Kate expected a detailed and cynical catechism from Aunt Gilliver but received none, other than the caustic comment, 'So, you are back at last. And worn out, no doubt, by wickedness and dissipation.'

London, so it seemed, was not to be a topic of conversation. Kate was intrigued but not sorry. She returned the diamond brooch (unworn) and produced a packet of the much-admired knitted silk stockings. The glittering gems were repinned to the dusty bodice and the stockings were received without comment. Kate would never know if Aunt Gilliver wore them.

Widemarsh Manor soon absorbed Kate back into its strange routines of herbal concoctions, dust and dark corners, with Mason ever vigilant.

And the tragic story of Isolde continued to worry and fascinate her.

On a fine morning which promised at least a few hours free from late April showers, Kate took the opportunity to don an old riding habit that she found stored in a clothes press and an all-enveloping cloak, equally ancient but suitable if caught in a downpour.

'I know what you are planning,' stated Aunt Gilliver as their paths crossed in the hall. 'Isolde's grave. Am I correct?' Her eyes gleamed with shrewd interest. 'I knew you wouldn't be able to resist.'

Kate laughed. 'You are quite correct, my percipient aunt. Am I so transparent? And perhaps you would consider coming with me for a little fresh air?'

Aunt Gilliver shook her head. 'My riding days are long gone. It is my intention to send Mason into the herb garden to see if the rain and wind has left us anything we can salvage and use. It will keep us busy. But the exercise will do you good. Go on, before the sun disappears. The secret places of the Priory will not go away. You can afford a day off from your investigations.'

Kate made her escape. It was true. Her knowledge of the Priory had widened considerably, but she had still found no secret caches, no priest holes, no hollow panels—nothing that contained anything like a will. Marlbrooke had left her to it, apart from an occasional amused enquiry as to her progress or a comment on the cobwebs that she was apt to collect in her hair, but it was all very disappointing. A collection of old recipes on yellowed pages in the still-room was the best she could achieve and Mistress Neale had refused to consider any of them, claiming them unfit for the establishment of a gentleman. But the sun encouraged her to cast off her low spirits and anticipate an exploration of the estate parkland.

She had sent word to her aunt's stable of her impending ride so that the elderly retainer who doubled as head groom and coachman was awaiting her when she arrived.

'Morning, mistress.' He touched his cap and gave a nod to a lurking stable lad who promptly scurried into one of the stable boxes.

'Good morning, West. Will it rain?'

'Sure to. Here we are.'

'But that is not my horse!'

'Aye, it is that, mistress. She's been sent over from the Priory for you—since you be intent on riding back and forth so much like.'

'But...' Of course. Marlbrooke!

'He says I mustn't take no for an answer. You are to ride her.' West's cunning eyes twinkled as he saw that she was torn between pride, which demanded that she refuse the gift, and instant infatuation. Infatuation won with no real contest.

The stable lad stood at the head of a pretty chestnut mare, saddled and bridled, ready for use. Her coat shone in the dancing

sunbeams and she tossed her head with flighty intent. Kate
rubbed her hand down the satin neck and threaded her fingers
through the rough dark mane. For a long moment she was
speechless with pleasure. How did he know just what would
please her? Only this week she had gone to make use of the still-
room at the Priory to discover that he had arranged for the thorough cleaning of the long neglected room. The window gleamed,
the bench and floor had been scrubbed and she had found it
restocked with jars and dishes and containers, all suitable for
storing herbs and fruit. And a book to record her preserves and
recipes. He had said nothing about it, of course, nothing to provoke her gratitude. He had simply *done* it. And now this.

'But she's beautiful,' she managed at last. 'Is she truly for
me?'

West bent to take her foot and give her a lift into the saddle.
'That's so, mistress. His lordship says you're to ride Goldfinch
here. She's flighty—just like a woman, he says—but she'll look
after you.'

'I have never owned anything so perfect.' Kate sighed with
pleasure, ignoring the adverse comment on her own sex, and
gathered up the reins. The mare pricked her ears, tossed her head,
eager to be gone.

'His lordship knows his horses. Will you go far, mistress?'

Kate shook her head. 'Only to blow the cobwebs away. I shall
ride across the park to the East Wood. And then I shall call at
the Priory to see how Lady Elizabeth does.' She arranged her
skirts, anchored the cloak tightly around herself and prepared to
encourage the mare into an active walk. 'I will be back before
the next downpour. If luck is with me.'

'The lad will accompany you then, mistress.'

'The lad?' Kate looked down at West with some surprise.

'Aye.' West jabbed a finger towards the boy who was now
lounging against a stable door, boredom writ large. 'His lordship
says you must not ride to the Priory unaccompanied. Too many
thieves about. So Josh is to go with you.'

'Nonsense! I do not need protection.'

'That's as his lordship said you'd say!' West nodded in acceptance of the inevitable difference of opinion. 'But he must go
with you.'

'But surely—'

'It's no good, mistress. I dares not cross his lordship. He would not be pleased. The lad goes with you.'

Kate's response was suspiciously like an unladylike snort of impatience. She did not want an escort. She *would* not have an escort. And certainly not today. But then, she realised, in all fairness, to refuse would bring down the Viscount's wrath on innocent heads. She could not do it. But perhaps on this one occasion... She smiled and nodded, waiting for Josh to mount and follow her. Once outside the stable yard, she stopped and beckoned.

'Today I have an errand. It will be much quicker if I go alone. Do you understand?'

Josh merely looked confused.

'Never mind.' Kate hid her impatience to be gone. 'Go by the main track. Wait for me at the old oak on the Common. I will meet you there and you can escort me on to the Priory...as the Viscount wishes,' she added as Josh appeared to be about to refuse. 'In an hour at the most! Do you understand?'

'Aye, mistress. By the old oak.'

She gave him no time to change his mind, but urged Goldfinch into a canter across the park. She would speak to Marlbrooke about this. She was perfectly safe and did not need a shadow who would report her every move back to him. She then forgot the problem in the delight of Goldfinch's silken paces as the mare lengthened into a gallop.

The mare headed across the open pasture in the direction of the far belt of trees. Kate was overcome with the sheer exhilaration of the moment. West was right. The mare was keen and lively, but had no vices. Owning Goldfinch was an unlooked-for blessing from her betrothal to Marlbrooke. So many surprises. Following Aunt Gilliver's directions, she followed the edge of the park, skirting the woodland where primroses were beginning to emerge in sheltered spots. Gradually she eased the mare to a walk since the clearing she sought might well be overgrown and almost unrecognisable after so many years. She doubted that anyone would have taken on the care of Isolde's grave. The prospect of both Widemarsh Manor and the Priory were lost to her behind a gentle rise in the ground, leaving her alone apart from the tumbling rooks and rabbits nibbling the spring grass.

The clearing was as overgrown as Kate had feared, choked by

low bushes and young saplings, but still accessible to someone with determination and agility. She dismounted, tied Goldfinch to a fallen branch where she could graze and pushed her way through the undergrowth. Brambles tore at her cloak and her habit was soon covered with cleavers and old dried seedheads, but she had little care for her old shabby clothes and persisted until she was eventually able to distinguish the outline of a weathered block of marble within a group of slender silver birches.

The dappled shadows and the rustle of new leaves in the light breeze gave no hint of the tragic circumstances commemorated by the grey stone and the single crumbling figure of an angel, head bowed in sorrow, which kept watch over the earthly remains. Otherwise the stone was plain and crude with no attempt at carving or decoration.

Isolde Elizabeth Harley

Kate traced the name with her finger. No date. No cause of death. Below the name she could just decipher the only epitaph for this poor lost girl.

Mourn her Grief
Pray for her Soul
God have Mercy

Nothing more. Only a drift of delicate windflowers to mark the slight mound beneath the rough grass. It was a tranquil place, silent except for the birdsong and the ripple of the birches. 'But you are not at peace, are you?' Kate spoke quietly, pressing her hands to the eroded surface of the stone. Wherever the essence of Isolde was, racked by inconsolable frustration and grief, it was not here in this sun-warmed glade. She added a silent prayer for Isolde's unquiet spirit and slowly retreated through the matted branches to the edge of the wood. 'I am not sure what I expected to find here,' she informed the indifferent Goldfinch, who nuzzled her shoulder affectionately. 'Perhaps Isolde is destined to remain a mystery. Let us go on to the Priory.'

Kate used a fallen tree to hoist herself into the saddle and turned to ride towards the Priory. She allowed the mare to walk slowly on a long rein, enjoying the sunshine and lost in her own thoughts. She was startled, therefore, by the sound of rapidly approaching hoofbeats, which made her uncomfortably aware of her isolation. Someone was riding through the park, and clearly in haste. She guided the mare into the protection of a young copse and turned to face the trespasser. A horse breasted the rise before her. Fears were banished and her heart filled with surprise and pleasure as the fair rider was instantly recognisable.

'Richard!' Kate lifted her arm in greeting and emerged from the shadows.

Her cousin changed direction immediately and approached, pulled his horse to a standstill and dismounted with fluent ease.

'Good morning, Mistress Harley.' He removed his hat and swept her an elegant bow with gentle mockery. 'I hope I find you well?'

'Oh, Richard. Help me down.' She held out her hands and slid down into his waiting arms. Too late she realised where her impetuosity had led her and she tried to push herself free, but Richard tightened his hold.

'Dearest Kate.' His smile made her heart beat uncomfortably fast inside her laced bodice. How could she have banished him from her thoughts for so long? It was so good to see him again. *But do you love him?* The insistent little voice in her head was not what Kate wanted to hear. She no longer knew the answer.

'I had to come and see you,' Richard continued. 'Tell me that you have thought of me as much as I have thought of you.'

Kate returned his smile, responding to the warmth and unaccustomed spontaneity in her cousin's appeal. 'It is true that I have longed to see you,' she admitted. 'How many weeks it seems since we walked in the garden at Downham Hall.' Her smile was replaced by a troubled frown. 'I did not expect to see you here.'

'Why not? Surely it is entirely appropriate for a close member of your family to pay a social visit. To enquire if you had recovered from the accident. We did not know until Sir Henry received Marlbrooke's message, and then we learned that you were away from home—that you had gone to London. But now I am here, to see you for myself.'

Richard's arms were still about her waist and, as she continued to smile up into his face, he drew her even closer.

'You are more beautiful even than I remembered. In spite of the hair!' He traced her cheekbone lightly with his thumb. 'Dare

I ask? Do you still love me or have you been seduced by the advantages of a marriage with Marlbrooke?'

Kate turned her face away. 'It is a useless cause. I am entrapped into a political liaison with no hope of escape.' She wondered fleetingly if Richard was aware that she had evaded the question. But apparently he was not.

'Are you certain?' Richard's response surprised her, but she could read nothing in his enigmatic expression.

'Of course. You must see that we cannot allow our... attachment to continue. The contracts have been signed and exchanged. My betrothal to Marlbrooke is now legal and cannot be broken. It is merely a matter of fixing a date for the ceremony.'

'I see nothing except the sapphire of your eyes and your lovely face. And I know that, before death, I am not willing to give you up.'

Before Kate could shake her head in denial, Richard tightened his grasp, holding her firmly and lowering his mouth to hers. She pushed her hands against his shoulders, but he was unyielding and his lips became more demanding, so that she ceased to fight, but lay quiescent in his arms. He released her, but only to trace a series of kisses along her jaw and the line of her neck until he was prevented by the collar of her riding habit.

'Well?' he murmured. 'Is it a useless cause?'

Kate searched Richard's face with eyes full of turmoil. Dear Richard. He was so dependable...so fine and uncomplicated in his care for her. She had known him all her life and had been willing to see her future mapped out with his. But now... She tried to banish Marlbrooke's avowal of love and his passionate demands on her body without success. Still, she shook her head a little to rid herself of that unwelcome presence and tried to give Richard an answer that would make sense of her feelings and could be given in honesty.

'No...yes... Oh, Richard! This only makes an impossible situation even more painful. For both of us.'

Richard released her, but retained her hands in his strong grip. 'Answer me this, Kate. Do you trust me?'

'Of course.' There was no problem here.

'Then keep that thought close to your heart. Will you do that? Whatever happens in the future?'

Kate nodded. She read such calm assurance in Richard's eyes. Whatever happened she knew that she would always find a haven in his arms. He was her one rock in the shifting sands of her present existence. She leaned forward to kiss his cheek shyly in gratitude.

'Thank you, dear Richard.'

'I am at your service, Mistress Harley, now and always. Come.' He tucked her hand under his arm, gathering up the reins of the two browsing horses. 'Let us walk a little way.' They strolled across the short flower-strewn turf, quiet for a little time, enjoying each other's presence.

On a sudden thought, Kate broke the companionable silence. 'How did you know where to find me? I cannot believe that it was pure chance.'

'No. I am not omniscient.' Richard smiled down at her. 'I went first to the Priory where Verzons directed me on to Widemarsh Manor. Mistress Gilliver told me where you would be.'

'So you have been to the Priory?' She frowned. 'Was Marlbrooke there?'

'I do not know. I did not stay to do more than dismount and speak to Master Verzons.'

'I see. I am going to the Priory now.'

'Then I will escort you.'

Kate contemplated attempting to dissuade Richard, but she detected a particularly stubborn tilt to his jaw. After all, it could do no harm for Marlbrooke to meet her cousin. Could it? A cool breeze touched her spine with its icy fingers.

'Very well.' She smiled suddenly. 'We must ride towards the Common first—I have something to collect on the way.'

The mare made her way back enthusiastically to the lure of a warm stable and Kate found herself soothed by the welcome of warm stone gilded by the pale sunshine and the glitter of the mullioned windows. She and Richard trotted side by side down the beech avenue, the stable lad duly collected from under the old oak and following at a respectful distance, and turned into the stable yard to find it surprisingly busy. Kate saw Jenks, who was hovering innocently outside one of the open stable doors, but otherwise there was any number of grooms and stable lads who had seen fit to gather within hearing of a conversation taking place within one of the stalls. There were raised voices; one of them, calmer than the other, was recognisable as Marlbrooke.

'So what I want to know, my lord, is what do you intend to do about it?'

'I sympathise with the situation, Mr Moreton, and the immediacy of it, but it will take time. I have already had the Reverend Peters here to discuss the problem at length, demanding that I take personal responsibility. I can and I will. But I cannot remove every highway robber between here and Kington in the blink of an eye.'

'I take your point, my lord, but the trade in Winteringham is going to rack and ruin. Good folk won't turn up to the market any more. They won't cross the Common and they will certainly not travel after dusk.'

'Mr Moreton, with the best will in the world, I cannot—'

'The old Harley family was quick to support the local community. Now we need *you* to take action.'

At this point they emerged into the sunlight, Marlbrooke and a tall, lean gentleman with a florid complexion.

Marlbrooke sighed.

'When I spoke with the Reverend Peters about it,' Moreton continued, outrage heavy in his sharp tones, 'all he could say was that he would offer up prayers on Sunday. Prayers, I ask you! I lost twenty head of sheep last week, driven out of my home pasture in broad daylight. And he is going to pray over me! A few harsh words from the pulpit on hell and damnation for those who steal the property of God-fearing men would be more to the point!'

'As I informed the Reverend Peters, I will do what I can, but I cannot promise instant success.' Marlbrooke became aware of the grinning audience. 'Is there a problem here? Have you no work to be doing?' His voice remained quiet, but his eyebrows rose. The grooms and lads vanished, except for Jenks, who came to hold the head of Goldfinch for Kate to dismount.

'Can I offer you a mug of ale, sir, before you leave?'

'Thank you, but no.' Somewhat mollified, Moreton's voice softened from its previous harsh tones. 'I am sorry to burden you with this, Marlbrooke. As a JP, I can deal with thieves and highwaymen when they come before me in court, but robbery on the King's highway? It is beyond my expertise.'

'I will employ some of my retainers to ride patrol and keep watch for a week or two. See if we can flush them from their haunts of wickedness! Does that sound sufficiently Biblical to satisfy Peters?'

'It should! And I would be grateful.' Moreton smiled his appreciation and offered his hand. 'Good day then, my lord. Mistress. Sir.' He bowed briefly to Kate and Richard, swung on to his mount and rode out of the stable yard.

'I suppose you heard the general gist of that conversation.' Marlbrooke looked up at Kate with a rueful smile. 'It would appear that the Harleys were far more competent than I in upholding law and order. Now why did I think it would be any different?' Taking the mare's reins from Jenks, he possessed himself of her hands as she dismounted. He raised them to his lips.

'Perhaps. I envy you your confidence in dealing with such a major task.' Kate smiled, her face lighting up, before his touch sent such a jolt through her system that she instantly sobered. It was immeasurably different from the quiet warmth when Richard had kissed her lips not an hour ago. She was aware of the colour in her cheeks as her blood ran hot and the pulse that began to flutter under the fragile skin of her throat. She frowned, but did not pull away as she found her gaze captured and held by the naked emotion that warmed his grey eyes. It took her breath away.

'Was I confident? I did not think so. Should I perhaps enquire from Mistress Gilliver, as a Harley born and bred, you understand, the methods that she would recommend in dealing with our local thieves, footpads and so forth? Blood of bat, do you think? Carefully sprinkled around the Common with suitable spells and curses?'

'You could.' Kate breathed carefully to regain her composure and still her heartbeat fast. 'But in all honesty, I doubt that Aunt Gilliver would be the best authority. I doubt that she would even show an interest!'

'God help me if she did! I think your aunt would be more likely to turn *me* into the bat than give me any assistance.'

Kate chuckled, eyes alight with mischief, and found herself returning the warm pressure on her hands. 'I will ask her for you, if you *truly* wish it, but don't expect a polite reply.' Then she remembered Richard, who had dismounted and was now standing behind her, and turned to see him watching this interchange with an arrested expression. 'Can I introduce you, my lord? This is my cousin Richard Hotham, come to see how I am. Richard, my lord Marlbrooke.' She felt a need to explain further. 'I met Richard in the park on my way here.'

Marlbrooke released her hands, bowed. His voice was clipped, giving nothing away. 'Kate has spoken about you. I expected that you would pay us a visit sooner rather than later.'

'Indeed.' Richard moved forward to stand beside Kate and touch her arm in a proprietorial gesture. 'When we received the message concerning Kate's whereabouts, the family asked that I come.'

'I was more than a little surprised that Mistress Harley was allowed to journey to her aunt's house on her own without an escort of any degree.' Marlbrooke's voice had taken on a glacial quality that Kate rarely heard.

'That was my own choice,' she intervened quickly, 'you know that it cannot reflect on the concern of my family.' She felt compelled to come to Richard's defence.

'Of course. But it would not, my dear, be *my* chosen course of action. I will not allow you to put yourself in such a position of potential danger in the future, you may be sure.'

The tension between the three was a sharp as a honed knife. Kate frowned at Marlbrooke and moved away from Richard's grasp so that she stood between them. The gleam in Marlbrooke's eye indicated that he was aware of her deliberate stand and she knew he was not one to resist a challenge. He did not disappoint her. His response was unsubtle and forthright.

'Your cousin needs no protection from me, dearest Kate.' His sardonic humour was most pronounced; Kate flushed and resisted a sharp reply. The Viscount turned to Richard. 'Do you intend to stay long, Mr Hotham?' It was a bland enquiry, his expression suspiciously friendly.

'Mistress Gilliver has offered me a bed at Widemarsh. She was very welcoming. I will perhaps stay for a few days.'

'I would not expect otherwise.' Again that enigmatic response, Marlbrooke showing his teeth in a smile that held neither warmth nor humour. 'Mistress Gilliver is very predictable in her loyalties.

I expect I shall see you again at the Priory. Now, if you will—'
There was a clatter of shoes on the cobbles of the stable yard
and a sharp cry from Elspeth, the kitchen maid, who appeared
from the house at a run laced with panic.

'My lord! My lord! You must come.'

'What is it, Elspeth?' He turned to face her.

She came to a halt before him, hands clenched in the folds of
her apron, gasping for breath.

'It is her ladyship. She is taken bad, my lord, very bad. Mistress Felicity is beside herself. Mistress Neale says you must
come at once.'

Without a backward glance or further discussion, Marlbrooke
thrust the reins of Goldfinch to Jenks and strode towards the
house.

Marlbrooke took the stairs at a run. Kate followed as quickly
as she could, hitching up her unwieldy borrowed skirts and abandoning Richard in the stable yard, to follow or not as he saw fit.
A terrible foreboding smote her, deepened by the stricken look
on Elspeth's face and the unwillingness of the kitchen maid to
meet her eyes, making her heart beat faster and her palms become
damp. When she reached the open door of Lady Elizabeth's bedchamber, her worst fears were confirmed. It was, she thought, a
scene out of hell.

The atmosphere was unpleasantly close, not helped by a
brightly blazing fire, numerous candles and closed curtains. Lady
Elizabeth lay on her bed, motionless except for her head, which
tossed from side to side in jerky, uncontrolled seizures. Mistress
Neale stooped beside her, trying with soft words and gentle
hands—but without success—to calm the desperate actions. Verzons, initially summoned to help carry the lady from the floor
where she had collapsed, stood helplessly at the foot of the bed,
for once his face less than impassive.

Marlbrooke now stood beside him, attempting to wring some
sense from a weeping Felicity who knelt by the bed, hands
clasped in fervent prayer.

Kate's entrance had an unforeseen dynamic effect on the terrible scene. As Felicity's tear-drenched eyes focused on her she
abandoned her petition for mercy from the Almighty and stag-

gered to her feet, patches of raw colour staining her habitually sallow cheeks, her hands clenched into fists as she approached to challenge this perpetrator of all their evils. Her voice rose to a harsh shriek as she addressed Marlbrooke.

'Would you let *her* into this chamber? She is the cause of all this.'

'Mistress Felicity...' Marlbrooke tried to reach out with a calming hand, to prevent what might indeed become a physical attack, but it was knocked aside with careless violence.

'It started when she arrived. She came into this house under false pretences, pretending such innocence. And from one of those damned Puritan families! She ensnared my lady and enticed her with potions of the devil. I warned her of how it would be—but would she listen? My lady was far too trusting and Mistress Kate was far too clever for that. She made my lady dependent, soothing her pain, giving her empty promises—and then she fed her this poison. Now she will die and it is all her fault.' Hot tears of passion dripped unregarded down her cheeks.

'Felicity, you have no proof of any of this.' Marlbrooke tried to be gentle in the face of such vicious emotion, but to no avail.

'Oh, no, I have no proof.' The vicious, breathy voice continued as Felicity dashed away the tears. 'But I have watched. I have seen her smiles and gentle ways. The way she has twisted my lady round her finger so that my lady favours her above me. Gives her gifts. Laughs with her. Takes whatever potions and ointments are given to her with honeyed words of deceit.' She paused for breath to point at Kate, finger stabbing. 'And now *she* is in league with that witch Gilliver Adams. And you talk to me about proof. I do not need any more proof! And neither will you if my lady dies.'

'I have never—' Kate's face was as pale and drawn as the wax of the candles, with a faint sheen of perspiration on her brow and upper lip as panic held her in its ferocious grip.

'Never? Can you deny that you have given my lady poison? She drank that—' Felicity pointed to a small glass container beside the bed '—left by you—and look at her. She will die.' Felicity covered her face with her hands and sobbed.

For the time it took to draw breath, those in the room were struck dumb by the force of the accusations against Kate, but then Marlbrooke broke the tension. 'We will deal with all that later. For now it is more important that we—' Before he could say more, Felicity emerged from her bout of hysterical weeping and flung herself at Kate, her thin, wiry body gaining speed and agility from her intense distress. Kate was too surprised to defend herself and felt Felicity's fingernails catch and rake down her cheek. She cried out in pain and surprise, stepping back. Marlbrooke hastily intervened before more damage could be done, grasped the lady's wrists and half-led, half-dragged her to the door. His face was stern and drawn as he turned to Verzons.

'We do not need this at such a time. Please convey Mistress Felicity to her room. And lock the door if you have to.'

'Certainly, my lord.' As relief swept his features with the prospect of action, the steward took the distressed lady by the arm and led her protesting and weeping from the room.

Kate stood where Felicity had left her.

'What do we do?' Marlbrooke demanded, turning to her, face set in grim lines. 'What has she drunk?'

'I do not know.' Kate felt dazed by the attack and accusations, incapable of either sensible thought or action. Her mind simply refused to function, swamped by the bitterness in Felicity's words and manner. 'I do not have enough skill or knowledge. She thinks I poisoned her. She thinks I would kill her.' Her eyes were wide, fixed in horror on the agony of the lady on the bed. 'I cannot help.'

Marlbrooke wasted no time. Ignoring his surroundings or the presence of servants, he seized Kate by the shoulders and shook her.

'Listen to me,' he said through clenched teeth. 'Look at me,' he ordered, waiting until she did so, ignoring the fear in her eyes. 'You are our only hope here, Kate. Forget Felicity's words. Use what you know. If anyone can save her, you can.' He shook her again to reinforce his words, forcing himself to ignore the blood that oozed from the livid scratches or the panic-stricken grief in the violet depths of those eyes, which pleaded with him for compassion. He could not afford to give way to impulse, to soothe and stroke and gather her close in his arms.

She looked at him in shock. His eyes were hard, his face implacable, his fingers bruising her arms where they gripped. Doubtless he too thought she was responsible.

'Kate!' His fingers dug into her flesh with painful intensity.

She pulled herself back from the brink of hysteria and out of his grasp.

'Of course. I will do what I can.' She drew herself upright, wiping the back of her hand over her dry lips and walked to the bed, trying to order her thoughts to draw on her limited experience and the skills her mother had instilled in her.

With decision came calm. She noted with a strange remoteness that she was beginning to think and plan. If Marlbrooke truly believed that she had poisoned his mother, there was little she could do to remedy it. But she could do all in her power to offset the effects of whatever had been drunk.

'Open the curtains and douse the candles—let the light in,' she ordered, her voice gradually gaining strength, 'and we will let the fire die a little. Open one of the windows, Elspeth. We need some air in here.' She moved to the ravaged bed and sat on the edge to look at the stricken lady who continued to thrash on her pillows.

The heavy drugged eyes opened. There was no recognition in her glazed stare.

'Tell me what you know, Mistress Neale.'

'Mistress Felicity sent for me,' the housekeeper explained, hovering at her shoulder. 'Her ladyship became very hot and flushed. And then she seemed to lose her wits, her words made no sense and were slurred. But she said her arms and legs hurt—I remember that. Not her joints like usual—but stiff. That's why she fell, I think.'

Kate nodded and bent to look more closely at Elizabeth. Her face was now pale but her lips were flushed and distinctly swollen. There were no other markings or rashes on her body. 'What did she drink?'

'This.' Mistress Neale took the green glass phial in her hand and passed it to Kate, who took out the stopper and sniffed. No scent here that she could detect. She inserted a finger, wetted it and tasted it. Bitter! Fortunately, the bottle still held more than half the liquid—Elizabeth could have drunk much more.

'How did she take it?'

'In wine, I think, mistress. She said that her tongue felt swollen, and her eyes were staring from her head. And then she fell to the floor. That is when Mistress Felicity sent for me.'

'What is it? Do you know?' The Viscount's query was brusque.

Kate thought over all she had seen and heard. There seemed to be only one answer, however much she tried to close her mind against it. 'I believe it is wolf's bane,' she replied simply.

'Is it fatal?'

'Yes.' What was the advantage in telling lies in such a case? 'It can be if enough is drunk. I have seen its effects. A small child at Downham Hall ate some of the plant—it is monkshood and is often grown in cottage gardens for its flowers. It can also be useful to make a potion to bathe bites by venomous creatures—it takes out the venom and soreness and is most soothing—but to drink it is poison.'

'Did the child die?'

'Yes.'

Marlbrooke bent to smooth his mother's disordered hair. 'Can you do nothing?' He could not hide the note of despair in his voice or the lines of strain around his mouth.

Kate turned to Mistress Neale. 'Fetch me pen and paper.' And to Elspeth, 'Send to see if Mr Hotham is still here. If not, I need someone to ride to Widemarsh Manor immediately.'

There was an instant scurrying of activity. Kate scrawled a hasty note and it was dispatched, she presumed, with Richard. 'Tell him to ride fast. It is imperative.'

'What have you sent for?' Marlbrooke looked up from his mother's pain-racked body, brows drawn in a heavy frown.

'Devil's bit.' For a long moment Kate's eyes locked with Marlbrooke's: then she turned away and with set face set about the task of ridding Lady Elizabeth's body of a potentially fatal dose of wolf's bane.

Kate kept Elspeth with her, but banished Marlbrooke unceremoniously from the room.

'This will not be pleasant and I think you must allow your mother to retain some dignity. When she recovers, she would prefer it.'

Reluctantly he accepted the truth of it, and noted the optimistic wording, whether she believed it or not. He spent the day pacing the corridors, paying an unnecessary visit to the stables and pretending to look at accounts in the library. Finally he gave up and simply sat and brooded. He sent in wine and food to Kate and Elspeth at regular intervals, but otherwise stayed out of their way, until anxiety got the better of him, and he prowled outside the bedchamber until Kate sent him away again.

Kate used her own infusion of white willow to try to curtail the severe vomiting and purging that soon struck. Boiled and strained to a clear liquid, they forced their patient to drink it at regular intervals. She did not seem to respond, her body constantly attacked by shivers and spasms, but Kate did not expect an immediate miracle. Kate and Elspeth worked silently, but their anxiety was evident as their eyes met when holding Elizabeth's shoulders as once more the poison sent convulsions through her.

'Oh, Mistress Harley, it gets no better, the poor lady.'

'I need to hear from Aunt Gilliver. How long does it take to ride from Widemarsh? The longer it takes, the stronger the poison's hold.' Kate paced the room restlessly, feeling helpless.

'Not long now, I expect, mistress. I reckon you are doing all you can. Perhaps she is a little easier already.'

'Thank you, Elspeth.' Kate's smile was weary but genuine for this show of confidence, even if she questioned the truth of Elspeth's observation. 'Go to Mistress Neale. Fetch some pot-pourri, lavender, anything sweet smelling. And bring some wine.'

The reply from Mistress Adams arrived—a scrawled note in her distinctive neat handwriting, and a small linen bag. Kate thanked the breathless stable lad who had ridden at speed and hurried back into Elizabeth's bedchamber. She was still unconscious, delirious, and they found it increasingly difficult to force liquid between her swollen lips. Kate set the contents of the bag—an unpretentious knobbly root—to boil in the fireplace in a pot of wine. She drew off some liquid quickly, as soon as steam began to rise, and cooled it with water to make it drinkable. The rest would be more potent when boiled longer and allowed to cool naturally, but Kate thought it necessary to introduce some of the liquid into Elizabeth's exhausted body as quickly as possible before she lost all her strength to fight against the deadly wolf's bane.

'Now, Elspeth.' Kate approached the bed with Aunt Gilliver's remedy.

Elspeth tried to raise Elizabeth in her arms but it was clear that she had not the strength. She pushed the hair back from her face in despair. 'I cannot hold her still, Mistress Kate. She is too restless. Do I get help?'

Kate sighed 'Perhaps you should send for Mistress Neale. No...wait. Fetch the Viscount. He may be in the library.'

Minutes hardly passed before Marlbrooke entered, appalled at the scene before him. It seemed far worse, far more degrading, than wounds or death on a battlefield. And Lady Elizabeth, his gentle, courageous mother, looked so frail, so far beyond their help. Kate saw the shock on his face: without giving him time to think, she issued instructions.

'We need to get your mother to drink this. You must hold her—she is very restless and Elspeth can not manage alone.'

Marlbrooke sat at the head of the bed and lifted his mother to rest against his shoulder, her flailing arms pinioned at her sides. He held her firmly, as gently as was possible, one hand to keep her head still so that she might drink. Kate tilted the cup and between them they managed to pour most of the warm liquid down her throat.

'There. Now we must simply wait.' She glanced towards Marlbrooke, lifting her shoulders in quiet despair. 'Thank you. I think we can manage now and it should become easier to administer the draught as she grows quieter.'

'Do you wish me to stay? Surely there is something I can do to relieve you of the burden.'

'No. There is no need. Elspeth and I will do very well now.'

'But you must be so tired...'

'I think your mother would prefer it if you were not here,' she said gently.

There was no arguing with her, but he beckoned her outside the door before he left. 'Tell me what you are attempting.'

She told him, briefly and explicitly, with none of the fear that was almost paralysing her showing above the surface. 'It is wolf's bane poisoning as I thought. My aunt agreed and has sent the root of devil's bit. Most still-rooms keep it as a root—it is not yet in flower until high summer. Aunt Gilliver says to give it boiled in wine—it is very powerful against all poisons and fevers.'

'Will it work?'

'It will make her sweat. This will bring the poison out through the skin and will also reduce her temperature. Aunt Gilliver swears by it and I know my mother used it. Master Culpeper recommended its use in all such cases.'

'Then all we can do is wait.'

'Yes.' There was nothing more to say between them. She turned on her heel and re-entered the bedchamber before she could read the accusation in his eyes.

Day passed slowly, crawling through the hours, and turned into night. Marlbrooke left them alone, knowing that Kate would send word when there was any change, for good or ill. If there was any change. Elspeth and Mistress Neale came and went from the bedchamber, but Kate did not. The Viscount fell into an uncomfortable doze in the library.

As dawn approached, a mere lightening of the sky in the east, he was awakened by a cool hand on his.

'What is it?' The only light in the library was from a dying fire, but instantly he knew who stood beside him.

Kate looked down at him, her face solemn, and he could not read it.

'Well?'

'We have done it. She is sleeping naturally. She is weak and will need care, but there will be no lasting ill effects.'

He breathed deeply, savouring the relief that poured through him and threatened his composure, but his control held firm. As he made to rise, she gripped his arm to stop him.

'Allow us half an hour. Lady Elizabeth is awake, but we need a little time. You understand?'

'Of course.' He rubbed his hands over his eyes, then looked up at Kate. 'She did not deserve this. I should never have brought her here. She would rather have stayed in London.'

Kate shook her head, but did not question his implication. She turned silently and left him.

* * *

When he entered Lady Elizabeth's chamber some time later, the horrors of the past twenty-four hours had been mostly put to rights. The room was pleasantly cool, dimly lit, with the scents of lavender and summer pot-pourri uppermost in the still air. The signs of sickness had been cleared and tidied away and Elizabeth, washed and clad in a fresh chemise, lay between clean linen. Kate had brushed her hair. She was startlingly pale, her eyes dark with remembered pain and fatigue, deep shadows below, deep lines engraved around her mouth. But she was awake and lucid, a faint smile on her ashen lips when her son walked through the door.

'Marcus. I am so sorry.' Her voice lacked its usual light timbre, but was clear enough.

He sat beside her and took her hand. 'And so you should be. You have given us all a fright.'

'You look tired.' She raised her hand to touch his cheek in maternal concern.

'We are all tired—but you are better now.' He captured her wrist and pressed his lips to where the pulse beat, slow but steady, refusing to consider the hours when he had feared that it would beat no more. 'You have been well nursed.'

'I know it. It would not have been pleasant...' Her voice died away as exhaustion took its toll. 'They have been so good. And Kate...'

But Kate had already moved slowly, unobtrusively out of the room, closing the door silently behind her. There was now no place for her there. And the repercussions of the day had still to come.

Chapter Eleven

The sky had just begun to pearl with the promise of a late spring dawn, faint streaks of pink appearing where the sun would eventually rise. Marlbrooke left his mother sleeping under the watchful eye of one of the kitchen maids with the sole purpose of finding Kate. He followed the sound of voices in soft-toned conversation, which led him to the top of the main staircase into the hall. There she stood, below him, with Verzons in attendance, fastening her cloak and pulling on her gloves.

'Katherine!' His voice from the stairs stopped her and she turned to face him.

Even from this distance she was almost transparent with tiredness, her face pale, the fragile skin below her eyes bruised with violet shadows. He had had little sleep, but he knew that she had managed even less and had worked tirelessly. As he drew close he could see the angry scorings on her cheek from Felicity's vengeful nails. She had never looked so desirable to him.

'What are you doing?'

She looked up, startled, her eyes wide with apprehension. 'I must go back to Widemarsh Manor. It is almost light now.'

'Hardly. It is not fit that you should leave.'

'I tried to dissuade her, my lord.' Verzons bowed and melted into the shadows as the Viscount descended the staircase.

'There is nothing more I can do now.' She held herself well, shoulders braced, a touch of defiance in the proud carriage of her head.

'Stay.' His voice was low, but held a note of command.

'Indeed, my lord, your mother will recover without me.' She felt as if her lips could hardly form the words, but she needed to remain strong before him and make her escape from the Priory—from the condemnation that she expected to see in his eyes. She would not show him the desolation that threatened to engulf her when she considered that he might actually believe Felicity's venomous words. She took refuge in cold formality. 'I have spoken with Mistress Neale. Lady Elizabeth is quite comfortable and Mistress Neale knows what needs to be done.'

'I would prefer that you stay.' She might be calm and withdrawn, to erect a barrier between them, but he was equally determined that she should not. He stood before her now, his emotions—what they were she could not guess—rigidly contained. His face was stern, brows drawn into a black line above stormy grey eyes.

'No. I will not.'

'Why not?'

'Because...'

'Would you rather return to Richard? Is that how it is?' The harshness in his tone jolted her from her trance-like state.

'Richard?' Kate frowned. She had to concentrate, on his words, his meaning. Exhaustion seemed to be robbing her of all power to think rationally. She had not given Richard a thought since that terrible moment in the stable yard. 'Why, no. I had not thought...'

Her confused denial eased the spark of jealousy that burned in his gut, which he would not acknowledge, even to himself, but which had been there since the moment he had seen them together in the stable yard. His voice gentled with the lessening of tension.

'Why will you not stay?'

She could repress it no longer, the words spilling out in a torrent. 'Mistress Felicity accused me of poisoning Lady Elizabeth. I am sure that you have considered that it could very well be true. I certainly have had every opportunity to do so. You probably believe it. After all, can you really expect honesty from one of *those damned Puritan families?*'

'I have never said that I believe her accusations.' He strove to keep his voice cool and flat, but he watched her intently to judge her reactions.

She laughed. A little harsh, definitely without humour. 'You did not have to say it. I saw it in your face. I am obviously devious enough to hide my sins if I am in danger of being discovered! What a pity that Lady Elizabeth did not drink *all* the potion before she was discovered. That would have been a triumph indeed for me!' The desolation swept through her but she faced him squarely, meeting his eyes, a denial in her own.

He knew he must handle this carefully. So much room for misunderstanding and misinterpretation here. Tired she might be—indeed, her eyes were almost blurred from it—but nervous tension held her in thrall so that she constantly drew her leather gauntlets through her fingers. He knew that if he touched her he would feel the hectic pulse of her blood through her veins. She was hurt, and thus beyond sense and logic.

He stepped closer, stretched out a hand to run gentle fingers down her damaged cheek. She flinched, but he persisted, then surprised her by stepping even closer still. Instead of cursing her he drew her forward and pressed his lips to her forehead. He felt her sigh beneath his hands. His eyes captured hers, fierce, vital, making his next words a command rather than a request.

'You are not fit to ride to Widemarsh Manor—and certainly not alone. I want you to stay. With me. Do I have to beg?'

There was a heartbeat of silence between them. To him it lasted a lifetime.

'No.' He recognised her weary resignation to a stronger force and would take advantage of it.

'I think we need each other.'

Without another word he took her hand and turned to lead her back up the staircase. Slowly. She followed as if the trance had settled on her again. When she stumbled from fatigue at the bottom step he simply swept her into his arms and carried her up as he had on that first night. She lay passively against his chest, her head resting on his shoulder, her hand clutching his shirt. He passed the room that she had then occupied and had become her own and strode on down the corridor to his own room, setting her down in the middle of the floor as he closed the door and lit a candle, choosing to leave the heavy curtains drawn against the growing light. She simply stood immobile, impassive, unable to summon the energy to make a decision for herself. He removed the gloves from her unresisting fingers, untied the cloak and laid them on a chair.

'You are so very tired,' he murmured as she watched him, aloof and distant with a glazed expression.

'No.'

Yes, you are, he thought, but could see the pulse beating wildly in her throat. She would not rest with so much tension tearing her apart, but he would make her.

He lifted her again and sat her on the edge of his bed, then stood back to look at her, hands fisted on hips. He made some rapid decisions, acting on pure instinct.

'Sit there,' he ordered as she attempted to slide to her feet.

'But—'

'Don't argue with me, Kate.'

She did as she was bid, hands clasping and unclasping convulsively in her lap.

He left her and walked to the court cupboard to pour a generous pewter goblet of wine. She would refuse it, he knew, but there were ways of getting round that. He returned to sit on the bed beside her.

'You need to relax a little.'

'I cannot. And I don't want wine.' Her voice sounded to her own ears as if it were a million miles away.

'I know you don't, but it will do us both good.'

'Why?'

'Don't argue. You are very difficult!'

He took a drink from the goblet and then passed it to her. He frowned at her momentary hesitation so she decided that obedience might be the best policy. She sipped.

'Good.' He took the cup, took another swallow, and handed it back again. 'Take another.'

She did. She watched him with a detached interest as he left her side to pour water from the ewer into a bowl, wet a cloth and return to gently cleanse the scratches. They were not deep and would not scar, but they were painful and she winced.

'Be brave, little one. This is the least you have dealt with this night.'

'I thought she would die!'

'So did I. But she did not.'

'But I was responsible. If she had not come to trust my remedies, she would not have taken the draught so unquestioningly.' There. She had said it.

'I know. Stop thinking for a little while. Drink a little more.'

She obeyed as he removed the bowl, then returned to assess the affect of the wine. He took the cup from her. Colour had come back to her face, her cheeks were faintly flushed and her eyes had lost their glaze. More important, the rigid tension had gone from her body. She looked soft and pliant and suddenly impossibly young. His impulse was to push her back on to the bed and take her, submerge his own intense needs in the sweetness of her slight body—but that was no way forward. He sat again on the edge of the bed and took her hands in a light clasp, careful not to reveal his urgency, which might frighten her.

'Look at me, Kate.' She raised her eyes to his with a faint question but without hesitation. 'I want you. I want to feel you in my arms, to take what is mine. With the contracts complete, the law now sanctions it.'

He bent his head to press his lips to the soft skin at her temple, her cheekbones, along her jaw, her throat, the lovely long line of it, dwelling at the place where her pulse beat like a fluttering bird below her skin.

'I don't know what to do,' she whispered as his mouth brushed hers in a soft caress.

'Fortunately I do.' There was a ghost of a laugh in his reply.

'I suppose that's a good thing.' She blinked at him. 'I suppose you have known a lot of ladies at Court.'

'I am sure it is a good thing. And, yes, I have. And it would be better for both of us if you do not see my every move as that of the enemy.' There was the slightest question there.

'Are you?'

'Am I what? Sure or your enemy?'

'Both. Neither. Perhaps I should not have drunk the wine.' There was the faintest of laughs. It made his heart turn over in his chest and he thanked God for the power of a judicious measure of wine in releasing impossible tensions.

'I am not your enemy, Viola.'

'I know.'

With fingers that suddenly felt clumsy, he dealt with the fastening of her bodice, and allowed her skirt to fall free so that he might push it down around her ankles, leaving her in her linen chemise.

'Can I ask something?'

'Whatever you desire. As you see, I am at your feet.' He had knelt before her to remove her shoes and roll down her stockings, allowing his hands to stroke her elegantly slender legs and feet.

'Will you put out the candle?' she asked in all seriousness.

'Of course. In a moment.' He rose from his knees to sit beside her. 'Before I do, I would like you to unfasten my shirt.'

He grinned at the surprise on her face, the quick frown at his deliberate distraction. 'It is very simple.'

She was not shy, he thought. She applied herself to the laces with utmost concentration, frowning a little, to push the heavy linen from his shoulders. She let her hands linger on the broad well-defined planes of his chest. She felt his body tense, his breath catch, as she allowed her palms to slide down his hard body.

Then she pushed herself from the bed to stand beside him, surprising him by leaning against him to release the black ribbon that confined his hair. She ran her fingers through it with a little purr of pleasure as it brushed his shoulders in heavy dark waves.

'I like it better than mine.' She smiled and leaned again to touch his lips with her own in the lightest of movements. It was a touch of such delicacy and sweetness that his blood ran hot. At that, with an abrupt gesture, he doused the candle and engulfed the room in darkness.

Kate found herself lifted and placed in the middle of Marlbrooke's bed, her chemise drawn efficiently over her head to be cast aside, the sheets cool against her skin. She shivered.

'Are you cold?'

'No. I am afraid, I think.' But, in truth, the warmth of the wine, which had spread through her blood, unravelling the knots in her muscles, releasing the tensions in her mind and body, made her thoughts anything but clear.

He rapidly stripped away the remainder of his clothes and stretched beside her.

'Your hair is beginning to grow.' He allowed it to curl intimately round his fingers before clenching his fists and holding her powerless while his mouth sought hers. For Kate it began a journey of initiation, an emotional awakening, conducted with the most exquisite tenderness and consideration. The memory of it would haunt her for ever. And the Viscount's loving possession of her would be branded on her soul.

Marlbrooke's self-control was limitless, subjugating his own urgent desires, the need to drive on to his own fulfilment, to bury himself in her. Did she realise the enticement of her delicious body as she relaxed and warmed under his hands? No, she would not, he realised. Not now. But in the future he would have the pleasure of showing her.

'Viola.' His hands skimmed down her body, all satin curves and dips and hollows, surprising him by their femininity in such a slight frame. He let his palm brush her breast, his gut and loins tightening when he felt her sigh and tremble in his arms. He abandoned her soft lips to touched his tongue to a nipple, savouring the taste of her, the instant reaction when she became taut and erect. She was so slender, so finely boned but gloriously feminine. She clung to him and buried her face against his shoulder.

'Marcus,' she gasped, 'I cannot...' But she did not know what she could not do. She felt totally serene, her fears banished by the confident touch of his hands, the strains of the day far distant. He had told her that he was not her enemy, and at that moment she believed him implicitly. What she could not believe was the intense pleasure created by his hands touching, stroking, soothing. It was disturbing, perhaps a little frightening, but so enticing. And he was so careful with her. She was conscious of the control in the muscles of his back and arms. So hard. So smooth. He seemed to know every sensitive place in her body. She flushed from her head to her feet at the intimate invasion of some of his caresses. She was grateful indeed for the darkness.

'Yes, you can. It is so easy. Just let me pleasure you.' He let his hands stroke hip and thigh, the dip of her waist, and then return to her tempting breast. When his thumb encircled her nipple she gasped and would have pulled away, the first hint of alarm in her response, but he was sufficiently sure of her now that he would not permit it. He took possession of her lips once more, this time forceful and possessive, holding her still under the increased demands of his touch. He was hard for her and knew his control would not last for ever.

'We would get further if you would spread your thighs for me,' he murmured against her mouth.

She did not know how to react to that—to be shocked or to laugh—but she opened to him and felt his fingers slide along the soft skin of her inner thighs. The heat in her body, the intense ache and tension in her belly startled her, but she did not resist. She held her breath.

'What do I do?' she whispered when she remembered to breath again.

'Nothing. Just let me show you.'

He lifted himself above her, taking the weight on his arms. She was aware of nothing but his nearness, the solid mass of his body, the exquisite touch of his fingers, the outline of his broad shoulders above her in the greying light.

His invasion of her body was not easy. He had not been able to promise her that it would be, but he did his best. She would have cried out at his first thrust, at the shock, the thorough possession of her body, but he covered her mouth and absorbed her tangled emotions into himself. Then held himself still to allow her to become accustomed, to tolerate his size and weight. He stroked her, comforted her until he felt her relax around him and her breathing settle again.

'Hold on to me. I will not hurt you now.'

He began to move slowly, easing his way further into her, withdrawing and pushing forward again, as smoothly and gently as might be, his skin damp with the effort of holding back from his desire to possess and conquer. Until his hard-held control finally snapped. He surged deeply within her, shuddering into his own climax. She simply lay in his arms, stunned by the events, but surprised at her own relaxed acceptance of what was a shockingly intimate act. But she had trusted him, and he had not hurt her—well, no more than she could bear. The warmth and closeness gave her a sense of profound well being. She turned her face into his soft hair, pressed her lips to his throat and breathed in the male scent of him. And smiled a little.

He withdrew from her to lie beside her and gather her close. 'Kate? Did you survive?' She could hear the concern in his voice—but there was something else there that she did not recognise.

'Oh, yes. It was not so very bad after all. I did not need to be afraid, did I?'

'Thank you for your compliment! Now why had I expected flattery from you, of all people?' He recognised the extreme tiredness in the slight slurring of her words. She felt totally warm and relaxed against him and he knew she would sleep. He had been successful in at least one of his aims.

He felt her smile against him in the dark. 'I did not dislike it, my lord.'

For a virgin initiation, and given the circumstances, that, he supposed, was as good as it got. He felt a surge of intense masculine satisfaction spread through him. He gathered her into his arms and kissed her with gentle intensity. 'I did not dislike it either. Perhaps we will suit. I promise that it will be better next time.'

'Yes.' She was drifting into sleep. 'I would like that.'

As he drew her head to rest on his shoulder, a faint sly shiver of dread touched his skin. It had been a deliberate and calculated decision to tell her that he loved her, to put his future into her hands. And such pretty hands they were. He closed his hand warmly over the one that lay on his chest. But where would he be if she could never return his love, but always saw him with suspicion and hostility as the damned Oxenden who had destroyed her family? It would leave him empty, emotionally adrift, when what had just occurred had shown him the splendid possibilities in a future lifetime of loving her. And yet she had turned to him with trust and had not disliked the experience. He shrugged mentally. He would do all in his power to make her happy and hope that love would follow. When she murmured against him, he pressed his lips lightly to her hair and she smiled.

He allowed her to sink into sleep, her body pulled close against his, and gradually followed her.

Kate woke, alone in Marlbrooke's bed, with clear light illuminating the dark panelling and heavy drapes which at some time had been pulled back. She pushed herself up on the pillows and tried to collect her scattered thoughts as she registered the sly aches and pains in her body. She felt that she had slept deeply, a sleep of exhaustion, and thought that it must be near to midday. The events of the previous day and night seemed so distant and out of focus, as if they had involved someone else. Or been in another lifetime. But she knew that the outcome of the near tragedy was very much her concern and she must face it. Her heart began to beat more rapidly at the prospect and her mouth dried.

And now there was Marlbrooke to consider. What had she done? It was all his fault!—and the effect of the wine that he had given her, which had so effectively smoothed out the nervous tension, destroying her reserve in her dealings with him. Colour flooded her cheeks. She would not think about it—not yet. What she must do was find some clothes to put on so that she could escape to Widemarsh before Marlbrooke returned, or any of the servants discovered that she had not slept in her own room. Legal contracts were one thing, the blessing of the Church was another. She wondered idly what her mother would say if she knew—but somehow it did not matter. She tore her mind away from the image of her body in Marlbrooke's arms, the caress of his fine hands as his lips blazed a pathway from ear to throat to breast... She would not think of him. But her innate honesty compelled her to accept that she no longer hated him. Nor was she merely indifferent. Marlbrooke was no enemy of hers. She pressed her fingers against her tender lips as a delicious shiver rippled through her body.

She needed a chemise—and focused on the one lying across the foot of the bed. She pulled it towards her with some relief—but this was not hers. It was beautiful. Her fingers stroked the soft creamy linen, sewn with such tiny stitches and marvelled at the fine lace trimming the narrow cuffs. For want of anything else, she pulled it over her head. How could she resist such an exquisitely feminine garment? A pattern of roses and honey-suckle rioted in pink silk embroidery round the neck and laced opening. She sighed with pleasure at the softness of it against her skin.

The smile still lit her face when the door opened. Marlbrooke entered, dressed hastily and informally in breeches and unlaced shirt, carrying a tray. He placed it on the bed beside her and surveyed her with raised brows. She returned his gaze, refusing to succumb to the nervousness that threatened to overwhelm her and reduce her to an embarrassed silence.

'I have a headache,' she informed him accusingly. 'It was undoubtedly the wine you gave me last night.'

'I thought you might have. I wager you ate nothing yesterday.' He sat on the edge of the bed and removed the cloth to uncover the tray. 'This should help a little.'

'I don't want food.'

'Yes, you do. I have discovered, my dear Kate, that you can be very difficult. Eat this.' He handed her a piece of bread cut from a new loaf.

'And you can be—'

'Masterful!'

'The word I was thinking of was manipulative!'

He grinned, his eyes alight with laughter, and touched her face, skimming his fingers over the curve of her cheek with a gentleness that made her catch her breath. 'You look rested this morning. And undoubtedly very pretty. The chemise looks well.'

She blushed and dropped her eyes as embarrassment won. She could no longer blank out the intimate demands of his hands and lips and the manner in which her body had responded. She obediently ate some of the bread and took a sip of the weak beer.

With a smile he left her to eat and strode to the window to look out over the gardens. Her eyes followed him. He might smile at her but his shoulders were tense, and she sensed a preoccupation in his manner. Kate knew that she must talk to him about the poisoning. That she must be prepared to see condemnation and suspicion return to his face when he looked at her. How could she bear it when she had seen such tenderness and understanding?

He turned to face her, leaning back against the window frame, arms folded. 'Better?'

'Yes.' She took a deep breath. 'How is Lady Elizabeth this morning?'

'Weak. Tired. Looking very fragile but sitting up, and asking to see you. I told her you would come in a little while.'

There was no criticism here in Marlbrooke's comment or his expression, but Kate feared the worst and could not remain silent. The words spilled out. 'I did not poison her. I did not leave the jar of aconitum. I know there is no proof and that I have both the knowledge and the opportunity—Mistress Felicity had the truth of it—but I would never—'

He moved quickly to cover the space between them and his firm hand on her arm stilled the words. 'I know it. There is no need for you to distress yourself. I do not need proof or arguments. I know that you would never harm my mother, Kate.'

'But Felicity said that—'

'If you had left the poison,' he interrupted, his voice gentle but inexorable, 'I doubt that you would have worked so assiduously to rid her system of the deadly essence and so heal her.'

'Perhaps.' Her fingers tightened in the bed linen until he covered them with his own to still them.

'Whoever prepared it and left it in her bedchamber knew that my mother would drink it without question, believing it was from you and so would bring her relief. It is not your fault. You were used, as much as my mother was used, most likely to attack me. I have to accept that I have enemies. Now leave it.'

'I cannot bear to think that—'

'I do not hold you in any way responsible for so cowardly an act, dearest Kate. Does that satisfy you?'

'Very well.' There was nothing more she could say, but she was determined to do all in her power to discover the culprit. 'I think I need to talk to Aunt Gilliver.'

'Yes. I think you do.' His expression became flat and cool for a moment. 'She has never hidden her hatred of us or her desire to see the Priory back in Harley hands. Perhaps you will tell me the outcome of your conversation.'

Kate nodded. 'Of course. You must know that I would tell you the truth.'

He took in her rigid shoulders, the anxiety in her compressed lips and the deep line between her brows and increased the pressure on her hand with his own in compassion. 'I have never thought otherwise. How could I find it in me to love you if I did not trust you?' He smiled with delight as she quickly drew her hand away from beneath his and pretended indifference—although the blush that rose from the lace edging of her chemise unquestionably denied it.

'And now I must get dressed.' Anything to prevent him from looking at her with such concern and understanding.

'Why? I like you as you are.'

He simply sat, watching her solemn face as the flush tinted her cheeks a delicate pink. Smiling, he leaned forward, closed his hand around the nape of her neck, so vulnerable with her short hair exposing its elegant curve, and pulled her gently towards him. She was irresistible in the embroidered chemise, her dark eyes lustrous and unfathomable, her body still pliant and warm from sleep. And so shy when he made his feelings obvious. He rubbed his lips softly over hers, pleased beyond measure when she made no move to pull away. Since she did not, he feathered the lightest of kisses from her ear, along her neck to the slope of her shoulder. Always gentle, keeping his own hunger hidden. When he returned his attention to her lips, he felt them curve under his in anticipation.

'You are too enticing,' he murmured as he used his tongue to trace the delicate outline, brushing her soft lower lip with his teeth. He laughed aloud at the look of surprise on her face; she was so unaware of her attraction, of the lure of her innocence. He found himself suddenly arrested by his determination that she should enjoy his body as much as he had enjoyed hers. He had never expected to feel such needs about a wife. One of the accommodating ladies at Court, perhaps, or a much valued, worldly-wise mistress—but not a wife who was in the way of a mere necessity. And certainly not an innocent unawakened girl who had acquired none of the Courtly arts to attract and seduce. He moved his hands to the unlaced neckline of her shift, intending to push it from her shoulders and expose her exquisite breasts when he caught the faintest hint of unease in her expressive eyes. He let his hands fall. Of course. It would not be an act of consideration to take her again now. He smiled ruefully, brushing his hand longingly over her slight bosom. She did not resist, but he could not.

'I expect,' he explained his reticence, 'that you have discovered a number of tender aches this morning, Mistress Harley.'

She bit her lip in some confusion. 'Why...yes, my lord.'

'Then I will not impose myself on you, however great the temptation. But I promise you that it will be a more memorable experience next time.'

'I think I should not...that is to say, we...' She floundered helplessly.

'There is no need for guilt, Kate.' He understood immediately. 'Legally you are mine, complete with seals and signatures and all the force of the law. My body merely confirmed that. Does that help?'

'Yes. I think so. You are very kind.'

'No.' He frowned a little, unnerved by such a level of trust. 'It seemed a good time to take you to my bed,' he explained simply. 'And I believe the effect on you was beneficial.'

'Yes. I slept well.' She smiled up at him. 'But I must get up. Where are my clothes?'

'You will find some on the chest by the window.'

'But they are not mine!' She looked in some consternation where he indicated, at the deep blue velvet skirt and bodice that had been laid out for her. The sleeves were tight, ending in a deep lace-trimmed cuff, the skirt full but plain without decoration. The scooped neckline was rendered more seemly by a deep lace collar. It was the perfect outfit for riding. Beside it was a matching cloak in the same velvet but lined—oh, luxury—with sables. 'I cannot wear something so...so magnificent!' But her eyes said different.

His brows rose. 'Why not? I see no reason why you should not look delightful in a colour that so clearly mirrors your eyes.'

Kate wilfully ignored the compliment. 'And I would wager they never belonged to Lady Elizabeth. Could you be trying to buy my compliance, my lord?'

'I did not realise that I needed to. Not after last night! You were splendidly compliant.' He stroked his hand along the curve of her throat and shoulder for the sheer delight of seeing her shiver with pleasure. 'But, no, that was not my intent. I merely thought Goldfinch deserved better.'

'Goldfinch?'

'Certainly. Something is owed to her breeding. Where did you get the horror you were wearing yesterday? I refuse to have my wife resemble nothing so much as a scarecrow.'

Kate tried to suppress a laugh, without success, as she saw his meaning. 'I found the horror, as you so eloquently put it, in a clothes press at Widemarsh. I had nothing else suitable for riding in inclement weather. Except the breeches I came in, of course, and Gilliver forbade me to wear them. She can be surprisingly prudish and made some of her usual very uncomplimentary comments on my upbringing.'

'Well, now you have something suitable. And I am sure you will look charming in it.'

'Why?' She frowned at him. 'Why have you given me so much?'

'Because it pleases me to do so and it gives you pleasure. I have never yet known a woman who did not enjoy parading herself in fashionable feathers.' He leaned down to plant a kiss on her indignant lips. 'The law now states that I am allowed to give you pleasure and I will continue to do so. You might grow to like it, dear Kate, if you allow yourself to do so.'

As a parting shot it was most effective. Ruffled at his undoubted ability to do so, Kate was reduced to silence.

Kate felt nervy and uncomfortable as, clad in a glory of sapphire blue velvet, she presented herself in Elizabeth's bedchamber. The lady was pale and drawn, but making a gallant attempt to drink some of Mistress Neale's nourishing chicken soup. But she gave up, waving away Elspeth and the spoon with some relief as Kate entered the room.

Sitting beside the bed, Bible open on her knee, was Mistress Felicity. Angry colour flooded her face and her stare was baleful, but she closed her lips into a straight line. It was clear that she had been warned against repeating the previous day's outburst, but her views on Kate's involvement had not changed.

'Kate. I hoped you would come before you returned to Widemarsh.' Elizabeth's voice was a mere shadow, but she tried for a smile.

'Of course, my lady.' Kate continued to hover by the door, reluctant to approach the bed where Felicity held sway. What could she say?

Elizabeth realised the problem and remedied it 'If you please, Felicity, I would have a private word with Kate before she leaves. I know that you will understand.'

Felicity did not understand, but knew that she had little choice in the matter, short of outright refusal. 'Whatever you wish, dear Elizabeth, but are you quite sure that I should not stay within calling distance? After all, you are still very weak.' She smiled at her cousin and completely ignored Kate's presence. 'I would feel better if I remained here.'

'No. Indeed, why should you? You are not to be at my beck and call all day. I am quite comfortable.'

'It's witchcraft!' Felicity hissed, all attempts at congenial manners suddenly vanishing. 'Meddling with herbs and charms and such like—it is not suitable for a God-fearing household.'

'Lady Philippa, my mother, would never have been involved with anything unseemly.' Kate likewise abandoned her intentions to be conciliatory and held Felicity's hostile stare with a calm certainty. 'Her family was of the strictest. Yet it was thought that the gift of healing should be practised for the benefit of others. That is not witchcraft. She had remarkable skill, which I could never emulate. She would never hurt anyone—and neither would I.'

'But can you say the same for Mistress Adams?'

And there lay the problem! 'I know little of her. I had not met her before two weeks ago, but I see no evidence of witchcraft at Widemarsh Manor.'

'I do not trust her.'

Or you. Kate read the implication perfectly. She shook her head, finding nothing to add.

'If you please, Felicity. I wish to speak with Kate.' Elizabeth's voice might be weak, but there was no doubting her authority.

Felicity gave a little shrug of acceptance and stalked past Kate, her eyes averted, taking the Bible with her as if Kate might contaminate it with her presence.

'Oh, dear!' Elizabeth sighed with a resigned grimace. Her words of warning to her cousin had clearly fallen on deaf ears.

'I suppose that she thinks I am a minion of the devil. I expect that she has been reading about stoning sinners to death!'

'I am so embarrassed. I know what she has said. Please let me apologise on her behalf.'

'There is no need.' Kate's face was stiff.

'There is every need.' Elizabeth leaned forward and held out her hand. 'Do not distance yourself from me, dear Kate. I value your company and your potions. Don't stop. And I know that I owe you my life. I am grateful to Elspeth, who told me about your efforts on my behalf last night.'

Kate shook her head, but approached the bed to touch Elizabeth's hand with her fingers and forced her facial muscles gradually to relax into a faint smile.

'I will only help you if you promise not to take anything that I do not give you personally. Otherwise there is too much opportunity for malevolence.'

'Very well. I promise.' She plucked at the covers in frustration. 'I feel so tired.'

'You need to rest. You were desperately ill. Tomorrow you will probably be strong enough to rise and take up your tapestry again.'

A faint smile touched Elizabeth's lips—but then she startled Kate by covering her face with her hands.

'What is it? Are you in pain?'

'No.'

'Will you tell Mistress Felicity?'

'No!'

'Then tell me. Is it the cold spirit that still troubles you?'

'Yes.' She let her hands fall helplessly in her lap, to be followed by tears that ran unchecked down her cheeks. And the words came flooding out.

'I cannot rest, Kate. She was here again last night when I was at my weakest. Her spirit surrounded me with such a weight of despair. I still feel it pressing on my heart.'

'My aunt says that she is Isolde Harley,' Kate explained, holding Elizabeth's hands comfortingly. 'She is an unquiet spirit who took her own life here at the Priory over a hundred years ago. For some reason she has returned now.'

'It becomes worse as the days pass—much worse. Such sorrow floods from her. I cannot sleep because I am waiting for her. And I am afraid that one day she will do more than just *be,* but will extract some terrible revenge from me. I have not caused her anguish and yet I feel that in some way she holds me and mine to blame. I wish you could do something to remove her, as you can remove my pain.' Elizabeth continued to fret in her weakened state, holding on to Kate in her distress.

'This is dangerous work, my lady.' Kate found it difficult to turn away from the desperation in the lady's face.

'I know. Dealings with witchcraft can have terrible consequences, but living with this outpouring of anguish is too distressing. What would Mistress Adams say?'

'I do not know, but I will do what I can. I need to talk to

Gilliver. About a number of things.' There was an air of determination about her at odds with her slight figure. 'But I would be grateful if you spoke to no one about this. And certainly not to Mistress Felicity!'

Chapter Twelve

'Does she live?'

'Yes, she does.' Kate pushed the door closed against the chill evening wind and walked forward into the dusty interior. 'The devil's bit removed the poison and reduced her temperature as you advised. She is recovering.'

Mistress Adams stood in the timbered hall of Widemarsh Manor, jewelled fingers folded across her apron, diamonds glittering coldly on her breast, and nodded with satisfaction. Her appearance was as benevolent and smiling as ever and, as Kate knew, could be completely misleading to those who did not know her. Beneath the kindly exterior lurked all manner of disturbing qualities. And yet she had sent the means to care for her forsworn enemy without hesitation.

'Should I say that I am relieved?' Gilliver's smile grew but became thin-lipped.

'I would be happier if you did, Aunt Gilliver. But I would not know if I could believe you. We need to talk.'

'I see you have talked to Oxenden. Or more.' The sly glance and raised brows caused colour to flood Kate's face to her intense annoyance and embarrassment in equal measure.

'You have an aura,' explained Aunt Gilliver, inspecting her uncomfortable great-niece. 'But why not? You are his legally betrothed after all. And very pretty. Is he virile?'

'I...I will not discuss it.' Kate all but choked on her answer.

'Pity.' She sniffed. 'An attractive man, in spite of his family.

That is a very fetching gown. You did not find it in *my* clothes press—and you did not leave home in it yesterday morning. Perhaps he is trying to buy your favours?' She pursed her lips. 'Perhaps he is succeeding. And what will Richard have to say about that, I wonder?'

The fact that she herself had accused Marlbrooke of doing exactly that, and that she too had entertained guilt-ridden thoughts about Richard, did not make Kate more amenable to her aunt's jibes. Without finesse she changed the subject.

'Aunt Gilliver! Did you produce the wolf's bane and leave it at the Priory for Elizabeth to drink?'

Mistress Adams looked at her with interest, head cocked on one side, a gleam in her bright eyes. 'Now what would make you think that?'

'Because you have the knowledge and the skill. And I am sure that there will be a jar of dried aconitum root somewhere in your still-room if I searched. And because, if you remember, you offered to poison Marlbrooke for me when I first set foot in this house. Some would say that was fairly conclusive and damning evidence.'

'*Some* would be totally misguided. Come into the parlour where we will continue this most interesting conversation. It is too draughty and too public in this hall.'

They sat on either side of the oak table amidst the drying herbs, eyes locked in confrontation.

'I have the container, and what remains of the contents.' Kate removed it from a deep pocket and pushed it across the scarred surface between them, where it left tracks in the dust.

Gilliver took the green glass and held it to let the light play on the dark surface.

'No. I did not make this. I admit to a great temptation—but I did not. If I had given in to the impulse, I would have directed it at Marlbrooke, not at his lady mother. Why not strike at the heart rather than at one of the limbs? Marlbrooke is the one who has stolen our birthright.' She hesitated, and then, 'I am surprised to note your sympathy, your care, for the family.'

'I am tied to them whether I will it or no. And besides...'

'Well?'

'If you wish me to be completely honest, Aunt Gilliver, I have experienced more affection and concern for my well being from Lady Elizabeth than I ever did from my own mother. Once she had birthed me, I am afraid she had only a cursory interest in me as a person, much less as her daughter.' Kate's smile was wry, but with no hint of self-pity. 'Tapestries and herbal lore were far more amenable than the needs of small children who would cry and fret.'

'And so? Where does this lead?'

Kate tapped her fingers on the table. Why not ask? Gilliver could only refuse. 'If you are not moved to harm Elizabeth, will you in good faith help me to ease a considerable problem in her life?'

'What do you want from me? You can deal with pain relief and salves for swollen limbs without my aid. I said I would not administer poison, but do not ask too much of me.'

'It is Isolde. She troubles her.'

'Isolde!'

Kate nodded. 'The presence lingers in her bedchamber at night. And the Lady Elizabeth is afraid.'

Gillivers was silent, forehead wrinkling, lips pursed as she considered the situation. Then, 'What are you asking?' Her eyes narrowed, wary, suspicious of her great-niece's intentions.

'I am asking you to use what you know, to use your experience to put to rest a troubled spirit that pervades the corridors at the Priory. If she is in truth a wronged member of our own Harley family, perhaps we owe it to her. Can you not do something to keep Isolde at bay or to give her peace?' Kate spread her hands on the table, palms upwards in supplication. 'I am certain you can. I have seen the rowan over the doorways and the mistletoe in this house—I believe that you have the knowledge.'

'Quiet!' Gilliver all but hissed, leaning across the table, eyes narrowed to the merest dark slits. 'What you speak is dangerous. Too many ears are open, even in this place. Besides, why should I do anything?'

'Why not? Isolde is of our blood. Indeed, perhaps our own family drove her to take her terrible decision to end her life. Should we not, then, help the lady to rest? And if she brings distress to others, surely we are in duty bound to alleviate that distress.'

Gilliver still sat in thought, fingering a gold chain that rested heavily on her bosom, occasionally glancing at Kate sitting calmly across from her. She wondered if the girl really understood what she was asking.

'Will you help?' Kate persisted.

'I might. Let me think.' She rose to her feet, paced to the fire to stir the logs, and returned to consider the determination in Kate's eyes and the stubborn lift of her chin. Finally she nodded.

'Very well. I find that, unfortunately, I cannot fault the logic of your argument—however much I might detest your reasoning.' Gilliver frowned at Kate and showed sharp little teeth in a fierce grimace. 'Never mind—come with me.'

The door of Gilliver's still-room was closed firmly and locked behind them. Kate looked around with interested fascination, even though she had been allowed in this hallowed sanctum on other occasions. She recognised much of what she saw—the graceful umbels of angelica and fennel, untidy twiggy bundles of common garden herbs, dried petals of rose and calendula. But there were twisted roots that she did not know and dried leaves with pungent aromas which she could only guess at. The dark mass of substances in some jars defied identification. On a shelf before her, at eye level, a row of polished skulls gleamed softly and surveyed her through empty eye sockets. The sizes ranged from tiny—possibly mouse—to larger mammals—rabbit? Fox? And the beaks of small birds. When Kate put out a hand to touch them, Gilliver tutted and slapped at her niece.

'Better not to meddle with some things, my dear, or not until you know their purpose. And perhaps it will be safer if you do not know…'

Kate rapidly put her hands behind her back.

'What passes between us here must remain between us. Do you understand?'

'Yes.' Kate shivered.

'I do not want either of us to be the subject of an unpleasant and probably painful trial. Or to see a witchfinder take up residence in this area, to start asking questions. What people do not know cannot harm them, but in the wrong hands… I need hardly explain.'

'I will take care. It will be my security as well as yours.'

'Well, then. As long as you are sure.' She glanced quickly at Kate and appeared satisfied with what she saw. 'Let us talk witch bottles.'

Kate's breath hitched and she closed her eyes for a moment. What would Sir Henry say if he was aware of what she was about? And as for Simon Hotham... But it seemed to Kate that there was no other alternative. Isolde was real and her presence was a cause of distress.

'But Isolde is not a witch.'

'No, she is not. But the power is the same—to ward off all evils, all troubled spirits, whether it be ghost or witch. If we make up a witch bottle, we can keep her power contained. We cannot stop her from entering the Priory—it is far too big—nor can we lessen her powers or give her the peace she needs for her spirit to return to the dead, but we can bar her from a particular room, such as a bedchamber.'

'Very well. Show me. And God have mercy on us!' Kate inspected the array of jars crowding the shelves in front of her. 'I see you have the aconitum,' she remarked drily.

'Of course. Very useful it is too in some circumstances. Now concentrate, my girl.' Gilliver refused to be drawn or embarrassed, but took a small glass container with a wax stopper from the depths of a cupboard. 'We will choose a selection of suitable plants and herbs and seal them in this bottle. It must be either buried under a doorstep—not in this case, of course—or placed over a door frame. Can you do that?'

'I expect so. What do we put in it?'

'Don't be hasty. Let me think. It is many years since I...'

Gilliver began to run fingers quickly and knowledgeably over the pots and jars before her, choosing and discarding, keeping up an informative commentary for Kate's education.

'St John's wort is essential against all types of ghosts, devils, imps, enchantment—even thunderbolts—but I don't expect we will be troubled by those.' Her eyes twinkled with a depth of malicious mischief. 'And blackthorn, excellent properties here. A few twigs will do. Now—houseleek? Perhaps not in this case. There are better. Penny royal prevents hysteria and enables the sufferer to remain calm—a pinch of that—as does fumitory—so a pinch of that too. A piece of oak leaf and holly, of course—

waxing and waning, you understand, so it will give all-year-round protection. What else? A little angelica, a sprig of rosemary? Yes, both powerful against evil or restless spirits. Perhaps I should give *you* a handful of this?' She shook a bottle of dark leaves and removed the seal.

'What is that?'

'Periwinkle, to achieve a happy marriage. But I anticipate it will take more than a pinch of dried leaves to bless this union.'

Kate snorted and pushed the jar of periwinkle back on to the shelf, successfully hiding a smile at her aunt's caustic humour. 'Is that all?' She picked up the witch bottle and held it to the light—a harmless bunch of twigs and leaves to the uninitiated. She shrugged. 'And I place it over the door frame of Elizabeth's bedchamber.'

'More or less. What were you expecting? Toad's blood and raven's bones? But this also.' She opened a drawer and took a twig that had been wound and tied into a simple knot while it was still supple.

'What is it?'

'A tree loop. Rowan, of course. It has special protective powers.'

'Very well. Tomorrow I will hide them.'

'You must close the doorway to Isolde first.'

Kate sighed. 'I thought there must be more. I don't suppose you...'

'Now what would be the reaction if *I* turned up at the Priory, to mutter incantations over doorways? How foolish you are! If you want Isolde restricted in her movements, then you must do it yourself. Listen carefully. It is not difficult.'

'And I suppose I must not be seen?'

'On no account! It is vitally important.' Gilliver's eyes were suddenly fierce, a deep line engraved between her brows, her clawlike hand closed around Kate's wrist. 'This is the first time I have shared my knowledge and it leaves an uneasy feeling. To know and to share is not always to have power. It can lay you open to attack.' She considered Kate's face for a long moment. 'I suppose I can trust you. Perhaps I have gone too far already?'

'I will not betray you, Aunt.' Kate's eyes were solemn and she met her aunt's questioning gaze directly.

Gilliver nodded. 'Good. There is no artifice in you. This is what you must do. I will give you a solution of salt and water, which I will consecrate for you. All *you* have to do is anoint the door frame and the door sill with the words *No Spirit can enter here. All Evil is turned back.* Now, repeat after me.'

Kate did so, carefully memorising the simple charm.

'If you could do the same around the windows in the room it would be even better, but that may prove to be too difficult. With the witch bottle and the rowan, your precious Lady Elizabeth should enjoy some peaceful nights. Her fears should be assuaged. As for the Lady Isolde—I know not what will restore her peace. It is in the hands of God.'

'Amen to that.' Kate turned to regard her aunt. 'Lady Elizabeth may no longer be afraid, but *I* am—at the extent of your knowledge, the ease with which you handle all this—' she indicated the array of bottles '—and my involvement in this witchery!' She drew in a sharp breath, once again horrified at her casual involvement in something so potentially explosive.

'Nonsense! As a Harley you are quite capable of dealing with this. But not a word to anyone!'

Kate grimaced. 'There is no need to warn me, Aunt Gilliver. For there is nothing Mistress Felicity would enjoy more than to find me dealing in spells and witchcraft! It would indeed be an answer to her prayers!'

Kate rode to Winteringham Priory next morning, her saddlebags carefully packed, containing the witch bottle, the rowan loop and Gilliver's secretly prepared bottle of salt and water. The parting between aunt and niece was tense and serious—what they were planning was not to be undertaken lightly. The joy of riding Goldfinch on a bright April morning, even with the ever-attendant Josh, would normally have distracted Kate, but not this morning. She rode oblivious to her surroundings and tried to quell the nervous flutters in her belly. The sooner she arrived at the Priory, the sooner she could complete and turn her back on this unsavoury task. And if Elizabeth could sleep easily and regain her strength, then it would have been worth Kate's guilt and anxieties.

It had been easy for her in the end to avoid Richard, with

Gilliver's help, as she left Widemarsh. But he had given her a few uneasy moments.

'Perhaps you will allow me to accompany you on your ride to the Priory this morning, Kate?' They sat at breakfast and Kate was immediately lost for words. Richard's presence was the last thing she had wanted in the circumstances. Indeed, Richard's presence and her feelings toward him were beginning to trouble her considerably. She promised herself to give it serious consideration as soon as Isolde had been dealt with. Yes, she loved him—of course she did—after all, he was her cousin, and had she not always known and loved him? Had she not hoped to be united with him in marriage? But Marlbrooke dominated her thoughts as he had claimed her body as his own. It was all too complicated. She could not think of it now.

'There now, Richard.' Aunt Gilliver came to the rescue. 'And I was hoping to make use of your strong arms this morning. I have an oak chest that I need moving. It is far too heavy for myself and Mason.'

'Of course, Aunt Gilliver. I am at your service.' Richard had not looked pleased at the prospect. Surely Gilliver could make use of one of her servants for such a task. He opened his mouth to suggest it, caught Gilliver's eyebrows, raised in amazement that he should even consider refusal, and lifted his hands in acquiescence. He glanced wryly at his cousin. 'Perhaps, Kate, you could postpone your visit until later in the day when I shall be at leisure again?'

'I am truly grateful for your concern, Richard, but I feel I must go immediately.' Kate hid a smile. 'I hope to see how Elizabeth has fared during the night. I would not wish to wait.'

Richard had bowed his head, accepting retreat before a superior force, hiding his dissatisfaction behind a light smile. And Kate had escaped. All she prayed now was that Marlbrooke was somewhere out on the estate, giving her unobserved freedom to limit the extent of Isolde's power.

She left Goldfinch in the stable yard where Jenks informed her that, unfortunately, she had just missed his lordship, who had ridden out towards Stoke Lacey and would probably not return before noon. She hid her guilty sigh of relief. Perhaps fortune would be with her after all.

Her first visit was to Elizabeth. She was asleep, with Elspeth sitting sewing beside her bed. In a whispered conversation she informed Kate that her ladyship had slept poorly through the night, leaving her irritable and anxious. But she had broken her fast and was sleeping peacefully now. She was much improved on her condition of the previous day and would no doubt wish to see Kate when she awoke.

Kate smiled, registering the improved colour in Elizabeth's cheeks, and promised to come back later. If Gilliver was correct and accurate in her preventative knowledge, that would be the last sleepless night that Elizabeth would suffer due to Isolde's anguished presence.

Outside the bedchamber, she placed her saddle-bag behind one of the wall hangings for safe concealment from any passing servant. Satisfied with this precaution, she walked quietly from one end of the corridor to the other, listening, senses stretched to pick up any sound or movement. She lingered nervously outside Felicity's room and listened. Nothing. No sign of Verzons or Mistress Neale either, or any of the other indoor servants. This was the best opportunity she could hope for. If she could manage only ten minutes of uninterrupted solitude, all would be accomplished.

She stood with her back to the wall opposite Elizabeth's bedchamber, took a deep breath and assessed the oak door and wood panelling of the corridor. No difficulty here. There was a carved ledge above the door, intricate with incised roses and leaves, a perfect place to secrete a small glass bottle out of the view of all, even an industrious maid who might feel the need to clean and dust.

She dragged a heavy, straight-backed hall chair to stand to the left of the door. What should she do first? Did it matter? Aunt Gilliver had not said, so she must presume it to be irrelevant. She took out the salt solution, unstoppered the bottle and dipped her linen handkerchief in the liquid. She hesitated again. No sound. The dust motes hung motionless in the sunshine that bathed the corridor in gold. Quickly, she wiped the handkerchief along the door sill, whispering Gilliver's words. Then, re-wetting the linen square, she did the same for each side of the door. Finally she removed her shoes, climbed on to the chair and anointed the door jamb. Finished! She would have to be content with the door—the windows would be too difficult. She could not imagine what Elspeth would think if she began to anoint the window ledges in Elizabeth's room. Besides, Isolde seemed to have her feet planted firmly on the floor. To Kate's knowledge, she did not fly through windows. She prayed it would be enough.

She swallowed, relief flooding through her as she returned the linen and bottle to their hiding place. Now for the rest. Climbing once more on to the chair, Kate stood on tiptoe, reached up and carefully placed the witch bottle on the wooden ledge, and anchored the rowan twig behind it. It seemed secure enough. Not even a draught would dislodge it. And if it did, then Kate could claim ignorance along with the rest of the household. After all, it was only a collection of decomposing twigs and leaves. Perfectly innocent. She took a another deep breath and closed her eyes, resting her forehead against the cool panelling, before climbing down.

'Treasure hunting again?'

She froze in horror, still perched on the chair.

'Any lost wills? Priest holes?'

He had moved like a ghost himself, silently, to stand behind her. She had no idea how long Marlbrooke had been there, watching her. She turned on her chair to face him, looking down from her height advantage, trying to compose her face and her thoughts to bland indifference.

The expression on his face reduced her to helpless silence. Her mouth was dry and any excuses she might have used for standing on a chair outside Lady Elizabeth's bedchamber were still-born. What she saw was anger, cold deadly anger.

'What are you doing?'

'Looking for my father's will.' Her voice sounded raw in her ears as she told the blatant lie. Better that he should believe that, than realise that she was conniving in Gilliver's witchery.

'The will, of course.' He laughed harshly, his grey eyes ablaze. 'Are you never going to give up this ridiculous search? The Priory will be yours, to live in, to enjoy, to pass on to your descendants, through our marriage. Do you really need to constantly throw the gift back in my face?'

His words revealed to her the depth of hurt there as well. How could she have been so blind to it?

And she could not tell him the truth. She must ignore the ache that began to spread in her heart as she saw his pain. It was better that he blame her than that he investigate more closely what she had been doing. The prospect of his future wife on trial for witchcraft was not to be contemplated.

She deliberately set out to stoke the anger, to turn his attention from her actions. 'I do not want the Priory as a gift. It should be mine by inheritance. And you only want me because you know that it should be mine.'

'I do not understand why it should matter so much to you when you will have what you desire.' He remembered the softness of her body in his arms, her submission to his caresses, her willingness to respond. And yet here she was, only twenty-four hours later, behind his back even, doing all she could to undermine his position as owner of Winteringham Priory. He thought she had accepted their union. But she had not. Self-mockery washed over him, biting deep. How could he have allowed himself to do something so foolish as to fall in love with her?

'You clearly continue to have a very low opinion of me, and of my motives in taking you as my wife.' There was no hiding the bitterness in his words. 'Perhaps I must finally accept that it is impossible for me to win even your respect, much less your love.'

'What do you care about my opinion? You have everything. Look around you, my lord Marlbrooke!' She knew that she was being outrageously unfair, deliberately cruel, but could not stop, must not stop. 'How would you understand how I feel? The restoration of King Charles has restored to you everything your family lost, and more. A house in London, the Priory, the power and wealth that goes with it. And the King's personal favour, of course. How would you understand what it is to lose everything, to have your property and inheritance destroyed, to be seen as traitors and outcasts in society? You need only listen to Mistress Felicity's opinions of me to see how true Royalist families regard traitorous nonconformity.'

Well. She certainly achieved her objective. His eyes were lit with ripe fury, his lips compressed into a thin line. But she was still taken by surprise when he reached up, grasped her wrist and pulled her ungently from chair to floor. His grip tightened, to prevent her stumbling, oblivious to her sudden squeak of shock.

'So you think I do not know loss and pain and destruction! You think I have lived a charmed life of comfort and privilege!'

There was a white shade around his lips from hard-held fury, at her unwarranted attack and at himself for allowing her opinion to matter so much.

'Put on your shoes.' The order was snapped out.

She did.

'Now come with me.'

He half-dragged her along the corridor, down the staircase and out along the terrace and into the stable yard. She had to run to keep up with his long stride, but he showed her no mercy, keeping his hold on her wrist. He was beyond the usual consideration in his dealings with her, but she had to acknowledge that it was her own fault.

'Where are we going?'

He ignored her, but ordered Jenks in clipped tones to bring out Goldfinch and his own dark bay stallion.

'Get up. This will not take long.'

He threw her up into the saddle, mounted, and set off down the avenue at a brisk canter before she could find her stirrups and arrange her skirts. She encouraged Goldfinch to follow after, as much intrigued now as concerned.

They rode for perhaps half an hour. In silence. Kate dare not break it and Marlbrooke had no inclination to do so. The delights of the spring day made no impression on either of them. Kate concentrated on keeping up with the punishing pace set by the Viscount.

They rode away from Widemarsh Manor and the village of Winteringham and soon left the confines of the estate. Kate did not know the countryside, but took no heed until Marlbrooke reined in at a spot where the path they were following passed between two small rounded hills and wound down into a gentle depression. The horses blew and tossed their heads, still eager to run.

'Do you know where you are?' They were his first words since they had left and his expression was no more compromising than when they had cantered from the stable yard.

She shook her head and looked about her.

It was an idyllic scene. The sun shone on the small wood before them, filtering through the bright new leaves to highlight the jewel colours of new grass and shy primroses. Tree trunks of young birch gleamed white in the soft light. There was the glint and splash of running water below, beckoning them on, and through the branches to the left, where the slight valley flattened out, Kate could see the mellow golden stonework of a large house.

'This is Glasbury Old Hall. You would not remember it. It is the inheritance—the home—of the Oxenden family—*my* family.' His face was set and cold although the anger had faded. 'I do not care to come here, but today I think it is necessary.'

She did not understand but, when he nudged the bay into a walk, followed him down the slope. But then, as they emerged from the shelter of the wood, into the parkland and formal gardens surrounding the house, she understood only too well.

The Hall was a ruin.

The setting was beautiful, a bright frame for an elegant and valuable treasure. But the jewel in the setting was a terrible outrage. The sunlit stone that Kate had seen, golden and welcoming, was simply the remains of what once had been a gracious house. Dismantled, robbed out, disfigured by cannon fire, engulfed by flames, the walls were tumbled around them. Blind windows were open to the elements, the glass long shattered, and the roof had collapsed inward to fill the interior with a hopeless mass of rubble. There were still remnants of wooden timbers and beams, but charred and rotting, like the broken ribs of a skeleton. The balustrade along the terrace had for the most part collapsed into the garden below. And as for the garden—it had reverted to wild and uncontrolled nature. Paths had disappeared, the box edging of the knot garden had grown ugly to overwhelm the delicate plants that had once thrived, the lawns were choked with weed and rank grass. The abandoned state of the orchards and kitchen gardens glimpsed behind the ruined frontage Kate could only guess at. Here was no romantic reminder of past ages, but a hopeless remnant of a once beautiful home. Desolation and sadness pressed down on her with the oppression of a thundercloud. And she had accused Marlbrooke of not understanding loss.

Marlbrooke dismounted, leaving his horse to graze on what had probably once been a well-tended flower bed, and strode up the broken steps to where a great oaken door, now lying in riven pieces on the floor, would have given access to his home. The Oxenden coat of arms was still visible above the stone lintel, the three falcons spreading their stone wings in perpetual flight. The symbol of power and dominance mocked the reality of collapse and depredation. Kate hesitated, then followed the Viscount to where he stood below the carved escutcheon.

'This is my home. Not the Priory. It will never be the Priory.'

He leaned on the crumbling remains of the balustrade, head bent. She saw the white tension in his fingers, heard the bitterness in his voice, and her heart wept.

'I am so sorry. I did not realise.'

'How should you?' He straightened, took her arm to guide her over the uneven surfaces and walked round the terrace to the side of the house, to look out over a formal parterre.

'We should not be here.' He looked up at the dangerous state of the walls. 'We are probably under threat from falling masonry. It is almost twenty years since its destruction.'

The steps into a rose garden had long gone, but the Viscount jumped down and reached up to lift her beside him. His hands were firm, but gentler now about her waist; although the intense anger might have faded from his face, it had been replaced by an acceptance that was more moving to her than grief.

They walked through a wilderness, which had once been a pleasure garden, down to the landscaped banks of the tiny stream, turning to look out over the open pasture to the distant hills, now gilded in sunlight, rather than at the heart rending ruin at their back.

'I remember my childhood here. It was a happy time. My mother loved these gardens—they are very much her creation. My father had no interest in flowers. But they lost it in the second year of the war. A Parliamentarian siege, just as your family lost the Priory to a Royalist force. But the Hall was destroyed in the skirmishes. After that... My father was ailing and embittered after the war and rarely responded to my mother's care. She lost a much-loved husband and a stillborn child. And for many years I was not the son she wanted. I left her in London, neglected and alone except for Felicity's companionship, while I...' He shrugged. 'Well, the pleasures of the Court—in exile at first— and then here in London when Charles returned were far more exciting for a young man with time on his hands. I do not understand how she can still be so generous, so untainted with bitterness. Especially as she has been so stricken with pain and loss of independence.' He looked down at Kate as if, for a moment, he had forgotten that she was beside him. 'Both sides have suffered, you see—and what have any of us gained?'

'Forgive me, Marcus. I accused you deliberately, to wound you, and I am sorry. I did not mean it and I should never have said it. I have received nothing but kindness at your hands—or Lady Elizabeth's. I wish with all my heart that I had not stirred up all this sadness for you.'

He turned to face her, away from the lovely scene, a wry smile touching his lips. 'You did so, very effectively. And I had come to believe that you did not hate me so much.'

She flushed at the implied question in his voice. 'No. I do not hate you.' Her voice was a little gruff and she could not force herself to meet his eyes.

He laughed a little. 'Such a confession!' and ran his hands up her arms from wrist to shoulder in one long caress to pull her close against him, enfolding her, resting his cheek against her hair.

'I used you very badly today. We have not done well by each other, have we?'

She could only shake her head but he felt the tiny movement against his shoulder.

'Look up.'

When she did so he lowered his lips to hers in a kiss of such compassion, such astonishing tenderness, that it all but took her breath away. He raised his head to scan her face with narrowed eyes.

'You are quite beautiful. I once told you that but did not know it and you accused me, quite rightly, of mere flattery. I know it now and hope you will accept my words as truth.'

'Why, yes. For you are looking at me this time.' She smiled up at him.

'I have been looking at you for some weeks!' He tightened his hold and claimed her mouth with his once more, but this time the flash and heat engulfed her. Her senses remembered the urgency of his hands and body against hers, remembered her own responses to him. And this time there was no embarrassment. As he pressed her hard against him, she clung and melted, aware of the blood in her veins, from head to foot, turning to molten gold, which rivalled even the bright sunlight around them. His mouth was completely demanding, completely possessive, proving ownership of her, and she shivered with longing. Her lips opened under the pressure of his to allow his tongue to caress and explore. He changed the angle of his kiss in response, delighted by her acceptance of his lovemaking, forcing her to acknowledge her desire to surrender to his every demand. Her tongue met his, shyly but without hesitation. He felt her sigh, a purr of sheer pleasure in her throat, and tremble against him, and he wanted more.

Marlbrooke was shocked by the surge of pure lust in his gut and a responsive stirring in his loins. He was painfully ready for her and knew that she must be aware of it, so closely was she moulded to him. He would like nothing better than to take her here in the sunlight, in a secluded patch of palest primroses, exposing her body to his gaze and his touch beneath the soft leaves. But this was not the place. Too much ruin, too many shattered hopes lay around them. It would be sacrilegious to celebrate love within sight of so much destruction. She deserved better and he made a silent promise.

He drew a slow breath and released her to press his lips to her brow. 'Let us go back. I want you, Kate, you must know that, but there is too much sadness here.'

'I am sorry that you will never see the Priory as your home.' Her brow was furrowed. What would their future together be if that was so?

'Did I say that? Perhaps. The future might change that.' He was not to be tempted into any more disclosures.

They did not speak again until they had returned to the gentle pass between the hills where they had first halted above the Old Hall.

Kate looked across at this complex man with whom her future was now tied. He now rode in a more relaxed manner, the reins held gently, the muscles of his back and shoulders less rigid. But there was a shuttered expression, a brooding quality, in his eyes that hurt her. She did not know him well enough to know how to remove it. But she would try.

'I have not had the opportunity to thank you properly for this lovely mare,' she informed him. 'I think we should try her paces.'

He glanced across, a glint of interest, an eyebrow lifted. 'You fit well together.'

'I know.' She laughed. 'I think we should see what she can do.'

'Can it be that my strictly reared Puritan wife is suggesting a race?' The interest had changed to humour.

'Why not? I wager I can beat you back to the stable yard. Do you accept?'

'What will I win when the Falcon beats Goldfinch out of sight?'

'I do not know. I will have to think. Besides, that presumes that Goldfinch cannot beat the Falcon. I do not accept that.'

'Very well. It is not my usual practice when assessing the odds, but for love I will take your wager for an unspecified prize.'

'But on one condition. That you do not allow me win.'

'Never!' The answering grin was all she could have hoped for.

The horses took no urging across the open pastures towards the estate. They flew in the bright sunlight, neck and neck, hooves striking the drying ground. It was glorious, exhilarating. It mattered not to Kate who won. She had seen the lifting of the mood from Marlbrooke's face and that was enough. It struck her that she was becoming very manipulative—and enjoying the sensation of power where the Viscount was concerned.

Once inside the Priory estate they took to the open parkland and gave the horses freedom to extend. Kate clung tightly to Goldfinch as the mare gripped the bit and stretched into a headlong gallop. She gave Marlbrooke a run for his money. But there was no gainsaying the Falcon. Stronger and heavier, the Viscount had already dismounted at the stables when she trotted in, windswept, dishevelled but laughing, her eyes sparkling with the exercise and sheer delight.

She slid down into his waiting arms. 'We lost, but I love her dearly and cannot thank you enough.'

'My pleasure. And my trophy, Mistress Viola?'

Instantly she responded, on impulse, without thought. She flung her arms round his neck and pressed her lips to his. Then, still laughing at the amazed expression on the Viscount's face at so public a display, she lifted her skirts to run on ahead into the house. He followed, aware of Jenks's grin behind him, the cold knot of anger in his belly dissolved, his thoughts on the girl who had achieved it and her delightfully devious methods.

He did not see the still, watchful figure of Richard Hotham, behind him in the open door of the stables. Nor would he have believed the turbulent depth of emotion that swept those calm features as he witnessed the uninhibited kiss between his cousin and the Viscount.

Later in the day Kate managed the last of a number of private conversations with Jenks. The result was to the satisfaction of both and led to some minor manoeuvring between the stables and the house. An hour later there were further repercussions for the inhabitants of the Priory.

'Why would you wish me to come in here, Kate? You are being very secretive—I suspect some deep developments.' Lady Elizabeth glanced at the Viscount, who had chosen to accompany the two ladies out of a lively interest to see just what his intended bride had been about, but she received no enlightenment. Kate opened the door to a little-used room in a more recent wing of the house, a saloon, chill and barely furnished.

'Do not look for any explanation from me, ma'am. I am afraid that I was foolish enough to give Viola *carte blanche* and now we have to bear the consequences.'

'We haven't used this room since we returned last year.' Elizabeth entered the room, brow faintly furrowed. 'I do not know why, but it never seems a very comfortable room. Perhaps it simply needs to be lived in.'

Kate had to agree, but for her present purpose it was perfect since it was one of the few rooms to give direct access to the flagged terrace through full-length windows.

'There is something I wish you to see. I hope it will find favour with you.' Suddenly she was attacked by nerves. What if she had misread Lady Elizabeth's temperament? She thought not, but...

Before the window was an object, shapeless and bulky, draped in rough cloth, which had been used to wrap it on its short journey from the stables.

Kate approached it, a sparkle in her eyes. 'This is it. I hope you will find it of use.' She pulled at a corner of the heavy cloth so that it fell to the floor. Inside the package stood a chair.

Elizabeth approached.

There appeared to be little remarkable about it. A chair. It had been fashioned by a local craftsman under Jenks's supervision, sturdy rather than elegant, but there was simple carving of intertwined leaves and scrolls on the arms and the struts of the back. The oak was well polished and gleamed in the sunlight that beckoned through the windows. On the seat was an embroidered cushion, commandeered from one of the Priory rooms, stitched by some long-dead Harley lady. Nothing to demand a personal inspection by the Oxenden family in the middle of the afternoon.

Elizabeth circled it and a smile touched her lips as she saw the purpose of it. For at the end of each leg had been attached a sturdy wheel, and attached to the front stretcher was an extra rail as a foot support for added comfort.

'When you wish to go into the gardens,' Kate explained the obvious, a little uncertain how her idea would be accepted, 'but you do not wish to stand for too long or walk too far, then this is your means of transportation.'

'Well, I had not...'

'My uncle Simon was too proud to use such a chair,' Kate continued anxiously before Elizabeth might refuse to consider it, 'even on the days when the pain crippled him completely. He thought that it was beneath his dignity to have to ask a servant or Richard to help him. But I thought you would enjoy being able to oversee your gardens again—and I would willingly push you. It would never be a burden to me.' Her fingers were clenched into fists of tension at her sides.

'Kate. It is a lovely idea.' Elizabeth's eyes lit with pleasure. 'I am not too proud. Indeed, I would value the means to escape these four walls.'

Marlbrooke laughed, delighted with her initiative. 'So that is why you needed to converse with Jenks. I would not have guessed.' He took his mother's hand and helped her to sink back on to the cushion whilst Kate arranged her skirts becomingly, tucking them away from the wheels. 'All you need now is Felicity to push you along the terrace.'

'Oh, dear. Could you not find someone a little more—sympathetic to the occasion?'

'I am sure we can.'

'I will lend you Josh, my constant shadow.' Kate smiled in

relief, knowing how difficult it was for some to accept infirmity. She need not have worried. 'I would be delighted if you could find use for him.'

'Josh stays with you,' Marlbrooke responded immediately with a bland smile and calm voice, but a glint in his eye that made Kate once again aware of the steely determination which she could not avoid. 'But since the sun shines and I am here to lend the muscle, let us try this ingenious contraption. And if it collapses, tipping you into a flower bed, my dear, you can blame Kate!'

For Kate, that was a moment of revelation. Emotions that had been insidiously creeping into her thoughts and dreams suddenly crystallised into something hard and bright, causing her heart to leap in her breast. The light fell on Marlbrooke as he opened the window to the terrace, illuminating him in vivid detail: the breadth of his shoulders, his dark hair falling forward in gleaming waves as he bent to unfasten the catch, the strength in his hard-muscled but graceful body. The beauty of his elegant hands on the back of the chair took her breath away. And the care and affection in those spectacular grey eyes as he joked with his mother over his ability to push the chair with any degree of safety.

Kate saw all this in the space of a heartbeat—and knew that she loved him to the depth of her soul. In spite of all her intentions to resist his charm, his physical beauty, she had fallen in love with him. And since he loved her, her world was suddenly filled with a glorious radiance that sent fire through her blood and a flush to her cheeks.

She turned away from her companions for a moment to hide her intense reaction. She needed a little time to come to terms with this devastating development.

Chapter Thirteen

It promised to be the perfect spring day and Kate's heart was light as she waited for West to saddle Goldfinch and roust Josh from his tasks in the depths of the stables. The ride in sparkling sunshine with the gentlest of breezes would be exhilarating and would lift her spirits. And she would see Marlbrooke. She longed to see him. Since that moment in the chilly saloon her thoughts had been full of him. He disturbed her sleep, robbed her of appetite, causing Gilliver to prod and pry with sly glances and obvious comments. How could her feelings towards the Viscount have undergone such a cataclysmic change in so short a time span? She did not know, shaking her head in disbelief, aware only of her need to see him, to feel the touch of his hand on her arm, to see the soft gleam of his eyes when he looked at her. A twist of guilt ate into her happiness. Richard! What she had felt for him was not love. Her affection for him was so mild compared with the flames that engulfed her when she thought of Marlbrooke's lips on hers. In her innocence she had not known. And Kate knew that she must put it right with Richard. But she did not know how. She had no wish to hurt him, but he would blame her—and rightly so. But for now she would ride to the Priory. And she would see Marlbrooke again. Her heart leapt.

But the day that promised so much rapidly became one of disastrous confrontations.

'I would not criticise your actions, Kate, but it seems to me that you spend far too much time at the Priory.' Richard had come to join her in the stable yard, soft-footed and amenable, and now requiring a reply that Kate did not feel able to make with any degree of equanimity. 'I understand your wish to live there, of course, but it seems that perhaps you find the company of Lord Marlbrooke more than acceptable.'

'I do not expect to see Marlbrooke,' Kate replied with what she hoped was a casual shrug of her shoulders. 'My mission is to take a new balm of Gilliver's for Lady Elizabeth to try. It is a new one distilled from germander leaves and helps to relieve rheumatic pains. I shall not stay long.'

'Then I will see you on your return.' Richard helped her up into the saddle and handed her the reins. But he kept his hand on hers for a moment, compelling her to meet his eyes. 'I can understand that a young girl, innocent of the ways of the world, would decide that marriage to Viscount Marlbrooke would be an attractive prospect. He has considerable presence.'

'Perhaps. But as you are aware, our marriage is purely political.'

'I am aware of that.' His face was stern but his voice gentle and uncritical, revealing no vestige of inner turmoil or the rampant jealousy that was a constant gnawing pain. 'I would simply warn you of a man of his sophistication. Don't put your trust in him. I have seen him in his dealings with you. He uses great charm—but he may court you now only to gain your compliance in this contract. When you are married and carrying his heir, he will have all he desires from you. Do not be surprised if his attention turns rapidly to neglect. He will assuredly wish to return to London and the Court. I would not wish to see you hurt, my dear cousin.'

Like a lightning bolt, Kate was struck by an image of Marlbrooke, standing as she had seen him in one of the magnificent reception rooms at Whitehall, backed by sumptuous damask hangings and Mortlake tapestries. In his hand was a glass of wine, his face alight with pleasure as he conversed with friends and acquaintances. Richly clothed, at ease, socially adept. A stab of anxiety pricked at her happiness.

'I shall not be hurt.' She managed to smile down at Richard and returned the pressure of his fingers. If he had intended to kiss her, she was able to avoid it without a confrontation. 'It is very kind of you to be concerned on my account, but there is no need. I expect nothing from Lord Marlbrooke.'

But she did! She could not deny it. Nor was she being totally honest with Richard, which distressed her. In the light of Richard's warning and her own duplicity, the clear spring day suddenly seemed to have lost some of its brilliance.

Felicity, dressed with her usual drab propriety in dark satin, met Kate on the flagged terrace as she made her way from stables to house. Kate was more than a little surprised to see a smile lighten the lady's thin features. Relations between the two ladies had not improved, Kate remaining ever polite but wary, unwilling to be the source of any further friction between Lady Elizabeth and her companion, Felicity for the most part silent, but with no mistaking her suspicion and hostility towards the newcomer.

'Mistress Kate.' Felicity addressed her with surprising warmth. 'Lady Elizabeth is sitting in the sunken garden. I will walk with you if you permit.'

'Of course.' Kate returned the smile with a lifting of her heart. Perhaps she had been wrong in thinking that Felicity would never accept her. Perhaps it was true that time would heal some of the wounds. They turned their steps to walk together.

'It must be a satisfaction for you to have returned to your family home at last.'

'Yes. It is a beautiful house. And the gardens. I have enjoyed exploring it.'

'Then marriage to my lord Marlbrooke will be a definite advantage for you.'

'Yes, of course.' Kate raised her eyebrows a little and glanced at Felicity, not quite following the gist of this. But perhaps Felicity merely wished to make conversation.

'I expect that you will not object to living here alone—when my lord and dear Elizabeth return to London.'

'I did not know that Viscount Marlbrooke was planning to leave the Priory in the near future.' Kate felt a cold hand close around her heart. 'He has said nothing to me.'

'Not immediately, of course, but soon enough.' Felicity's smile widened, but Kate could not ignore the lack of warmth in her eyes. 'Once you are wed he will return to Court. I understand that his Majesty enjoys my lord's company. And of course my lord enjoys Court life, as you are aware—he would not wish to absent himself for long. It would not be politically wise to do so, as I am sure you will agree. Now that he has secured the estate, there is no need to spend much time in the depths of the country, and certainly not when the weather can be so inclement. Life in London is so much more comfortable, do you not think? Of course, dear Elizabeth does not enjoy country life. She has so many friends in town who miss her and look for her permanent return rather than a brief visit.'

'I see.' What else could she say? The words echoed Richard's warning, turning her heart to ice.

'Did you think to accompany him again?'

'I had not thought. But, yes, I can see no reason why I should not.'

'Perhaps you will. But once you are breeding, Marlbrooke will assuredly wish for you to remain here in peace and comfort.' She laughed in shrill tones at Kate's stricken look. 'Do you expect my lord to dance attendance on you once he has secured the succession? You do not think that, surely. Once he has an Oxenden heir he will have achieved what he wanted from the marriage. Or did you expect him to love you? He has such excellent manners, does he not? No one would ever believe that his emotions were not engaged. But the wounds of war are far too deep. It is my opinion that he will find it impossible to ever forgive the supporters of Parliament for the devastation of his home and family. My lord's father was destroyed by the war, you understand.' Felicity's conversational tones, dripping with malice, went on and on, coating Kate's emotions with deadly despair. Would she never stop? 'He went into a steady decline, you realise, into premature old age. Which also hurt dear Elizabeth, causing her great distress from which she has not recovered, or ever will, I suspect.' She turned to face Kate and touched her arm with an apparently sympathetic hand. 'He will never love you, you know. It will be better for you if you accept it. I have seen you look at him—it would be foolish of you to open yourself to casual and painful rejection.'

Kate felt as if all her dreams lay in dust at her feet. She might, of course, have simply rejected Felicity's warning out of hand as a malicious attempt to sow discord, to destroy any chance of happiness. But the lady's words merely confirmed her own deeply buried fears. She had seen for herself the lure of the Court. What a fool she had been. She realised with sudden clarity that she must never forget her position here. Never be seduced by Marlbrooke's attentions, his kind words, his apparent care and concern for her welfare. It all meant nothing. Even his declaration of love. Perhaps at Court fashionable people were willing to say such things without any depth of feeling and she was too innocent and without the worldly wisdom to realise it. Perhaps he had said the exact same words, an avowal of love, to Alicia Lovell in a brief moment of flirtatious charm, with no intention of proclaiming a serious commitment. And presumably Mistress Lovell had accepted those words in a similar superficial light. Kate closed her eyes momentarily against the blinding truth. It was surely time that she realised that she was merely a legal necessity and the woman on whom he would get lawful children to ensure the continuity of his family name. How could she have been so naïve as to believe that she saw anything other in his laughing eyes when they rested on her or sense any other motive than possession in the drift of his hands over her body? And had not Richard only that morning warned her of hoping for too much, for being misled by his sophisticated manners? Yes, he was kind. But that was all. And she was a fool!

She turned to face Felicity squarely, drawing on her pride to hide her humiliation and shattered emotions.

'Of course, Mistress Felicity. You are perfectly correct in your reading of the situation. I expect nothing from this marriage other than the legal terms agreed between my lord Marlbrooke and my uncle.' She kept her voice flat, her expression closed. 'But, yes— I will enjoy living at the Priory—under any circumstances. It is my home.' But the ownership, once so desirable, was suddenly as ashes against her tongue.

She met Marlbrooke later in the day on the long corridor at the top of the main staircase. 'My lord.' She curtsied, eyes downcast. 'I would ask you—have you decided with my uncle on the date of our marriage?'

'Next month. I do not know what you will need to do, but women always seem to need more time than they have. Will that allow you sufficient time to prepare? If not, it can be changed to suit your convenience.' He smiled at her, an appreciative glint in his eye, unaware of her inner turmoil, unable to see her expression in the shadowy upper reaches of the house.

'I am surprised that you care to wait so long, my lord.'

Now he picked up the strained quality of her voice and gave her a quizzical look. Where had that hint of anger come from?

'The sooner you wed me,' Kate continued in the same strained tone, 'the sooner you will be able to return to London.'

'But I have no plans to return to London as yet.' He simply stood, wary, waiting for enlightenment.

'No, but when I am breeding there will be no reason to stay here. And I believe that your mother would wish to return.'

'Has she told you so?' He frowned a little at her directness.

'Not as such. But I doubt that either of you would wish to stay here permanently once the inheritance is secure.'

'So you think it is my intent to get a child on you and then leave you here in seclusion.' She should have heard the warning in the quiet voice, but was too wrapped in her own distress.

'Why not? I am willing to remain here, of course. It will be an arrangement that will suit us both. You can return to Court—and your previous life. I know that you find it far more entertaining than life here at the Priory, now that I have experienced it for myself. Indeed, I am surprised that you have seen fit to remain here as long as you have.'

Marlbrooke covered the ground between them in two long strides. 'Who have you been speaking to? Who has put these ideas into your head?' He gripped her shoulders in a painful grasp as fury flooded through him. Why should she suddenly doubt his intentions enough to accuse him of such a blatant lack of sensitivity? What had he done to deserve this? Whenever he seemed to make some progress towards winning her troubled heart, she struck at him for some unforeseen slight or insult. And on this occasion with no foundation for her accusation.

'Why, no one, my lord. Surely it is perfectly obvious and understandable. Please release me.' She winced a little as his fingers dug into her shoulders. 'It is my intention to return to Widemarsh before noon.'

If anything, he tightened his grip.

'Let me go, my lord.'

'No. Not until this matter is clear between us. You cannot make such unfounded accusations and then run away. You are no coward, Kate. I have no intention of returning to London as yet. When I do, you will accompany me—if it is your wish. As for getting a child on you—I would desire it, but we are both young and it is not a matter of immediacy.'

'Really, my lord?'

'Really. So rid yourself of the Puritanical notion that marriage is merely for the procreation of children. It has other benefits, as I had hoped you were coming to appreciate. It would seem that I was wrong.'

'I do not see any benefits. And I simply presumed that you might wish to return to the company of Alicia Lovell.' There! She had said it! Kate swallowed against the misery that threatened to rise from her heart to choke her. 'It has been clear to me from the beginning that you wished to marry me for one reason only.'

She was shocked out of her own misery by his reaction: the flash of anger in his eyes, the tension in his jaw, the tightening of the muscles in his shoulders.

'So you expect me to bed you, get an heir on you and leave you here alone while I return to the delights of Court? To break my vows to you in sins of the flesh?' He had never spoken so harshly to her.

'Yes,' she answered in defiance of his challenge.

'Then I would hate to disappoint you, Mistress Harley. Or Richard Hotham or Gilliver—whoever has sown this unpleasant seed in your mind. You clearly have little regard for my feelings towards you and are more likely to listen to their words rather than mine. I was clearly foolish beyond measure to tell you that I love you. How could I have been so careless of my own happiness as to drop that little gem into your hands and hope that you might return my regard?' His words were a lash of bitterness, his mouth twisted into a sneer. 'But understand this, Katherine. Alicia Lovell means nothing to me. Nor has she since the day I asked for your hand in marriage. I am not guilty of such deceit.'

'No. I never meant that. It was just that...' She floundered into silence as she realised the enormity of what she had allowed herself to be driven to do, now that he had painted the truth of it in stark black and white. She had been wrong! She had misjudged him beyond forgiveness. And he now thought, with terrible justification, that her family was guilty of poisoning her thoughts against him. She dare not tell him of Felicity's cruel words, calculated to hurt and undermine. Her thoughts were in turmoil, more so when he clamped his hand around her wrist and dragged her back along the corridor to thrust her into her own bedchamber, locking the door behind him.

'Please...'

'What do you want from me? Compassion? Pity? I doubt it.' His voice was clipped, harsh, hiding the amazing depth of hurt that assailed his heart. 'I presume you and your family think me incapable of such a sentiment. And yet you would accuse me of such monstrous selfishness—it is beyond bearing.'

He pounced on her with all the elegant strength of a hunting beast. Before she could register his intent, he had unlaced her bodice with deft fingers, pushing her chemise from her shoulders to expose her breasts. He took her mouth in a hot angry kiss, forcing her lips to part beneath his, his tongue invading, plunging deep. When he pushed her back on to the bed she fought against him in sudden panic, struggling against his hard hands, pushing ineffectually against his shoulders. He stepped back from her, but merely to strip off his coat in one fluid movement. When she tried to slide away across the bed, he lunged to grasp her skirt and pull her back.

'Oh, no, Mistress Harley. If you will fling down the gauntlet, you stay to face the consequences.'

And she knew she must. She struggled no more, but waited for the onslaught. But she could not stop the tears sliding down her cheeks into her hair. What had she done? She had no reason to suspect him of neglect, thoughtlessness, lack of consideration. He had always treated her with kindness and respect for her difficult situation. Yet she had allowed Felicity—and Richard— to push her into false accusations. She trembled at the heat of his mouth on her shoulders, the roughness of his hands as he pushed her skirts and chemise above her thighs. She dare not look at him, to see the anger and rejection in his brilliant eyes, of which she had been the cause. She closed her eyes against reality.

Then she was crushed beneath him, his body pinning her to the bed, the ridge of his erection strong and powerful against her thigh, mouth hot and hungry on her breast, the scrape of his teeth against her sensitive nipples. Although her mind rejected his assault, her treacherous body heated beneath him, her nerve endings shivering with sensation.

Then she became aware that he had frozen above her, his touch stilled, his breathing caught. Kate opened her eyes to see his face, an expression in his eyes she had never seen before as he looked down at her. Horror primarily, and an abhorrence too deep to be expressed in mere words. He saw the tears on her cheeks and wiped them away with gentle fingers, which trembled with the realisation of what he had almost done. Her eyes were wary, watchful. But there was no fear. Regret, perhaps.

In God's name, what was he doing? How could he have allowed himself to be driven to such a wanton act? Was his self-control so diminished in his dealings with her?

'Kate... As God is my witness, this was not how I meant it to be between us. I have hurt you beyond redemption and that was never my intention.'

'I know that you would never mean to.' Her voice might catch on a sob, but her eyes met and held his calmly.

He looked down at her, trapped beneath him, his weight doubtless crushing her. What was he doing, treating her no better than a London whore, without consideration or finesse? He knew better—he knew how to deal with a woman, especially the one whom he loved above all else in life—and yet had been for that moment prepared to use her in his anger and frustration, his sense of betrayal, to destroy her innocence. He closed his eyes momentarily against the wave of guilt that swept over him. He deserved to suffer the unending torments of hellfire for his thoughtless cruelty.

'I am so sorry.' He took his weight on to his elbows so that she might breath again. His own breathing was still ragged, but his control was once more in place. 'I have probably just proved to you that I am guilty of all the things you have believed me capable of doing.' He closed his eyes momentarily to blot out her concern and bewilderment. 'Apologies will never put it right.'

'I should not have said what I did. I did not really believe it. But she said—' Kate broke off before she could say more, before she could lay her own faults on to Felicity.

Marlbrooke smoothed her hair with gentle fingers, pushing back the wayward curls from her forehead.

'No. There is no blame attached to you—how could there be? My behaviour has been unwarrantable and I deserve all your reproaches.'

He moved further, pushing his body to take his weight from her, to release her and free her from his demands.

'No.' To his astonishment she dug her fingers into the heavy linen on his shoulders. 'No! Do not leave me like this. I could not bear it.'

'After what I have done?' He watched her carefully, in disbelief, momentarily stunned by the fierceness of her response, not understanding its cause. 'I can think of no way to make amends. I deserve no kindness from you.'

'Don't go.'

She did not want him to leave her with this terrible emptiness that seemed to have occupied all the spaces in her heart, in her very soul. She wanted him to hold her and caress her as she remembered from the first time he had taken her to his bed with such finesse. And, most of all, she wanted to wipe away the bitter self-mockery and disgust in the lines around his grim mouth. On impulse, she reached up to touch her lips to his in a featherlight kiss. To him it was the ultimate sign of forgiveness. To her—her heart turned over in her breast. And she knew that she could love this man who possessed her—and would love him until the day of her death.

'Don't leave me,' she repeated, a catch of panic in her voice.

'If you are sure.' He kissed her gently now, her tear-stained eyelids, and felt his heart swell with tenderness and a depth of love that shocked him to the core.

'I am sure.' It was little more than a whisper, but enough. He was hard, aroused, and she was so very desirable. He eased himself into her and began to move slowly, savouring the heat, enclosed in glorious silk. Now he deliberately gentled his touch, taking his weight from her so that he could watch her face as he claimed her. One sign of distress, he promised himself, and he would withdraw, end it. But her willing softness seduced him utterly. In all honesty he would not be able to stop. When she arched her body instinctively to meet him he was lost and had no choice but to drive on to his completion, totally enslaved by her female powers, albeit wielded with such innocence. He was overwhelmed by her generosity of spirit when he had almost forced her against her will.

For her, it was just as she had remembered yet more intense. His kisses woke unbearable tremors through her body so that she forgot all her fears, swamped by the knowledge that he had taken control of her heart as he had her body. She moved in response to his thrusts, delighting in the union of their bodies, absorbing him, imprisoning him in the silken chains of her body as he reached his own powerful fulfilment.

Her mind accepted her lack of reticence without surprise. She gloried in his demands and felt a need both to give and take more. Not understanding, she was content for the moment with the flow of golden warmth and satisfaction through her veins. Yet the heat in her belly and thighs lingered and beckoned.

Afterwards he held her in his arms until their breathing settled, content to just have her near him, enjoying the memory of her asking him to stay, to continue the union of their bodies. Her head was comfortably turned into his shoulder, one hand clasped firmly in his.

'I would never use my body to punish you, Kate. You must know that.'

'Yes. And I would never believe…what I accused you of. It was unforgivable of me to do so.'

'You humble me, Katherine. When I have used you ill—and have not yet been sufficiently unselfish to awaken you fully.'

'No?'

'No. It should be breathtaking. Magnificent. Shattering.' He laughed softly at her raised eyebrows. 'Or something like that!' He closed his hand over her breast to feel the nipple begin to harden again against his palm.

'Then I will wait,' she remarked, somewhat breathless at her immediate response to his touch.'

'Not too long,' he murmured the promise against her hair.

They remained silent for a little time, enclosed in their own world of drowsy pleasure.

And then, 'Was it Felicity?' He remembered her hastily suppressed words.

'Yes.' Kate did not pretend to misunderstand.

He kissed her hair and the sensitive skin on her temple. 'I will not ask you what she said—but there is something you should know about Felicity.'

He kissed her again, taking possession of her hands and holding them against the steady beat of his heart. 'I know how she appears, bitter and suspicious, quick to blame and condemn, but she was not always so. She was once betrothed. It was not a love match, but it was very suitable and she wanted it. It would have given her a home and family, which is what she desired above all things. Perhaps it would have tempered her sharp words and intolerant opinions. But he was killed at Edgehill by a musket ball in the very first charge of the battle. There has never been any hope of another marriage for her. So, as you see, she has not been dealt with kindly. And her hatred of Parliamentarians is inordinate. You must not mind her words, Kate.'

She sighed a little at the justice of his explanation. 'We all have burdens from the war, do we not?'

'There are few families who do not. She has had much to contend with, and being a dependent is not enviable. As you should know.'

She turned her face into his chest. 'I deserve that. I should not have been so quick to judge her and you are right to chastise me.'

'Never that, Kate.' Marlbrooke tightened his hold to press her close. 'But you should understand why she finds it difficult to like anyone, except my mother, of course, who rescued her from penury—she has Felicity's total loyalty and service. But do not expect too much for yourself or honesty from her. She will see you as a thief who has stolen what she sees as being rightfully hers—and that is my mother's gratitude and affection. To Felicity you, my love, are a usurper who has taken her role in the household. She will not be quick to forgive.'

'I understand. And I am sorry I doubted you.' Kate kept her face hidden against him.

'It is not easy, is it, Kate?' He felt her shake her head. 'Smile at me.' He tilted her chin with gentle fingers to make her look up. 'Perhaps one day you will believe me when I tell you that I love you.'

He was so handsome, so caring of her. Her dark eyes were

trapped in the clear grey depths of his and she smiled. For the first time their future together seemed to be filled with brilliant promise.

She was so lovely, he thought, and did not realise it. His heart tightened as he realised her growing power over him. And the guilt that he had almost been driven to hurt her more than she deserved or could bear remained with him with unexpectedly sharp claws.

Chapter Fourteen

'Her ladyship is resting. She should not be disturbed.' Mistress Felicity stood firmly, determinedly, in the half-open doorway to Elizabeth's room to bar the way. Her face was set, her eyes angry, her lips compressed. She stood like a dragon guarding its young.

Kate recognised defeat and turned to go. She had little alternative, short of forcing her way into the room. It would never be possible to find some common ground with Elizabeth's companion, not now, after her deliberately destructive and malicious taunts when Kate had last visited the Priory. Felicity folded her arms in triumph.

'Felicity? Is that Kate come to see me?' Elizabeth's voice sounded from the depths of the room. 'Let her come in.'

'But you should rest, dearest Elizabeth.' Felicity turned her head to look over her shoulder, but did not move her body. 'It is too soon—'

'I wish to speak with Kate.'

Felicity stood back and allowed the door to swing open. Kate tried not to be affected by the hatred that shone in the lady's eyes. She walked past her into the bedchamber.

Elizabeth's first words were for Felicity's compliance. 'If Kate comes to see me, unless I am asleep, I do not wish you to refuse. I know that you have my comfort and safety at heart, but to refuse is to presume too much. I am sure that I make myself clear.' Although the tone was as tolerant and mild as ever, there was a distinct edge. Perhaps Elizabeth's patience was wearing thin. For perhaps the first time Kate saw a clear similarity between Marlbrooke and his mother.

'Of course, dear Elizabeth. I would never do anything against your wishes. I only—'

'I know. Let it rest.' The smile that accompanied the words was kind and understanding, but did not win Felicity over. Elizabeth, with the slightest of shrugs, turned her head to address Kate. 'Come and sit. Tell me what you have been doing.'

Elizabeth was on the mend, seated in the window embrasure before her favourite view, a piece of intricate embroidery on her lap.

'You look well.'

'Indeed I am and so pleased to be on my feet.' The grey tinge to her skin had quite faded, her cheeks had a delicate flush and her grey eyes were bright once more. Perhaps she had lost a little weight, but nothing to signify.

'Look.' She held out the pattern of tiny stitches, interwoven flowers and leaves, with all the eagerness of a young girl. 'See how much better my fingers are. This morning I walked in the garden with Marcus, and, when I grew tired, used the chair along the paths and the terrace.' Her face lit with pleasure. 'It makes so much of the gardens accessible to me.' Elizabeth hesitated, almost shyly. 'Will you help me to restore them? When you live here permanently?' She stretched to touch Kate's hand. 'I would like it if you would.'

'Of course.' Kate returned the pressure.

'Perhaps we could make some changes. Become *fashionable*.' Elizabeth's eyes twinkled.

Kate laughed. 'Why, yes. What did you have in mind? Cascades and fountains and such like? I must admit to knowing little of such things.'

'Well!' Elizabeth's enthusiasm, liberated by her improved health, began to take over. 'I believe that it is all the rage to create a wilderness—although perhaps we have too much of one here without any effort on our part.'

'A wilderness?'

'Groups of trees and shrubs to give shade in summer, with walks to entice you to enter. Shall we make one?'

'But yes. And perhaps a wider range of flowers in the beds at the side. Roses for perfume in the evenings. And lilies.'

'What pleasure we shall have spending Marlbrooke's money!'

'And columbines—my mother grew them at Downham Hall and I always thought them so pretty. They are also soothing for sore throats—and, if the seed is steeped in wine, it helps for speedy delivery in childbed—'

Kate fell silent as she felt colour begin to rise in her cheeks.

'Dear Kate,' Elizabeth responded, with only the slightest curve to her lips. 'Then we must certainly grow columbine.'

Kate's colour deepened further, so she adroitly changed the direction of their conversation to a matter of some immediate concern to her. She glanced towards Felicity, who had busied herself on the far side of the room, as far from the intruder as she could politely manage. Now was her opportunity.

'Are you sleeping well?' she asked quietly, knowing that she would be understood.

'Oh, yes.' The sigh of relief spoke for itself. 'So much better. I won't ask how you achieved it—but I feel so safe and secure at night. The atmosphere is so much more calm and untroubled—it makes me think that perhaps I imagined the...the problem before.' She frowned. 'Do you think it was mere foolishness on my part?'

'No, I do not. I know what you experienced. It pleases me that I could restore your rest.'

'Do I presume that your aunt was...useful?'

Kate laughed ruefully. 'Yes—with some persuasion. The extent of her knowledge frightens me. She was able to tell me something about Isolde, the grieving presence who took her own life. She threw herself from the roof here and because of her torments, whatever they were, she did not rest. Her family had her spirit imprisoned and sealed by the bishop in a pottery vessel, which was rumoured to be kept here in the Priory—although Gilliver knew nothing of it. Gilliver could not say why Isolde has suddenly returned to this place. Perhaps she—'

The expression on Elizabeth's face cut off Kate's words. It was one of dawning horror, which robbed her cheeks and lips of blood.

'What is it? What have I said? Do you know something of this?'

'A pottery vessel, you said? Kept here at the Priory?'

'Why, yes. Gilliver thinks that...'

'Kate.' Elizabeth pushed her stitchery aside with an impatient gesture. 'Listen to me. I was in the still-room—some time before you came here. And found an old earthenware jug in the bottom of the cupboard. And—' Her words stopped as she lifted her hands to her mouth, her memory of the event suddenly emerging with painful clarity.

'What happened?'

'I dropped it. It smashed on the floor. I remember it had a sealed stopper in the neck, but it was empty. I was concerned because I was unable to bend to pick up the pieces. But perhaps it wasn't empty after all. What if—?'

'What if it was Isolde's troubled spirit, confined and sealed?'

The two ladies looked at each other as they acknowledged the possibility.

'I think perhaps I was not aware of the cold and grief until after the accident. It would explain everything.' Elizabeth's eyes were wide and troubled.

'It would.'

'And, if so, it is my fault that Isolde haunts these rooms.'

'It may be.' Kate tried to smile reassuringly. 'But you must not blame yourself. How could you have known?'

'I could not, of course. But I wish I had never found the pottery jug!'

The discovery would clearly continue to worry Elizabeth. Kate could say no more to comfort her. The deed was done and, as she had said, there was no blame. So she changed the subject once more by producing a small pottery bowl. 'Gilliver suggested a new salve for your joints, my lady. It is angelica—my aunt's still-room is a place of wonderful treasures. I have tried the mixture myself—I believe it will be most soothing and remove the redness from your knuckles. It has a lovely perfume, too.'

'I promise I will try it.' Elizabeth raised the pot, sniffed the pale green paste and smiled. 'What will you do now? Have you seen Marlbrooke?'

'No. I came to see you. Now that I know you are so much improved, I shall go back to Widemarsh before it is dark.' She rose to her feet to take her leave.

'He took you to Glasbury, didn't he?' Elizabeth's sudden question startled her for a moment.

'Yes, he did.'

'He should not have done it. It has too many unhappy memories. I would not want your relationship to be coloured by our past—you have too many tragedies of your own to face.'

Kate sighed a little. The lady understood so much, it touched her heart to be shown so much sympathy. 'I am glad he did.' She bent to kiss Elizabeth's cheek in warm gratitude. 'It makes it easier for me to understand him.'

Elizabeth considered her, as if she would have said more, but simply shook her head and smiled. 'He is his own man and must work out his own salvation, but do not judge him too harshly, my dear. And now you had better go home. Come and see me again, dear Kate.'

'Of course. Do you need anything before I leave?' Felicity had gone from the room.

'No. But, yes… I think I left a book in the Long Gallery, most likely on a window seat. Would you look for me? I am reading the poems of John Donne and enjoying them so much.'

'If I find it, I will bring it.'

The Long Gallery was empty but for a gathering in the corners of evening shadows, imparting a shaded, mystical air to the vast room. The portraits looked silently down in stern judgement. Kate's heels clicked softly on the oak floor, echoing, the only sound in the empty space. There was no trace of the missing book. Kate fisted her hands on her hips, impatience simmering as she realised that she must not linger, mindful of the short days and approaching night.

In a whirlwind of activity she lifted cushions on the window seats, swept aside and searched behind curtains, riffled through the pages of music on the spinet, opened the lid of Felicity's workbox and sifted through the bright silks. Nothing. Perhaps Lady Elizabeth had been sitting beside the fireplace and the slim volume had fallen between cushion and arm. She pushed aside the heavy oak chairs, hampered now by encroaching shadows, and managed to unbalance a fire-screen in the process so that it fell to the floor with a loud clatter that filled the vast room. She bent, hissing in frustration, to right it. And stopped, a little guilty, at the voice from the doorway.

'What are you doing now, Viola? Destroying my property?'

He was standing there, watching her, little more than a silhouette in the gentle dusk. Tall, physically imposing, arrogant even, elegantly clad in silver-laced black velvet... She drew in her breath at the sight of him. She was instantly reminded of her first meeting with him, his total mastery of the situation. Her heart picked up its beat, but not from fear.

'You startled me, my lord.'

'Forgive me, Mistress Harley.' He swept her a formal bow, all grace and proper respect. 'It was not my intention. I did not know you were at the Priory until Verzons told me. And so I sought you out.'

He kept the distance between them so that she could not read his face.

'I have seen Lady Elizabeth. I was looking for her book—the poems of John Donne. It is not here. And I have just managed to—'

'Katherine.' His voice stopped her. It was soft with an allure which she could not resist.

'Yes, my lord?'

'Will you dance with me?' He held out a hand, his request charmingly formal, but a demand none the less.

'Dance? Now?'

'Why not? You can dance the pavane—you have been well taught!' She saw the unexpected flash of his grin, which instantly turned her knees to water. 'We do not need music. Come.'

She obeyed, taking his hand, turning to face him to begin the stately measure.

It was one of the strangest experiences of her life. Caressed by soft shadows, enfolded in silence, except for the brush of their feet and her skirts against the oak boards, Marlbrooke led her through the steps and movements of the pavane. She curtsied, stepped, circled with grace and elegance as if to some unheard refrain. Their bodies touched and moved apart, their hands clasping and unclasping, palms meeting, a mere whisper of flesh against flesh, as they trod the length of the Gallery. She moved as in a dream, her senses completely submerged in the tone and texture of this heart-stirring courtship. Her heart beat rapidly, her skin felt flushed with an inner heat, but her mind was clear, her focus on Marlbrooke intense. As her hand touched his, the cool sliding of flesh against flesh, she felt the tingle of excitement spread in her veins. She could not have spoken, did not need to speak. Conscious of the soft whisper of her satin skirts, the evening light absorbed into his dark velvet coat, she abandoned herself to the glory of it all. Her awareness was centred on the silver glitter of his eyes as they caught the light, the soft touch of his breath on her cheek as they drew together, the unexpected emotions that filled her body and demanded a response. His eyes never left hers, so that she danced as if under an enchantment. It brought her close to tears from the sheer beauty of it.

By common consent, they drew the dance to a close. The Viscount kept possession of her fingers and raised them to his lips. She was so lovely. And she was his. And whether she realised it or not, she had begun to trust him—perhaps more than that. She looked at him now, her face bright and glowing with pleasure. He could see the glorious sapphire eyes, the wilful mouth, the elegantly arched brows. Blood surged through his veins, dispersing an elusive happiness into every cell of his body. He pulled her gently forward to take her into his arms, to kiss those eminently enticing lips, to wipe away the tear that clung to her lashes. When he smiled down at her, she returned it without hesitation.

And then froze. All her muscles tightened as the familiar chill settled on the nape of her neck, on her arms, around her shoulders. A shiver ran through her. And then the Viscount was startled to see tears gather in her eyes, to overflow and trace a slow, silvered pathway down her cheeks.

'Kate, my love. What on earth is there to distress you here? I would not hurt you for the world. You know that.' He took her shoulders in a gentle hold, astounded by her reaction.

'It is not you, my lord. Can you not feel it? She is so sad. It breaks my heart.'

'Isolde?'

'Yes.'

The chilled air around them heralded Isolde's presence as spectator at their dance. The atmosphere was thick with her grief. Even Marlbrooke felt the weight of it.

'Don't cry.' He took out a handkerchief to catch Kate's tears.

'I thought it was my lack of skill at dancing that had reduced you to such misery.'

She smiled through the tears at the absurdity. 'Never that. She has gone now. I am sorry I was so foolish.'

He wiped away a final tear with the pad of his thumb.

'I do not understand why she is so anguished, so inconsolable,' Kate said thoughtfully, 'when I am so—' She stopped abruptly.

'So...?'

'I don't know.' She turned her face away, suddenly shy.

'Yes, you do. If you are not sad, dearest Viola, then what?'

Colour suffused her face. She shook her head. She would not admit to him the effect his nearness had on her treacherous heart.

But he knew. And it was enough. Smiling, Marlbrooke traced the outline of her lips with a finger. 'Don't look so unhappy, little one. It is enough for now. But some day, do not doubt it, I will demand more from you. And you will tell me exactly how you feel.'

She stepped back, to put space between them, embarrassed at the urge to tell him what was truly in her heart. Instead she became all practicality. 'I must put the chairs back again. And the fire-screen.' She turned and stooped to lift it. 'I think I may have damaged the frame when it fell.'

'It is of no consequence.'

'Yes, it is! Felicity embroidered it!'

'And incredibly ugly it is, too. Her choice of embroidery is not complimentary.'

She choked back a laugh. It was true. The intricate *petit point* leaves, wrought in dark greens and browns, did nothing to enhance the overly ornate carving of the walnut surround with its pillars and finials. But that was irrelevant!

'It is easy for you to say, my lord! If she discovers that I caused the damage, she will hate me even more.'

'Then I will tell her that I kicked the screen in a fit of pique and temper when you refused to listen to my fervent declaration of love.' He hesitated and then added, a trifle pensively, 'She would probably believe it too. I fear that her devotion to my mother does not always extend to me. She considers me to be far too shallow, worldly and lacking in any moral values to be worthy of her consideration.'

'Ha! Perhaps she has the truth of it.' Kate used all her will power not to smile. 'Are your shoulders broad enough to bear the weight of her displeasure?'

'For you, Katherine, they will take on any burden. You should know and accept that by now.' For a moment his flippancy was gone, his handsome face unusually stern and set as he lifted her to her feet, to stand before him.

'Marcus...'

They remained caught in each other's gaze, flies in amber. She drowned in the clear intensity of his eyes, and he in the beauty of hers.

'I must go,' she managed at last, but made no effort to move.

'My lord.' A voice and light at the end of the Gallery broke the spell and announced the arrival of Verzons. 'Perhaps you need some light in here. Dusk has fallen quickly.' He carried a branch of candles high in his hand.

'Thank you, Verzons.' Reluctantly, with a wry smile, the Viscount gave his attention to his approaching steward. 'The corner of this fire-screen has been inadvertently damaged. Perhaps you could see to its repair? I believe it is a favourite of Mistress Felicity.'

'Of course, my lord.' The steward lifted the frame from Marlbrooke's hands and leaned it against the wall. 'I will see to its removal. Should I also see to the repair of the panelling, my lord?'

'Panelling?'

Verzons indicated with his hand the place where a section of the linen fold had collapsed inward when struck by the heavy screen, leaving a dark blank cavity.

Marlbrooke turned to look at Kate, an unreadable expression in his eyes.

'Well, Mistress Harley. You hoped for a secret cache. And here it is.'

The cavity, revealed by Kate's fall and now illuminated by Verzons's candles, contained a wooden box, which fitted snugly against the stonework of the house. Marlbrooke knelt and lifted it out, covered with dust and cobwebs. There was engraving on the lid on a silver plaque, but it was black from long enclosure and disuse.

'Documents?' His brows rose.

Kate nodded at the miraculous possibility.

Marlbrooke's face was impassive as he gave his orders to Verzons. 'If you would be so good as to arrange for this box to be taken to Mistress Harley's bedchamber. And organise a fire there—and some candles.'

Verzons departed, leaving them alone with the box on the floor between them. The Viscount looked down at it with an expressionless face.

'You hoped to find a will, Mistress Viola. Perhaps your hopes are to be realised after all.'

When Marlbrooke entered Kate's bedchamber some hours later, it was to find her seated on the floor before the fire, candles on the mantel and at her elbow. The wooden box stood open and empty, the contents spread around her. Some had been arranged in neat piles; others still lay scattered in haphazard fashion. She looked up briefly as he entered, smiled vaguely, obviously preoccupied, and returned to a perusal of the document in her hand. Marlbrooke poured wine for them both, setting her goblet beside her, and stretched himself at ease in the high-backed chair beside the fire. He stretched out his legs and took a sip, watching her.

She made a charming picture of intense concentration as she sifted from one yellowed document to another, dismissing some quickly, lingering long over others. He studied her face, realising that for the first time since she had come to the Priory, her skin was clear and without blemish. No bruising now, no lingering scratches from Felicity's nails. Her dark hair was beginning to curl on to her neck and would eventually allow her to arrange it in becoming curls, if not exactly fashionable ringlets. She had buried her teeth in her bottom lip as she concentrated, a line between her dark brows. She seemed oblivious to his presence, for which he was sorry, but he enjoyed the luxury of watching her without her being conscious of his scrutiny.

He sipped again at the wine, contemplating the delight of carrying her to the shadowed bed, removing that pretty satin dress, kissing those slender limbs until she grew warm and supple and would shiver beneath him. He grew hard at the thought and grimaced, amused at his intense reaction to her—and to the fact that she was totally unaware of her effect on him.

He loved her. By God, he loved her.

At last, Kate put down the final document and sighed heavily.
'No wills?' he asked gently.

'No.' She looked directly into his eyes, hers surprisingly dark with a swirl of emotion. 'No. But there are some letters here that you should read.'

'If you wish it.' He held out his hand. 'But why? Surely they are family documents—Harley documents.'

'Yes, they are. But I have discovered that they touch on your family too. And they explain much. Things that even Gilliver did not know of.' She picked up a small pile of curled and stained parchments and shuffled through them.

'Read this one.'

Marlbrooke took it and angled it to the light to pick out the faded words. The opening of the letter caused him to look up at Kate sharply. She simply nodded and so he continued.

To My Lord Marlbrooke

Following our discussion of last week, I have had conversation with my wife. We have come to an agreement that a marriage between my daughter Isolde and your son and heir, John Oxenden, would be of advantage to both families. The future running of the two estates in tandem would bring wealth and security. I suggest that we meet next week to discuss terms and settlements and draw up contracts for the forthcoming marriage.

I know that the outcome will be as much to your liking as it is to ours.

Your servant
Francis Harley

'I see.' Marlbrooke frowned over the document. 'And this was when? Some time last century?'

'Yes. There are dates on some of the letters...here it is—it was in 1563. Now read this.'

He took the next document she offered.

To My Lord Marlbrooke

The situation over the completed contracts has now become very difficult. My daughter has refused to consider marriage with your son, even though it has come to our attention that she carries his child. She claims that she was forced by your son against her will and now holds him in abhorrence. She will not willingly enter into the agreement. I have counselled her on the advantages of this marriage, but she is stubborn. I believe that it will be the best for all parties if the marriage goes ahead. Ultimately, of course, Isolde will obey her father. We should rejoice that an heir has already been conceived to ensure the future inheritance.

Your servant
Francis Harley

The next letter was brief.

To Sir Francis Harley

I agree that the situation is unfortunate, but happily not without redemption. My son claims that your daughter was willing. I agree that the marriage should go forward as quickly as might be.

Your respectful servant
Edward Oxenden

'And this one,' Kate selected a final page, 'explains the tragic outcome.'

To My Lord Marlbrooke

It is with regret and great sorrow that I must inform you of the death of my daughter Isolde. The circumstances are most delicate and I know that I can rely on your keeping the matter close. Last night she fell from the roof walk of the Priory and was found on the stones of the terrace. I believe that her mind was disturbed by her condition. There can be no other explanation. I trust your compliance in preventing the spread of scandal in this matter—something that would be of advantage to both our families.

Your servant
Francis Harley

'Poor lady.' Marlbrooke returned the document thoughtfully. 'So this is our revenant. It explains her refusal to be at rest. She is certainly not a comfortable presence.'

'No, she is not at rest. Her heart is torn and has yet to be healed. Perhaps it is torn beyond redemption.' He saw the grief mirrored in Kate's face. 'Did you know that she is buried in a glade on the edge of the estate? I have seen the monument. And it seems that she has always been something of a problem. This note explains in part what happened when she died.'

Kate hesitated a moment, aware of a sudden shadow that darkened Marlbrooke's eyes. 'What are you thinking?'

He frowned down at the letter in his hand and then turned to Kate with a clear, candid gaze. 'I am thinking that I almost forced you against your will. It does not sit well with me and touches my conscience. Particularly when I read of the effect on Isolde.'

'But you did not.'

'No, but—'

'I am nothing like Isolde,' Kate insisted, determined to erase the lingering guilt and repair the balance between herself and the Viscount. 'She cared nothing for the Oxenden heir. Whereas I...'

'Whereas you?'

Her answering smile and the gleam in her expressive eyes were deliberately full of flirtatious mischief. 'Why, nothing, my lord. Finish the letters—and then I may explain!'

It had the desired effect. The harsh lines around Marlbrooke's mouth relaxed and he picked up the next piece of correspondence with a wry smile of understanding. His betrothed, he was discovering, had a well-developed skill for manipulation to get her own way.

My dear Wife,

I have arranged, as we agreed, that his Grace the Bishop will take steps to limit Isolde's presence and confine her tormented spirit in some way. God's servant is the only authority that might achieve a resumption of peace both for our poor daughter and for our family. My suggestion of reburial in consecrated ground was not met with any degree of support, so we must put ourselves in his Grace's hands and his suggestion of a confining ceremony. I hope this will relieve your mind and restore much-needed tranquillity to your thoughts.

Your loving husband
Francis Harley

'Which would explain,' Marlbrooke commented, 'why she has not been seen since 1563. But does not explain how or why she has returned.'

'*I* know the reason for her return.' Kate shuffled the documents together in an efficient manner and replaced them in the box, closing the lid, then proceeded to tell the Viscount of her conversation with Elizabeth.

'Do you truly believe that Isolde's spirit was contained in that abandoned pot in the still-room?'

'Yes. I think I do. It fits with Gilliver's folk tales and rumours.'

'So she was released by my mother's hands.' Marlbrooke leaned forward with the ghost of a laugh, arms resting on his thighs. 'It is ironic, is it not?'

Kate nodded. She ran her fingers thoughtfully over the tarnished escutcheon. Then looked up at him. 'I would like Gilliver to read these letters. Would it trouble you?'

'Of course not. They are your family documents. And since it is unlikely that Mistress Gilliver will set foot here, unless it is over my dead body, I will arrange for them to be carried to Widemarsh for you.'

'Thank you. How strange it all is.'

'Mmm?'

'History repeating itself. You know, a marriage between Harleys and Oxendens.' Her voice was a little pensive as she frowned into the remnants of the fire.

'I trust it will not repeat itself.' There was humour in his voice, which made her glance up at him. 'You must inform me if you feel any desire to throw yourself from the roof. I have to say that I will do all in my power to stop you.'

Kate smiled. 'Poor Isolde. No, I will not follow her example.' She dropped her eyes, a little embarrassed, more than a little aware of the Viscount beside her.

Marlbrooke leaned forward and reached out a hand to pull her to her knees beside his chair. 'Besides, I do not believe that I forced you.'

'No!' she agreed with some asperity. 'I remember you gave me wine so that I was not totally aware of my actions!' But he saw the glint in her eye. His lips curved.

'And I would wager that you did not dislike it as much as Isolde appears to have?'

She shook her head shyly. 'No. I did not dislike it.'

He stood at that and drew her to her feet. 'You are quite lovely.' He framed her face with his hands and bent to brush her lips with his, a mere whisper of a caress.

'I should go. It is late.' Her instinct was to pull back, to escape a flood of emotions that threatened to engulf her.

'Too late,' he murmured the words against the pulse in her throat. 'Far too late for both of us.'

He lifted her and carried her to the bed, to lay her back on the soft pillows. 'I believe it may be too late for both of us to claim that this marriage is merely for political expediency.

'What do you mean?' Kate frowned at him, shivering at his touch.

'Have you not realised yet? His voice was gentle, his hands stroking down her arms from shoulder to wrist. 'I love you, dearest Kate. And I find it impossible to believe that you are indifferent to me'

'I...' She shook her head in denial, unable to find words. 'I don't...'

'I know you don't.' His smile was a touch wry. 'But I will wait. At least you have told me that you do not hate me any more.'

'No.' Encouraged by his light touch, she smiled up at him.

'Then let me make love to you. Let me show you the pleasure that a man can bring to a woman.'

Her arms tightened around his neck and she lifted her mouth to his, wordlessly granting him all the permission he needed.

It took little time for him to remove his own clothing and hers, even without haste, and then she lay in his arms, her head resting against his shoulder. He held her close to stroke her hair and press his lips to her temple where a nerve throbbed below the delicate skin. When he felt her relax against him, the tension dissolve from her body, he began his thorough campaign to show her, as he had promised, how much pleasure he could give her.

He was careful with her. Gentle but firm, setting the pace

slowly to arouse and seduce until she had no will of her own under the skilful assault of his hands, and would answer every one of his demands. His clever fingers smoothed and caressed, exploring every inch of her body, exploiting every delightful response to his touch. When she sighed, his mouth took hers into submission until her lips were soft and swollen, willing to open to the pressure of his tongue. Her skin was like finest silk as it warmed to his touch. He allowed his palm to cup a breast, to enclose the gentle swell of it. It fit so perfectly into his hand, how could any man resist. His thumb teased her nipple until it hardened with keen desire. When he replaced his thumb with his mouth she caught her breath at the explosion of heat, spreading through every limb, but then wound her hands into his hair to hold him there. He closed his teeth over her in the gentlest of bites, feeling her shiver and melt against his hard flesh, pulling him even closer as her arms slid around him, chaining his body as she had unwittingly chained his heart. He trailed his fingers lingeringly over her stomach, her muscles trembling, to touch her thighs, the intoxicating flare of her hips. She instantly opened for him, against his every expectation. He groaned, turning his face into her hair, in anticipation of his ultimate possession. His fingers slid along the impossibly soft flesh of her inner thighs and into the hot wetness, as delicate as any flower petal. When he took her, opening her with urgent fingers, he covered her mouth with his to swallow her cry of shock and amazement that her body should feel such heat, such delight, such need.

He continued to touch, to caress, to slide deeper into her, until her body began to move beneath his, until she lifted her hips against his hand in urgent demand. Her fingers gripped his shoulders, her nails scoring him, as she fought against a sensation for which she had no experience.

'Don't fight it, Katherine. Let go,' he whispered, his mouth against her throat where the pulse beat with such intensity.

'I dare not.'

'Yes, you dare. You have no choice.' He supported himself so that he could witness every emotion in her eyes as he drove her on. 'I will give you no choice.' His arrogance took her breath away, but she had no doubt of his determination to command her senses.

Power swept through him, surging through his blood, as he

held her captive and continued his assault, with confidence and certainty, even when she would have twisted away from him, afraid of the feelings that were quickly overwhelming her. He drove her on now, without mercy, until her whole body tensed and shuddered against his hand and she muffled her cries against his chest. As her hands slipped limply from his shoulders, her breathing settled, he covered her face with kisses, moved beyond words at the depth of her trust in him.

'Marcus?'

'Mmm?' His teeth grazed a tingling path along her throat to her collarbone, returning to nibble at the soft skin beneath her ear.

'That was incredible. Was it...wrong?'

'Wrong?' He lifted his head in surprise, his brows raised, but his lips curved in an understanding smile.

'Well, so many things that I have found to be enjoyable—are sinful. Or so my uncle says.'

'And did you perhaps discuss this particular matter with your uncle?'

'Of course not!' She laughed at his deliberate foolishness, a sound of such joy that his heart clenched in his chest and his hold on his self-control slipped a little. He took her face in his hands and captured her gaze.

'No. It is not wrong. How could something so glorious between us be anything but right?' He touched his mouth to hers in the softest of caresses as her lips curved into a smile. Then he rolled to kneel between her spread thighs, feasting his eyes on her relaxed flushed body, pinning her hands to the bed at her sides with his own. He was now driven beyond reason by the urge to bury himself within her.

'Touch me, Kate.'

He took her hand and closed her fingers around his erection, guiding her, showing her how to use her caressing touch to maximum effect, to his own pleasure. He closed his eyes and stifled the groan, a low growl in his throat when her cool fingers stroked and enclosed. It was too much.

He could command his responses no longer. He lifted her hips and thrust into her, holding her still as she gasped at his invasion, at the intensity of the sensations that gripped her. But this time there was no difficulty, no resistance. She was more than ready to accept, to enclose. He withdrew a little and drove deeper still, slowly so that she might savour every moment, lifting her so that her legs wrapped naturally around him, to allow him greater access.

'Look at me, Kate. I will never hurt or reject you as Isolde was hurt and rejected. You are mine and I will never let you go.'

She kept her eyes open on his, betraying every emotion as his thrusts became stronger, harder, his breathing more ragged. Each thrust claimed her as his, a declaration of love and commitment. She clung, moved with him, answered him, giving herself to his every demand until, with a final powerful thrust, he could hold back no longer. At that moment he thought that he had never known such intense happiness.

And then he could not think at all.

It seemed to Kate that her emotions were shattered into a thousand crystal shards, glittering in the candlelight. As he finally allowed his desire to take complete mastery over his body, she locked the glorious sensations that he had given her inside her heart, astonished at her capacity to give and receive such sensual satisfaction. When he lay spent beside her, she stretched like the little cat he sometimes called her, curling into his side.

'Marcus,' she whispered his name as she sank into sleep.

Marlbrooke remained awake, watching the patterns created by candles and fire on the softly glowing panelling. Shattered by the capacity for love that she aroused in him, he could not believe that she did not return his feelings. And yet she had never said so. She had never used the word love. Was he condemning himself to a life of frustration and anguish by loving her so unconditionally, by putting into her hands a weapon that could be lethal if used with careless intent? Knowing that she could destroy him if she wilfully rejected his gift? No. He could not believe it when she returned his lovemaking so ardently. He must not believe it. He drew her sleeping body close, swamped by a need to love and protect as she stirred in his arms.

'Dearest Kate.' He pillowed her head on his shoulder. 'History will not repeat itself this time. Oxenden will wed Harley.'

He let himself fall into sleep beside her.

Chapter Fifteen

'My lady.' Verzons bowed. 'There is a gentleman here to see your ladyship, and have conversation with Mistress Harley. Mr Richard Hotham asks if he might present his compliments to you.'

Lady Elizabeth glanced across at Kate, noting her surprise and a sudden flash of anxiety in her candid gaze, but she pushed aside the tapestry frame, pleased at the prospect of a new face and new conversation, and nodded to Verzons.

'Certainly, Master Verzons. And perhaps you will bring wine.' She smiled at Kate, who had recovered her composure. 'So. I have learned something of Richard Hotham from you. Shall I like him?'

'Why, yes. I was brought up with him as a small child. His family live very close at Staunton Court and were always made welcome by Sir Henry at Downham Hall, so I saw much of Richard and my Aunt Lucy. He was always a very splendid figure as my older cousin. I was allowed to ride with him.' Kate smiled slightly at the happy memories but Elizabeth saw the faint line between her brows and was reminded of her previous evasion of certain pertinent matters.

There was no further opportunity for discussion as Verzons bowed Richard into the Long Gallery where the ladies had chosen to spend the afternoon hours.

'Your ladyship. Kate.' He bowed over their hands with charming grace. 'It is very good of you to receive me.'

'We are always pleased to have company with new topics of gossip and affairs from the outside world. You are very welcome, Mr Hotham.'

'Mistress Gilliver asked me to enquire of Kate's welfare and escort her back to Widemarsh if she intends to return today.'

'Of course.' Elizabeth gave him a warm smile and indicated a chair.

Richard took the seat and accepted a glass of wine from Verzons. Kate was left free to watch him as easy conversation flowed between her cousin and Lady Elizabeth. Yes, he was as pleasing to look at as ever. And she had as much affection for him as she had when she had lived at Downham Hall. She had once told him she cared deeply for him—would be more than willing to wed him. She remembered the rain-washed day in the gardens. But love? What had she known of love in those days before she had come to the Priory, before she had met Marlbrooke? Her thoughts strayed unhesitatingly to the dark glamour of the absent Viscount. To the beauty of his face, the touch of his elegant hands on hers. She repressed her wayward thoughts, but could not prevent the warmth that lodged in her belly and spread its fingers through her veins to her very fingertips at the memory of their nights together. And it struck her again, a sharp lance of pain and wonder, as she scanned her cousin's fair hair and pleasingly regular features. She knew without doubt where her heart was given. Her feelings, a childish affection and hero worship for her cousin, now matured into respect and friendship, paled into insignificance beside the turbulent passion that threatened to overwhelm her as she sat with outward composure in the Long Gallery, deaf and blind to what was going on around her. It was Marlbrooke. She had claimed to hate him. But it was now many weeks since he had stirred an entirely different emotion in her. She pressed a hand to her lips as she relived the searing caress of his mouth on hers. How could she possibly have mistaken her youthful admiration for Richard as love?

'Dear Kate? What do you think?'

She blinked as she came back to the present, letting her hand fall into her lap, and flushed when she found Richard's eyes on her, a questioning gleam in them.

'Forgive me. I must have been daydreaming. How rude of me, to be sure.'

'We were talking about family,' Elizabeth explained gently. 'Mr Hotham, of course, remembers the Priory from earlier days when he came here as a small boy. Is that not so?'

'Why, yes.' His voice continued, casually conversational, a smile in his eyes as they rested on Kate. 'I would be six or seven at the time of the siege.' He spoke blandly about the painful past, without inflection. 'My mother, Sir Thomas's sister, you understand, frequently visited, particularly when my father was engaged in the war. I was often here. But that was before Kate was born, of course.'

'So your family will be in the portraits here?'

'My mother should certainly be here somewhere, as a child, if not later in life.'

'Kate, my dear, why don't you show Richard the portraits where you know the subjects. I am sure he will be interested—after all, it is his family as much as your own.'

Kate smiled, rose to her feet and obligingly led Richard down the Gallery, leaving Elizabeth to follow them with her eyes, a speculative look hidden by her lashes.

They went to stand before a large family portrait of Harleys, with Sir Thomas as a small boy sitting next to his sister Lucy, Richard's mother. But Kate could sense her cousin's lack of attention as she explained who was who.

Finally he stopped her with a light touch on her arm. 'Kate. Do you intend to return to Widemarsh today?'

'I am not certain.' For the first time in their long relationship she felt nervous in his company.

'I think we need to talk.' His lips were compressed and the look in his eyes were serious. But she did not want a serious discussion with him at this moment when her own feelings were so new, so overwhelming. And how could she possibly explain her apparent change of heart to him? What words could she possibly use to condone her betrayal of his love for her? She shrank from the prospect.

'Look at me, Kate. I need to know—'

Kate cast around in her mind for some distraction. Fortune smiled on her and she was able to interrupt in what she hoped was a matter of normality as she spied the edges of a book partially concealed by a cushion.

'Why, look. There is John Donne, under the cushions all the

time.' She escaped from Richard's grasp to go to the window seat and rescue the lost volume. 'Lady Elizabeth has missed this. Let us return—'

And then Verzons was bowing before her.

'Mistress Harley.' His eyes glanced at Richard, but with no emotion or interest other than the ordinary. 'Forgive me for the interruption, but I believe you might wish to know. I have arranged for the transport of the box to Widemarsh Manor as instructed. It should be in the hands of Mistress Gilliver by late this afternoon.'

'Thank you, Master Verzons. You are very kind.' Her eyes followed him with a thoughtful expression as he retired once more from the Gallery. Then she started to walk back to Elizabeth.

'A box?'

'Yes.' Richard's enquiry recalled her attention. 'Last night we found a box hidden in a wall cavity behind the linenfold.' It surprised her that she did not wish to explain further.

'And in it? I presume it was of interest if you have sent it to Widemarsh.'

'Harley documents. Letters and such. Most of them very old and indecipherable.' Kate shrugged, a light gesture, indicating a matter of no account. She had no intention of being any more specific. 'I have sent them to Gilliver—I thought she might wish to read them as they touched on a family matter that we had discussed.'

'I could have taken them for you.'

'Thank you, Richard, but no need. Verzons has seen to it, as you heard.'

'Well, Mr Hotham. Did you find your mother in the portraits?' As they had returned to Elizabeth's side, Richard dropped the subject of the documents.

'Yes. As a little girl with a finch on her wrist and a wicked twinkle in her eye. She had great charm, although her brother appeared to view her with some suspicion—or so the artist presumed.' He laughed, as relaxed and courteous as ever.

'Perhaps you would stay and dine with us, Mr Hotham? I am sure Kate would enjoy your company and she can take you round the Priory and gardens, if you should like it. To renew your acquaintance. We have made plans for some changes on the east side and would value your opinion.'

'You are kind.' Richard smiled and bowed over Elizabeth's hand with regret. 'But I must not encroach on your time longer. I have other errands in the area and the days are still short. If I may, I will return another day.'

After that the leave-taking was rapid. In no time at all Richard's soberly clad figure was striding from the Gallery.

'Now, what errands do you suppose he has here?' Kate's brow wrinkled as she kept her eyes on the retreating figure in some surprise.

'Kate?'

'Why, nothing, Lady Elizabeth.' Kate smiled and handed over the errant book. 'It is just that…it seemed to me that Richard had intended to stay longer. But perhaps I was mistaken.'

Kate came across Marlbrooke in the Hall where he had just come from the stables. On seeing her he immediately swept her a flamboyant bow, feathered hat sweeping the floor, taking her hand and proceeding to cover it with extravagant kisses. Kate chuckled at his levity and tightened her fingers around his in warm response—and yet there was a preoccupation about him that was almost tangible.

'What is it, my lord? Have you received bad news?'

He registered her perception and frowned slightly. 'I am not certain, but I have an uneasy feeling… I have just spoken with one of the stable lads. He rode in, the horse in a lather, as I was there. He said he had been sent on an errand last night—with a letter—with instructions to make haste. He had just returned.'

'Where did he go?'

'To Mr Simon Hotham at Staunton Court.'

'Simon?' The faintest finger of disquiet feathered down Kate's spine. Her eyes widened and flew to Marlbrooke's face. 'Who sent it?'

'The lad did not know. Neither did Jenks—he thought it was at my instigation. The letter was left there in the stables with a covering note and Jenks simply handed it over as instructed. But I have my suspicions… What is it, Kate?' His eyes narrowed. 'Do you know something of this?'

'I don't know...do you think it could have been Master Verzons?'

'Why do you ask that?'

'Because—' Kate stated her fears as calmly as she could '—he is the only one who knows about the box of letters apart from the two of us. Besides that...I know that he still retains a deep-seated loyalty to the Harley family. He might have seen it as his duty to inform my Uncle Simon if he suspected the existence of a will had come to light.'

Marlbrooke enfolded her hand for comfort within his own, but his tone was clipped and flat. 'I believe our thoughts run together on this.'

'Will you ask Master Verzons?'

'I must.' He cast his hat and gloves on to the side table. 'There is no place here in my employ for a steward with such obvious divided loyalties. I have accepted much after the complications of the war and interregnum, but not such a deliberate show of interest that is against my own—and possibly against yours.'

'Would he tell the truth?'

'I know not.' His brow furrowed in frustration as he released her hands to pace the floor. 'But the letter has been sent. We must now await to detect its content.'

'There is something I should tell you.' Kate lifted anxious eyes to the Viscount. 'Richard was here a little time ago. And left suddenly.'

'Why so?'

'Master Verzons had just informed me, in Richard's presence, that he had sent the box of documents on to Widemarsh for me, to Mistress Gilliver.'

'I see. And he told you when Richard was present. Did you tell Richard what was in the box?'

'Apart from family papers, no. I made no mention of a will.'

Marlbrooke glanced searchingly at her. 'Kate...'

'What are you thinking?' The anxiety now wrenched at her heart with sharp claws.

'Apart from yourself—' he chose his words carefully '—who would be interested in the discovery of your father's will? Who might benefit if the courts could be persuaded to grant the Priory back to the Harleys?'

'No! I won't think it.' She stepped back, away from him.

'Kate! Don't pull away from me. Think! Was marriage ever suggested between you and Richard? Was there ever an understanding between you?'

'Not an understanding exactly, but...'

'You must tell me. There could be a danger here.'

'My uncle. Not Sir Henry—he believed the political allegiance of the Hothams was too dangerous to attempt a closer alliance. He would not consider it. But Simon Hotham would have pursued a marriage. Indeed, I know that he tried to persuade Sir Henry to agree with him. Marriage to me would unite the families and strengthen Richard's own claim to the property through his mother.'

'So the Hotham interest in the Priory has always been an issue.'

'Yes. And I too—' She stopped, gripped by sudden embarrassment and looked away.

'I wondered. Tell me, Kate.' His voice was gentle, full of compassion, which encouraged her to speak from her heart.

'I believed I was in love with Richard. Before I came here, I thought that...'

'And are you?' He had already noted the tense she had deliberately chosen to use in her confession.

'No. I liked him. I knew he cared for me. But I did not love him. I did not know what love was until...'

'Until? Look at me, Kate. I think now is the time for truth between us.'

Obediently she raised her eyes and said simply, 'Until I knew you, my lord.'

He remained motionless for one long moment, suspended in the clear, unmistakable emotion that shone in her eyes. The relief that swept through him melted the sharp crystals of doubt which had plagued him for weeks. He had been right all along. She had come to love him. In spite of the urgent matters of the moment he could not prevent the intense joy warming the chill grey of his eyes or curving his lips into a tender smile. Marlbrooke raised the fingers in his clasp to his mouth in a quick salute.

'Kate—I could kiss you for that, and promise that I will—but there is too much urgency here. What do you presume Richard intended when he left here?'

Her cheeks flushed and her eyes remained fixed on his, stark fear in their depths. 'I know what you are suggesting, but I cannot believe it. Surely...'

'Think, Kate.' He curled his fingers around her wrist in a harsh bracelet. 'Why did Richard leave so quickly? What could be of such interest to Simon? If a will exists, the Hothams would be concerned to discover its content. Have *you* ever considered that, in the difficult circumstances of war, your father might have willed the property to a male line—to Simon Hotham, in fact?'

'I think...' The blood drained from her cheeks and she swallowed painfully as she accepted the terrible conclusion of her thoughts. 'I think that I need to go to Widemarsh now. I need to see Gilliver.' Her hand covered his, not in protest at his grip, but in a need for unity with him. 'Marcus, I feel a terrible premonition.'

'I am coming with you. We will see Gilliver together. Go and fetch a cloak.'

As good as his word, Marlbrooke lingered only to cover her mouth with his own in one hard, heart-stopping caress before collecting gloves and hat once more and returning to the stables.

They rode fast, side by side, their horses fresh and eating up the ground under impatient hooves. No words were spoken between them, but there was none of the exhilaration, the sheer joy of living of their previous ride together. The fear in their hearts was very evident. It was deep dusk now, the shadows echoing their dark concern, which grew with every second, with every hoofbeat.

At Widemarsh Manor Kate would have pushed open the door and entered, but Marlbrooke, close on her heels, held her back.

'It might be better if I go first.'

'What do you fear?'

He merely shrugged, unwilling to voice his concerns. The house was gloomy, with a closed-up feel. There were no lights to welcome them, no barking of dogs, no shadowy Mason to emerge and watch. Marlbrooke pushed open the door to the parlour. 'Mistress Gilliver?'

And stopped in the entrance. For there was Mason, standing by the table with one candle in her hand. There was no other light in the room for the fire had not been tended. No sound came from her, but tears streamed down her ravaged cheeks, her whole body shaking so that the candle flame flickered widely to cast grotesque shadows on the plastered walls. Wax fell unheeded on to her hand and cuff, spattering on her skirts.

'Mason?' The lady did not respond. And then Kate focused on the dark shadows at her feet.

'Aunt Gilliver?'

She lay face down, the glitter of her gems obscured. Around her, documents were spread in untidy profusion as if thrown there by a careless hand. On the table a familiar wooden box with its tarnished silver plate stood open, and empty.

And around Gilliver's head spread a dark pool of thickening blood.

Kate fell to her knees beside Gilliver's still form, heart thudding in her chest, unable to take in the evidence of extreme violence before her. In her sheltered life, she had never witnessed violent death before and her mind refused to accept it. She swallowed hard against the rising sensation of nausea and breathed deep to calm her stomach as she took in the amount of blood that had spilt from so small a body.

'Gilliver!' she whispered.

She laid a hand on the elderly lady's cheek, shocked at the blue-tinged pallor and ice of her skin. Marlbrooke came to stand behind her and, on seeing the extent of the injury, gently pushed Kate aside.

'Let me lift her.' He held the woman who had attacked him with actions and words, with dogs, and had called him her enemy, and turned her over with the utmost care. And then crouched beside Kate. The injury was now clearly visible. The blood congealing round it had seeped from a heavy blow to the side of her head, which had crushed her skull like fragile glass. Without doubt Gilliver was dead. Marlbrooke laid her back again.

Kate buried her face in her hands, not wanting to see the terrible destruction of the old lady who had been her great-aunt and had shown her some kindness and been willing to take her into her home, whatever the underlying motive.

'I am so sorry, Kate.' Marlbrooke lifted her to her feet, hands continuing to support her when her legs threatened to give way. 'There is nothing we can do.'

'I know.' Kate's eyes were dry and raw with harsh grief. Later she would cry for this vindictive old woman, but not yet: now was not the time. Her throat was choked by the horror of it.

She looked down at the face, once so bright, so alive, so full of both mischievous and malicious possibilities, now wiped clean of everything but the remnant of great pain and terror.

'But look at her,' Kate murmured, her fingers grasping Marlbrooke's sleeve. 'This was not a robbery, was it?'

'No.' For Gilliver, in death, still carried a treasure house of precious stones. The diamonds still winked wickedly on her breast, the pearls gleamed amidst the folds of the dusty black bodice of her gown, the clasp in her hair still picked up the glitter of light from the candle, through the mask of blood.

'Who would do this?' Their eyes met. There was no need to put their shared suspicions into words.

Marlbrooke pushed Kate into a chair and turned to Mason, who still stood, a silent witness to the scene. When he would have approached her she flinched from him, scurrying like a small frightened animal with bared teeth to put the width of the table between them. But she never once took her eyes from the lifeless form of her mistress.

Kate instinctively stood and moved to stand beside her, reaching out to take her hand. Mason flinched, but allowed it. It seemed to Kate that her flesh was as cold as Gilliver's. Meanwhile Marlbrooke left the room, sword drawn, to ensure the murderer was not still in the house.

'Mason.' The sound of Kate's soft voice did not register in Mason's eyes but Kate persisted. 'Mason. Who did this? Did you see?'

Mason simply stood, as if she did not hear. Instead a high keening began in her throat, a thin inhuman sound that set the hairs on Kate's neck on end.

'Did you see, Mason? Did you see who struck Gilliver? Were you here when it happened?'

Nothing, other than the eerie sound of extreme distress.

Kate looked helplessly at Marlbrooke, who had returned with a quick shake of his head and had taken a shawl from the back of a chair to place it over the figure at their feet, covering the face with its staring eyes. Gilliver had not died easily.

'What do we do?'

The sound of wheels on the drive and the hurried beat of horses' hooves caused them to stop and listen. Their eyes locked as the approaching carriage drew nearer and came to a halt outside.

'Who?'

'I wager we know the answer.' Marlbrooke's voice was cold and grim. 'I believe that we are about to receive a call from Mr Simon Hotham. How very convenient that we found Gilliver's body first.' Kate drew in her breath to steady her nerves as he went himself to open the door for the travellers. She remained where she was beside Mason, listening to the voices, trying to regain her composure.

The voices grew closer. Marlbrooke re-entered the parlour, his expression giving nothing away, followed by Richard. And then came Simon Hotham, slowly, painfully, back bent, using two sticks held in claw-like hands. Without ceremony, without a word to Kate, he dragged himself to a chair and collapsed on to it, drawing in his breath through his teeth.

'Uncle! I did not expect to see you here.' Kate could not disguise her surprise at this unlooked-for visit, or her sense of foreboding. Whatever the content of the letter, she had not expected him to make so difficult a journey and with such speed.

'Perhaps not. In fact, I am sure you did not! But it seems that I arrive at an opportune moment. I trust you are well, Katherine, in spite of your precipitate and unwise flight from Downham Hall—what can you have been thinking of? And you are Marlbrooke, I take it?'

'Mr Hotham.' The Viscount acknowledged him with a curt inclination of the head and nothing more.

But he surveyed the man before him with interest. Once tall, well muscled, imposing, a soldier in both bearing and training, now bent and wasted, fair hair thinning to show the gleam of his scalp, face hollow-cheeked and lined. He was a mere shadow of the man who had earned a name for puritanical zeal and military prowess in the service of Parliament. But his eyes were still keenly intelligent and alive as he took in the scene. His body might suffer the ravages of ill health, but his mind retained its purpose and instinct for command.

'What has happened here?' Simon demanded.

'As you see, Mistress Gilliver has been attacked.'

'Robbers? She should not have been living here alone, but she never would listen to reason. She is dead, I take it?' He stared with little obvious sympathy at the pathetic shrouded body on the floor.

'Yes, she is dead,' the Viscount confirmed in measured tones. 'But no, her jewellery is still in place. She was not robbed. Perhaps I might ask the reason for your presence here at Widemarsh Manor, Mr Hotham?'

'Gilliver asked me to come.' He shrugged as well as he was able and fixed Marlbrooke with a hard stare. 'A matter of family business, I presume—she did not make it clear.'

'*Aunt Gilliver* asked you to come?' Kate's eyes flew to Marlbrooke's face to find it bland and shuttered. She turned back to her uncle. 'It must have been a serious matter to bring you here, Uncle. I know that you rarely travel such distances now.'

'Very true,' he agreed, with a sharp glance at his niece, dropping his sticks with a clatter on to the floor beside him. 'A glass of wine would be more than acceptable, Katherine.'

Richard had uttered no word since his entrance into the parlour. He took up a position behind his father's chair, tall, powerful, in stark contrast with his infirm parent, his gaze moving critically between Kate and Marlbrooke, perhaps the faintest of smiles on his lips. Kate noted it and raised her brows in surprise.

'Did you not see Mistress Gilliver after you left me at the Priory, Richard? Was she not still alive?'

'With hindsight I regret that I did not come back here.' Richard shook his head sadly, leaving Kate uncertain of her previous impression. 'Obviously, now I wish I had. But I was expecting my father to arrive and so rode across the Common to meet him.'

'You did not say Uncle Simon was expected!'

'There was no reason to do so.' Richard was unconcerned. 'Did no one see who killed Gilliver? Had she no visitors today?'

'Mason was here, but if she saw anything she is not saying.'

'Then I may never know what she wanted from me.' Simon struggled to his feet. 'Perhaps I should look through her papers—there may be some clue. I don't suppose I shall get much of good sense from Mason unless she has changed since we last met.' He bent awkwardly to pick up one of the documents near his foot, to give it a cursory glance, and then cast a frowning stare on Kate. 'I shall stay here tonight. We must have some conversation about these matters, Katherine.'

Kate merely nodded, anticipating an uncomfortable interview.

'I shall take Kate back to the Priory with me,' Marlbrooke spoke quietly, interrupting Simon's immediate plans. 'You are free to stay here, sir, but this is not the place for Katherine to be tonight.'

'There is no need, my lord. She would be perfectly safe here under my protection.'

'She goes with me.' There was no arguing with that tone of voice or the glacial chill in the Viscount's eyes. He did not concern himself to ask Kate's wishes or even look at Simon for his acquiescence. 'I will send some of my people to care for Mistress Gilliver and make arrangements for her burial.'

With brisk efficiency the Viscount collected up the documents from the floor, shuffled them into an untidy pile and handed them to Kate. They might only be personal letters and the sorry tale of Isolde, but instinct directed him and he had no intention of leaving them in the possession of Simon Hotham.

'Those documents should remain here,' Simon objected. 'They may include the reason for Gilliver's summons. Give them to Richard, if you please, Katherine.'

'No.' She shook her head, holding the papers tightly. 'They belong to me. They are not pertinent to Gilliver's affairs.'

'I still think…'

'The documents belong to Mistress Harley. They can have no possible bearing on your business with Mistress Gilliver since the lady was unaware of their existence before this afternoon.' Marlbrooke's voice was again quiet but implacable. After the briefest of hesitations Simon Hotham merely nodded in acceptance.

'Mason, will you come with me?' Throughout the conversation the lady had remained silent, withdrawn into the shadows by the fireplace, her gaze fixed on her mistress's lifeless body. Kate now touched her gently on the shoulder. 'It would be better for you to be with me at the Priory than to stay here tonight. You can not help Mistress Gilliver now.'

Mason stepped back, startled, focusing on Kate's face for perhaps the first time since she had arrived, and then ran from the room with her strange graceless gait.

Kate shrugged, looking helplessly at Marlbrooke, and prepared to leave. But Mason returned almost immediately, carrying a cloth-covered package. She shuffled to stand in front of Kate, ignoring the other occupants of the room, looking up at her with wild eyes as her mouth twisted in an agony of grief. Her tortured gaze searched Kate's face carefully, seemed satisfied with what it found there and then allowed the covering to slip from the package on to the floor to reveal a small cedarwood box, highly carved. More a jewel casket than a document box. She pushed it into Kate's hands and fled once more into the dark regions of the house.

Kate left with Marlbrooke, a brief farewell curtsy for her uncle and cousin, carrying the box and the documents with her.

It was late when they returned to the Priory and Verzons waited on them in the entrance hall. He relieved them of their cloaks and took the documents and casket from Kate with calm efficiency and care for their comfort. Nothing disturbed his composure.

'Lady Elizabeth has retired, my lord. Will you have wine? I will arrange for it to be sent to the library, if it is your wish,' he added, aware of Marlbrooke's habits.

'Thank you, Verzons. Before you go—' as the steward turned to leave '—do you know anything of a letter that was sent from here last night?'

'A letter, my lord?'

'To Staunton Court. To Mr Simon Hotham.'

'I have no knowledge of such a letter, my lord. I will enquire for you.' His reply was everything Marlbrooke could expect from a loyal and trustworthy steward.

'If you become aware of any knowledge, I would be grateful if you would inform me. It has become a matter of some importance.'

'Be assured, my lord.'

'As a result of the letter,' Marlbrooke continued, 'Mr Hotham is at present residing with his son at Widemarsh Manor.'

Verzons's eyes flickered in what might have been surprise, but his control was firm. He inclined his head. 'There is a family connection with Mistress Adams, of course.'

Kate walked forward to stand beside Marlbrooke and placed her hand on his arm. It was clear that the deliberate gesture of unity with him was not lost on Verzons, as had been her intention.

'No, Master Verzons.' Her voice was low, but she fixed his pale eyes with a clear gaze. 'There is now no connection. Mistress Adams is dead. She has been murdered this night.'

The steward's pale skin became even more colourless as he looked from Kate to his employer and back again. 'I hope that you will accept my condolences. Has the murderer been apprehended?'

'No. But, before God, he will not go unpunished.' Kate felt Marlbrooke's muscles bunch under her hand.'

'Assuredly. As he will undoubtedly answer before God for this most wicked of sins, my lord.' Verzons bowed and walked from the room.

'Go to bed, Kate. There is nothing you can do now. I will see to matters for Gilliver. The rest can wait for tomorrow.' He enfolded her in his arms to give her comfort, brushing his lips lightly over her hair. She rested her head against his chest, grateful for the warmth and simple closeness of his body. 'It has been an exhausting evening for you. You must be tired.'

'A little.'

She turned to go as she was bidden—and then looked back.

'I finally realised tonight. Richard's words meant nothing. They never did. He told me that he loved me, that he would always love me. I was naïve, was I not? He wanted the estate, not me.'

She did not wait for his reply. Indeed he did not know what to say. His own initial relationship with her had been based on equally mercenary principles. But at least he had not compounded it by vowing his undying love for her—until he had come to know her. But that would be of no comfort to her tonight. He felt the weight of her sadness on his soul as he watched her climb the stairs to her bedchamber.

Chapter Sixteen

'Where do you suppose she got all this?' Kate examined the contents of the cedarwood box in amazement. She had spread them out on the table and now sat back to raise an enquiring eyebrow at Elizabeth.

On her return to the Priory the previous night, she had fallen into an uneasy sleep, her dreams haunted by unpleasant suspicions and bloody deeds. Waking early and feeling unhappy and unrested, she was glad to rise, wrap herself in a cloak, and walk in solitude round the gardens. It was not pleasant, there being a chill wind from the east, but she needed the space to collect her thoughts and grieve for Gilliver.

She found it difficult to shed tears for the old lady. She had not known her well and had found many of her ideas and opinions suspect, if not immoral and against the teachings of her childhood. But she had given her unknown niece an easy affection and the method of her death had sent a shock wave through Kate. She should not have died in that fashion.

And then there was the inexplicable matter of her Uncle Simon and Richard, arriving most opportunely. When she had believed that Richard would go back to Widemarsh earlier in the afternoon after he had left her at the Priory. She blocked off the trend of her thoughts. It could not be.

But the one insistent thought, which returned again and again to trouble her, was that if Richard wanted the Priory for himself, had always wanted the Priory, then he had been willing to use her without principle to achieve it. And whereas she had suffered the torment of guilt that she had once, misguidedly, promised him her love, he had had no qualms in persuading her that he looked for her hand for her own sake. And a further sly thought insinuated itself in her tortured mind. Had not Marlbrooke done the same? He had said that he loved her, and she had come to believe that it was true. And to desire it above all things. For the one brilliant, shining fact amidst all the lies and deceit was that she loved Viscount Marlbrooke. Furthermore, she had discovered to her chagrin that the events of the past had no bearing whatsoever on her present feelings towards him. When had it happened? When had love stalked her, like Isolde's spirit, to invade her senses, her heart, her very soul? Perhaps it was that moment at Glasbury when she had seen the ruin and desolation in his own life and she had accepted the vibrant joy that he could bring to hers. Or perhaps it was simply the touch of his hand on hers which set her pulses racing beyond her control. Whatever, she loved him, and had to hope that this new, bright love could withstand the bitter shadows of the past.

Marlbrooke had sent Elspeth and two other servants to Widemarsh as he had promised to care for Gilliver's remains and see to the needs of the silent Mason and the Hothams. Elspeth had returned at daybreak with the news that Mason was nowhere to be found. There was nothing that Kate could do about it but await the turn of events.

But for now she was seated before a smoking fire, the wind being in the wrong direction, as usual, in the Long Gallery with Elizabeth at one of her endless pieces of stitchery and Felicity picking out a mournful tune on the spinet. And in front of her lay a fortune in precious metals and jewellery.

'Just look at this.' She picked up a gold pendant, enamelled in green and white, set with diamonds and pearls. Inside were two miniatures of a man and a woman in Elizabethan dress. A delightful keepsake, if not quite in the modern taste. 'And she was wearing as much again, if not more, when she was struck down.'

'Do you suppose they are Harley heirlooms?' Elizabeth trailed a rope of fine pearls through her fingers, holding them up to the light.

'I was not aware that we had any. And unless my mother

recognises any of them it will be impossible to tell. Gilliver must have been like a magpie, picking up every sparkling object that she could find.'

'This looks very old.' Elizabeth touched a gold pectoral cross with a gentle fingertip. 'And certainly it needs a good clean. These are emeralds, I think, but the setting is broken and badly tarnished.'

'And this—' Kate picked up an intricate collar '—is positively mediaeval!'

'I regret her death, Kate.' Elizabeth frowned at the hoard as she chose her words carefully. 'She was not an easy neighbour to live with, but she did not deserve to die as she did. And for what? If you are correct in your assumption, nothing was taken and no search seems to have been made or anything broken at Widemarsh.'

'No. Only the letters were scattered around, and that may simply be that she dropped them when she fell.' Kate fell silent, fingering a pretty silver-and-enamel ring with entwined hands and a heart. 'I am sure that Mason knew, but she would not say. Indeed, I am not sure that she *can* speak, but she seemed too afraid to communicate in any way other than to push this box into my hands as I was leaving.'

'Would the documents be of interest to anyone—other than you and Gilliver?'

'If they knew what they contained—then no. They were only family letters.'

'I see.'

Kate looked up from the ring and fixed Elizabeth with her cool, clear gaze. 'My uncle and Richard arrived together at Widemarsh after we did. We had already found Gilliver's body. Richard said that he had not returned to Widemarsh earlier in the day.' It was a statement of fact with no inflection in her voice.

'Of course. So they are not involved in any way.' Was there the faintest question in Elizabeth's voice?

The same thoughts struggled for acceptance—or denial—in both minds.

'Would it be possible—this is very difficult—that whoever did it...that he thought that a will was there amongst the letters too?' Elizabeth continued to arrange the jewels before her on the table.

'It is possible,' Kate acknowledged. 'Only Marlbrooke and myself knew that there was no will.'

'Inheritance of valuable property can cause terrible rifts in families, dear Kate.'

'Yes.' Kate smiled a little as she felt an inner warmth within her heart at the delicate sympathy expressed by the older woman, but she could not find the words to tell her that Verzons had probably informed Simon of the box of documents on the previous day, and had ensured that Richard was aware. She grimaced and turned back to the box, lifting a final chain of tarnished gold links from the bottom. 'Another medieval treasure. I wonder who wore this hundreds of years ago.'

And then she became very still, the links of the chain falling from her hand on to the table.

From the bottom of the box, creased, folded and bearing a crumbling red seal, Kate drew out an official document. Her fingers were unsteady as she opened and spread it on the table amidst the gems. Her eyes scanned the close-written lines rapidly. Then she handed it to Elizabeth.

'Aunt Gilliver had this all the time.' Kate's voice was without expression.

'A will!'

'Why did she not say so? Why did she not show me? Instead she wove some tale of it being hidden in a priest hole at the Priory—she even gave me the keys, you remember. I cannot understand her motives. When she wrote to me, did she intend to give me this? If so, what changed her mind?'

Elizabeth read the document through twice and then returned it to Kate, her expression grave. 'I confess that I am as bewildered as you are. But more important—I believe that this complicates matters for you on a personal level. Am I correct?' Written early in 1643, mere weeks after the birth of his baby daughter, the will was a sharp reflection of Sir Thomas's deep concerns for the security of his family and property in the event of his untimely death.

'It is not what I had hoped for. Why did my father do this?'

'For safety in a time of great danger?' Elizabeth reached out to cover Kate's hands with her own as they rested on top of the document. 'If he feared for his life, he would have done everything in his power to protect his young wife and baby daughter.'

'I suppose so.'

'The entail would not necessarily be broken. It would simply be a sensible arrangement with you as ward of your uncle Simon, leading to a dynastic marriage when you came of age.'

'With Richard.'

'That is what your father envisaged, certainly.'

'And Simon holding the reins until I reached my majority. Or even longer if I became his daughter by marriage. It puts a different light on Simon's involvement, does it not? He could hardly claim to be disinterested in the outcome of my inheritance. Do you suppose that he knew of this?'

Elizabeth sat quietly for a moment and considered the sensitive matters thrown up by the contents of Gilliver's box.

'We cannot know. But more importantly—would you wish for this, Kate? For marriage with Richard?'

'No.' Kate kept her eyes on the document before her. 'I will marry Marlbrooke. After all, the contracts are all drawn up.'

'I am not talking expediency, Kate! Forgive me, but I had thought that you were not indifferent to your cousin.'

'That is true,' Kate admitted in a low voice. 'He had spoken to me of marriage, and before I came here I thought that...but I do not love him. I realise that now.' She ran her fingers round Marlbrooke's ring on her finger. 'And I cannot rid myself of the gravest suspicions about Gilliver's death.'

She began to pack the jewels back into their box, a deep line between her brows, but left the sealed letter on the table.

'What do I do with this?' she asked. 'I am much in need of advice.'

They were interrupted by Verzons's soft footed approach. 'My lady.' He bowed, indicating the two figures standing in the doorway behind him.

'Forgive me, my lady. I took the liberty of admitting these gentlemen, knowing them to be closely related to Mistress Harley. Mr Hotham requires urgent conversation with her about Mistress Gilliver's affairs.'

'Of course, Verzons.' Lady Elizabeth smothered a sigh. 'You did right. Bring wine, if you please.' She turned to acknowledge Simon and Richard Hotham, but remained seated. 'Welcome, gentlemen. Kate's family will always be welcome here. Please sit. I understand your complaint, sir.' She inclined her head towards Simon as he lowered his limbs to a chair with a grunt of pain. 'I too suffer. Kate's knowledge has helped me greatly.'

He inclined his head. 'She was well taught by her mother in herbal lore.'

'Indeed. What can we do to help you? Marlbrooke is expected back at any time, but I will help all I can. I trust that you will accept my condolences on the sad death of Mistress Adams.'

Richard too sat. His face was solemn, as might be expected on so difficult an occasion, but Kate noted that he made no attempt to engage her attention or meet her eyes. His concentration was all for his father.

'This is not altogether in the way of a social visit, my lady.' Simon's words were impatient to the point of brusqueness and barely polite. 'I have demands on my time and I do not wish to linger at Widemarsh longer than absolutely necessary. The house is too damp for my liking and comfort. Katherine took some papers away with her yesterday. I find that I have a need to see them.'

'As I explained, Uncle Simon...' Kate executed an elegant curtsy '...they are personal family letters, from last century for the most part. They have no bearing on Gilliver's affairs.'

'If I could inspect them, I can satisfy myself and will return them to you instantly. Then the matter will be closed.'

'I am sorry, sir.' Her voice was gentle, but with a level of determination that could not be misread. 'They are not for general perusal.'

Simon clearly tried for patience. 'But surely they are not secret, Katherine? This is such a small matter and not one to lock horns over.'

'No, indeed, sir. Surely not!' Elizabeth tried to smooth over the growing ripples of confrontation. 'They are personal letters. I have seen them—there is nothing of value except for family gossip.'

Simon ignored the interruption. 'I demand to see the letters, Katherine.' There was a snap of anger now.

'Why?' Kate raised her chin. 'What do you expect to find?'

A glance passed between Simon and Richard. It was Richard who spoke.

'We believe there is a will—written by your father in the last year of the siege when affairs were difficult in the war. We understand that he left the care of the Priory to my father, to administer in your name. And he gave his blessing for our union.'

Kate shook her head. 'I do not have such a document.' Her innate honesty flinched at the blatant lie, but she spoke it without compunction. 'It was not in the box discovered at the Priory.' At least here was truth!

'Gilliver was a cunning woman with her own devious ends,' Simon continued. 'I believe that she hid the will. Could I hazard a guess that you have indeed found it? I will not leave this house without it!'

Kate shook her head, barely breathing when she saw the direction of Richard's gaze. The document with its revealing red seals, momentarily forgotten, lay on the table beside her, obvious to anyone who cared to look.

'Tell me about *that,* Kate,' Richard requested in deceptively mild tones. '*That* document is not simply a family letter, is it?'

Kate stood defiantly. 'It is my property.'

Richard rose to his feet and stepped forward. 'I would hesitate to use force, my dear cousin, but you must see that in the circumstances you have no choice but to hand it over.' His smile caused a finger of fear to trace its chilling path down her spine.

'Really, sir! What can you be about?' Elizabeth pushed herself to her feet in an attempt to intervene. Felicity had already abandoned the spinet and was fussing with anxious movements behind her ladyship. 'Am I to be threatened in my own home?'

'There is no need for any unpleasantness.' Richard barely glanced at her. 'Give me that paper, Katherine.'

'I will not.'

As Richard moved determinedly to take the letter, Kate snatched it up and backed away, holding it behind her skirts. Richard pursued, intent and dangerous, all trace of conciliation vanished in his need to secure the document

'The will, Kate!'

He lunged quicker than she could react, to grasp her wrist in a painful hold, to drag her closer. It would be so easy to wrest the paper from her. In that moment Kate knew that she could not allow the document to fall into Simon's hands, to give him the opportunity to make her a tool for his manipulation. She wrenched herself away from Richard and with a sure aim, born of panic, flung the paper into the fireplace.

There was a bright flame. A sizzle of red wax. The paper sank to ashes. As did all Simon's plans.

'You fool,' Simon gasped, lips drawn back from his teeth in a snarl, hands clenched on the chair arms, furious at his inability to rise. 'What have you done? You have ruined any chance we had of turning the courts in our favour and reducing this Royalist vermin back to the gutter where they belong.'

Richard's self-control snapped as the quick flare of fire died away. Eyes blazing with uncontrolled fury, he raised his hand and struck Kate, an open-handed blow to her face. There was a sharp report of flesh against flesh and she fell to the floor to cower at his feet, more in shock that he should use force against her than in actual pain.

'What have you done?' he echoed his father. His face was contorted with rage. 'It could all have been ours. Yours and mine. The law would uphold your father's wishes. What possessed you? Has marriage to Marlbrooke become so desirable? Has he seduced you with his Court ways? Has he bought you with his body? I would not have thought you so shallow, little cousin.' He seized her arm to pull her roughly to her feet, shaking her as a dog would shake a rat. 'Yet you were prepared to accept my love and devotion not so long ago—when there was nothing else in your life. It seems that a title and a fortune can make any woman fickle in her affections. You disgust me!' He shook her again, his self-control in tatters.

Kate shrank from him, afraid of further violence from a cousin whom she no longer recognised. There was no escape.

'If you have any more illuminating observations on the nature and inclinations of the female sex, I suggest that you address them to me!'

Marlbrooke stood unobserved until that moment in the doorway. In the emotionally charged atmosphere no one had heard him enter. There was temper in his face, all the more deadly because of his icy control. He had not been present to see the attack on Kate but he sensed the uncontrolled violence in Richard's stance. His voice was low, calm, but there was no doubting the lash of command.

Silence fell on the room as he walked forward with deceptive languor. He went first to Kate, removing her without difficulty from Richard's grasp, pushing her back into a chair with determined gentleness and a brief caress to her hair. His smile, for her alone, reassured her, but she was aware of the tangible aura of danger that shimmered around him. He laid a reassuring hand on his mother's shoulder, and then turned to his guests with an elegant Court bow.

'I dislike your behaviour towards my family in my house, and I particularly dislike your actions and words towards my betrothed wife.' He might have been discussing the weather or the value of a horse. 'How unfortunate that I was not at home earlier. So much unpleasantness could have been avoided. It amazes me that, as gentlemen, you should feel the need to threaten these ladies with physical coercion.'

'She destroyed the will!' Richard was still rigid with fury, face flushed, hands clenched into fists, but now watchful, impressed, despite himself, by Marlbrooke's arrogant mastery of the situation. He ran a finger between the lace and his throat where his cravat suddenly seemed too tight for comfort.

'Since it was Mistress Harley's property, I suggest that she had that right.'

'It is my right—'

'You have no rights here. I call you to account for your conduct. To lay hands on a lady in such a fashion is unwarrantable. You will answer to me for this, sir.'

'If I had my youth and health, I would make you pay for this interference in our affairs, my lord Marlbrooke,' Simon raged, in his impotence of age and infirmity.

'But you cannot.' Marlbrooke inclined his head courteously, his desire to react, to destroy, to demand recompense in blood for Richard's treatment of Kate held in check. 'Therefore your son must answer to me for your sins.'

'Gladly.' Richard's anger carried him on into uncharted waters.

'Then there is no better time than here and now, I suggest.' The deadly glint in the Viscount's eyes made his intent clear to all.

'No. You must not!' A silent witness of events until this moment, Elizabeth pushed herself to her feet in distress. 'You must not prolong the battles of the war. It should have all been buried long ago. Violence will solve nothing—merely cause more pain.'

Marlbrooke shook his head, the pleasant smile on his lips at odds with the expression in his eyes. 'There is really no choice in the matter, madam. As I am sure Mr Hotham will concur.' He stripped off his coat and waistcoat, tucked up the lace ruffles at his cuffs.

'I await your pleasure, Mr Hotham.' He drew his sword with a deadly hiss as the steel left the scabbard—and waited.

Without hesitation, driven by a deadly combination of intense disappointment and a keen sense of failure, Richard stripped off his coat likewise and drew his sword. The two men faced each other, worthy adversaries, of similar height and build. Perhaps Marlbrooke was a little taller, but neither man had a true advantage in either reach or weight. Both had experience of swordplay. As the son of a notable soldier, Richard had been well groomed by his father, who had accepted nothing but his son's best efforts to master the military skills worthy of a gentleman. Marlbrooke's experience was more varied. As a young man he had seen action in the final years of the Civil War, albeit very young, and later at Worcester. In more recent years at Court he had been able to indulge his skills and pleasure in fencing in more light-hearted contests.

But this clash of interest was real, no sham for the entertainment of idle courtiers. Both men now recognised the inevitability of this meeting. A sudden shaft of sun glanced through a window to touch Richard's fair hair and regular features with flame as in a blessing. But Kate's eyes were all for Marlbrooke's dark magnificence as he stretched and flexed the muscles in his shoulders and sword arm. The blood seemed to be congealing sluggishly in her own veins and she had to remind herself to breathe when the potential for untimely death hovered so close to them.

Their swords hissed together in an initial kiss of steel against steel. Then Marlbrooke lowered his and stepped back as if he had come to a difficult decision. 'I believe, Mr Hotham, that this challenge is also in retribution for the death of Gilliver Adams.'

Richard also drew back, his expression carefully controlled; no hint of either guilt or regret. 'You have no proof for such an accusation.' His voice was clear and steady.

'No?'

'We know that no one was present when Gilliver died.'

'Mason was,' Marlbrooke reminded him quietly. 'Mason knows who killed her.'

'But she will not speak.' Richard was confident now, a triumphant smile on his lips. 'I repeat, you have no proof. You cannot set yourself up as my executioner for a crime that you are unable to prove that I committed. If you kill me, it is murder, my lord.'

'Mason may not speak—but she can write.' Marlbrooke raised a quizzical brow.

'I do not believe you!' But Richard's fair brows drew together.

'Kate, if you would oblige me.' The Viscount never took his eyes from Richard. 'Search in the pocket of my coat. You will find a document.'

Kate hastened to do as instructed, fingers suddenly clumsy. She searched the pockets and brought out a folded sheet of parchment.

'That is the proof,' Marlbrooke explained in conversational tones. 'Mason wrote down the name of the murderer. She was there and saw who struck Gilliver down—a cowardly act against a defenceless old woman—when she refused to hand over the documents.'

Kate opened the folded document, looked briefly at the contents, and placed it folded again on the table at Elizabeth's elbow.

Richard looked towards the document; the possible repercussions of such evidence slapped at him. His previous control wavered and disintegrated at the prospect and he snarled at Marlbrooke, his face contorted in anger. 'Gilliver was an interfering old witch. She knew all about the will. She had it all along. She was manipulating us all, pulling the strings to make us dance to her tune. She enjoyed every minute of it and laughed in my face. She had no intention of doing right by the family, and when I asked to look at the letters she refused. She did not know the meaning of truth—all she wanted was to weave her own little plots and schemes like a spider in a web. Well, I was not willing to play the fly who was caught up in her sticky spinnings merely for her own entertainment. Yes, I killed her! And I have no regrets.'

It was an outpouring as revealing as it was shocking to those listening, who thought they had known this well-mannered, moderate young man whose hands now shook with violent intent and whose words burned with vitriol.

'Enough, Richard!' Simon broke into the silence, harsh and grim. 'The old woman is dead. Let us get this over with.'

'By all means. I call you to account for the blood of Gilliver Adams. I am at your service.' Marlbrooke saluted with easy grace and took guard.

They circled each other, watchful, wary. Elizabeth sat in silence, anguish in her eyes, hands clenched in her lap, ignoring the sharp complaint from ill-used knuckles. Kate took up a position behind her, hand lightly on her shoulder in mutual support. Even Felicity left the spinet to stand irresolutely on the edge of the scene, her eyes darting from one to another of the major players in the drama. Simon sat forward, willing on his son, wishing that he had the physical strength to have taken on the responsibility himself, eyes never leaving the conflict before him.

They came together in a rush of adrenaline-fired action. Quick thrust and parry, boots thudding on the oak boards where Kate and the Viscount had trod the measures of the pavane. But now it was a deadly dance of death. Cut. Parry. Slice. The blades swept low then high, sparks glinting blue as their edges scraped and clashed. They fought with controlled agility, eyes locked, their skills honed and polished and now used to such murderous intent. They circled, blades testing for any weakness. Richard was the first to see an opening and lunged. Although Marlbrooke reacted within the blink of an eye, the sword whispered along his ribs to be followed by a crimson line that seeped through his shirt and into the sash around his waist.

Richard lowered his sword, point to the ground, and stepped back. 'You are hit, my lord. Are you now satisfied?'

'It is of no account.' Marlbrooke's response was clipped. 'Gilliver's death will not be so easily avenged.' He wiped the sweat from his eyes with his sleeve and renewed the attack.

Fierce, relentless, forcing each other back and forth along the extent of the Gallery, the challenge continued. Sweat dripped and blood stained. They were indeed well matched and there was no sign of weakness in either man. But the exertion was, by its very nature, beginning to take its toll on both. Muscle and sinew strained and their breath became laboured and harsh. The contest could not continue indefinitely, and both knew it. The end must come for one of them. It was a duel to the death. The watchers knew it too and were fixed with horror at the prospect.

The contest continued along its deadly path. Thrust, parry, re-treat, each protagonist concentrating on nothing but the eyes and sword of his opponent. Searching for a weakness, a hesitation, a stumble, any opportunity to allow access and claim victory. The fine steel kissed and scraped, seeking to bury itself to the hilt in blood and flesh.

Inevitably it came. Feeling the first twinge of strength begin to drain from sword arm and wrist, Marlbrooke played his hand. He feinted to the right, as if to attack Richard's unprotected left shoulder, only to change direction to threaten his ribs below the heart. Richard read the intention and parried, successfully beating the thrust down. Marlbrooke recovered with lightning speed, thrust again and, expecting another feint, Richard hesitated. For one fatal moment he held back, his eyes meeting the Viscount's in horror as he read the intention there and realised that his judge-ment had faltered. He had fallen into the trap. Marlbrooke con-tinued the thrust. And his sword, driven on with all the force of his body, buried itself in Richard's chest.

Without even a cry, Richard fell to the floor, sword arm out-flung, face ashen, lips drained of all colour as his body was drained of life. The only movement was the slow spreading of bright blood to soak into his shirt and pool on the floor beneath him.

Marlbrooke stood, head bowed, sword in hand, blood dripping from his ribs to the floor. He raised an unsteady hand to wipe the sweat from his face. An agonised groan from Simon, his dreams in shreds at his feet, struggling to his feet to reach his stricken son, went unnoticed. Kate darted forward to kneel beside her cousin, to touch his face, his hands with nervous fingers.

'He is dead. So much blood.' Her voice was soft, almost a caress, drowned in disbelief. She looked wildly round, unable to take in the tragedy beneath her hands. 'Richard is dead!'

There was no one to help her, to remove this second burden of death. Her immediate impulse was to escape from this deadly turn of events. She sprang to her feet, gathered her skirts in her hands, heedless of the smears of blood, and fled the room, heels clicking on the polished boards.

'Kate!' Marlbrooke knew in that moment that he must prevent her, knew that she would need some source of solace in her grief.

But she gave no response, did not even turn her head, but continued her flight.

'But the paper. Mason's confession.' Felicity had picked up and now held out the folded sheet, which she had just unfolded, and broke the ensuing silence in an uncertain voice. 'There is no name here.'

'No.' Marlbrooke's austere response did not encourage discussion.

'So Mason did not name the killer?'

'No, she did not. But she did not have to, did she?' He looked down at the body of Richard Hotham, his expression shuttered and unreadable. 'The culprit was perfectly willing to confess, after all. I suppose justice has been done.'

But there was no victory in it. He would see Kate's white face and shocked eyes in his nightmares. Just as she would undoubtedly see Richard's blood on his hands.

'Oh, Marcus! What an impossible situation this is.' Lady Elizabeth closed the door firmly behind her when she finally ran her son to earth in the library. He had been avoiding her with some success for the past several days. She seated herself in the chair next to his desk, arranged the folds of her stiff brocade skirts to her satisfaction as if she intended to stay, and smiled innocently in answer to his raised eyebrow. He would avoid her no more. She would stay until her planned conversation with him was complete and to her liking.

'I know it. It is damnable.' Marlbrooke sat behind his desk, estate papers strewn before him, accepting the inevitable when he saw the determination in his mother's face. He smiled ruefully and put down the quill pen, which he had not been using to any effect.

He looks so tired, she thought. He covers it well, but the strain is beginning to show. In spite of the tragic circumstances, it amused her that her notorious son should be disturbed to any degree by the vagaries of a woman. She hid a smile at the prospect, effectively disguising her inordinate fondness for him, as she allowed her eyes to linger on his stern but handsome features.

'We seem to be living in a nightmare from which there is no escape.' She folded her hands in her lap and fixed him with her clear gaze, which he had inherited. 'I cannot believe that you actually fought a duel and killed a man, here in this house.'

'It was not my obvious intention, ma'am.' He was cool, non-committal, any expression in his face carefully hidden from her. This was not going to be an easy interview. 'In fact, I remember that it was a near-run thing. I have a painful scratch along my ribs to prove it. Would you perhaps have preferred that Richard had killed *me*?'

'Of course not! You know I did not mean any such thing! I wish we were back in London.' For an unguarded moment Elizabeth picked fretfully at the lace edging of her deep cuffs. 'Life seemed so much more predictable there.'

'I will transport you back there whenever you wish. It would probably be a good idea for you to leave this place.' His tone was perfectly conciliatory, perfectly distant.

'That was not what I meant either! You are being obtuse, Marlbrooke!' It was time to be more direct if she wished to force her son in to any sort of personal comment or show of emotion in this duel of words. 'Should we, do you think, have allowed Simon Hotham to return home?'

'Why not? We could not have detained him. It is better that he is not here in the circumstances. Whatever his involvement in recent events, he has lost his son. He would not wish to be away from home.'

'Do you really suppose he was responsible for Mistress Adams's death?'

'Simon or Richard? In all probability Simon was the instigator. Without doubt, he is a man driven by ambition, disillusioned over the past and fearful of the future. Embittered and vengeful. I remember Kate's words and she had the right of it. All his hopes were pinned on Richard, the will and an alliance with Katherine. With Richard as the tool to carry out his devious plotting, Gilliver was an easy target if she was alone and refused to hand over the relevant papers.' He pushed his fingers impatiently through his hair. 'And now, with Richard dead and the will destroyed, his plans have gone awry and he will have lost his hold on the future. Nothing left to him but his pride and his declining health. I should feel compassion for his loss—but I cannot find it in my heart to do so.'

'No. You should not try too hard, Marcus. Simon has brought

fatal harm and distress to too many to deserve our sympathy. And we still have no idea where Mason is.' Elizabeth pressed on. They would reach the nub of the problem eventually. 'I feel in some sense responsible for her.'

'There is no reason why you should—but I understand. I too feel that we should give her some protection. She is probably in hiding in the attics or cellars at Widemarsh.'

'I suppose.'

Giving in to the silent criticism that sat so elegantly before him, Marlbrooke pushed back his chair and strode to the window to look out over the drear scene of cloud and rain, which so perfectly mirrored his mood. And he knew exactly what his mother intended. With a shrug of compliance, he turned to face her, a dry and not particularly pleasant smile curving his lips.

'You have not—very tactfully, if deliberately—mentioned the worst part of this débâcle, my dear mother. Perhaps you should spell it out before we both die of anticipation!'

'I know.' She sighed a little. 'We both know. It is Kate.'

The Viscount strode back and flung himself into his chair once more, his dark brows meeting in a heavy frown as the memory of his recent efforts to see Kate flooded through him.

On the third abortive visit to Widemarsh Manor, having been refused entry on the two previous occasions by a firmly bolted door, there was a dangerous light in the Viscount's eye, but he kept his temper reined in. There was, after all, he admonished himself, nothing to be gained from frustrated aggression. He dismounted in the courtyard, handed the Falcon over to a stable lad and knocked on the door. This time the door opened a merest crack; the dark eyes of an elderly servant gleamed through.

'Yes, m'lord? I didn't expect you again so soon.'

'I would speak with Mistress Harley.' Marlbrooke felt that he was reliving a nightmare. He had been here before.

'Mistress Harley is not receiving visitors, m'lord.' The door closed in confirmation.

Marlbrooke's patience finally snapped. He hammered on the door with the haft of his riding whip as if to wake the devil. 'Open the door or I will surely break it down.' His voice remained remarkably calm, but there was no denying the change in temperature.

The door opened again almost immediately. 'The lady says she's seeing no one, m'lord. I can do nothing for you.'

Before it could be closed on him again, Marlbrooke put his shoulder to the door and pushed so that it smacked back against the wall. The servant retreated hurriedly. Marlbrooke advanced.

'Be so good as to tell the lady that I do not leave this place until I have seen her.'

From her concealment in the parlour, amidst the dusty neglect and bunches of herbs, Kate listened to the potent exchange. She would have to see him, but what would she say? The muscles in her throat tightened at the prospect. She felt torn apart. She longed to see him, to feel the touch of his hands, to hear his voice—just to be in his presence. But, engulfed with guilt and remorse, what would she say to him that would make any sense and that he would understand? She must pay for her pride and wilfulness. Perhaps the price was too great to be borne—how would she exist if she never saw him again? She loved him so much, yet she had damned them both with blood and she would have to live with it. For the first time she knew some of the torment that kept Isolde from her grave.

Gathering her courage, Kate stepped from the parlour into the hall. 'There is no need for Crofton to carry your message, my lord. I am here.'

Marlbrooke's frustration remained, but his anger evaporated at the sight of her. She looked so drained and vulnerable. Her eyes were wide with apprehension and something that he could not name. He wanted nothing more than to take her in his arms and smooth away all her fears, kiss the shadows beneath her eyes, but he could not. There was too much between them, an invisible barrier, impossible as yet to breach.

'Katherine.'

She stood back so that he might enter the parlour. She followed, but remained at some distance, a stretch of oak boards between them.

'What do I say to you, Katherine?'

'Why, nothing, my lord. I do not blame you for what happened, but rather myself. Because of our marriage and my determination to pursue the claim of the Harley family, two people are dead. Whether it is your fault or mine I truly know not. But I carry their deaths on my heart.'

'Will you let their deaths come between us, then?' He placed his hat and gloves carefully on the table beside him, thinking rapidly of any argument that would carry weight with her in her distress.

'I feel that they are between us whether I wish it or no.'

'My love for you is not enough?' It was as if he were fighting his way through an impenetrable mist that held his limbs captive and allowed no progress.

'Your love is magnificent, but I have repaid it with murder.'

'Then will you let me comfort you?' He wanted to hold her, just to touch her but could not. What was he to do? 'Do you return my love?'

'I love you. But there is no comfort and I cannot talk about it. Not yet. The guilt is too strong. What right have I to be happy when I have caused such distress? Richard and Gilliver dead. Mason lost somewhere. Simon wrapped in grief. Why should I take my happiness at their expense?'

But what about my happiness? The response echoed in Marlbrooke's head, yet he chose to remain silent. Such a question would merely compound the issue.

'Kate—I can do nothing to help you.' She was such a slight figure to carry so much burden on her own. But he could not fight her resistance. He turned to pick up his hat and gloves from the table. He hated to leave her alone at Widemarsh with her memories. 'Would you at least come to the Priory with me?'

'No.'

He bowed in acknowledgement—but vowed that he would not leave her unprotected. He would send some of his own people to keep watch. He took possession of her hand and raised it to his lips. It was cold, so cold. He could find no words to ease her heart or his own. He bowed again and strode out.

Kate remained in the parlour. She refused to watch him ride away, but stood, tears once more coursing down her cheeks, unable to decide what to do next, now that she had wilfully destroyed her one true hope of happiness. And she did not know how much will power it took for him not to bundle her into a cloak and carry her off to the Priory.

The gulf between them was vast.

* * *

'What do you want me to say?' the Viscount demanded of his mother. 'You know the situation! When I forced the issue I could not get through to her. It was as if there was an unbridgeable chasm, with the bodies of Gilliver and Richard between us. And since then she refuses to see me. Even to open the door. I have been to Widemarsh three times since, but short of battering down the door I cannot force her to come out. I will admit that I am tempted to do just that. God save me from stubborn females—and managing ones!' He returned his mother's placid smile of triumph with a wry grimace.

'Is there nothing you can do? She is probably as unhappy as you are.'

'Unhappy! Ha! You do not know the half of it!' He surged to his feet again and took a hasty turn about the library. 'Short of standing on the gravel beneath her window and shouting my requests for all the world to hear, I can do nothing. What is she thinking? Is she able to sleep? Is she eating?' As he turned to look at his mother, hands clenched in frustration, she realised the true depth of his concern and impatience at his forced inaction. 'I feel helpless!'

'She is hurt. Do you remember her words as she ran from the room?'

'Of course I do. They are engraved on my soul.' He turned his back on her. 'And the horror in her eyes when she looked at me with Richard's blood on my sword.'

There is so much blood. I cannot bear it!

'And so she sees her cousin's blood on *my* hands,' he continued, spine held rigid beneath the soft velvet coat. 'This is no basis for marriage. Her husband guilty of killing the man she loved.'

'Marcus—' Elizabeth's voice might be gentle, but the tone was strong with conviction '—Kate did not love Richard.'

'No?' His tone was bleak. 'Probably not. But his blood is still on my hands.'

'She told me that she did not. Affection, yes. Family loyalties, of course. And a lifetime of upbringing when they saw much of each other. She thought she did—I believe it was a strong case of hero worship—but it is many weeks since she believed that she loved him.'

'How can I know that?' He could barely disguise the hint of

desperation as he raised his eyes to his mother's. 'How can I know what to do?'

'Don't forget, Marcus, she deliberately destroyed her father's will. If she had wanted Richard, wanted her father's wishes to be carried out, why not simply hand the document over to Simon as he demanded? She had the choice, and chose not to, but to destroy it.'

'Yes. Of course.' He sat again, some semblance of calm restored. 'It breaks my heart to think of her alone at Widemarsh.' Their eyes met and held. He remembered Kate's recognition of Elizabeth's grace and generosity in spite of all she suffered. And marvelled at it.

'Do you want me to interfere?' Elizabeth asked finally. Anything to heal the hurt buried beneath her son's carefully controlled features.

'What's this? Are you asking for permission?' His smile at last was one of genuine amusement. 'I do not believe it!'

'Of course. I have an idea.'

'Will I approve?'

'Not at all! But sons do not have to approve their mother's actions.'

'I mislike the tone of this.'

'Leave it to me!'

A comfortable travelling coach pulled by four matched bays drew up before Widemarsh Manor. There was only one occupant. Jenks jumped down from the box to open the carriage door and give his strong arm to the lady who descended with careful steps. She shook out her skirts, pulled her cloak around her, and nodded to her coachman with perfect equanimity.

'Knock on the door, if you please, Jenks. Loudly.'

Thunderous knocking from the haft of Jenks's coaching whip echoed round the courtyard.

No answer.

'Knock again.'

Jenks complied.

'Katherine. Open the door. It is Elizabeth Oxenden.'

The shortest of moments passed and then the came the sound of keys and bolts. The door swung back.

Kate stood there in the doorway. Her face was pale but composed, her emotions well in hand.

'You will not see my son,' Elizabeth explained. 'I can understand that. But will you allow me to enter?'

Without a word, Kate stood back and led the way into the parlour.

There they stood and looked at each other.

'For you to make such a journey, matters must be very grave.' Kate's voice was a little husky, strained with frequent tears and disuse over the past days.

'Of course they are grave, my dear and foolish child! When the two people I care about most are so clearly unhappy, it is of the gravest!'

The mild endearment and Elizabeth's exasperated smile were Kate's undoing. Despite her best intentions, she covered her face as tears began to slide down her cheeks. She could do nothing to stem them.

'Come here. Dearest Kate. What is so terrible to make you cry so?'

Kate sobbed uncontrollably in her arms as Elizabeth guided her to the settle before the fireplace. They sat and Elizabeth continued to hold her, stroking her hair, allowing her to weep.

'What distresses you so? There is no need.'

'My own mother would not come to see me.' Kate gulped and sniffed. 'But you did.'

Elizabeth was stricken, reduced to silence, now aware of the depth of Kate's isolation.

'She never even sent a letter with Simon. I know I left Downham Hall without her knowledge, but I thought she might have written...'

'There, now. Perhaps she did not know that Simon planned to come. I have come instead.' Such meaningless words in the circumstances. Elizabeth held Kate as the tears still racked the slight body, murmuring more empty words of comfort, but giving her the solace of her enfolding arms. When the sobs began to abate, she produced a handkerchief, dried her cheeks and fetched a glass of wine from the court cupboard.

'I am so sorry.' Kate sniffed, now embarrassed. 'I did not intend to inflict myself on you in such a way.'

'Nonsense! Who better to dry your tears. Now.' She gave her the glass of wine again and watched as Kate sipped obediently.

'Better? Good! Then let us try to put everything to rights. When are you going to see my son and allow him to talk to you?'

Kate had not expected such a direct approach, but decided on honesty after all. 'I do not know that he wishes to see me,' she explained simply, her eyes on her fingers clenched in the handkerchief in her lap.

'Of course he does not want to see you! He has only been here—how many times in as many days?—and returned home in a temper with you and himself when you have barred the door. Of course he does not wish to see you! At this moment he has gone rough shooting and is pretending that he is enjoying it! He snarls and snaps and drinks too much. He is perfectly happy!' Kate had to smile at the heavy irony. 'Do see him, dear Kate. It will make life better for all of us. I have never known him be so concerned about the affections of a woman before. You have made quite an impression on him!'

'I do not know what to say to him. My family have so much to answer for—he may have decided that he could achieve a better marriage after all.' Kate continued to sniff at the doleful prospect.

'We do not choose our families, dear Kate.'

'No. But murder. Lies and deceit. If I had not started this quest, would Gilliver still be alive? And Richard! I cannot bear to think of it.'

'You must not blame yourself.'

'But I encouraged Richard to believe that I would marry him. He thought that I loved him. I am not guiltless in this.'

'No, but his actions went far beyond anything you could be held responsible for.'

'But he is dead. My cousin is dead!' She held tight to Elizabeth's hands as tears threatened to fall again. 'I know that he probably killed Gilliver, but I cannot forget his kindness and companionship to me as a child.'

The two ladies sat in silent grief and, although Elizabeth inwardly winced at the fierce grasp of her hands, she would not have loosed that hold for the world.

Eventually, sensing a restoration of calm to Kate's overwrought emotions, she took control of the situation again. 'So, when are you going to put my son out of his misery? You realise that he thinks you hold him to blame him for your cousin's death?'

'No. Never!' She shivered with the return of vivid memory. 'I know that Marcus had no choice but to defend himself. If he had not, Richard would assuredly have killed him.'

'But he blames himself. He needs you to help assuage his guilt.' Elizabeth raised a hand to touch Kate's cheek in a gentle caress. 'Surely you know that he loves you. That he adores you.'

'He has told me so.'

'And do you believe him?'

'Yes.' Kate's reply was unhesitating, but little more than a whisper, as if she hardly dare admit it to herself.

'Well, then.' Elizabeth smiled. 'Tell me what is in your heart, Kate.'

'I wish we had met in different circumstances. Then we could have loved freely without the horrors of deception and violence.'

'But can you love him at all?'

'Yes. Oh, yes.' Kate smiled at last, her face transformed by joy at the recognition of what was indeed in her heart.

'Good.' Elizabeth nodded, satisfied at last. 'Then I will tell him to come.'

Elizabeth made ready to leave. 'You should know. My son has arranged for the burial of Gilliver.'

'Where will she rest?'

'At the Priory, of course.' Elizabeth understood Kate's anxieties here and answered gently. 'With the rest of the Harley family. She has always thought that the house was hers, so it is right that she should return there at the end.'

Of course. Kate bowed her head in acknowledgement of the news she wished to hear. He would think of that. And carry it out quietly and efficiently. She should have expected no less.

'Does Marlbrooke know you are here?' Kate asked finally as she accompanied Lady Elizabeth to the door.

'No. He does not.' Elizabeth answered Kate's shrewd question with a bland smile.

'And Felicity?'

'Certainly not!'

'What a devious lady you are.' Kate managed a chuckle. 'I think I might be surprised to learn how often you get your own way without anyone realising it!'

'I have had considerable practice!' Elizabeth leaned over to kiss Kate's cheek, but then frowned down at her gloved hands. 'One thing before I go. I believe it might help you if you realise that we all have difficult families, to some degree or other.'

Kate registered her surprise.

'Shall I tell you who poisoned me? Not really intending to give me enough to kill me, you understand, but enough to frighten me and lay a trail of guilt to you.'

'I thought it was Gilliver. She said not—but I think it was not easy to know what was truth and what was justifiable deception in her mind.'

'I *know* who did it. It was Felicity.'

'Felicity? Did she tell you?' Kate was shocked at Elizabeth's calm acceptance of her companion's duplicity. 'Are you sure?'

'I am very sure. And, no—she did not tell me. She did not need to. I know she was guilty, from her manner, from her re-action to me, and to you, after I recovered.'

'But why? Why would she do something so outrageous? I thought she was devoted to you.'

'I believe she is. But that made her jealous of you. What better way to get rid of your influence over me—as she saw it—than to make it seem that you had poisoned me with one of your potions? I shall tell no one of this and I would be grateful if you too remain silent. Felicity and I understand each other very well. She is a sad person, but she has given me her time and her patience when I have been intolerant and thoughtless towards her. I will not turn her off. And I know that she will never do such a thing again. So, you see, you are not the only one with relatives you wish you need not lay claim to!'

Chapter Seventeen

Kate dressed herself with utmost care for Marlbrooke's visit. She was in no doubt that he would come. Nerves tingled through her body, bringing a flush to her pale cheeks and a delicious sparkle to her sapphire eyes. For the first time for days her mind was dominated by something other than the memory of her cousin's lifeless body and Marlbrooke standing with blood dripping from his sword. And her uncle's anguished cry as he had fallen to his knees beside his son, regardless of the agony from his stricken joints. Instead the Viscount's tall, elegant figure, his night dark hair, his striking features, all filled her mind with nervous anticipation.

She scolded herself for foolishness. Yes, he would come. Lady Elizabeth had said that he wished to see her and doubtless she would know. But they would simply talk. And decide whether to complete the contracts with a marriage ceremony. There was no need for her to be so flustered. And to shiver with longing when she remembered the slide of his hands over her breasts and the heat and demands of his mouth on her skin. And the hard planes of his body as they held hers in submission, luring her into such responses that shocked her with their intimacy... No need to think about that at all! All they would do was have a sensible discussion.

Nevertheless she dressed carefully and made her preparations.

She bathed and washed her hair in fragrant rosemary and lavender, grateful for Gilliver's stores of dried flowers and herbs.

Then she chose one of the gowns given her by Elizabeth, although as before she doubted its previous ownership. By now she not only suspected, she knew without doubt that Marlbrooke could be amazingly devious in his methods. This was no gown sewn by a local seamstress for a comfortable evening at home— it had all the marks of London and high fashion stamped on it. The separate bodice and skirt were made of the most extravagant, and beautiful, cream silk and silver tissue trimmed with applied bands of costly Venetian point lace. It was a dress, Kate decided in all honesty, she could not resist. And her Puritan uncle would surely disapprove of it with forthright comment on the pursuits of the devil. The bodice was tightly laced with rigid boning, emphasising Kate's slight bosom. The low neckline, low enough to reveal her shoulders and a considerable portion of her bosom, made her blush, but the deep lace collar was very beautiful. The skirt was full and rustled delightfully over the layers of petticoats needed to do justice to the gown. The elbow-length sleeves were also trimmed with a fall of lace to draw attention to Kate's slender arms and fragile wrists. It was far too formal and extravagant for a quiet evening at Widemarsh Manor, but Kate had no hesitation in choosing to wear it. And if beneath it she donned a particular chemise with roses and honeysuckle embroidered in rose pink silk, no one but herself would be aware. She would not contemplate any other possibility! A pair of matching brocade shoes decorated with pretty rosettes completed the ensemble.

She studied herself in a faded mirror. The foxing could not hide the glory of her appearance and she blushed with pleasure. Her cheeks were still pale, but her skin was glowing and her deep blue eyes held a sparkle of excitement. For her hair, there was no hope and she could not pretend otherwise. It was still far to short for fashionable ringlets, but she was able to thread a cream ribbon through her curls to tie in a provocative bow by her ear. A fan finally, decorated round the edge with violets. She clutched the ivory sticks with their painted flowers as if her life depended on it.

She was ready far too early, so she sat and waited for him in the parlour. It seemed like a lifetime. And then tensed as she heard the sound of a coach on the carriage drive. So he had not chosen to ride from the Priory.

She stood in nervous apprehension, suddenly wishing that she could refuse him entry once more. She could sit no longer, but paced the length of the parlour, trying to still her beating heart, chiding herself for her cowardly reaction. The knock on the door stopped her mid-pace, fan flattened against her breast. The slow footsteps of Crofton echoed in the hall. Voices. What would she say? What would he expect of her? Her heart still beat painfully within her laced and boned bodice. She found that she was holding her breath.

The door to the parlour opened on a brief knock.

'Lord Marlbrooke to see you, Mistress Harley.' There was a knowing gleam in Crofton's eye, quickly hidden. 'Would you be wanting anything further, mistress? Or can I be off to my bed like all good Christians?'

Kate shook her head distractedly and focused on Marlbrooke, who still stood in the shades of the hall. 'My lord.' She swept him a formal curtsy, worthy of the Court gown, her full skirts billowing as she sank gracefully to the floor.

As she rose she lifted her gaze—and stood transfixed, her polite social smile frozen on her face. He stood in the doorway now and he too had dressed for the occasion. And he was magnificent. The situation reminded her forcefully of that day—so long ago, it seemed, and yet perhaps not so—when he had bowed himself into her uncle's library and she had decided that he was no more than a pampered courtier whom she was free to hate. How wrong she had been.

He remained in the doorway, a faint smile on his face, an appreciative gleam in his eyes as if he could read the trend of her thoughts.

If she was tricked out in latest Court style, then without doubt so was he. The sleek black brocade coat and waistcoat swept from neck to knee, showing his figure to perfect advantage. Gold embroidery ornamented the heavy turned-back cuffs and buttonholes whilst a gold-fringed sash confined the waistcoat. His black breeches were gartered at the knee, the impression of wealth and elegance completed by silk stockings, and black leather shoes with high red heels and decorative ribbon rosettes. A white silk shirt displayed extravagant lace ruffles at throat and wrist. Finally, his own dark hair was arranged to fall in a profusion of heavy curls and ringlets to his shoulders. He carried a black wide-brimmed felt hat, ostentatiously decorated with ostrich plumes and ribbons, and a costly dress sword. He flourished the hat in elegant style as he swept her a magnificent salute.

Then they stood and looked at each other.

Marlbrooke broke the tension. 'I decided that since my errand was to woo you afresh, I should dress the part. I am relieved. Otherwise you would have quite cast me in the shade, Mistress Harley.'

'Impossible. You are far too splendid for me, my lord.'

'Are you intending to invite me into this room, or do you wish me to leave now?'

'Forgive me, my lord...'

'Oh, Kate!' He abandoned the rigid formality and approached to take her hand and lift it to his lips. 'How could I have forgotten in three days how very beautiful you are?' He turned her hand over to press his lips to her palm and then to her wrist, where her pulse beat against his mouth. It pleased him inordinately that she was wearing the sapphire ring.

She was flustered. 'Please sit, my lord.' She fluttered the fan somewhat inexpertly and tried for composure.

He sat.

'Perhaps a glass of wine?'

'Thank you.'

She poured the wine with formal courtesy and placed the glass carefully at his elbow before taking the seat opposite.

'Well, Mistress Harley?'

'I do not know what to say.' Kate's formal manners deserted her and she frowned at him. 'This is most unfair of you. You have me at a disadvantage, sir.'

'How should that be, Viola?' His smile was quick and utterly disarming. 'You have kept the door locked against me for the past few days. Your servant looks at me as if I had crawled from under a stone and he would like to crush me as he would a cockroach under his boot. I have turned out tonight—in my coach, no less—wearing this extremely inappropriate outfit for country life, and you talk of disadvantage.'

She came rapidly to her feet, dropping her fan. 'I know. I am sorry I was so disobliging but I... What do you want from me?'

He came gracefully to his feet, bent to pick up the fan and placed it on the table out of her reach. 'Nothing that will make you uncomfortable, dearest Kate.'

He took her hands in his. His smile had vanished, his face now serious and a little strained. It seemed to Kate that perhaps he had enjoyed as little sleep as she had.

'Look at me,' he commanded gently when her eyes fell before his. 'It is no very great matter, Kate. Simply this. Do you love me enough to put the past behind us?' And here was the crux of the problem. 'Do you love me enough to live comfortably with me, even though you know that I challenged your cousin to a duel and that my sword was the cause of his death? If you feel that you cannot, then I will not hold you to the settlement. We will end the agreement, break the settlement, whatever it is that you wish. I will not force you into a union that you cannot bear and which would ultimately destroy us both. I love you too much to allow that.'

Her eyes were locked with his now, overwhelmed by the sacrifice that he would make for her. 'Would you indeed do that?'

'Of course.'

'Your generosity takes my breath away.'

'Dearest Kate.' He frowned down at their joined hands. 'You must also be able to forgive yourself for the past tragedy. And, indeed, there is no blame attached to you. You must not take on the burden of the sins of others. Richard and Simon must be allowed to carry their own responsibility in this.'

'I know. I have thought about this.' Her voice was low but certain. 'I was wrong.'

He surprised her by releasing her hands to drop to one knee at her feet, head bent in supplication.

'I told you once that I loved you. That has not changed, nor ever will. Will you love me, Kate, and accept my love in return? Will you do me the honour of wedding me?'

She touched the dark silk of his hair, savouring the warmth in her heart that began to melt her fears. He waited in some trepidation, realising that he had never wanted anything as much as he wanted this woman to give her heart and her hand to him. The silence between them seemed to stretch endlessly.

Then, 'Yes. I will marry you. I will love you and take your heart for my own.'

He looked up at her, seeing the glint of tears in her eyes, but her lips were smiling. 'Do you realise that if you had said no, you would have condemned my soul to endless night?'

'Oh, Marcus!' She opened her arms to him. 'I have loved you for longer than I would admit to myself—and I have been so lonely here without you.'

'I know.' He rose to his feet and gathered her against him, his arms enclosing her, turning his face into her hair as waves of relief swept through him. 'I have spent the last week prowling aimlessly round the Priory, driving my mother and the servants to distraction.' His hands swept down her back with more than a hint of possession. 'I suddenly find it impossible to live without you.'

His mouth found hers in a kiss that devastated her and left them both shaken with the depth and intensity of emotion between them. 'You know what I want,' he murmured against her lips.

'And I.'

He took her hand, linking their fingers. 'Show me where your room is.'

She led him up the darkened staircase to her bedchamber. Kate knew that it was now free of dust and herbs, polished and tended for this one occasion, the linen laundered and fragrant with lavender, but it would not have mattered. They had eyes for no one but each other.

Without words, he undressed her carefully, laying the magnificent gown aside with the lightest of touches, even though his hands trembled from the iron control he exerted. He wanted to drown in the glory of her body. To claim what was his and possess her completely. He forced his will and his heart to rule his senses.

When she stood naked before him he pressed his lips to her forehead, holding her away from him with gentle hands on her shoulders as he looked at her.

'Forgive me, Kate. I want you so much. I will try to use you gently and with the courtesy you deserve, but I fear that this night my need may be greater than my control.'

'I am not afraid.'

'You should be.' His eyes blazed. 'For I am. Afraid of the depth of desire that I feel for you.'

'Then take me, my lord. For I am yours. And I love you with all my heart.' Her smile was one of total trust and love. And she reached up to press her lips to his with a whisper of mouth against mouth.

He removed his own finery and would have led her to the bed, but she stopped him with a hand lifted to his shoulder.

'What is it?' He searched her face in concern but saw only her glorious smile.

Kate came to stand before him, and touched in tentative recognition the vicious line of the raw scar that still scored his ribs. She ignored his sharp intake of breath as he realised her intent. Leaning in to him, she bent and traced its path with her lips, caressed the length of the newly healed wound with tender kisses. She touched him slowly, lingering over her task. It was the last visible remnant of Richard and the ugly deeds that had almost destroyed them, almost divided them irrevocably. Kate's deliberate act of love purged the bitter memories and obliterated the final division between them.

It was Marlbrooke's undoing—his absolution and his salvation. The depth of her understanding and love took his breath away. And when he finally lifted her to the bed, and covered her with his body, his fierce passion had been overlaid by an overwhelming tenderness that reduced her to amazed delight.

'Tonight is ours,' he promised, framing her face in his hands. 'No shadows will threaten us. Not Gilliver nor Richard. Not Isolde. Tonight I will fill your thoughts, your body, your whole experience. Only me. I adore you and I will drown myself in you.' His mouth sealed the promise, a searing heat.

With utmost care and finesse his hands and mouth touched and awoke every part of her to mind-shattering pleasure. And she responded without restraint to caress and smooth, delighting in the hard, well-defined muscles of his arms and shoulders. When she allowed her lips to brush his throat, along the flat planes of his chest, her sweet breath whispering against his skin, she drove him to the edge of that hard-won control.

He caught his breath as her breasts tightened under his palms, as her nipples hardened into peaks of desire under the assault of his lips and tongue. He allowed his fingers to feather along her soft belly, his senses swamped by the instant quiver of her muscles. She purred, a low sound of pleasure, deep in her throat, when he used his knee to open her thighs so that his hands could glide over that impossibly satin skin and taste the hot wetness of her body's responses to him. He felt her gasp in wonder as his accomplished, skilful fingers touched and caressed before finally sliding possessively into her receptive body. Such an intimate touch ignited fire to flame through her body's myriad of nerve endings. In reply she arched, moved beneath him in unspoken demand, letting her hands drift to touch where they would. He set his teeth against the immediate instinct to answer her demands, but continued to touch and taste, replacing his fingers with his mouth and tongue until her breath came in agonised gasps and her fingernails scored his shoulders. His seduction was complete and he gloried in it, the fact that she could accept the worship of his body without restraint.

Uncontrollable shivers overtook her, racing through her blood to engulf and finally explode through her very soul as the fragments of a meteor spangled the heavens.

'Marcus!'

He slid to take possession of her mouth with his once more, capturing her breath, tasting her delight, as she cried out in the devastating splendour of the sensations that shook her from head to foot.

Finally, impossibly hard and ready for her, he could withstand the invitation of her body no longer, but lifted her hips and slid into the velvet depths of her. Then held himself still, looking down at her radiant face.

'Open your eyes. Look at me, Kate.' He waited until she obeyed, every muscle taut. 'Say it. Tell me that you love me, Katherine. Tell me when I am inside you. Tell me that I may believe it.'

Her eyes looked deep into his, allowing him into her soul. 'I love you,' she breathed and arched her body against his in instinctive response, lifting her hips to take him deeper yet, to allow him to fill her.

'You are mine. You always will be. Do you accept it?' He forced himself to remain motionless in spite of the pulsating heat that surrounded him and demanded his response.

'Yes!' It was little more than a sigh but it was all he needed to hear.

Desire now overtook control, mind giving way to demands of the flesh, and he thrust again and again with long smooth strokes to fill her completely, driving her over the edge of feeling once again, absorbing her response as it shimmered over her skin, the pleasure over her face.

'And I am yours,' he answered, feeling the ripples of her muscles as she surrounded and enclosed him in her glorious heat.

Her skin glowed beneath his, her body warm and supple, answering his every need with instinctive anticipation, shining with a love far more brilliant than he could ever have imagined or dreamed of.

He lost himself in her, hearing only her words as the tremors overtook again with overwhelming sensations. 'I love you, Marcus. I love you.'

'And I you.'

A final thrust brought his own release, plunging into the raging torrent, to drown there, as he had promised.

Chapter Eighteen

'Katherine, my love. You look rested. In spite of everything.'
Marlbrooke rose to his feet, his eyes alight with pleasure as they
rested on her. 'I gave Bessie instructions that you were not to be
disturbed.'

He had brought her back to the Priory from Widemarsh Manor
in the early hours of the morning, putting her to bed and ordering
her to sleep. Elizabeth had rejoiced—and found something time
consuming to occupy herself and Felicity in the far reaches of
the house, to give her son and his reunited love time and space
together.

'I feel well.' Kate walked forward into the library where Marlbrooke had been sitting at his desk before an array of documents,
coming to stand beside him and placing a hand on his arm.

'I am relieved to hear it.' He stood, smiled down at her, still
not quite daring to believe that she was here with him at the
Priory. Reaching for her hand to lead her to the window, he
watched as the light fell on her face, gilding the soft planes and
curves. She was pale and there were faint smudges of violet
below her eyes, reaction to the long days of grief, self-doubt and
heart-searching after Richard's death. It worried him, but she
looked content, at ease, within the circle of his arm.

'I liked you in your court finery...' he touched her sleeve
'...but this suits you very well.' She had exchanged the formal
cream-and-silver creation of the previous night for a pretty bodice
and skirt in pale blue watered silk. The low neckline that

skimmed the swell of her breasts was stylishly obscured by a deep lace collar, but it could not hide the blush which rose to her fair skin as she read the latent desire in his eyes and remembered their night at Widemarsh. He ran a finger down her cheek, grinning at her confusion, and then raised her hand to press his lips to the fragile skin on the inside of her wrist.

'I thought it better to bring you here—I could not leave you at Widemarsh. And you will now stay here with me. Until we are wed.'

'Of course.'

No argument here! It pleased him that she accepted his arrangements without question. She smiled up at him, love and trust in her clear gaze. They had come a long way together since their first meeting. He felt the familiar surge of blood through his veins at the realisation that she was his—for the moment, at least. He quelled the quick surge of renewed fear in the region of his heart, working hard to hide his emotions from her.

'Come with me. I want us to do something—together.' He would say no more, so she lapsed into silence at his side, content simply to be near him. He led her to the Long Gallery, guiding her to stand in the centre where sunlight gilded a pathway along the dark oak boards. There, he turned her to face him, took her hands firmly in his own and searched her face to see if she would read his intent.

She did. With a jolt of surprise and not a little fear, she tightened her clasp. 'Isolde?'

'Yes. Call her.'

Kate did so, her voice clear, echoing slightly in the empty spaces of the vast room. They waited. She called again. 'Isolde.'

The creeping chill touched them, raising awareness along exposed flesh. And the sorrow engulfed them. Kate trembled, taking comfort from the Viscount's strength and staunch presence.

'She is here.'

Now Marlbrooke took over. He had thought carefully about this, about the revelations in the family letters. He would use that knowledge, if it were possible, to allow the pain-stricken creature to rest finally. 'Isolde.' He kept his voice low and gentle. The cool air swirled and the depths of emotion in it. 'Leave us in peace, Isolde. I love her and she loves me.' He lowered his eyes to Kate's face as he spoke the words, making of it a solemn vow.

'I will never force her or hurt her.' He cast about in his mind for the right words to reach the spiritual remains of the wronged girl. 'Any child Kate bears will be desired by both of us, created out of our love. Your history will not be repeated here. There is no future for your sorrow here. My heart is in Kate's hands, and hers in mine.'

There was no sound in the Gallery.

'Rest in peace, Isolde.' Kate took up the theme, moved almost beyond words by Marlbrooke's declarations. 'You have carried your grief too long and deserve to rest. Marcus and I will unite our two families at last, willingly and with love.'

In confirmation of the promises, they moved together and kissed, lips to lips, a solemn vow.

Imperceptibly, the chill ebbed. The atmosphere lightened. The heartbreaking emotion dissipated into the sunlight, to leave only silence and tranquillity.

'She has gone, hasn't she?'

'Yes, I believe she has.' Marlbrooke pulled her gently on to the window seat beside him.

'Do you think she will return?' Kate leaned comfortably against his shoulder, a little breathless at what they had just done, overwhelmed by this evidence of the Viscount's love for her and concern for the poor tormented spirit of Isolde.

'I don't know. Perhaps.'

'But she is not here now. I know it.' She sighed a little. 'I hope she has found some element of peace somewhere.'

They continued to sit as the sunlight warmed the room, savouring the stillness, the silence that settled round them as in a blessing.

'Marcus?'

'Hmm?' Marlbrooke folded her into his arms. He needed her close.

'About Isolde. Perhaps it was not such a tragedy after all that your mother dropped the vessel—and so released her to walk these corridors again. Do you believe in fate?'

'Perhaps.'

'It came to me that it was Isolde's destiny that she should be released from her captivity *now*—when you decided that you wanted me for your wife.'

'So that we might have the chance to lay her unhappy spirit

to rest for eternity.' Picking up her train of thought, Marlbrooke turned his cheek against her hair as he contemplated the possibilities. 'It is a pleasing thought.'

'Yes. Perhaps it was destiny that we should love—and that our love should free her from the grief and betrayal of her past. That our love should heal her wounded heart.' Kate pushed against her lord's shoulder so that she might look up into his face, her own bright with happiness. 'Perhaps it was fate that took a hand in our union.'

'Dearest Viola! You are a constant delight to me.' Marlbrooke smiled down at her, touched her cheek with gentle fingers. 'I will willingly believe in fate or destiny, if you would have it so. Whatever the driving force behind it, you hold me captive in your pretty hands, as surely as Isolde was confined in her clay prison. Have I told you today how much I love you?'

'No. I knew there was something missing.' She laughed and her eyes sparkled with mischief.

'You are my love.' He was now deadly serious. 'For ever. I cannot imagine not loving you—in this life or the next.'

'That makes me happy.' She turned against his restraining arm. 'When shall we be wed?'

He did not answer, causing her to glance up at his stern profile. 'Marcus?'

'There is something you need to see. I cannot keep it from you and I am determined that there will be no secrets between us.' He pulled her to her feet and, without further explanation, ignoring her demands for enlightenment, led her back to the library, back to the desk and its weight of documents.

'These are the contracts. You and your heirs will be suitably provided for as your uncle Sir Henry Jessop and I agreed. It is a very generous settlement, as is your right.'

'Of course.' Kate was puzzled by this turn in the conversation, but failed to detect the reason for it. 'As you know, I have only given my consent to marriage because you are outrageously wealthy.' She glanced at him from under her lashes and reached up impulsively on her toes to press her lips to his cheek. 'Tell me what is wrong?'

There was some shadow here. She could not quite identify it, but he was not at ease.

'You are too astute,' he admitted at last, an unexpected harshness in his tone. 'I have something for you.'

'A present? You will find that I can be very mercenary, my lord.'

He did not return her smile, her attempt to keep the conversation light for fear of stirring muddied waters, but unlocked a drawer in the desk.

'It is no gift. It is something I have no wish to give you. But I know that I must.' He held a discoloured document in both hands as if he would not willingly give it up. He raised his eyes to hers. They were stern and bleak, his handsome face set in uncompromising lines. 'I am afraid of the consequences.'

'If you admit to fear, then I too must be troubled.' Anxiety clawed at her throat, a fretful beast, a frown marred her forehead. 'What can be such a threat now after everything that has happened?'

'Verzons gave me this. It seems that I have misread his loyalty in the past and that I appear to have become acceptable to him as a suitor to a Harley after all. He said that he entrusted it to me in the certainty that I would give it to you. It was found in the back of the cavity behind the Long Gallery panelling. It must have been put in there, but not in the box itself—and slid down behind it.'

He held it out to her. 'Take it. It is yours.'

Kate took the document, knowing instinctively what it must be; opening it, she read slowly the heavy black script that she now recognised as that of her father.

Marlbrooke discovered that he could not simply stand and watch, could not anticipate her reaction, which might be one of pleasure and so might destroy his hard-won plans. He turned his back on her, strode to the fireplace and stared down at the smouldering logs, one arm resting on the high mantel.

The silence stretched between them until he could stand it no longer. He turned his head and looked across at her. She stood where he had left her, neat and composed in blue silk and old lace, document in hand, eyes on him.

'Well? It is what you had always hoped for.' His tone was flat and cool, perfectly disguising what he felt, but emotion was stark in his eyes.

'Yes. You know that it is. The recognition of my claim to

Winteringham Priory within the wardship of my uncle Sir Henry Jessop until my majority. Then it would be mine without restriction, as if I were a male heir, with no strings of a marriage attached. That is how it should be.' Her voice was quite calm, her eyes soft, a smile playing round her lips.

'So, Kate!' He straightened and looked fully at her. 'Will you fight me through the Courts?'

So that is what he feared! Kate took a deep breath as she realised what he had done. What sacrifice he had been prepared to make. She found the need to swallow hard to keep tears from welling and spilling down her cheeks at the magnificent gesture.

'It gives you a very strong claim,' he continued, 'and, with the resources of the Priory behind you, enough money to bribe the most mercenary of judges to decide in your favour. Harley has a far weightier claim historically than Oxenden. You could very well win. Particularly if you exerted your considerable charm on King Charles. I doubt you would lose!'

'And then there would be no need for me to marry you. Or pressure from my family for me to do so.'

'No. The contracts could be destroyed if both parties are in agreement. If that is what you wish.'

'What do *you* wish, Marcus?' She joined him before the fireplace, moving lightly to close the space between them. So close that he could smell her flowery perfume, almost touch her. But he would not. His muscles tightened as he strove for control amidst the personal storm.

'I want you, Kate.' Now was a time for honesty, not dissembling. 'I want you more than I have wanted anything in my whole life. But not against your will. If you would rather claim this inheritance in your own right without marriage to me, then I will abide by your decision. I told you when we first met in your uncle's home that I did not want an unwilling bride. And again at Widemarsh. Now, even more so, I will never coerce you.'

'Would it hurt you if I reneged on the agreement?' She placed a hand on his sleeve, intensely aware of the taut muscles beneath her light clasp.

'Damnably!' His smile had a sardonic twist. 'But I would accept it.'

'I thought you understood me better than that.'

Her head tilted a little as she studied his face. So handsome, so masculine. Heartstoppingly so—she took a deep breath to still the shiver along her spine. She could not believe such generosity, which could allow her the final decision about their future. She opened the document again, heavy with its seals and ribbons and signatures, smoothing her finger over the date inscribed beside her father's name.

'Do you not see? He changed his mind.' The smile that touched her lips was a mingling of old sadness and a new satisfaction. 'This was his final decision, before he left us. It pleases me, more than I can express. That my father had enough faith in me that, at the end, he believed I would be the most suitable heir for the Priory. I shall never know what made him change his mind, from Simon and Richard to me—but I am glad he did. I never knew him, nor he me, but this makes me feel closer to him.'

She looked up. Marlbrooke had a quizzical expression, one brow raised.

'And I now realise *that* is all that matters,' she explained.

'What are you saying, Kate? You are not making it easy for me.'

'But I am. Very easy.'

Marlbrooke read the intention in her eyes before she moved. But too late. With a quick turn of the wrist, she let the will fall into the fire. It was only a single sheet, dry and curled. In a moment it was gone into ash and smoke. His attempt to catch her wrist, to intercept the paper before it touched the flames, failed.

'There. It is done.'

'Katherine, I... Whatever I thought you would do, it was not that. What do I say?' He could not find the words, simply looked at her, mouth firm, every muscle held in check.

'Why, nothing.' She tightened her grip on his arm. 'You gave me the freedom to make a choice. I will never forget that. And I have made it—so that is the end to it.'

He took her face in his hands, to search her expression with fierce eyes. Then he lowered his head to kiss her, his mouth soft and warm, seducing her into raising her arms to wind them around his neck and hold him close. She sighed when he released her, yet still keeping his arms around her, his cheek resting against her hair, her body held protectively close.

'Do you need to know how much I love you?' she asked, feeling the rapid beat of his heart against her own. 'I could not fight you through the courts. Not now. Nor will I charm the King. The Priory is yours—and mine, if you want me.'

'Katherine!' He turned his head to press his lips to her hair. 'I love you more than you could ever believe.'

'And I thought you loved Viola!'

He heard the laughter in her voice, muffled against his coat. He smiled at the release of tension. 'Ah, yes. I fell in love with Viola. I have very fond memories of her. She was not as wayward or strong willed as Katherine. I remember her sweet gentleness, her good humour, her willingness to accept my advice without question...' He grinned and winced as Kate's heel found a tender place on his instep and exerted not a little pressure. 'But I believe I can find room for both Viola and Kate in my heart. Will that satisfy you?'

She lifted her head and answered with her lips on his, brushing her hand along his glorious hair in a tender caress. A faint crease appeared between her dark brows.

'What is it, my dearest love?'

'You once told me that you could never see the Priory as your home. That Glasbury would always hold the central place in your heart.'

'I remember.' A shadow touched his face, but was quickly gone.

'I understand why, Marcus. But could you perhaps bear to live at the Priory occasionally? Even if some day in the future you decide to rebuild Glasbury?'

'Yes. I can do that.' Marlbrooke's face was solemn, his eyes holding hers, as if committing himself to a binding oath. 'As long as you are here with me, the Priory will be my home. In spite of Isolde and all the works of man, Harley and Oxenden will finally be joined.'

'I would like that.'

A ghost of a smile flittered across his mouth, quickly suppressed. 'And, of course, we are now honour bound to keep my solemn vow to Isolde.'

'Did you make one? I do not remember.'

'I did indeed. That a child of our union would be desired and cherished, a celebration of our love.'

'And you believe, of course, that we should attempt to keep your vow?'

'Assuredly! Vows should always be taken seriously.'

Kate laughed. 'And you claim that I am devious and managing!' Her eyes glowed with love. 'I will agree to keep your promise, Marcus—but only if you marry me first!'

'I can also do that!'

'Well then, my lord!' She took his hand, linking her fingers with his in a promise of unity before she allowed him to draw her more firmly into his arms, lifting her face for his kiss.

*   *   *   *   *

If you enjoyed what you just read,
then we've got an offer you can't resist!

Take 2 bestselling
love stories FREE!
Plus get a FREE surprise gift!